**HESTERWINE, TEXAS, 1943**

# HESTERWINE, TEXAS, 1943

*Dot Ryan*

Copyright © 2016 by Dot Ryan

*Hesterwine, Texas, 1943*

All rights reserved. No part of this book may be used or reproduced by any means, graphic, electric, or mechanical, including photocopying, recording, taping, or by any information storage retrieval system, without the written permission of the publisher, except in case of brief quotations embodied in critical articles and reviews.

*Hesterwine, Texas, 1943* is a work of fiction. All characters, names, and events, as well as all places, incidents, organizations, and dialogue in this novel, either are the products of the author's imagination, or are used fictitiously.

ISBN:
978-0-9831197-6-0 (dj)
978-0-9831197-7-7 (sc)
978-0-9831197-8-4 (e-book)

Published by Checkered Swan Publishing, LLC

dotryan5@att.net
checkeredswan@att.net
dotryanbooks.com
United States of America
Library of Congress Control Number: 2015939762

*"Here's to women of every age and stage whom life has made a little crazy ... or a lot."*

*Etta Ruth Morley*

## ACKNOWLEDGEMENTS

A special thanks to D'Lyn Fraser Suggs, an extraordinarily kind and generous young woman to everyone with whom she comes in contact. I was a beneficiary of D'Lyn's generosity this past year when she promoted my books to a wide group of readers who otherwise might never have heard of them. I thank you with all my heart, D'Lyn.

Last, but never least, thanks to my husband, Sam. He is always there for me, no matter what, and usually with trusty dictionary in hand.

# 1

"DINAH DOESN'T ... TREAT HIM RIGHT ... but if he'd shave ... Dinah-mite ... Burma Shave!" The male voices rose in sequential thunder each time another of the small red-and-black shaving cream advertisements came into view along the highway. The signs, five in a row and usually one hundred feet apart, seemed like beacons to the uniformed men—army, army air corps, navy, marine, and coast guard—peering from the windows of the hot, overcrowded Greyhound bus that had lost its air-conditioning a hundred miles back. Thirty months into world war, the multifarious variety of catchy little Burma Shave limericks were undoubtedly welcome diversions to the question likely on the mens' minds: How soon would they be fighting Hitler's Nazi Germany or Hirohito's imperial Japanese forces on all the continents of the world except Antarctica and South America?

However, the signs were much more than welcome diversions for two young non-military women on the bus, one white, one black, neither of whom knew each other. For both, each new Burma Shave ditty meant the distance between them and trouble was widening, and the farther they could get, the better.

To Leeta Bulow, plastered into a sweaty, airless corner of the *colored* section at the back of the bus, each new set of signs literally meant the difference between life and death. Her lack of a suitcase or other type of luggage, other than her pocketbook, chronicled the urgency with which she had left the south side of Chicago behind almost three days prior.

*Hesterwine, Texas 1943*

Hunched low on that first bus out of town, she hadn't stopped trembling long enough to take a deep breath until several hundred miles lay behind her. Afterward, at each stop on her way to California—and safety—she hid in crowded bus terminal restrooms until only seconds remained to board ... always crazy-scared that she would open one of those bathroom doors and there he would be.

On this hot afternoon, it seemed as if she'd been traveling forever, and she still had to cross the rest of Texas, and then New Mexico and Arizona, before reaching California. Along with being hungry and in a bad mood, she was exhausted and ached all over. She'd been in such a hurry to get out of Chicago that she thought she might have sprained something in her efforts to keep from *running* all the way to the bus station instead of walking normally, as if only out for a morning stroll. Fear had slowed her steps, even though every part of her body was fighting to run—fear that if she seemed in too big of a rush, someone who knew *him* would see her and would tell.

She stretched to get the kink out of her back and then groaned inwardly. *Shut up 'bout a few aches and pains, girl. You're lucky you made it to that damn bus station at all, walking or running!* She slapped at a fly buzzing around her head. *Lucky? There ain't nothing lucky 'bout you, Leeta Bulow. Never was, and never—.* She glanced out the window. *Where in hell am I?*

Leeta's right eyebrow shot up in agitation as the bus slowed and she leaned forward to peer out at the dilapidated outskirts of a small Texas town. She jerked open her pocketbook and stared into the messy jumble of necessities inside—a lipstick, Maybelline "spit" mascara, rouge, compact with a cracked mirror, three Indian head nickels, a single dime, two copper pennies—and a bus ticket with no more miles left on it....

She tugged at the large crimson bow that hung in wilted creases from the deep V-neck of her blouse. *This damn burg gonna be your getting off place for a while, Leeta Bulow ... unless you get lucky and the driver forgets you're back here.*

Her disgusted gaze fell on a three-tiered sign dangling between two extremely tall and ragged palm trees. The first tier advertised *Hesterwine, Texas - Population 3,025*. The second tier bragged *Home of The Hesterwine Medallions since 1861*. Leeta snorted, thinking, *Ain't medallions coins? Maybe I can get my hands on some of 'em coins and buy me a bus ticket outta this hole.* The third tier, just as large but not nearly so faded as the first two—indicating a regular application of fresh paint—informed, in big, black letters: **NO VAGRANTS ALLOWED**. Leeta's eyes glinted with familiar rebellion. *I may be running out of time on this earth if Mandingo Q. Mann catches me, but I ain't no damn vagrant!* Still scowling, she mumbled under her breath, "That sorry Negro ain't no descendent of Mandingo royalty from West Africa like he's always crowing he is. Before he call himself *Mandingo Q. Mann*, he was just plain o' Dewayne Peet—just another cotton-pickin' *Negro* from Georgia on the lam from the law."

"You talking to me, gal?"

Leeta jerked her head at the dour-faced elderly man crowded next to her on the communal seat. "No, I'm talking to myself. Ain't you ever done that?" She sounded as hostile as she looked.

He said, "Huh!" Then he looked straight ahead.

Flopping back in the seat, she directed an angry puff of breath at the swatch of sleek, fake curls dangling over her forehead and then, hoping she had overlooked a compartment of hidden cash in her fake leopard-skin pocketbook, she dug down into every section and came up with another nickel. Her fingers recalculated her finances. *Thirty-two cents. Maybe enough for a hamburger and a Coke.*

She glanced at the *Whites Only* sign in the window of a small café. Identical signs hung from the doors of adjoining buildings—an unusually narrow chiropractor's office wedged between Hair by Cinderella and Baldy's Pool Hall. In front of the pool hall, a tiny Negro boy swept the sidewalk while a stubby-looking white man wearing a gray apron over his big belly used a flyswatter to point out the spots the boy missed.

*Oh, Lord, I feel a déjà vu coming on,* she thought, suddenly reminded of the Mississippi town she had called home... until Chicago and *Mandingo Q. Mann.* She'd been as pure as little Orphan Annie on the morning of her thirteenth birthday, but by eleven o'clock that night it was no longer true and she had escaped Mississippi forever... or thought she had, until today. Working for Mandingo Q. Mann at his Southside Chicago nightclub had not been ideal employment for a gullible child of thirteen, nor had the eye-opening years that followed been something to write home about. She was twenty now, but she hadn't felt young in a long time.

As always when trapped by circumstances over which she had lost control, Leeta's eyes blinked rapidly as her thoughts bounced from one agitated topic to the next: *I always said if I ever talk about going* South *again somebody shoot me, please!* She'd have to find a job quick, but, so far, she'd seen nothing through the bus's windows that looked like any place she'd ever worked. *Guess it gonna have to be washing dishes or scrubbing toilets for a while*—there would be plenty of her kind of work in Los Angeles when she got there. *You'd think forty bucks woulda took a body farther from Chicago than raggedy-ass-looking Hesterwine, Texas!*

She tugged at her blouse, pulling it away from the sharp points of her satin bra. *Sha-ee-it! It's hot back here! Is that pee I smell? I smell pee!* She glanced at the elderly man now dozing next to her. *Jesus-Pete! Has that old Negro got pee-pants? Scoot over!*

As quickly as she nudged him, his eyes flew open. He gave her a scathing once-over that started at the top of her upswept hairdo and traveled down to her fake leopard-skin platform heels with the chartreuse-and-black ankle straps that perfectly matched her fake leopard skin belt and pocketbook. His attempt to wither her further into the corner of the crowded communal seat only served to stiffen her neck. Like Joe Louis about to defend his title, she jerked her shoulders back, lifted the two points of her small bosom to their utmost height, and remained that way until he administered a final glance of scorn, then made a point of staring straight ahead.

Leeta turned aside with a grunt. It wasn't the first time her own kind had judged her and condemned her all in one fell swoop. She felt a twinge of the hurt that she had long ago trained herself to replace with indifference. Dry-eyed, she stared at nothing in particular; she'd stopped crying over the certainty of her life years before. *I shoulda got off in New Orleans. A girl can get by in New Orleans—especially a Billie Holiday-type blues singer with big-city smarts and Houdini nerves.* Even before the thought ended, a fresh line of perspiration popped out on her brow. *But New Orleans is probably the first place that crazy bastard gonna look!*

A smothered giggle came from a few rows up. Leeta glanced at a sailor and a blond-haired girl—maybe his wife, maybe not—covered to their chins by a big pink blanket despite the heat. She eyed the gyrating blanket and shook her head. *I done it in a lot of places but never on a Greyhound bus!* She let out a low laugh. *Bonkin' on a Greyhound—somebody oughta tell Glenn Miller to put some music to that!*

She assessed the other passengers one by one, making a game of trying to figure out which of them, if any, would be getting off in this *hick-looking town. Bet it won't be that puny white gal in the green hat three rows up. Look at her. She's sunk so low in that seat she look like she melted to it. Wonder what's the matter with her? Little whitey gonna need some ice for them puffy red eyes of hers. And if that ain't the ugliest green hat she wearing I ever did see! Look like an old lady's hat!*

The hostility on Leeta's face appeared as though it had been slathered on with a heavy brush; somehow, it helped her to be mad at people she didn't know. She shivered, despite the ungodly heat on the bus. With barely enough room for her narrow butt on the communal seat, she couldn't tell if it was *her* sweat she was feeling on her clothes or that of the old man next to her. She glanced at his scowling face; he was still staring straight ahead. *Lordy, that old Negro sure stink like pee!* She waved her hand in front of her nose none too subtly. *Maybe it's the upholstery. Maybe some damn kids peed on it.* The smell reminded her of the thin cotton mattress she and her brothers and sisters had slept on, all four of them stuck together like sticky noodles in a pot on those unbearably hot Southern nights when a breeze was as scarce as supper. She glanced past old "Pee Pants" at the three Negro soldiers sharing the same long, back-of-the-bus seat. *Hope them fellers don't think it's* me *stinking like that,* she thought, as she caught the hem of her short skirt and used it to fan her long legs, then swished her hands over her damp calves. *These stockings are burning me up!*

She flopped back on the seat. *Bet that puny white girl in the ugly green hat up there in the good seats ain't got no silk stockings like mine. Shoo! Get off me, fly! Ouch! The goddamn thing bit me! No you don't! Gotcha!*

She wiped her fingers on the window, her agitation growing with each small-town store and vacant lot the bus rolled past. Another sign, Hesterwine's Leather Goods Since 1852, caught her eye. *This damn town's older'n God's grandma! I don't like old stuff. When I get to California, I ain't gonna have nothing but new stuff 'round me. New cars, new clothes, new everything—I done had enough old shit!*

The bus's hydraulic brakes hissed, as if in warning. Nineteen-year-old Mary Kenny's fingers trembled as she stuffed a damp ringlet of thick, auburn hair under her grandmother's green felt fedora—*a beautiful old hat,* she thought as she tugged the brim close to her forehead over her right eye like her grandmother used to wear it and slowly drew herself up to look out the window. She reached behind her and pulled the wet, dark-blue linen of her dress away from her shoulder blades. Several times during the day, she wished she had accepted the rattan fan offered by the sailor sitting across the aisle from her, but then she would have had to talk to him, and she could not. She hadn't talked to anyone in days other than the few words it took to buy bus fare or order a sandwich; her mind was too busy trying to make sense of the past year to make any sense at all in a conversation with a stranger. Besides, she had never been much of a talker. "Come out of your shell, little turtle," her grandmother used to say while tapping lightly on her head. If she had been a talkative child, she might have told her grandmother that because of all the screaming, yelling, and *talking* going on at home, she had learned at an early age that she fared much better if she kept quiet.

Mary suddenly felt guilty. Neither had she acknowledged the young marine who had occupied the seat next to her all the way from New Jersey to Florida. Instead, she had turned aside and stuck a magazine in front of her face the instant he sat down. He kept rolling and unrolling another magazine, pausing from time to time to glance at the cover, which showed a line of amphibious-type boats, like those appearing in the newsreels at the movies, loaded with combat-geared marines and approaching a beach strung with barbed wire and ramparts, shells streaking in all directions. Maybe he was thinking hard about what was to become of him, wondering if he would make it through this war alive, what with the Nazis and the Japanese trying to take over the world. She should have shaken that boy-faced marine's hand, talked to him as long as he wanted to talk, told him how grateful she was to the men and women in uniform. Who was she to feel so sorry for herself and worry that she had no future, when *their* futures were on hold and in danger of abruptly ending on the battlefield? At least she was able to move on with *her* life ... even if she had absolutely no idea of what that meant, or how to do it.

Her gaze shifted to her mother's beige-and-brown-striped Samsonite suitcase that she had placed on the seat the moment the young Marine vacated it. Everyone had memory triggers, and that old suitcase was one of hers ... beginning long before her eleventh birthday when her mother died. Before then, that scratched and scraped piece of luggage was hastily packed so many times she had lost count, and always in an atmosphere of her mother's tears and her father's yelling. "Get the hell outta here and take the kid with you! Go crying to your crazy old mamma again and see if I give a goddamn!"

And they had gone, only to go back when he showed up at her maternal grandmother's brownstone apartment in New Jersey, contrite and with promises to do better ... until her mother died without him ever having made the attempt. Then it was just her and the suitcase making those trips. The old Samsonite was so scarred it looked like it had *bounced* all the way from her father's upstate New York dairy farm to her grandmother's Newark, New Jersey, brownstone. Her father always thought he was punishing her for some misdeed each time he sent her away, but she had been glad to go and sad to return.

Mary Kenny drew a trembling breath—the kind of deep, halting breath that always made her feel as if her lungs were resisting the effort. Aside from all those memories of traveling back and forth, she could not look at that tattered old suitcase without remembering how it got its latest scars. She could still see her father slinging it down the stairs as he ordered her out of his house for the last time. As usual, she fled to her grandmother in New Jersey, glad to be with someone who loved her, glad never to have to return to her father. Six months later, the much-loved woman sat down in her favorite wing-backed chair for an afternoon nap and died in her sleep.

The realization that she was now alone, and forever without her only ally in this world, struck Mary a blow that had yet to heal. She quit her wartime factory job in New Jersey and opted to seek one of the same in California ... as far away from her past life and a chance meeting with her father as she could get.

Mary's teary gaze dropped to the large brown paper bag between her feet. Inside were possessions that would not fit into the suitcase—the only items she had taken from her grandmother's ghostly silent apartment after the funeral: a glow-in-the-dark alarm clock, a small electric toaster, and a tiny sewing basket. Safely wrapped in cellophane in the bottom of the bag was her grandmother's legacy to her; a copy of John Erskine's *The Private Life of Helen of Troy* and one of Erskine's essays, *The Moral Obligation to Be Intelligent*. Grandmother was an intelligent woman and, unlike her father, a forgiving woman, never a harsh judge of people's errors. Mary squeezed the brown paper bag between her ankles, feeling her sweaty thighs tighten hard against each other ... as if to hold inside what had already been lost.

The bus's brakes squeaked again, and Mary gave the brim of her green hat a final tug before lifting the brown paper bag to her lap, then curling her fingers tightly around the handle of the old Samsonite.

The bus rolled slowly down Hesterwine's broad main thoroughfare and past a smattering of gas stations and vacant lots. Small, unassuming dwellings lay strung like imperfect beads between large, pretentious old homes with encircling balconies on their upper floors and wide, sweeping porches below. She looked straight ahead, using the bus's windshield as a frame; the town looked like a shabby painting, a picture not deserving of a place over the mantel but worthy of examining if only because of its melancholy scruffiness. A five-and-dime store with a big, bleached red-and-white sign was most prominent among the array of faded brick and wood storefronts of white, brown, or dusty rose, all standing beneath soaring wooden facades that reminded Mary of an old cow town she'd seen in a Western movie. On both sides of the street, tar-roofed awnings hung low over the sidewalks, coupling the buildings to one another like a train of sun-bleached circus cars.

Shade provided by those old canopies was likely most appealing on a blistering day like today, but few townspeople seemed to be taking advantage of them except for two unsmiling, blue-haired old ladies, with hands gesturing and mouths moving, while standing in front of a huge *Lassie Come Home* billboard. The soaring facade above the elderly women boasted a multicolored neon *Rialto Theater* sign—perhaps the town's tallest and brightest adornment when lit, other than the courthouse a few blocks back that looked more like an old, weatherworn castle than a court of law.

The bus turned right at Goldrod's Corner Drugstore, air brakes hissing again as it slowed to let a big white dog with a red collar and a blasé air trot across the street. Mary Kenny watched the dog as it jogged along the sidewalk, same speed as the bus.

Perched on the edge of the communal seat in back, Leeta Bulow also watched. The bus and the dog took a right turn into a wide, oil-spotted, concrete alleyway that separated the drugstore from a triple set of railroad tracks about a half-block back from the drugstore's rear. The brakes hissed again as the bus rolled to a stop and the driver, a tall man with pockmarked cheeks and dark glasses, pulled the lever and popped the door open. He flicked the visor of his blue cap and called out: "Hesterwine, Texas! It's a thirty-minute stop, folks. Soda fountain and food right through there."

He pointed at a set of dark-green doors framed by identical plate-glass windows. A sign over the doors stated *Whites Only*. To the left of the entrance and its adjoining plate-glass window another sign, COLORED *Get Food/Bus Tickets* HERE, dangled over a small opening with a sliding service door. The military men and civilians filed off the bus, some of them laughing and joking as they disappeared into the drugstore. The colored soldiers strolled across the railroad tracks to the depot where a Negro family—one of them holding a sign that said *Christ Emanuel Baptist Church*—beckoned to them with upraised sodas and sandwiches. Pee Pants followed the colored soldiers across the tracks. The driver hoisted himself back up the high metal steps, curled his forefinger in a beckoning wiggle, and yelled toward the back of the bus.

"End of the line for you, back there, gal!"

He softened his expression when he looked at Mary Kenny. "For you, too, miss," he said. "Unless you plan on buying some more ticket."

# 2

"I TOLD YOU, CLARA, BUT YOU SELDOM LISTEN ANYMORE. The Rialto does not open on weekdays until *five*."

"Justine Hesterwine, you know good and well we came at 1:00 p.m. last week, saw the entire thing, newsreel and all, and were having our root beer at Goldrod's by four o'clock."

"It was Saturday, Clara."

Clara Hesterwine sighed, then pretended to adjust her silver-rimmed spectacles but was actually reading the sign over the ticket window.

Justine waited until she finished reading. "See? The Rialto opens at *one* on Saturdays, *noon* on Sundays, and *five* on Monday evenings through Friday evenings—I told you that before we left the house."

"No, you did not tell me. We both forgot, and don't deny it. We shall come back when the feature changes next Saturday." She smiled while patting the image of Lassie on the billboard. "I really didn't want to see Lassie again, did you? I believe Rube got his feelings hurt when he saw what we were up to." She looked up and down the sidewalk. "Where did he go?"

"He went on ahead when he saw the bus coming. You know how he likes to greet the passengers in hopes they will toss him a morsel."

"You have spoiled him feeding him those table scraps, Justine. He's getting too fat."

"You are quite mistaken, Clara. He is a healthy dog is all."

"He *jiggles*," Clara insisted.

"Not true," Justine retorted as she glanced down the street at the corner bank. "Perhaps we should avoid the Rialto awhile, Clara. You saw how

Banker Prickett kept turning around in his seat and staring at us last week. I felt quite embarrassed."

"It's none of his business if we attend the cinema, Justine. Just because we are a few months late with the mortgage payments doesn't mean we can't enjoy ourselves occasionally. Besides, on my way to the restroom last Saturday I saw *Mrs.* Prickett in the lobby and made certain she heard me tell the little Newton boy—as loudly as I could without being common—that we had won the cinema tickets at Goldrod's fishbowl drawing, the same as last time. Being the town's most prolific gossip, other than cousin Etta Ruth, I am certain Betty Prickett told her husband what I said."

"You have just ruined what is left of my entire day, Clara," Justine huffed. "Obviously, you've forgotten that we decided never to mention that woman's name again. She is so mean to me, Clara!"

"*Who*? What on earth are you talking about?" Clara was just as huffy.

"*Cousin Etta Ruth*, Clara! We said we'd never speak of her ever again, and we'd only speak *to* her if we accidently crossed her path somewhere and could not avoid being polite."

"For heaven's sake, Justine, I only mentioned her name in comparison to Betty Prickett," Clara sighed with overdone exasperation.

"Anyway, Clara, I feel we have as much right to enjoy the Rialto's refrigerated air as anybody."

"Well, *yes*, and why would we not?" Clara eyed Justine as if she had voiced a truth so evident that it should have gone without saying.

Justine was unperturbed. "By the way, do you know that Ruthie Benweider bought one of those big water-driven window fans to cool her parlor, the kind you hook up to a hose outside and the fan blades whirl behind the dripping water? Well, her piano was completely ruined by all the dampness coming off that fan. The keys warped, the wires rusted, and that once beautiful wood is now as curdled as clabber."

Clara rolled her eyes. "I *know* what happened to Ruthie Benweider's piano, Justine. I was standing right next to you when Maude Hapner told us. I'll say again what I said then and which you have evidently forgotten that I said: 'One would think Ruthie would have noticed what was happening to her piano long before it got ruined.'"

"Well, Clara, like *I* said, in reply to your remark that day, in case *you* have forgotten, 'How could Ruthie possibly know what was happening to anything in her house since she hasn't dusted a stick of furniture in it but twice since her tyrant of a husband died in thirty-seven.'"

"Al Benweider *was* a stickler for cleanliness. Just plain mean the way he nagged poor Ruthie into being such a drudge. He certainly put the years on her. My heavens, she's wrinkled as Old Man Abelson at the shoe shop."

"No wonder she planted that cactus on his grave," Justine said.

The sisters gazed up at the *Lassie Come Home* poster and Justine sighed. "No need to see Lassie a third time, great dog that he is ... where's Rube, Clara?"

"For heaven's sake, Justine, I asked you that very same question not a whole minute ago." She lifted the watch pinned to her white lace collar, squinted at it, and then smoothed the collar and the watch back into place over the gauzy lavender-and-white print of her roomy, ankle-length dress. Justine did the same to the identical watch on her own white lace collar, then they both looked toward Goldrod's Drugstore on the opposite corner while calling out, "Rube ... here boy! Here, Rube...."

Clara drew back and fanned herself with an open hand, her beckoning to Rube fading as she glanced toward the bank. "My! I do indeed need a refreshing drink! And since Banker Prickett would be quite amused if we offered him the few nickels we spend at the cinema, I suppose we should show Goldrod's our appreciation for the cinema tickets by having our nice, cold root beers as usual."

"So true, Clara, and besides, Rube is surely waiting out back for one of us to bring him his usual cup of ice water."

They patted their petite crochet belt buckles, making certain the clasps aligned perfectly with the row of tiny white buttons down the entire front of each garment. Beneath their dresses and their two-ply layers of thick cotton slips, long whalebone corsets bolstered the inherent tradition of the Hesterwine sisters' modesty. Nothing ever jiggled except Miss Clara's softly weathered sixty-nine-year-old cheeks; the same was true for her sixty-seven-year-old sister, Miss Justine, whose gauzy dress was resplendent with tiny white roses on a pale pink background. Miss Clara's dress was almost identical in style to her sister's dress except that it was lavender with white daisies. Miss Clara's modest-sized black purse, with the suitcase-type handle, like her sister's purse, matched her black, laced-up shoes, with the sturdy one and one-half inch walking heels. Neither woman ever lamented the sleek silk stockings that were no longer available in these times of war, because *their* stockings, past and present, were cotton, pure and simple, just like the long, fingerless stocking-like gloves that protected their very white arms when they worked in their garden. *"Waste not, want not,"* was their creed: Holes in toes of stockings easily converted into finger holes, and what once concealed the lower limbs did further service in protecting the upper.

Years ago, when the family fortune petered out, they recouped by turning their lofty-ceilinged kitchen into a home bakery. Twice weekly—as loyally as butter melts and sugar caramelizes—they sold their delicious cookies, cakes, breads, and canned preserves, such as tomato, grape, and fig jellies, jams, and watermelon pickles from the front porch of their rambling old mid-nineteenth century mansion.

Unfortunately for the Hesterwine ladies, their past ability to pay a latter obtained mortgage on the ancestral family home ended with the war's rationing of the very thing that had allowed them to stay current—*sugar*. Sugar was the first consumer commodity rationed by the onset of war, and thereafter limited to one half-pound per person per week. The last bake sale was six months ago and Banker Prickett, of The First Loan & Trust Bank, was threatening to foreclose on the mortgage.

Since the townsfolk considered Clara and Justine Hesterwine owners of a bona fide bakery, the sisters could have received rations of almost seventy percent of their normal usage, had not the local ration board decided to deny them bona fide bakery status. The rationing board consisted of volunteer workers selected by the town's leading officials. Unfortunately again for the Hesterwine sisters, Banker Prickett was top man on that oh-so-selective board, and he had ulterior motives: he wanted Clara's and Justine's property. Their historic old mansion, sitting on two hundred acres of what had once been lush farmland located five miles southwest of Hesterwine's city limits, was surrounded by several large plots of Prickett's own property—each plot foreclosed on over the years by him and his bank.

Clara and Justine, born in the old house as was their father, had inherited it from him. *He* had inherited it from his father, Civil War General Andrew Ignacio Hesterwine, the beloved founder of the little farming and ranching community of Hesterwine, Texas. The town's proudest boast—other than a couple of massive ranches that had been established before Texas was a state, and which now spanned several counties—were the deep, azure waters of the Gulf of Mexico right at the town's back door.

No doubt, had the townsfolk known about the pecuniary troubles that now worried the highly respected elderly granddaughters of the town's revered founding father, they would have gladly chipped in more than enough to get the banker off their backs. However, Miss Clara's and Miss Justine's unwavering adherence to absolute privacy when it came to their financial and personal affairs left the townsfolk no choice but to mind their own business.

Justine pointed down the sidewalk to the end of the block. "Oh my heavens, Clara, look! There's Etta Ruth! Quick! Hide!" She stepped into the doorway of Flora's Flower Shop and pulled Clara along with her.

"For God's sake, Justine! You nearly made me fall!"

"Is she coming this way?" Justine whispered. "You look."

Clara obliged, peeking cautiously around the door.

"She's pulling that little red wagon again, isn't she?" Justine asked, but it was more of a statement than a question. "And is she wearing her dead husband's pants?"

Clara squinted. "She's wearing trousers, but I can't tell from here if they're Clarence's." Clara stepped out onto the sidewalk. "You can come out now. She's turned the corner."

Justine emerged. "Remember what Vernell Watson told us, Clara? She said lately Etta Ruth wears Clarence's pants and shoes everywhere she goes—Piggly Wiggly's, Goldrod's, any place she shops, and she snaps the heads off anybody who looks at her. Who wouldn't look, in that getup? Furthermore, Etta Ruth has abandoned her automobile and pulls that little red wagon all over town well into the midnight hours, as if light and dark doesn't mean a thing to her. Everyone's suspected for years that she isn't right in the head, and she just keeps proving it."

"Knowing Etta Ruth, she's enjoying proving it," Clara quipped.

"Vernell said she accused her neighbor, Mr. Pepper, of trying to kill her cat. When he denied it, she whispered something in his ear that made him turn as red as a sugar beet. I hope he doesn't kill her cat now just to get even ... even if Beelzebub *is* the grouchiest old cat I ever saw."

"She's more likely to kill *his* cat."

"No, she likes cats much more than people—especially *men*," Justine replied. "Anyway, the next day she gave Mr. Pepper a basket of fruit and told him he could pick pecans from her trees this year. It was strictly against her nature to be so nice, Vernell said—which just goes to prove how erratic her behavior has become."

"Perhaps she was trying to follow the Medallion creed, for a change. You know—*kindness, honor, charity, fortitude,* and so on."

"After fifty years of being a witch spelled with a '*B*'? I don't think so. I still believe she only joined the Medallions because she liked the uniform. Anyway, I'd give a dollar to know what she whispered in Mr. Pepper's ear."

"*You would* squander a dollar on such nonsense," Clara snapped.

Justine jerked her chin in her usual dismissive manner. "Vernell said Etta Ruth seems to be mad at the world lately."

"*Lately?*" Clara yelped. "I wonder what sandbox Vernell Watson's had her head buried in all these years?"

"Or how she could have possibly missed Etta Ruth's lifetime of being such a meanie," Justine added.

Clara rolled her eyes. "Isn't that what I just now implied?"

"I have no idea what you implied, Clara. Sometimes it's hard to tell—the *words* you use."

Clara emitted a humorless titter. "Vernell's head in a *sandbox*? Oh my, yes, Justine, I can see how difficult that one is for you to decipher."

Justine gave her a look.

As the traffic light turned from yellow to red, they crossed the street to Goldrod's, smiling and waving politely to the few cars on all four sides of the intersection that had no choice but to wait patiently for them to pass.

If the Rialto was Hesterwine's most frequented place of respite for young and old in the area, then Goldrod's beautiful, rainbow-hued, 1941 Wurlitzer jukebox was the hub around which the town's younger generation gathered when not in the movie house. Only now, with most of the men volunteered or drafted into military service, the lonely girls converged on Goldrod's to sip sodas at the long, black marble fountain while staring sadly into space. They robbed their piggy banks in order to feed nickels, dimes, and quarters to the prized Wurlitzer, then jitterbugged wildly with each other until the buses or trains pulled in for a short stop and the military men crowded in through the back door. In a matter of minutes, the tunes on the jukebox slowed to a cozier, slower form of dancing. Songs like Glen Miller's "Moonlight

Serenade" and Artie Shaw's version of "Stardust" made for closer contact between the combat-bound military men and the heavy-hearted girls.

Such music was playing on the jukebox now as Clara and Justine walked past the pharmacy and cosmetics counters and into the crowded room of slow dancers. As they sat down at the counter, Justine looked around and sighed. "Every day the buses bring more precious young men through town, Clara. War is such a terrible thing. We should be thankful to Poppa that we never married and had sons."

"We should be thankful to *Poppa* for *that*?" Clara asked incredulously, her wizardly greenish-gray eyes suddenly hostile. "We both know who is responsible, and it was not Poppa."

Justine glanced at Clara as if she'd been wounded by the remark, but then she wagged her head from side to side, her eyes forming little slits of denial. "Think what you like, Clara, but *I* think we owe Poppa thanks for it, the way he acted after ..." She went silent.

Clara's reaction was an immediate, "Ha! We can blame Poppa for a lot, but *not* for that!"

"Maybe so, Clara, but it never helped that *we*, you and I, always wanted what the other had."

"Speak for yourself. When it comes to our wants, our minds have always been as split as Rutherford's atom. I never wanted anything you had. It was *you* who did the wanting—*and* the getting," Clara said before calling out to the soda jerk: "Our usual, Bobby—two root beer floats, not too much foam, and a half-jigger of vanilla extract in each. No more, no less, please. Vanilla makes one quite tipsy if one abuses its use."

"That is not true, Clara."

"Vanilla won't make one tipsy?" Clara quipped.

"I didn't always get what I wanted, and you didn't always just stand idly by getting nothing."

"Memory fails you, I suppose," Clara muttered, making a show of glancing curiously around the room.

Justine gave her sister the same haunted look she'd been giving her for the past twenty-nine years—since January 14, 1914, to be exact, and shortly before the beginning of World War I in Europe when she was thirty-eight and Clara was forty. Still years earlier, before *that* unsettling 1914 occurrence, there happened another unfortunate episode when Justine was twenty and Clara twenty-two. However, that first of Justine's girlish debacles was not as much in Justine's mind anymore because she had been so *young* at the time. Even so, she did not doubt that Clara had long ago combined the two hapless occurrences and, like that sourdough biscuit starter they'd had in the refrigerator for years, had been feeding off it.

"We keep promising not to speak of those long past events, Clara."

"It is you who keeps bringing it up, Justine, not me."

"Unintentional slips of the tongue, I assure you." She gave Clara's hand a nervous pat. "I suppose Rube is waiting out back for his cup of ice water."

"I shall take it to him in a while, since it is my turn," Clara said.

Bobby set their frosty mugs of vanilla-laced root beer before them. "Stardust" ended, and "Moonlight Serenade" began. The pair exchanged sweet smiles before turning on their stools to sip their root beers and watch the melancholy young dancers snuggle and cuddle on the dance floor. Occasionally, the two women's eyes widened in fleeting glances at each other, as if to decipher the thoughts in the other's head.

Apparently, there was much that Clara and Justine Hesterwine had forgiven—but not forgotten.

# 3

**O**UTSIDE, AT THE BACK OF GOLDROD'S, Mary Kenny stood in the shade on the *Whites Only* side of the building. Finally, drawn by the music coming from inside and unable to resist, she knelt on the long wooden bench beneath the plate-glass window and peered inside at the dancing couples. Other couples hovered in the booths that separated the small dance floor from the soda fountain, their laughter and friendly conversation sometimes rising above the tunes coming from the glowing Wurlitzer that occupied a corner of the room. Mary listened intently. She loved to dance, but it had been a long time since she had felt anyone's arms around her—well over a year and a half. She quickly abandoned the memory as she noticed a group of teenage girls staring up at her from a booth beneath the window. She spun around and sat down on the bench she'd been kneeling on. Clutching her paper bag tightly on her lap, she tried to relax to the pleasant tune coming from the jukebox.

Although she had not eaten since noon yesterday, she had decided before getting off the bus that she would not go inside the drugstore and spend any of her last five dollars. When the crowd cleared out, she would ask the soda jerk if he knew where she could find a job. This time, she would work long enough to buy a bus ticket *all the way* to California instead of working only a few days before continuing her journey. She had it all planned out. She would stay at a YWCA when she got to California, find employment, and work hard until she could afford a place of her own. She wondered if there was a YWCA in Hesterwine, Texas, that furnished rooms to women who needed them. If so, and if she was frugal, her five dollars would surely be enough to eat on until she found work and earned a paycheck; if not....

There was no hiding the fear in Mary Kenny's eyes as doubt arrived to chip away at her optimism. She was alone and nearly penniless in a strange town that, except for the paved streets, looked as if all construction—as well as the job market—had ended early in the nineteenth century.

With that thought, she dragged the battered old Samsonite onto the bench beside her and drew it close, as if it were a protective shield. The big white dog with the red collar that she had seen trotting down the sidewalk sat on his haunches nearby, and now he glanced up her. *A friendly face,* Mary thought as she warily reached out and patted him. He thumped his tail against the concrete several times before refocusing his attention on the green doors, obviously waiting for someone to come out.

After a while, Mary looked across the way to the unfriendly looking girl slouched against the "colored" service window waiting for the hamburger and Coke she had ordered. The girl returned Mary's curiosity with an inhospitable glance that said she did not consider herself a curiosity. Mary's face reddened, and she quickly focused her attention straight ahead. *That is the meanest-eyed girl I have ever seen. She must be mad at somebody... the entire world, looks like.*

Music and laughter floated from inside, along with the soft scuffling of shoes across the dance floor. Mary wanted to peek through the window again but, fearful she would draw more attention to herself from the girls in the booth, as well as the angry-eyed colored girl, she continued to look elsewhere.

After a moment she closed her eyes, wishing she could govern the brooding pondering of her mind as well as she controlled her physical movements. The chain of events that caused her to be sitting here on this bench today—alone, lonely, and wishing she was dead—was like an insect in her brain, a *memory bug* constantly on the prowl, stinging at will, and then moving too swiftly to be cornered and squashed. Familiar voices rose and fell amid the insect's tumultuous scurrying. One voice rose above the others, cutting her anew, just as then ....

"Darn it, Mary! I thought we were just having fun! I never said no different, did I? A guy's got to live a little ... and face it, Mary, you've been about to smother the life out of me!"

Claxton Mitchell had said those words to her as he removed her hand from his arm and all but threw it at her.

A month later, the draft board drew his number and he was gone. Shortly after that, she discovered she was pregnant.

Mary again felt the panic that had swept through her on that day of discovery, and as she fearfully recalled her father's words a few years earlier when he finally noticed she was no longer a child and had sat her down to give her his version of the "birds and the bees." Being without a mother, their important "father and daughter talk" consisted of: "There's just one thing you need to remember about the *birds and the bees*, Mary, so listen up. There'll be no bastards spawned in the Kenny family. If that ever happens, you'd better not let me find out about it—just fix it."

She got Claxton's address from his parents and wrote to him. *Claxton would be* happy *about the baby.* He had only been confused before, worried about the war and dreading induction into the army before he was ready. He would say he was sorry for saying those hurtful things to her. He would come home and marry her. *He loved her.* They had loved each other since high school, right on up through their sophomore year in college.

To this day, she cringed remembering how desperate, and *delusional,* she had been to cling so long to that kind of thinking.

She was well into her seventh month of pregnancy and hiding beneath winter's heavy sweaters and overcoats before she realized Claxton was not going to answer her letters. Even though numbed by despair, she sensibly acknowledged that the day was rapidly approaching when she would have to confide in someone. Her father was not stupid; one day soon, he would realize what she was hiding beneath those bulky clothes. She thought of her grandmother. The gentle woman would be saddened at how she had complicated her young life, but she would not disown her, nor would she demand that she "fix it." As always in the past when problems at home had sent her to her grandmother in New Jersey, she longed to pack the old Samsonite and go to her. But this was a problem like no other, and despite her desperation, she could not bring herself to burden her elderly and ailing grandmother with it. Subconsciously, beneath the honesty of that reason, she feared that this revered mentor in her life would be ashamed of her, even while supporting her.

Still, she had to confide in *someone*, and soon. The question of exactly *who* would be her confidant was resolved for her the day she stepped out of the old four-footed tub in her bathroom and Jessie, her father's girlfriend, carrying a stack of fresh towels, unexpectedly pushed the door open. Jessie was nothing like her gentle mother had been, and was a bit coarse in looks as well as speech, but she always seemed to be offering friendship in her joking, offhanded manner. After staring at Mary's swollen stomach as if she had never seen a pregnant woman before, Jessie promised to keep the forthcoming event strictly between them.

"No telling what your daddy would do if he found out. He'd probably bust a gut! I'll tell him you're gonna stay with me at my house for a while. He won't mind you being gone," she said, and immediately looked apologetic.

Mary remembered replying, "No, he won't mind, he never has."

The baby was stillborn. She didn't remember much about the birth after the midwife, Jessie's sister, gave her an injection that spun her into a dream-like state. She was aware of a final burst of pain, but then it was as if she was looking at the room through the distorting glass bottom of a Coke bottle. Lapsing into a deep sleep, she dreamed she had seen her father standing over her and holding a tightly wrapped bundle, his mouth moving on indistinguishable words that sounded like garbled explosions. Caught up in that dreadful dream, she struggled to focus on him through the Coke-bottle lens as he turned away with the bundle and disappeared.

"The poor little thing was a boy," Jessie said when Mary, feeling drugged and disoriented, awoke late the next day and learned her baby was dead.

"He's had a proper but very private burial. Me and my sister saw to it. The burial was this morning—a beautiful little casket, prayers, and a place in our family plot," Jessie said.

Then, as Mary sobbed, Jessie rocked her in her thick arms. "Don't think about it, Mary. It's gone and, after all, ain't it for the best ... for you and for *it*?"

"He wasn't an *'it'*, Jessie, he was a baby boy. *My* baby boy. I loved him! I wanted him!"

A week later when Mary had recovered enough to be up and about, Jessie took her home. Her father was waiting at the top of the stairs, his big hand clutching the handle of her old Samsonite. The instant she saw his face puffy with condemnation, she knew that Jessie had betrayed her. "I called your grandmother and told the old bat how you disgraced this family," he said. "Being the *bohemian* type that she is, she says you are more than welcome to live with her. So, get going!"

She had watched the old Samsonite bounce down the stairs, incurring more scars as it went before sliding to a halt at her feet. Jessie stood beside the front door, her car keys in her hand ... waiting to take her to the train station.

To this day, Mary loved Claxton. She knew it was foolish to love someone who did not care about her and had dumped her, but she had not learned yet how to stop being foolish.

Just then, the green doors opened and several couples emerged and strolled to a spot behind the bus. Trying to guide her thoughts away from the past, Mary concentrated on watching them. If she leaned forward on the bench and peered beneath the bus's carriage, she could see the couples' shoes nestled toe to toe as the girls offered passionate good-byes to the young servicemen passing through town. "War does strange things to people," Mary recalled her grandmother saying. "Proper young ladies, raised to be stingy with their kisses, are less inclined to be so reserved during war time when the boys who go away may not come back."

Mary's eyes filled with tears. Before she'd left her grandmother's empty apartment, a college friend from home had called and told her that Claxton Mitchell was "missing in action and presumed dead."

She dropped her chin to her chest and watched her tears make tiny stains on the brown paper bag in her lap.

Across the way, the small service window slid open and the aroma of fries and burgers wafted from inside. Mary wiped her eyes as her stomach announced its hunger in a long, incessant rumble. The white dog with the red collar looked at her, as did the girl standing at the *Colored Order Here* window, until the soda jerk rapped his knuckles impatiently on the shelf to get her attention.

"Thirty cents," he said as he shoved a small basket out to her.

"Keep the change," said the girl.

"Want a straw?" he asked.

"Yes, I want a straw, and some catsup, and a napkin, too, if you ain't gonna charge extra for 'em."

"They come with the order."

"That so? Well, then, why ain't you already give 'em to me?"

Mary knew without looking that the soda jerk was being jabbed with those ferocious black eyes.

Moments later, Mary drew back cautiously as the girl, unsmiling, sauntered toward her.

"I hate fries. I didn't order 'em. They came with the burger. You can have the damn greasy things." She thrust the little paper boat of fries at Mary, and even before Mary could reply, she added angrily, "What's the matter, you too good to take my fries? Maybe you think I touched 'em and got my *black* all over 'em!"

Mary quickly took the fries. "Thank you. I-I am grateful."

"You ought to be. I heard your belly howling. For a minute, I thought it was that old white dog." She tore off a piece of bun and tossed it to him. He sniffed it, then returned his attention to the green door.

"Damn dog thinks he's too good for my scraps."

"Most dogs are meat eaters, and ... and color-blind, I'm told." Instantly embarrassed to have made such a nonsensical remark, she felt her face redden.

The girl gave out a humorless titter, then eyed her. "You ain't Southern. I can tell by your talk."

"I am from New Jersey ... upstate New York before that." She set aside the fries and hesitantly offered her hand. "I am Mary Kenny."

The girl shook it briefly, more like a hand *brush* than a handshake, saying, "Leeta Bulow, from ... it ain't important where I'm from." She tilted her head and squinted at Mary. "You stranded in this damn hole, too, ain't you?"

Mary nodded as she slid her suitcase from the bench to the concrete in case Leeta Bulow decided to sit down. Just then, both girls looked toward the street as a battered old pickup truck, pulling a horse trailer that contained two saddled horses, rattled loudly across the tracks, took a sharp left, and pulled up beside the Greyhound bus. The air suddenly changed from diesel to manure.

Two men exited the truck; one of them a burly white man with a big belly, knee-high boots, and a wide-brimmed, silver-gray hat. Mary noted that his narrowed eyes had locked on Leeta Bulow. She glanced at Leeta, who was paying no attention to the man. Leeta's half-hostile, half-curious eyes were on the second passenger—a young colored man as dark-skinned as she was, only slightly taller, his pointed-toed high-heeled boots also up to his knees, and his *Hopalong Cassidy*-style hat just as big and black as Hoppy's but not near as clean.

"Well, I'll be a ring-tailed critter," Leeta said mockingly under her breath. "If it ain't a genuine pair of real Texas-style cowboys, horse shit and all."

Mary wanted to shush her but didn't dare as she focused her attention on the burly white man coming toward them. Plainly visible now was the sheriff badge on his sweaty khaki shirt.

"You, gal," he said to Leeta. "See that sign over there that says *Colored*?" He pointed to it, then looked at Mary, his pale eyes scowling as he scolded her. "You shoulda told that gal to get on her side of the building, miss. This here section is for whites only."

Leeta was already on her way to the colored side, stepping jauntily along with her nose in the air but looking straight ahead.

Next to the bench where Leeta plopped down, the stone-faced colored cowboy tapped at the little window and ordered a club sandwich and strawberry shake.

The sheriff made a move as if to kick the big white dog.

"Get on outta my way, Rube," he growled as he looked at Leeta again. "I know every Negro in Vander County, and you ain't one of 'em, not by a long shot," he added, looking her up and down from head to toe. "I'll just bet Hesterwine ain't the kind of town you're looking for, now is it, gal?" He opened the green door. "If you ain't on board that Greyhound bus by the time I come back out, I'll have some questions for you down at the jailhouse."

"*What ...?*" Leeta came up from the bench. "You mean you gonna throw me in jail just because I was on the wrong side of the damn—"

"Hush your mouth, gal!" the cowboy at the window growled, slamming his hand downward as if motioning her to sit as quickly as possible. "You gonna be heading for bad trouble if you don't."

The sheriff paused in the open doorway. "Good advice you're giving that gal, Posey," he said, then eyed Leeta. "I could take you in right now for *disorderly conduct*, if I wanted to," he drawled before going in.

Leeta, already in her Joe Louis stance, swung her glare to the cowboy. She waited until the door closed behind the sheriff.

"Ain't no shit-kicker like you big enough to make Leeta Bulow shut up! You wave that arm at me again, black boy, and I'm gonna rip it off and shove it up your black ass!"

Mary Kenny stared open-mouthed at her.

"You got a real dirty mouth, Leeta Bulow," he said quietly.

"Maybe I do, but I don't smell like horse shit!"

"Yeah, you do. I smell it from over here every time you open your mouth to speak," he said with a small laugh, and stomped one of his boots on the concrete. "I can clean my boots easy, just like that, but I reckon that smell you got ain't to be rid of so easy."

"You don't know me, *Negro!*"

"I know you. All I got to do is look at you. You are a walking, talking, big-city, street-corner advertisement. The sheriff is right. Hesterwine ain't your kind of town, gal ... unless you're gonna be looking for honest work." He eyed her from beneath his big black hat. "But I reckon you're gonna be getting back on that bus."

Leeta's retort was lost among the piercing, uninterrupted shriek of a siren, so loud it seemed to vibrate the air. Almost immediately, shades inside Goldrod's plate-glass windows came down, the music stopped, and the lights went out. Across the side street the same thing happened, as the shades went down in the windows of a shoe shop and the *Open* neon sign on the door flickered off.

"That's the air raid siren on top the courthouse!" the cowboy yelled over the sound.

"I *know* it's a damn air raid siren! I ain't stupid!" Leeta yelled back.

Mary clamped her hands over her ears. A few seconds later, the sirens stopped. The shades went up, and the music on the Wurlitzer whined back into song.

"We got bigger and louder sirens than *that* where I come from, and, so far, ain't nobody been dumb enough to set 'em off in broad daylight and scare the crap out of everybody," Leeta said. "If anybody gonna bomb us, it gonna be at *night* time. Ain't you seen them London newsreels? That's how them Germans do it."

"In Hesterwine, we believe that practice makes perfect, and folks will know what to do if them sirens goes off for real some *night.*"

"Oh, yeah? What if a real air raid happens? How you gonna know the difference, dummy, if you been hearing 'em sirens every damn day?"

"I'll tell you how, *dummy*. If we gonna get bombed for real, them sirens won't *stop* blaring the warning. They're just gonna keep blasting away. That's how we'll know it's for real ... *dummy.*"

"Huh! Ain't nobody gonna bomb this little burg, anyhow."

He grinned at her. "You're probably right, but it ain't no secret we got German U-boats coming into our waters and dropping off spies. Hesterwine ain't that far from the water, and them U-boats can get close enough to lop some bombs on us if they get a mind to."

Leeta scoffed again, sassily wiggling her hip as she did.

The cowboy's grin deepened. "Ain't nothing to worry 'bout though, 'cause the United States Navy and Marine Corps is on the job. We got three military bases right near here where they train navy and marine pilots round the clock. We got ships in the water and planes in the sky all the time, keeping the enemy from sneaking up on us. If our boats don't get 'em, our planes will. And they'll get 'em long before them U-boats can lob their bombs on our military bases." He snapped his fingers. "Get 'em just like *that*."

Mary watched as Leeta's big eyes blinked rapidly at him, as if she still wanted to fight, but was sidetracked by his sudden friendly talk.

Just then, both green doors opened wide and the crowd streamed out behind the bus driver. Some of the servicemen filed onto the bus, while others hung back with the girls they had danced with half an hour. The bus engine revved and then idled; waiting, it seemed, for the couples to separate. Finally, the driver delivered three short blasts on the horn. The men and boys piled onboard, and the colored soldiers came running from the depot. The bus pulled out and, for a brief moment, the choking smell of diesel overpowered the whiffs of horse manure coming from the trailer.

"I reckon you shoulda got on that bus, gal," the cowboy said.

"Shoulda, coulda, woulda," Leeta mumbled, and slouched back down onto the bench.

"The next bus don't come through 'til morning." He paused, as if waiting for her to reply, and when she didn't, he said, "You ain't got any luggage, so I don't reckon you're going far."

"As far west as I can goddamn get."

"With just the clothes on your back?" He shook his head. "I ain't even gonna ask."

"Good! So shut up, shit-kicker, and leave me the hell alone."

Even from where Mary Kenny sat across the way she could see Leeta Bulow's big eyes glistening, and they weren't looking so mean anymore; they were looking scared. Mary stood but then sat back down, thinking that maybe *whites* weren't allowed in the *colored* section any more than coloreds were allowed in the white section, and that the sheriff might take her to jail, too, if he came out and saw her over there. Anyway, did she really want to comfort that unpleasant girl? Remembering the *No Vagrants Allowed* sign at Hesterwine's city limits, she sobered even more. With no money, no job, and a total stranger in town, being white only made her a slightly better off *vagrant* than Leeta Bulow was!

Mary started as the green door swung open and the sheriff stepped out.

Behind him, clutching a cup of water, toddled one of the blue-haired old ladies she had seen in front of the theater. The elderly woman patted the big white dog with the red collar, then bent low to let him lap noisily at the cup of water.

"Well, well," the sheriff drawled, staring at Leeta Bulow. "Ain't you the one." He jerked a set of handcuffs from his hip pocket. "What you trying to prove, gal? Didn't I say you better be on that bus when it leaves town?"

The terrified look on Leeta Bulow's face as he snapped a handcuff on one of her thin wrists made Mary jump to her feet. She hesitated only a few seconds before shakily calling out to the sheriff.

"Sir! Mr. Sheriff! That girl couldn't buy a ticket because ... because her money purse and luggage were stolen at the last bus stop." Mary had told lies in the past, some of which were little white ones and a few that her father would have considered big black ones; she wasn't sure which this one was. She glanced briefly away from the sheriff as another blue-haired old lady came out the green door to stand alongside the first and stare curiously at everyone.

"It ain't the town of Hesterwine's problem she lost her money, miss," said the sheriff. "Point is, strangers of her kind ain't welcome in Hesterwine." He paused to look Leeta up and down again, his critical gaze traveling down her tight-skirted body to the fake leopard-skin platform shoes. "Ain't welcome here for obvious reasons," he finished, with a disgusted wag of his head. "She's going to jail and if she can't make bail in a week or so, she'll be put on the work detail 'til she works off her fine."

"'Til I work off my *fine?*" Leeta cried. "Fine for *what?*"

"Vagrancy," he growled. "After you've worked a couple months scrubbing the jailhouse floors, you'll be taken outside the city limits and can try hitching your way, or hoofing it, to someplace you might be welcome. Either way, you better not stand still for more than five minutes at a time, or I'm gonna slap you right back in jail."

As Leeta Bulow glared at the sheriff, her mouth twisting on words that she obviously dared not speak, Mary dared to approach the sheriff on the colored side of the building.

"Sheriff, my ... my relatives will pick me up soon. They will give this girl money for bus fare." *Another lie! Now what will I do?* Mary wondered as she watched him examine her just as he had scrutinized Leeta Bulow.

"What's your name, miss?"

"M-Mary Kenny."

"You got relatives here in Hesterwine, Mary Kenny? Seems like to me they woulda been here to meet the bus."

Mary stared up at him, unable to speak; his size alone was intimidating, let alone the harshness of his puffy face. She heard herself stammering, but she did not know what she was trying to fabricate this time. The next lie wasn't coming fast enough. If she answered yes, he would ask *who?*

"*Mary?* Is that *you*, my dear?"

Mary whirled in surprise to face the two blue-haired old ladies who stood side by side, smiling pleasantly at her.

"My goodness, Mary, how you have grown!" one of them cried. "We would have never recognized you if you hadn't said your name. I'm not a bit surprised you didn't recognize your Aunt Justine and me—since you haven't seen us since you were a baby."

"You the relatives she's waiting for, Miss Clara, Miss Justine?"

"Why, yes, but we thought she wasn't arriving until tomorrow."

Speechless, Mary stared at the strange pair; the only aunt she ever had was her father's older sister, and she had died years ago.

The sheriff looked from them to Mary and back again. "I didn't know you had any kin outside of Miz Etta Ruth Morley ... 'specially not somebody with a Yankee accent," said the sheriff.

"I dare say the Hesterwines have kin all over the United States, Sheriff Bloot," said one of the old ladies. "The Hesterwines *did* spread far and wide when they came to America as stowaways on the *Mayflower,* you know."

"You told me that story before, Miss Justine—*stowaways*—and that's why the Hesterwine name ain't on the passenger list with the original arrivals."

"Correct, and the family immediately branched out on their own as soon as their sturdy feet touched shore, which was likely why so many of them survived the pestilence that plagued their fellow passengers," said the one

Sheriff Bloot had called Miss Clara as she stepped up to Mary and gave her a hug. Miss Justine did the same.

"Come along, dear," said Miss Clara. She turned to Leeta. "You too, girl. We can't let you spend all that time in Sheriff Bloot's jail for absolutely no reason other than being without your money purse."

"Now wait just a minute, ladies," the sheriff said, throwing up a hand as if halting traffic. "I got to question that colored gal and maybe her *friend*, too." He shot Mary a disapproving look. "I gotta make sure they ain't up to something, them being strangers in town. It's my duty!"

Miss Justine scoffed as Miss Clara, staring at him as if in disbelief, cried, "I have told you who our Mary is. Do you not believe me?"

He seemed to hesitate. "You sure about that, Miss Clara? It's easy to make a mistaken identity when you ain't seen a person in years." As both elderly women pursed their lips at him, he added, "Anyhow, I suggest you take a long, hard look at that colored gal before you take her into your home." He mugged sourly at Leeta as he removed the handcuff, his squinted eyes taking in her attire from head to toe again as if to make a point, and he nodded knowingly at Miss Clara.

Obedient to the sheriff's suggestion, Miss Clara stepped back and gave Leeta a thorough going-over. Finally, she tapped her softly crinkled cheek with an arthritic forefinger. "I love your shoes, dear, but don't they hurt?"

Sheriff Bloot tossed up his hands and motioned to the Hopalong-Cassidy-style cowboy. "Come on, Posey, let's go." He turned to Leeta. "Watch your step, gal ... or you may get to see my jail yet. We don't tolerate coloreds with *big-city*, Yankee attitudes in Vander County."

"I was born and raised in Mississippi, Sheriff. I speck it ain't much different here than it was there."

He gave her a last hard look before stomping away.

The four women watched silently as he started the engine of his truck, made a wheel-screeching U-turn—the two horses in the trailer scrambling to stay afoot—and then rattled loudly across the railroad tracks before speeding off down the street much faster than when he'd arrived.

Mary looked cautiously at the elderly women. "Thank you for what you just did, but ... you do realize that I am not your niece, don't you?"

"Of course you're not our niece. We do not have a niece," said the taller one, Miss Clara.

The other, Miss Justine, with the curly permed hair and a round face that clearly had once been very pretty, nodded. "My sister and I are the last vestiges of the Hesterwine family, other than a disagreeable cousin in town, who Poppa always said inherited his in-law's *peculiar* gene." She made a face. "Of course, our dear mother was one of them, and she used to get furious when he said that."

Mary immediately had second thoughts. Her mother and grandmother had taught her never to talk to strangers, "Looks deceive, Mary ... and the most innocent-looking strangers, though outwardly kind, can be quite diabolical beneath it all."

Leeta Bulow narrowed her eyes suspiciously at the pair. "I'm just gonna come right out and ask it. How come you wanna take us home with you? You two ain't *funny* ladies, are you?"

"Why, my dear, you certainly *need* help, don't you?" Clara Hesterwine said. "For one, we are Hesterwine Medallions, a dwindling group of ladies here in town sworn to administer aid where needed and to set right the wrongs of the world if they should ever come to Hesterwine, Texas. Besides, Sheriff Bloot is *Banker Prickett's* son-in-law."

"Indeed, he is!" said her sister in a most agitated voice. Then she smiled sweetly at Leeta. "As to Clara and I being *'funny ladies,' I* possess a much better sense of humor than Clara does."

# 4

THE HESTERWINE SISTERS SAID their Buick was parked behind the lumberyard, a two-block walk down the side street from Goldrod's. They headed in that direction, the big, white dog, Rube, leading the way as if he knew exactly where he was going. Leeta carried Mary Kenny's old suitcase, Mary carried the paper bag, and the blue-haired old ladies carried the conversation. Mary and Leeta fell far enough behind so as not to be overheard as Leeta wondered aloud if they should be following these two old ladies to "who knows where or what?"

"They seem real nice," Mary whispered back. "The tall one, Miss Clara, reminds me of my grandmother."

"I'll figure they're real nice if they come across with some traveling money," Leeta grumbled. "I don't know why they didn't just open their purses and hand me some."

Clara and Justine Hesterwine could not easily hear each other unless they whispered rather loudly; therefore, Mary and Leeta heard every word they said.

"We will have to sell something, Clara. We certainly can't buy bus tickets for those girls with an empty sugar jar. And what about the mortgage, Clara? Frankly, we have more to worry about than *bus tickets*, with Banker Prickett prepared to take away everything we own." She glanced worriedly over her shoulder at Mary and Leeta, and then gave them a big smile before adding, "Maybe we should have left well enough alone and allowed them to solve their own problems."

"Shame on you, Justine. Are you not a Hesterwine Medallion the same as I? If our founding mothers heard you talk like that, they'd likely take your uniform away, as well as your lap flap."

"Clara Hesterwine, I am as much a Hesterwine Medallion as you are, and I am getting tired of you throwing our founding mothers in my face every time I say something you don't agree with! You hurt my feelings, Clara."

"If we had a dollar for every time you said I hurt your feelings, we could buy the Missouri Pacific Railroad."

"Could not."

Leeta grunted, then hissed, "Damnit! They ain't got any money! And I thought *Home of the Hesterwine Medallions* on that sign meant *dough*, the kind you can spend. But it's just a bunch of old lady do-gooders—and what the hell is a *'lap flap'?*"

"I guess it could be part of their uniform," Mary said, then put a finger to her lips for quiet so she could continue eavesdropping. "The poor things are in trouble."

"Anyway, Justine," Miss Clara was saying, "if you have any bright ideas about where we can get the money to pay Banker Prickett, I'm all ears."

"Well! Thank you for asking for a change, Clara," said Miss Justine in a mocking tone clearly meant to sound incredulous. "As a matter of fact, I was thinking of Mr. Klunk at Klunk's Junk. Perhaps, Clara, Mr. Klunk at the Klunk's Junk will buy the engine out of Poppa's old International tractor. What do you think?"

"I think it's worth a try."

"You do? On second thought ..."

"On second thought, *what?* It is *your* idea, Justine." Miss Clara was clearly agitated.

"I just mean that Mr. Klunk will probably want the whole tractor, but Poppa would not be happy with us if we let him have it."

"What do you think Poppa's going to do, rise up out of his grave and confine us to our rooms for the weekend? We'll go to the junkyard in the morning and ask Mr. Klunk if he will take the engine. It hasn't caught a spark in over twenty years, anyhow."

"Remember what happened to it in twenty-nine, Clara?" Miss Justine laughed cheerily. "In the pitch-black of night, those little Polpepper boys borrowed that old International and overturned it in the creek. After Mr. Polpepper gave the boys a fit tanning, he came over with his two oxen, pulled it out of the creek, and dragged it back to the barn for us."

"It wasn't twenty-nine, Justine. It was twenty-eight. And they didn't borrow it; they *stole* it. Their name was, and *still* is, *Poindexter*, not *Polpepper*—and it was a team of *mules*, not *oxen*."

"I am very certain that I am not mistaken," Miss Justine huffed.

"*I* am very certain that you *are* mistaken," Miss Clara shot back.

Leeta rolled her eyes upward and leaned close to whisper to Mary. "Like I said, them silly old ladies ain't got a dime. They ain't gonna be able to help either one of us. They probably live in a li'l old shack hardly big enough for *them*, much less us."

"Maybe we can find work tomorrow."

"Maybe somebody gonna hire *you*, but the signs I seen hanging everywhere ain't calling my name, and I don't reckon them old ladies feel any different when it comes right down to it. I don't trust 'em worth a damn. They're broke. They probably gonna try and make me work for nothing."

Mary gathered enough nerve to say exactly what she was thinking, although she was careful to say it softly: "You really should be more grateful, Miss Bulow. They spoke up to save us both from that awful sheriff's jail, not to get free labor."

"Gir-r-r-l, that sheriff wouldn't a drug your skinny little white ass off to no jail. If them old ladies hadn't showed up and seen what a helpless little scaredy-cat you was, he probably woulda took you home to his family."

"Well, Miss Bulow," Mary whispered back, "I guess those nice old ladies saw something just as helpless in *you*. They invited you along, didn't they?"

Leeta opened her mouth for another retort, but before she could voice it, one of the old ladies called out to them.

"There's our Buick, girls."

Not seeing the Buick, both Mary and Leeta looked at Clara Hesterwine to see that she was pointing across the street at a rambling lumberyard building surrounded by tall stacks of lumber that looked as if they had been there a while. In the shade of a giant oak tree stood an old relic of a vehicle that surely was among the very first horseless carriages ever invented. However, there was no Buick.

Silent, and with mouths slightly ajar, Mary and Leeta followed Clara and Justine Hesterwine across the street and right up to the antiquated jalopy.

"Isn't it a beauty?" Justine asked. "Poppa bought it brand-new for Clara and me. 'The White Streak' is what it was called. It was the only 1909 Buick Model Ten Surrey convertible in town back in those days. Poppa liked it because it resembled a fancy old horse-drawn carriage he had given Clara and me on her eighteenth birthday."

Miss Clara slapped the solid iron fender. "A four-passenger, double-roadster touring car is what it is," she said proudly. "We squeezed *nine* of our friends into it once when Poppa was out of town and drove to a dance clean over in the next county!"

"Just that once, though, because someone told Poppa on us," Miss Justine said as she frowned and tossed her chin, as if it had happened only yesterday.

"You mean it runs?" Leeta's half-hostile, half-flabbergasted eyes darted from front to back of the relic.

"Why, yes," Miss Justine smiled. "And thanks to Mr. Rudolph Valentino, it gets us wherever we need to go." She opened the driver's-side door and Rube jumped onto the front seat.

"Rudolph Valentino?" Mary said beneath her breath while wondering why the name sounded so familiar. Suddenly, she remembered that her grandmother had told her about a Rudolph Valentino—a star of the silent movie screen—an Italian heartthrob known as the Latin Lover. *But he is dead, isn't he? Grandmother said he died of a perforated gastric ulcer long before his time, causing mass mourning among his adoring female fans. Grandmother said she had shed a tear or two, but did not get ridiculously soupy over it.*

Mary looked around for the famous actor's namesake, suspecting he was the person who would crank the motor on the relic. The notion that an automobile as old as this one would still *run* suddenly struck her as funny, and she grinned ever so slightly, the first smile in a long time. However, she had no time to ponder further because a young Negro man wearing a baseball cap and overalls appeared from around the side of the building leading the biggest, meanest-looking Brahma bull she had ever seen, and headed toward them!

Mary heard Leeta Bulow's terrified screech an instant before she dropped the Samsonite suitcase, shoved past Mary, and scrambled onto the back seat of the old vehicle.

"Don't be afraid, dear," Miss Clara, said. "Rudolph Valentino is quite gentle ... as long as no one touches that ring in his nose."

Mary knew that the monstrous animal was a Brahma bull like the savage bulls rodeo cowboys rode—or attempted to ride—often to their peril. She had never seen a real rodeo, only a spine-chilling newsreel of such an event. The two-thousand-pound bull in the newsreel, with the sharp tips of his horns sawed off, had tossed the cowboy high into the air, gored him repeatedly, and then tried to do the same to the rodeo clown that came to the bull rider's rescue. The clown escaped by jumping into a big barrel that the bull then tossed and rolled all over the arena. This mammoth animal looked exactly like that ferocious, two-thousand-pound, pale-gray rodeo bull, except that the sharp points of this bull's horns were still intact!

Suddenly the bull made a long, low noise that resembled an ominous growl. Intending to clamber aboard, Mary shoved the paper bag at Leeta Bulow, then tried to do the same with the suitcase, but it became stuck between the door's narrow frames. Near panic, she was shoving and banging away at it when Clara Hesterwine pulled it free, went around back of the Buick, and tied it onto the luggage rack. "Thank you," Mary said meekly from her safe spot on the back seat next to Leeta, her eyes still warily on the bull as Miss Clara returned and smiled sympathetically at her.

"Both of you will be hugging Mr. Valentino before you know it, dear," she said.

Not convinced, the girls watched apprehensively as the man hitched the bull to the front of the old Buick via a singletree yoke and harness that had lain unnoticed in the deep grass. When done, the young man accepted the coins Miss Clara handed him, tipped his cap, and left. The ladies climbed onto the front seat. Rube sat on his haunches between them. Miss Justine suddenly twisted around to stare at the girls.

"For heaven's sake, we haven't been properly introduced, have we? How rude of us, Clara," she said to her sister, and then to the girls, "I am Justine Hesterwine and this is my sister, Clara Hesterwine. Clara's the oldest, as I am certain you have already determined," Justine said, smiling as she thrust her arm over the seat and daintily shook each girl's hand.

Miss Clara did the same, adding, "I am also the most *educated*, which *I* am certain you determined soon after Justine opened her mouth."

"I went to college the same as you did, Clara," Miss Justine said.

"Yes, but *I passed* the courses," Miss Clara shot back, and then smiled at Mary. "I know you are Mary Kenny because I heard you say so to Sheriff Bloot."

"Yes, ma'am, I am from New York. I was on my way to the West Coast because I heard factory jobs were plentiful out there."

"My goodness! Your family allowed you to travel alone clear across the country? I suppose times *are* changing," Miss Clara said, then sighed.

"Actually, I have no family ... to speak of."

"What a shame. Like you, dear, Justine and I have had no family '*to speak of,*' since Poppa died."

"Except for a dreadful cousin named Etta Ruth Morley," added Miss Justine. "And we do not speak of *her* at all." She suddenly looked agitated.

"And what is *your* name, my dear?" Miss Clara asked Leeta.

"*Willie.* Willie Holloway."

Mary's head did an instantaneous swivel at the girl who had previously said her name was *Leeta Bulow.*

"Wilhelmina?" Miss Justine asked.

"No, ma'am, just plain old *Willie.* I guess my momma wanted a boy. She's dead, and *I* ain't got no relatives 'to speak of,' neither."

"Clara and I can certainly sympathize with anyone whose family, *to speak of,* has passed on to their just rewards." Both women smiled warmly at them.

Moments later, with reins in hand that evidently controlled the big bull, Miss Clara frowned slightly over her shoulder at them. "I feel I must prepare you for the ride, girls. Mr. Valentino is not *always* a perfect gentleman. He detests traveling in this heat and will probably complain about it all the way home."

Miss Justine let out a loud, weary breath. "I surely hope he won't be so rude in front of our guests, Clara."

"Your *hoping* has never stopped him before, Justine."

"He ain't gonna go nuts, is he?" Leeta asked, staring past the sisters at the scary-looking Brahma bull.

"Heavens, no!" Miss Justine cried, as if Leeta's question was the most ridiculous thing she had ever heard. She turned round on the seat and, with raised eyebrows, made a sour face, fanning her hand in front of her nose. "Sometimes I think he does it on purpose."

Leeta did not have time to finish rolling her eyes at Mary because Clara Hesterwine—like an expert stagecoach driver in a John Wayne movie—launched the monstrous animal into a neck-snapping lurch that caused Leeta's arm to shoot out and wrap securely over the door. At the same time, Mary's hand flew up to clamp tightly over her green felt fedora.

"Giddy up, Mr. Valentino! Let's go home!" Clara cried. Then, as if doing his part, the big white dog, Rube, braced his paws on the dash and barked ... and barked ... until they had rolled through the red light at the intersection, turned onto Main Street, wheeled past Goldrod's, the Rialto, and all the small-town sights Mary and Leeta had seen from the Greyhound bus, and headed out of town.

"As soon as that damn bull slows down, I'm jumping outta this damn rattletrap," Leeta whispered to Mary.

"Sheriff Bloot would just *love* you doing something as foolish as that, *Willie Holloway*," Mary whispered back.

# 5

Three miles past Hesterwine's city limits, Leeta had not yet jumped out, but Rudolph Valentino had stopped "being rude" the instant he turned off the highway onto an obscure little dirt road next to a faded, arrow-shaped sign that said *Hesterwine Road*. Thankfully, the air was suddenly fresh, with only the aroma of greenery.

"We shall be home soon," Miss Justine yelled over the whistling sound of light wind that came up suddenly to ripple through the thick trees and other foliage that lined the heavily shaded lane. "I imagine you girls are tired and hungry; I know I am. I hope you like chicken and dumplings."

"Justine made them this time," Miss Clara shouted over her shoulder. "The dumplings turned to mush as soon as she dropped them in the pot."

"They did not! There are still a few nice, fluffy dumplings in there, and quite tasty, I might add."

"I love chicken and dumplings ... even if they have melted into soup," Mary called out, hoping to avert another heated exchange between them, and while thinking that her rescue by these two bickering, but kindly, women was certainly not the worst thing that could have happened. Feeling almost relaxed, she settled back to take in the sights. Aromatic whiffs of wild flowers punctuated the breeze, making the ride in the old Buick most enjoyable—except, perhaps, to the glum-faced Willie Holloway sitting next to her.

Miss Clara halted Mr. Valentino atop a steep hill that Miss Justine said was Windy Knoll. From there, the scenery ahead was less grown-over and, although dotted with mottes of oak and mesquite, looked more like farmland.

"One can see for miles from up here," Clara said, and pointed. "That's Corpus Christi Bay over there, only a mile from our house."

Justine chimed in, "And beyond the bay is the Gulf of Mexico and the Caribbean Sea. And after that, of course, is the Atlantic Ocean."

"I'm sure the girls don't need a geography lesson, Justine," Clara said.

"You don't know that, Clara."

Clara pointed again, this time to a massive three-story structure at the bottom of the hill. "There's our home, Hesterwine Place."

Mary stared. She had expected something unremarkable.

"*Pillars*, yet," Leeta muttered. "It's big as that old courthouse in town."

"Grandfather used to tell us what a grand showplace it was before that awful war with the Yankees. Poppa said Grandfather once owned a dozen slaves and their families," Justine said and then, looking horrified, slapped her hand to her mouth. She turned to stare regretfully at Leeta. "I am sorry I mentioned that, my dear."

Leeta rolled her eyes. Mary, knowing by now to expect sarcasm, dared to poke Leeta's ribs. Leeta glared at her and then smiled at Miss Justine.

"Oh, dat's all right, mis'ress," she simpered. "I'se jest gonna love bein' on de ol' plantation again! Grandma tol' me what fun she had scrubbin' dem flos and totin' dem bales."

Justine laughed and clapped her hands. "You have a fine sense of humor, young lady! I love it! I just love it!"

As they neared the looming three-story brick mansion, Mary leaned forward on the seat. The windows on all three levels were from floor to ceiling, and with huge stained-glass fanlights on the landings between each floor. All that kept Hesterwine Place from looking just as spectacular as the beautiful old manors featured in magazines was its peeling paint on the wooden shutters, a number of which hung askew. In contrast, the grounds stood picture-perfect in tastefully laid-out shrubs and flowerbeds. A rose garden lay to one side of the house. Mary gazed with appreciative eyes at the picturesque scene of another time and place. She surmised that the Hesterwine sisters were as genteel as their once opulent surroundings, despite harboring a deep-seated anger at each other. "Your yard—if I can call something so large simply a 'yard'—is magnificent," Mary said as they neared a scrolled iron gate.

"Our yardman, Flaco Rosales, deserves the credit. Of course, we work alongside him," Clara replied. "Flaco has the day off today. One of his nephews is being baptized over at the Mexicans' church."

"Flaco can neither speak nor hear," Justine said.

"Which doesn't keep him from being a master of flora *and* fauna," Clara added. "He takes excellent care of Mr. Valentino and the other animals, as well as grows the biggest, sweetest watermelons in Vander County. He sells them for us alongside the highway every summer."

Justine sighed heavily and pointed at the fields they had passed minutes earlier. "We used to plant cotton but, between battling the droughts and the boll weevils, we finally gave it up."

"I think the land was crying out for a rest, anyway," Clara added. "Overworked land can get as tired as overworked people, you know."

Justine sighed again. "Flaco will be selling the watermelons soon but, despite his green thumb, I'm afraid this year's melon crop won't be near enough to pay the—"

"Justine!" Clara interrupted, and then smiled as if she hadn't raised her voice. She pulled Mr. Valentino to a halt. "Go on into the house, girls. Justine and I will put the Buick away and unhitch Mr. Valentino."

Just then, a medley of loud braying came from the direction of a massive, old barn seventy-five yards or so from the house.

"That's a donkey," Leeta said.

"Yes, that is Lionel Barrymore welcoming Mr. Valentino home. Lionel gets upset if we keep him and Mr. Valentino separated too long," Justine said. "We brought Lionel home from the stockyard when he was just a baby. His leg was broken and they were going to shoot him. Well, we could not have that! We fixed him up with a splint."

"Yes, but then the chickens and turkeys in the barnyard began pecking at the bandages. You can imagine our surprise when, low and behold, Mister Valentino—snorting and raging like the big bull he is—started chasing them away. The feathers flew for a while, but none of them was injured too badly. He and Lionel have been best friends ever since."

Justine nodded in agreement. "He is coming, Lionel! Patience! Patience!"

Mary laughed. "Are you sure Lee—uh, *Willie* and I can't help?"

Leeta did the rib-poking this time, adding a ferocious look.

Miss Clara smiled. "That is so sweet of you, Mary, but no, you and Willie are our guests."

As Mary got down from the Buick and went around back to get her Samsonite, Leeta, carrying the paper bag, followed. When they were out of earshot of the sisters, Leeta poked her.

"Look, you, don't you volunteer me to do a damn thing around here! And just so you know, a donkey bit me once, and I don't like 'em worth a damn! I 'specially don't like that damn bull. So, don't be volunteering me to do nothing. You get that, girl?"

Mary frowned. "Suit yourself, Miss Bulow, but I intend to help out all I can. You should appreciate that they saved you from that sheriff's jail."

"Yeah, but saved me for *what*?"

Mary shook her head, deciding that Leeta Bulow, alias Willie Holloway, was not only the meanest-eyed person she had ever met but was also the most cynical.

"Another thing, don't call me 'Miss Bulow'! My name is *Willie Holloway*, like I told *them*." She jerked her thumb at the sisters up front in the Buick.

"All right, but my name is *Mary*, not '*girl*' ... or '*you*' ... or *helpless little scaredy-cat* ... or any of those other references you made to me."

"Are you girls having a problem unstrapping that suitcase?" Miss Clara called out to them.

They answered no and came forward to open the gate. However, they hesitated as a stern-looking, extraordinarily *black* Negro woman wearing a white apron and cap pushed open the screen door and stepped out onto the porch. At sight of the girls, she stuck both fists to her wide hips.

"That is Aunt Lucy, girls, our housekeeper," Justine said from the Buick. "She is colored."

"No shit?" Leeta said under her breath, then scowled when Mary lightly nudged her ribs again. This time, she returned the nudge.

Justine continued in a hushed tone, "If Aunt Lucy offers you a glass of buttermilk, you had better accept."

Clara laughed. "Aunt Lucy thinks anyone who doesn't like buttermilk is of poor character." With that she snapped the reins, and the big bull lumbered off toward the barn.

"I ain't drinking no buttermilk just to please some bossy old housemaid mammy!" Leeta hissed. "This ain't Tara, and I sure ain't Miss Scarlett! I damn sure ain't *Prissy*, neither."

Aunt Lucy ushered them into the massive foyer, and Mary's eyes widened at the Old World opulence of the stately room—gilded framed paintings on the walls, three massive chandeliers, and a curving stairway that must have been fifteen feet wide. Sheet-covered settees, chairs, and small tables lined the walls. Mary imagined that the gigantic foyer must have once served as a ballroom. She peeked under a sheet to admire a satiny brocade settee, then jumped as Aunt Lucy emitted a loud, "Harrumph!"

With a finger curled stiffly against her ample lips, Aunt Lucy did not appear to need the buttermilk test to pass judgment on Leeta. She made a point of examining her up and down, her eyes bulging with disapproval. However, before she could utter a word, Leeta cut her short.

"I think I met your husband on the bus."

"What! My Mista Robinson done been dead twenty years! What you mean by that kinda talk, gal?"

"A man I saw on the bus must be *some* kin to you, 'cause you both got that same look."

"What you talking 'bout, gal? What *look*?"

"The look that says I is shit and you is Shinola."

Aunt Lucy puffed up for a retort, but Miss Clara and Miss Justine came in the door and led the girls upstairs to their rooms, leaving Aunt Lucy scowling at Leeta's tight-skirted backside, which was now swinging defiantly from side to side.

Clara glanced over her shoulder. "We'll find something appropriate for you to wear, Willie, dear. You surely won't want to wear your… uh … fancy traveling garments out here in the country."

Leeta glanced down at her attire and shrugged. "If you was planning on helping me out with a bus ticket tomorrow, ma'am, and a little cash, I could be gone before I need a change of clothes. That sheriff told me to get gone, and I reckon he gonna make sure I do."

"He has a terrible disposition, doesn't he? He was just plain old mean, even when he was a boy," Justine said. "His grandfather was even worse. He was known as 'the hanging judge of Vander County' back in the days after the war between the North and South. Poppa said Judge Bloot hung so many Negro males that half the colored families in the county just up and moved away. The judge and the Klu Kluxers had them scared to death. If only someone would run against the sheriff next election; but everyone knows it would be a hopeless venture. I swan, I don't know how he keeps winning. I suppose just the name Bloot puts the scare in people, even if the hanging days are over."

"My grandmamma from Mississippi always said, for a Negro, there ain't no difference 'tween being *scared* to death and being *hung* to death. That's what happen to my great-grandpa. The Klu Kluxers came up on him while he was fishing in the creek and he got so scared he dropped dead."

"Oh, my dear Willie, how horrible!" Clara said.

Justine piped up, "But don't you worry; no one's been lynched in Vander County in years. I'm told the Klan is mostly just a social organization now, but their membership is still strictly white and Protestant, I hear—rather snobbish of them, I'd say."

"It sure is. Remind me not to apply for membership," Leeta said, and they all laughed.

Clara continued addressing the girls. "As to money for a bus ticket, our cash funds are a bit tied up presently, but we hope to free up a portion of them tomorrow ... after we see Mr. Klunk at Klunk's Junk."

Leeta whispered to Mary as they continued following the sisters up the stairs: "Yeah, they gonna free up some money but only *if* they can sell that old tractor motor we heard them talking about."

"Shush," Mary cautioned. "They will hear you. I would not mind staying a while if they let me. Maybe you should not be in such a hurry to leave, either."

Leeta gave her a sullen look. "Girl, maybe I got better reasons than you got for being in a hurry."

"My name is *Mary. Remember?* Call me *Mary.*"

"I got my reasons, *Mary*, for being in a hurry."

"Maybe so, but unless you plan to walk to California, or swim there, you are going to have to be patient. And it would not hurt you to be polite, *Willie*," she finished, proud that she was getting braver even while being threatened by those mean eyes.

"I'd set sail in a damn washtub if that was my only way outta here."

Clara, now at the top of the stairs, turned. "Did I hear you say you needed a washtub, my dear?"

"Yes, ma'am. I need a bath. The last hundred miles on that bus, the cooling conked out and I was scrunched up next to an old man who smelled like he had done gone and p—; anyway, I need a bath. Thank you for asking." She glanced smugly at Mary, as if she had just proven that she could be polite.

Justine laughed. "*Washtub* indeed! Shall we show them where we bathed on hot days like today when we were their age, Clara?"

"After Mary has put her things away in her room," Clara replied.

Mary had wondered if the rest of the house was as elegant as the downstairs foyer and the adjoining parlor that she had managed to glimpse, and it was. Her and *Willie's* rooms were directly across a wide hall from each other, both with massive mahogany headboards, marble-topped side tables, chifforobes, dressers, colorful lamps, and paintings. Heavy velvet draperies, drawn aside to let in the breeze, framed gleaming mahogany shutters.

"Poppa finally agreed to installing indoor plumbing in *ought one*, thank goodness," Justine said. "All the bedrooms have their very own bathrooms now, and a small dressing room as well. The rooms were so huge that adding the bathrooms and dressing rooms didn't cut down much on their size at all—most even have their own little parlors."

"This is the most beautiful house I have ever seen," Mary said. *And these kind ladies are in danger of losing it,* she thought, suddenly feeling sad.

Soon, the sisters led the way down the back stairs and along a path to a sun-bleached, rusty-bladed, old windmill that must have been as old as the house. Next to the windmill was a high platform, on which sat a huge wooden cistern with a ladder leading up to the very top.

"I ain't crawling up there and getting in that tank!" Leeta cried. "I'll drown!"

"Of course you are not getting in that tank, silly girl! That is our *drinking* water," Justine said, and laughed. She stepped under the tank and motioned to the girls as she pointed up to two spigots protruding from the bottom of the tank.

"Stand beneath your spigots, open them, and get as wet as you want," Clara said. "Lather up, and have a nice, cool shower."

"On a hot day like this, I used to practically *live* under my spigot," Justine said. "But then Poppa always hollered out the window, 'turn off the *blankety-blank* faucet and set the *blankety-blank* windmill to pumping before you use up all the *blankety-blank* water!' Of course, he did not say blankety-blank."

"I'm *sure* Poppa would want you telling everybody about his colorful language habit, Justine," Clara snapped.

"No he wouldn't, and I *didn't,* Clara—I said blankety-blank didn't I?"

"Oh, I'm sure the girls didn't catch on to *that,*" Clara said facetiously again, and then held out her hand to the wind as she turned back to Mary and Leeta. "One thing we have plenty of out here is wind. Great for the windmill, but terrible for the hair. It's because we are so close to the bay and the Gulf of Mexico. The *Gulf breeze,* we call it, even when it's blowing over forty miles an hour and feels more like a gale. Anyway, those rusty old windmill blades squeak and screech like blazes when it blows like that."

Mary glanced around at the only other dwelling in sight. "Someone passing by on the road could easily see us bathing under here, and there is a house not a block away."

"The house is empty. It's a rental house that belongs to Banker Prickett, but it's so rundown he hasn't been able to rent it," Clara said as she reached up to the wooden rim that encircled the bottom of the cistern and pulled on a rope. A dusty burlap curtain instantly dropped down to shield them from the world, neck to knees. "See, girls? No one can see you now," she said.

After the sisters left, Mary and Leeta undressed, turned on their spigots, and lathered up. With the two of them nude and sharing a bar of soap, Mary once again felt brave enough to say what was on her mind.

"*Leeta Bulow*—that really *is* your name, isn't it?"

Leeta stopped lathering. "Yeah."

"I hope you don't mind my asking, but why did you tell me your real name at Goldrod's, then tell the Hesterwine ladies you are Willie Holloway?"

"That was a slipup at Goldrod's. Like I said, I got my reasons, but I ain't gonna be around here long enough for it to matter to anybody. You just keep my name under that ugly green hat of yours, that's all. As soon as I get my hands on some cash, I'm gone, and that better be damn quick or my ass is—" She clamped her mouth shut and, for a moment, Mary thought she looked more scared than when the sheriff snapped the handcuff on her wrist.

Determined to banish her last remnants of nervousness when in this girl's steamroller presence, Mary continued, "You know what? I think I know what the matter with you is. You are running away from home, aren't you?"

"Ha! You might say that."

"I had a feeling when we got off the bus and you did not buy another ticket that we had a lot in common," Mary said as she handed over the soap that Leeta was motioning for impatiently.

"Oh, yeah? We got something in common, you and me? You got some mean-ass dude from back home that's gonna cut your throat or stab you or shoot you ... or maybe do all *three*, if he finds you?"

"No!"

"Well, *I* do! His name is Mandingo Q. Mann, and he's the meanest son of a bitch in Chicago, Illinois."

"Oh, wow!" Mary stared at Leeta Bulow with fresh unease.

"I need to get to Los Angeles, California. I figure that's as far away from him as I can get. Now don't ask me nothing else!"

"I-I won't," Mary whispered, trying to imagine how scared she would be if a bad man was looking for her with the intention of ending her life. She turned away from Leeta to stare over the curtain at the surrounding countryside, half-expecting to see Leeta's stalker sneaking up on them.

However, other than the dilapidated old house a scant half-block down the road, she saw only miles of rolling green grass and scatterings of trees, their leaves rippling peacefully in the light wind. Hesterwine Road lay tranquil and undisturbed except for a spiraling dirt devil that blustered up from out of nowhere and then dissolved across the field like an evaporating ghost. Except for the softly whistling breeze, everything was serenely quiet. Mary's eyes suddenly widened as she stared at the road—a road no one would know was there unless they were specifically coming out to see Clara and Justine Hesterwine. *And just how many visitors could the elderly sisters, with no living family left, have?—other than a disagreeable cousin they never saw?* Mary whirled around to face Leeta.

"You know, *Willie Holloway,* if Rudolph Valentino had not turned onto this tiny road, I would never have guessed it was there ... invisible as it is between all those low-hanging tree limbs. I doubt a stranger would find this place even if they happened upon the little town of Hesterwine, Texas." She hesitated a moment. "Los Angeles is a long way from here and it will take money to get there, and even more money to stay there. Maybe you should consider sticking around a while longer."

Leeta Bulow stopped lathering her arms and narrowed her eyes at Mary. "What you care where I go? I'll be staying, all right, but how long I'll be staying gonna depend on somebody named 'Mr. Klunk ... at Klunk's Junk.

# 6

"I'D JUST AS SOON HAVE THE WHOLE TRACTOR, Miss Clara ... Miss Justine. I'm in the business of selling junk, that's for sure, but I ain't had nobody come in here asking for a rusty old 1917 International tractor motor, nor any of the parts that's in it," said Mr. Klunk. "Maybe if that motor was in the tractor, some fool from over the drawbridge to Corpus Christi might want the whole thing as a collector's item, but waiting for that to happen would be chancy."

Justine nodded at Clara as if to say *I told you so*. Clara sighed. "All right, Mr. Klunk, you can have the whole tractor, but we shall need three hundred dollars for it."

"*What?* Why, no, I can't do that, Miss Clara. At that price, I may never recoup my money. I ain't a rich man, you know."

"You *shall* recoup your money, sir, if you promise that in twelve months you will sell Poppa's International back to us for ... shall we say, three hundred dollars?"

He grinned. "Why now, that sounds like a deal; if I don't sell it beforehand."

"No, Mr. Klunk. You shall not sell it before the twelve months are up, except to us. You may sell it only if we do not buy it back by the end of twelve months."

Justine nodded her approval of Clara's deal.

Mr. Klunk squinted at them, shaking his head. "So, what I'll be doing is giving you a twelve-month, *interest-free* loan of three hundred dollars."

"It is not an interest-free loan, Mr. Klunk. It is a verbal *contract for sale* ... with limitations, of course. After all, you will have the tractor the entire year," Clara said.

"I guess you'd expect me to use up some of my gas stamps to drive all the way out to your place, load it up on my truck and bring it here, eh? I'd even have to hire a couple of Meskins to work the block and tackle to get that heap of useless iron on the blame truck."

"Mr. Valentino could pull it here for you, if the tires can be pumped up and if they will still hold air," Justine offered.

He frowned while appearing to rethink the matter. "I'll tell you what I'll do ..." he began, but didn't finish the sentence. "Hold on a second. I'll be right back." He stalked into the back room of the 1937 Silver Dome trailer that was his home and office and returned a few minutes later to count out five twenty-dollar bills into Clara's hand.

"We agreed on *three hundred* for the tractor, Mr. Klunk," she said.

"Forget the tractor, I can't afford it. But I'll lend you a hundred. Pay me back whenever you can."

Clara primly laid the bills on his cluttered desk. "Certainly not. We Hesterwines do not borrow money."

"Now, Miss Clara, I know that ain't true, because I know you got a mortgage at the bank. Ain't that borrowing money?"

"I am surprised *and* disappointed in you, Mr. Klunk, that you would pretend to know our personal business, which is certainly none of yours. If you must know, that mortgage was our father's doing, not Justine's or mine."

"Absolutely true," Justine cut in. "Clara and I have never so much as borrowed a cup of sugar."

Mr. Klunk swept up the money. "Then, Miss Clara, Miss Justine, I'm just gonna *give* it to you." He thrust it at her. "Take it!"

"No, sir! Nor do we take charity." Clara fairly hissed the words.

"Never!" Justine agreed.

Clearly agitated, Mr. Klunk rubbed his stubbly cheeks. "Now, Miss Clara, Miss Justine, I do wanna help you out. My pa once told me that your pa took him up to his attic and showed him a grand set of old Civil War weapons—guns, swords, other memorabilia, including a set of battleground maps. As I recall, my pa said there was lots of old furniture up there fine enough to satisfy the taste of some of them customers who visit my warehouse looking for old stuff like that. I'd like to come out to your place and take a gander round that attic. I might make you an offer."

"There is nothing in our attic that is for sale, Mr. Klunk, nor shall there ever be," Clara said as the two of them turned, marched to the door, and hustled down the steps as fast as two elderly ladies *can* hustle. Once in the Buick, they both called out: "Giddy-up, Mr. Valentino!"

Well out of sight of Klunk's Junk, Clara glanced at Justine. "Stop that sniffling, Justine Hesterwine! We shall just have to ask Banker Prickett for an extension."

Justine drew a deep, sobbing, breath. "Oh! Why did Poppa mortgage our land and everything on it before he died, and without us ever knowing about it until he was dead and buried?"

"Because, God bless him, he was a drunk and a gambler, and very much a coward, that's why."

"Oh, Clara, don't say that!"

"Grandfather said it, and said it often. He was ashamed of Poppa's lack of moral fiber. 'A weak man is like a tree with shallow roots—destined, like the tree, to wither and then topple, usually doing damage.'"

Justine nodded in agreement. "Grandfather wrote those words in one of his ledgers. I saw it there. I often wondered if it was about Poppa."

"It was."

"And to think Poppa expected so much *moral fiber* from *us*, Clara, when he was certainly no saint." Justine dried her eyes with a corner of her handkerchief. "Sometimes, I just want to go straight to that cemetery and tell him so!"

"No need. I've done it several times," Clara said. Then, as if reciting poetry, she added, "A pusillanimous male ... does naught in moderation, not his drinking, not his gambling, not his quest for gratification."

"Did Grandfather say that, too?"

"No. I did."

"You were always the poet of the family, Clara. You should write that down somewhere before you forget it."

"That's right, Justine. Compliment me in one breath and then insult me in the next. I haven't forgotten it *yet*, have I?"

"*That* could be the problem, Clara. You remember things that you should have forgotten long ago, and you make me miserable because of it."

"*You*, Justine Hesterwine, are the one who always brings it up—like now."

"Perhaps that is because I think you still have those old feelings for *you know who*, and you are jealous, thinking that I still have them, too."

"Well, *don't* you?"

Wide-eyed, her chin beginning to tremble, Justine stared silently at her.

Clara jerked Rudolph Valentino to a halt. "I ought to make you *walk* the rest of the way home!"

"Ha! Just try it! I'm not budging!" Justine locked both arms tightly around the steering wheel, and only relaxed her grip when Clara snapped the reins and yelled for the big bull to "Giddy-up!"

Early the next morning, Mary and Leeta glanced at each other as Miss Clara explained again that the money would be "tied up" a bit longer. "Regardless, the two of you are welcome to stay as long as you wish."

"Maybe Willie and I could get a job in town," Mary said.

Miss Justine shook her head. "Hesterwine is such a small place. I'm afraid you being strangers and all, you'd have no luck getting hired—especially *you*, Willie, dear." She gazed apologetically at Leeta.

Clara nodded. "Justine is right. There is scarcely enough work for the locals."

"Yes, and those with automobiles drive over the bascule bridge to Corpus Christi for employment," Justine added.

"It's a *drawbridge*, Justine," Clara said.

Justine jerked her chin at her sister. "*Webster's Dictionary* says a *drawbridge is* a *bascule* bridge."

"One should call a drawbridge a drawbridge—unless they are trying to sound *French*, Justine."

"I shall call it a bascule bridge if I want to, *Clara*."

Leeta, wearing a skirt and blouse of Mary's and with Miss Justine's pink, pom-pom-topped mules replacing her fake leopard skin platform heels, slapped her hands on the kitchen table where the four of them sat drinking coffee. "As I see it, there ain't a da— dang one of us in this room that's got a dime."

"Not many dimes," Clara said. "Fortunately, though, we grow almost everything we eat. The cellar is full of canned fruits and vegetables. We have hens supplying our eggs, fryers for the skillet, and all sorts of seafood that Aunt Lucy's nephew brings to us nearly every week."

"Unfortunately, though," Justine added, "we need *sugar*, but the Rationing Board, headed by *Banker Prickett*, no longer allows us the amount we need."

"True," Clara said. "Until a few months ago, we operated a bakery and cannery out of this very kitchen. Twice a week we sold our goods. Why, half the town used to drive out here on Tuesdays and Fridays to buy our delicious cakes, pies, breads—all sorts of sweets, including jellies and jams ... sweet watermelon pickles, too, in season."

Leeta eyed Mary, as if saying, *so no one travels that little road, huh?*

"As you can see, sugar is *the* staple of our livelihood," Justine said. "Without it, we have no income, and thanks to our philandering father, there is a three-hundred-dollar mortgage on this very property that is now months overdue, and—"

"Justine!" Clara hissed, staring reproachfully at her. "Why don't you just take out an advertisement in the *Vander County Picayune*?"

"Well, it's the truth, isn't it? We *are* in dire straits, Clara."

"If *truth* was imperative in this house, your face would be as red as that tablecloth, Justine Hesterwine."

"Ha! Now *you* are the one who's bringing it up!"

"Oh, shush! I'm not going to dig up that old dead horse, but only because discussing one's vulgar little peccadillos from the past is as tasteless as prattling about one's *personal* finances!"

Justine swept up her empty cup, stalked to the sink, jabbed her fingers into a bowl of soap chips, dashed a few into the cup, and began scrubbing it as if it were her sister's face.

Clara turned to Mary and Leeta. "Times are difficult everywhere, but Justine and I are more fortunate than most. We are *privileged*, even, in comparison to many households. We have no right to complain."

Justine, her mouth set, turned around. "We might as well tell them how bad off we are, Clara. After all, they may have no other choice but to live here with us for a time, unless they want to become hobos of the road, and it's only fair that they know our circumstances." Without waiting for Clara's next remarks, she turned to Mary and Leeta. "We haven't baked or sold a thing in six months, and if we do not come up with the back mortgage payments soon, we will be put out on the—"

"Justine!"

"Oh, *Justine* yourself, Clara!" She turned back to Mary and Leeta. "On top of the mortgage being long overdue, there is a second *handshake* loan Banker Prickett says he made to our father for an *additional three hundred dollars* right out of his own pocket! We only found out about *it* this morning when the mailman delivered a letter from the bank saying we owed not just *three* hundred dollars on the mortgage, but, counting that handshake loan, a total of *six hundred dollars!*" She rolled her eyes helplessly and released a sobbing breath.

"That is quite enough, Justine!" Clara was fuming, but Justine continued.

"And yesterday, we tried unsuccessfully to do what we have never in our lives had to resort to—*sell* a Hesterwine treasure to Klunk's Junk!"

"That rusty old tractor is a *treasure?*" Leeta quipped, shaking her head. Mary softly elbowed her.

"Now we must go *begging* to Banker Prickett," Justine declared. "We must entreat him to renew Poppa's mortgage. And, as if *that* will not be humiliating enough, we must then plead with him to give us more time to pay that personal loan he made to Poppa."

Mary immediately began planning a secretive way to deposit her last five dollars into the Hesterwine sisters' sugar bowl that sat on a shelf over the cook stove. *Perhaps I should roll my five one-dollar bills together and drop them* behind *the sugar bowl,* she thought. *That way, the prideful Miss Clara will think that she or Miss Justine simply missed their target when dropping bakery money into it.* Mary smiled inwardly. Tomorrow, she would begin helping Aunt Lucy with the housework, as well as the cooking and anything else that needed doing. If it wasn't likely that she could get a job in Hesterwine and pay the kind ladies for their generous hospitality, then she would repay them with hard work.

"How dare you say such a thing, Justine Hesterwine!" Miss Clara was saying. "We shall not 'go begging,' nor shall we 'plead' for him to extend the mortgage and the loan! We shall *request,* and that is all!" Clara grabbed a large galvanized pail from the sink. "I'm going out to milk the cow! At least we shall have milk for our oatmeal, and butter for our toast."

Mary rushed to her and took the bucket. "Willie and I will do it, Miss Clara."

"*What?*" Leeta cried. "I don't know how to milk no cow!"

"I do," Mary said. "I've been milking cows since I was six. I was raised on a dairy farm. Come on, I will teach you. It'll be fun." She took Leeta's reluctant hand and led her out the back door.

Justine called after them: "Her name is Lillian Gish and watch out ... she'll put her foot in the bucket if you don't hobble her hind legs! She won't be a bit contrary as long as Mr. Valentino is nearby. Fetch him from his pen behind the barn and put him in the stall next to Lillian, but don't let Lionel Barrymore in there with them. He'll suckle Lillian if he gets the chance, and you won't get a full bucket!"

"Like I said," Leeta uttered beneath her breath, "I got to get the hell outta here."

Leeta stayed well back as Mary opened the gate and shakily called out to the massive bull. He turned slowly and looked squarely at her—a chilling sight, with his evil-looking eyes and spread of dagger-like horns. Mary thought he was staring at her longer than was necessary with those evil-looking eyes, but then he finally lumbered forward and, without prodding, went into the stall next to Lillian Gish.

After hobbling Lillian, Mary pulled up a stool, sat, and motioned Leeta over to watch.

"Didn't you hear them old ladies? That damn road out there ain't so private after all," Leeta said. "What if they get their hands on enough sugar to put 'em back in business? Folks gonna come out here to buy that stuff. That sorry Mandingo Q. Mann could find me!"

Mary smiled. "Is Mandingo Q. Mann fond of shopping for jams and jellies down out-of-the-way little country roads around Chicago?"

"Hell no, but—"

"Then why would he come here? Stop worrying. Come watch me milk this cow. It won't hurt you to get just a little countrified," she laughed.

"I wasn't *born* in Chicago, you know," Leeta retorted, squatting down and looking curiously at the cow's udder. "I was born in Mississippi, but we didn't have no cow ... no cow *juice*, either, most the time."

Mary leaned her head against Lillian's flank, and as soon as her hands gripped Lillian's teats, two streams of warm milk struck the bucket with a ringing, metallic sound. The sound grew fainter as a creamy layer of foam began to build. When the bucket was half-full, Mary straightened. "Let me see your hands." She shook her head as Leeta reluctantly held them out. "Your nails must be two inches long! Lillian will never stand for that." She resumed milking. "I'll show you how tomorrow morning after you have trimmed them."

"You mean we gonna do this every day? Who said? I'm going to town and see if I can find me a job. I don't care if it's washing dishes or cleaning white folks' toilets. It'll be better than slaving on de ol' plantation for free."

"It is not for free, Leeta. We will be earning our keep."

Leeta folded her arms across her chest and stepped backward to lean against a post. After a while, her eyes slid away from Mary to stare sulkily at nothing in particular. "Did I tell you what I was doing in Chicago?"

"I-I think I guessed," Mary said quietly.

Leeta fairly jumped at her. "Well, you guessed wrong! I ain't no prostitute! To be a prostitute you got to be willing to be one, and I wasn't!"

"I am truly sorry, Leeta. I do not know why I assumed that. I guess it was your clothes that fooled me."

"What the hell is wrong with my clothes? I *like* my clothes! They got color and style!"

"Okay. I really am sorry I hurt your feelings."

"I'll tell you what I am—or what I *was*. I was the best blues singer on the south side of Chicago. When the clubs found out I could sing just like Billy Holiday, there wasn't enough nights in the week to sing at all the joints that wanted me. But I couldn't sing at none of them places 'cause I was in deep debt to Mandingo Q. Mann. He owned the Big Man's Club, and that's where I had to sing seven nights a week. Mandingo Q. Mann kept my money, 'cept just enough for my rent. He had lots of girls working for him doing nothing but that thing you thought I was doing. One day he knocked me upside my head and said I gotta do it, too, or else he was gonna cut my throat."

"Oh, Leeta!"

Leeta's glittering eyes narrowed. "The day I was supposed to hit the streets for the first time, I woke up sick and tired and *mad*. I looked in the mirror and I kept seeing my momma. My momma wasn't no saint, but I knew what she would say if she knew what I done got myself into. I done heard her say it lots of times 'bout gals she knew done took to the streets.

Momma said, 'A gal just fine iffen she got a special man caring for her, but if she ever starts sinning with her body to take care of that man, then she a lowlife that ain't no better'n shit on a stick.' When I left my room that day, I walked straight to the bus station fast as I could go without running."

"So that is why you did not have luggage," Mary said.

"You talk funny, Mary Kenny. How come you pronounce every damn word like that? Forget it, 'cause I don't really give a shit. Anyway, on the south side of Chicago, there ain't no secrets kept from Mandingo Q. Mann, so I didn't carry nothing but my pocketbook so nobody would guess I was leaving town. He done beat up gals for letting it be known they was wanting to quit, and somebody always told on 'em. One girl I knew got strangled behind the club, then got dumped in the river."

Mary was still aghast, her eyes like big blue-and-white saucers. "You must have been terrified while waiting for that bus!"

"I was shaking so hard I couldn't hardly walk." Leeta sank down on a hay bale as if the memory had weakened her. Mary set the bucket aside and came over to stand beside her. She lifted an arm in a comforting motion but dropped it when Leeta, clearly showing an aversion to such pity, shot her a don't-touch-me look.

"Not long after I got the job at the Big Man's Club, I got word Momma was real sick and needed to go to the hospital. Mandingo Q. Mann said he'd pay the bill 'cause I was his girl. When Momma died, he drove me to Mississippi and he paid for the funeral. Later, he said he paid the hospital four hundred dollars, and three hundred for the funeral. He even charged me for the burgers he bought my brother and two little sisters before we dropped them off at my aunt's house in Hattiesburg. I knew the hospital and the funeral didn't cost near as much as he said, but I didn't say nothing 'cause by that time, I knew not to make him mad. He even charged me for the rubber on his tires and the gas it took coming and going, all the while taking everything from me that a bad man knows how to take from a dumb thirteen-year-old gal from Mississippi."

"Thirteen! You were just a baby, Leeta."

"That was seven years ago, and the interest on that hospital and funeral bill kept getting bigger and bigger, and he kept getting meaner and meaner." She touched a small, round scar on her cheek. "He liked to play darts, and anybody he got mad at was his target."

"Oh, Leeta, that is so awful!"

"I was gonna have a baby."

"Wha—" Mary whispered, the thought of her own dead baby dropping a familiar cloud over her. "You had a baby, Leeta?"

"I was *gonna* have a baby and I was glad, but when I told Mandingo Q. Mann about it, he 'bout broke everything in my room. I-I lost the baby pretty soon after that." She hushed, her eyes dimming.

Mary dropped her head, once again hearing Jessie break the news that her own baby was born dead.

"I didn't want any part of Mandingo Q. Mann anymore, but I did want that baby. To me, it was as if that brand-new little person was gonna save me ... take me away from there. I guess it was selfish of me, being all set to give an innocent little baby a burden like that."

Mary's tears came faster than she could wipe them away. "You believed if *good* came into your life, the evil would disappear."

"Dumb, huh?"

This time Mary did not hesitate to grab up Leeta's hand and squeeze it between her own. "Oh, Leeta Bulow, you think we haven't anything in common because you're colored and I am white and our lives have been so different, don't you?" Mary said through her tears. "I never had a Mandingo Q. Mann shoot me with darts or beat me up or try to send me out on the street corners, but I have more in common with *you*, Leeta Bulow, than with anyone I have ever known in my entire life!"

# 7

CLARA'S AND JUSTINE'S HEELS CLICKED a bit faster than usual on the sidewalk. With arms locked at their elbows and hands clutching their black purses to their chests, they walked quickly from the bank. Clara spoke through her tightly drawn lips.

"Don't you dare cry, Justine Hesterwine! He is watching out the window!"

"But *forty-five days*, Clara! Where will we ever get three hundred dollars for the mortgage, let alone *another* three hundred for that personal loan in forty-five days? Six hundred dollars, Clara!"

"I don't know! Let me think! Stop sniveling!"

They were in front of the dentist's office, and Clara jerked her arm from Justine's grasp, dug into her purse, produced two one-dollar bills, and thrust them at her sister. "You are almost late for your appointment. Now go in there and get that tooth fixed."

"Where did you get that money? We can't afford it, Clara. I'll suffer through."

"I found it behind the sugar bowl where you carelessly misplaced it. And you *will not* suffer through! We certainly could not afford dentures if you lose your teeth, and shame on you for suggesting it!"

"I didn't suggest it! For heaven's sake, Clara! Don't take your anger at Banker Prickett out on me. I am not the one throwing us out on the street in forty-five days. The last thing on my mind is *false teeth*!"

Suddenly staring absently at her sister, Clara's reply was as vacant as was her gaze. "Anyway, you would never wear them. Your gums would turn to flab and then you'd have a heck of a time chewing your ..." She paused. "I'm going to the cemetery to weed the family plots. I shall do your share of the weeding this time."

"But you didn't bring your gloves. Besides, it isn't our turn to clean the family plots, Clara. It is that awful Cousin Etta Ruth's turn. She's sure to be there, and you two will surely get into another of your fights." She waited for Clara's retort, then frowned when it didn't come. "Clara? Are you listening to me? I said Etta Ruth is likely at the cemetery today."

Clara shifted her empty gaze across the street.

"Clara?"

Clara's hand went up to rub and then tap at her temple.

Justine grabbed her arm. "My God! Clara! You're having a stroke!"

Clara shook her loose. "Get in there and get your tooth fixed. I'll meet you at Goldrod's after I finish the business of appeasing Cousin Etta Ruth."

"Whatever do you mean? Why would you even *want* to appease that horrible woman? She has never been anything but rude and mean to us even since we were all three of us children. And *you*, Clara, always gave her as good as we got."

"Well, God help me, today I intend to be nothing but honey and molasses, no matter what she says. Surely, you haven't forgotten how Etta Ruth pestered us to sell the house to her after Clarence refused to build her a bigger one. Perhaps I can convince her to buy a third of it."

"Clara! No! What if she wants to move in with us, and she might now that Clarence is dead and her children escaped her by moving far away and don't even come back for a visit."

"Living under the same roof with Etta Ruth would be a venture into hell, I am sure, but it beats the consequences of inviting Mr. Klunk from Klunk's Junk up to our attic to pick over our treasures," Clara said, then walked away.

Justine, sputtering helplessly, called out to her: "But, Clara, that woman is a born-again assassin of anyone who disagrees with her politics or does not attend *her* church. I don't think I could stand her thumping her Bible in my face every day for the rest of my life and calling me a sinner just because I'm a Methodist. Come back here and let us talk this over! You'd better stop and think what you'd be getting us into, Clara! Clara!"

Clara kept going.

Justine slowly turned away, muttering beneath her breath as she entered the dentist's office. "Cousin Etta Ruth does not like either one of us, Clara. She's *cracked*, Clara! I wouldn't be able to sleep a wink with her in the house!"

Eternal Rest Cemetery lay directly behind Hesterwine's architectural showplace, the Classical Revival-style courthouse, erected in 1914, fifty-five years after a Comanche Indian raid on the town gave the now historic graveyard its first customers. As grand as the old courthouse was, it had never superseded the little cemetery's importance to Hesterwine's citizens. Their loyalty was proven four years ago when the county commissioners, led by Banker Prickett, thought to turn the cemetery into a parking lot. No sooner had the *Vander County Picayune* and area radio stations announced the plan to disturb Hesterwine's founding citizens by digging them up and transplanting them to a later established cemetery on the outskirts of town than the entire county rose up in protest.

It was the first time that Clara and Justine stooped to a public demonstration in the streets. Justine's placard implored, *Please Leave Them in the Dust That They Have Become,* and Clara's placard threatened, *Defile the Dead and They Will Defile You in Eternity!* Sympathetic superintendents of schools turned out every high school in the county to join the protest. A rhythm band of kindergarteners from Saint James Catholic School stood on the courthouse steps banging away on their triangles, blocks, tiny cymbals, and tambourines. The only break in the somberness of the occasion was when Vernell Watson's five-year-old great-grandson, after a half-hour of squirming and tugging at his fly front, laid down his cymbals, ran to the side of the steps, and peed into the oleander shrubs.

Even Cousin Etta Ruth was there to defend the preservation of the old cemetery, but her camaraderie did not last. Days later, when the Coalition of Churches met—except for the Catholics and the Jews, who weren't invited—to plan the annual rummage and bake sale, Etta Ruth disagreed with Clara on the date for the big event. The following week, Clara received from Etta Ruth, in the mail, an invitation to drop dead. Clara had not bothered to RSVP, as the note further instructed her to do.

Dread swept over Clara as she entered beneath the cemetery's arched iron gates and realized that saving the old cemetery was the only thing that she and Cousin Etta Ruth had ever agreed upon—other than the carefully laid-out plan to take turns cleaning the family plots so that they would not accidentally run into each other. Yet, here she was, going against her innermost warnings and stepping into the viper's pit.

Suddenly, Clara ducked from the path to sequester herself behind a towering angel with a broken wing, the disturbing memory of the last time she and Etta Ruth cleaned the plots together all but rendering her backbone to jelly. The woman's spitefulness that day had gotten to Clara in a most surprising and unladylike manner, and she had reacted in a way that Etta Ruth would never be inclined to forgive and forget:

"Tell me, Clara, what happened to discourage you and Justine from ever trying to trap a husband?" Etta Ruth said that day, right out of the blue, her mouth working in that agitating little way she had of twisting it when being snide. "I always suspected some mysterious, long-ago event involving you two was the reason," she added.

Outwardly unruffled, Clara had replied, "Nothing sensational, I assure you, Cousin Etta. Certainly nothing involving the two of us."

"It is surprising, though, Clara, that neither of you ever married. In your younger days, there never was a lack of males around you two ... like flies on a busted melon, as I recall." She worked her mouth into a salacious grin. "I remember you two had quite a wild streak back then, although you hid it rather well."

"*Hid* it? Apparently not from *you*. Would you like to tell me exactly what you mean by that remark?"

"Oh, Clara, you should see your face!" Etta Ruth had laughed. "Don't be offended! I'm not referring to any *one* thing in particular." She parked half a buttock on a nearby tombstone and narrowed her eyes. "Tell me, Clara, whatever happened to that handsome Pendleton boy who was sparking you back in our day? The one we all had such a crush on."

Clara remembered jerking up a rake Etta Ruth had brought with her and clawing at the leaves around Etta Ruth's deceased husband's grave. "I have no idea what happened to him, Cousin Etta. The name hardly rings a bell." She raked harder. "I'll help you with this. You look tired and worn out ... positively *haggard*."

Etta Ruth had eyed her like a prosecuting attorney questioning a murder suspect. "Oh, come now, Clara. You and Boyd Pendleton were sweethearts all through high school and college. As I recall, you were wearing a ring on your left finger that looked very much like an engagement ring... until he just up and disappeared one day."

"Ouch!" Clara shrieked as a splinter from the rake handle she'd been choking stabbed into her thumb. She felt her face flame. "That is absurd," she had said, controlling her voice. "It must have been Mother's ring; I wore it for many years after she died."

Even as she spoke, a picture flashed across her mind's eye of herself... the wind tearing at her hair and the salty sea air stinging her teary eyes, as she sped onto the wooden bridge across Hall's Bayou in her father's brand-new Studebaker one-horse carriage and threw Boyd Pendleton's ring over the side into the devouring slough of mud below. She wished she had that ring now. She could sell it for more than enough to save Hesterwine Place.

"And you just ran off to Europe right away after he disappeared, didn't you? That was really quite baffling."

"No, Cousin Etta Ruth, I did not 'just run off' to Europe. I am sorry you were so baffled. I had planned the vacation trip for months."

Etta Ruth grinned doubtfully at her. "I also remember the day Boyd came back to Hesterwine some *twenty years later* to collect his inheritance from his dead father. Almost everybody we knew was long married by then and raising a family, except you and Justine, of course.

"Yes!" Clara fairly shouted. "We were free as birds and quite happy that way! Still are!"

"When Boyd Pendleton came back, you and he took up where you'd left off twenty years before, didn't you? 'The Pendleton heir with the savoir faire,' we called him. I remember saying to myself, 'My God! Poor Clara is *forty* and has waited for him all these years, and now he's turned up like a bad penny to raise her hopes again.'"

Clara remembered that her eyes had locked on Etta Ruth in a homicidal stare.

"Oh, he *was* deliciously bad, wasn't he, Clara? I allow he kissed every girl in Vander County, or at least gave them a good pinch, and we all adored him for it, didn't we?"

"I don't recall much about him at all, Etta Ruth."

"That's funny. Everyone thought it was *him* you would finally marry, even at that late date; when the bloom was off the rose, so to speak. I could have sworn I saw another ring on your finger ... that is, until, for the *second* time he up and disappeared again."

"It was still Mother's ring. I wore it until it wouldn't fit anymore." She held up her fingers and wiggled them as if to show Etta Ruth how arthritis had swelled her knuckles.

"Well ..." Etta Ruth had drawled. "I guess memory is selective, at best."

"*Yours* is, anyway," Clara snapped.

"I meant your memory, Clara. I'm still thinking of that first time Boyd Pendleton left town when you were barely twenty-two," she said, smiled, and in a scolding tone, continued, "Really, Clara? A hastily taken six-month vacation in Europe without a chaperone? Usually when a girl leaves town for six months, it isn't for a vacation," she said, then pointed at her little red wagon. "Hand me my lunch bag, will you? I'm hungry."

Today, hunkering behind the angel, Clara shuddered at the thought of what had followed. Shaking with anger at the woman's insinuation, she had grabbed up the brown paper bag containing Etta Ruth's lunch and slung it so hard at her chest that when it struck her, a squashed tomato rolled out. Not staying to listen to Etta Ruth curse, she had stormed out of the cemetery, and hadn't seen Etta Ruth since.

Clara squared her shoulders, stiffened her spine, stepped from behind the protective angel, and made her way through the rows of tombstones toward Clarence Morley's gravesite, her dreaded mission evident in the grim setting of her mouth.

She spotted Etta Ruth hunched over on all fours, spading up the dirt on her husband's grave. As usual, when she came to the cemetery pulling her red Radio Flyer wagon full of gardening supplies, she wore a pair of her dead husband's trousers. Luckily for Etta Ruth, Clarence had a rear end like a pachyderm.

Clara eyed her with disapproval. In addition to Clarence's pinstriped, cuffed trousers, she wore his fancy, two-toned wingtip oxfords with the tasseled shoelaces. *The woman loses more of herself every day*, she thought, then wondered what frame of mind Etta Ruth might be in this morning, since she was stabbing at the dirt as if she was killing garden snails.

Suspecting that Etta Ruth would not have forgotten any of their past disputes—especially not the squashed tomato incident—Clara halted and cowered a full five minutes longer before finally taking a deep breath and treading slowly to Etta Ruth's side.

"My goodness, Etta Ruth, you've got Clarence's spot looking quite... clean. I'm sure he would be pleased."

Etta Ruth glanced over her shoulder before twisting around on all fours to back up and plop her wide rear onto the dirt in front of Clarence's imposing headstone. She leaned back against it and spread her chunky legs out in front of her. Her black eyes, large, like Clara's greenish-gray ones and Justine's blue ones, flickered with hostility as they skimmed over her. Clara shuddered. Perhaps she'd begin by complimenting Etta Ruth on her family. As unpleasant as Etta Ruth was, there was an exception to her meanness—her misty-eyed boastfulness when espousing on the perfection that was her life: Her children were perfect. Her marriage was perfect. Her house, her car, and her cat were perfect. The message being, everyone should be quite envious of her flawless world and quite disgusted with their own. Clara opened her mouth to spiel a bit of sugary baloney but did not get the chance.

"Did you know that Clarence spent the last twenty-five years of our marriage trying to make me leave him, Clara?"

Clara wondered if her shock showed. She had no reply for such a question, except to shake her head no. Etta Ruth continued.

"He never came right out and said it, but after years of his constant fault-finding, and me having to make all the moves at"—she raised her eyebrows—"*you know what*, I finally figured it out." She flipped a handkerchief from her shirt pocket and blew her nose. "He was a big, fat hypocrite, afraid of what people would say about him if *he* left. He wanted to keep up his grand facade of respectability—make *me* the one to abandon *him*. He was on the school board, you know, and on the board of directors at the bank because of all the money his daddy left him."

Clara sat down on a stone bench at the foot of Clarence's grave. Was this happening? Who was this stranger occupying Etta Ruth Morley's rotund body?

"Be glad you never married and had to grow old with a husband, Clara. Old men require an exceptional amount of babying."

Clara assumed Etta Ruth paused so that she could respond. "Oh? I have heard that said a few times, Cousin Etta."

"Yes, especially one who wishes he had never married you. He never was a kindly man, but got meaner and more demanding the older he got. He constantly scolded me as if I were a child. I couldn't boil water without him standing over my shoulder to see if I was doing it right."

Clara wondered why Etta Ruth was telling her all of this *now*, after Clarence had been dead almost five years. Since her mouth was already open, Clara felt as if she had to say something, but Etta Ruth, staring off across the graveyard, continued.

"He'd scream my inadequacies at the top of his lungs—all the things that he said *drove* him to belittle me." She jerked her stare back to Clara. "If I defended myself in any way, he'd storm out of the house, and even though his parents were long dead, he'd drive two hundred miles to the old homestead where his older three bachelor brothers still lived. Most times, he'd stay a week or more. He once told me his brothers were, by choice, all as innocent as the day they were born. I took that to mean they were all virgins, except for…" she put up a hand and wiggled her fingers.

"I never met them," was all Clara could think to say.

Etta Ruth reached for the thermos jug next to her, uncapped it, and took a deep drink, the smell of liquor wafting from it. She stared off into the distance for a long moment.

"I'll tell you a secret, Clara. By the time I was fifty-five, my affection for Clarence had suffered so many blows it was like a stomped-on cockroach that, though barely alive and with its insides squashed out, *still* crawls off into a corner and tries to hang onto its sorry life."

"I would never have guessed it in a million years, Cousin Etta Ru—"

"How could you? I suffered in silence!" She fairly shouted the sentence, as if trying to notify the dead of her martyrdom, then blew her nose again.

"You poor thing."

"I would have been better off if I had just flipped belly-up, like that damn cockroach, and died!"

"Oh, please don't say that, Etta Ruth, *dear*."

"However, dying is what Clarence wanted me to do, and I wasn't about to let him control the *dying* part of my life, like he did nearly every blasted living day of it!"

"Thank heaven for your good sense, Cousin Etta."

"My dear mother convinced me that a martyred wife was preferable to a divorced wife in our family, and I *did* make several efforts to revive my old feelings for Clarence," she said, her mouth turning down at the corners as she stabbed at the dirt with the trowel. "He was reluctant, at best, and when he finally gave in and offered one of those frozen-lipped kisses of his, I felt as if my mouth was under attack. I don't recall in all the years we were married that Clarence ever touched my bottom, Clara."

"Oh my!" Clara gasped, hoping that was as far as Etta Ruth would go with *that* revelation.

"Tell me, Cousin Clara, what would you have said to me if I had told you about Clarence and me years ago?"

"I would have told you to demand that he treat you better, Cousin Etta Ruth."

"Your ignorance of married life is obvious, Clara. I made that demand many times over the years, but all it got me was another of his tantrums."

Clara wondered again why Etta Ruth was telling her all of this *now*, a half-century after the fact. For the first time in a long time, her eyes softened on Cousin Etta Ruth as the poor woman waved the trowel in one hand and brushed at the dirt on her cheek with the other.

"Etta Ruth, you said Clarence spent the last thirty years trying to get you to leave him. Did it ever occur to you that Clarence was exactly like his older brothers? The only difference between them and him was that *he* married ... married, even though his essential nature was that of a bachelor."

"Oh, Clara," Etta Ruth scoffed. "That's all you know! Are you really that stupid?"

"Well, I don't know why else he would have been so bad-tempered toward you," Clara lied, thinking Etta Ruth would drive any man to distraction.

"Because he was carrying on a thirty-year affair, that's why!"

"*Clarence?* And another woman? I don't believe it."

"Not another woman; that silly Old Man Abelson, at the shoe shop!"

As Clara gaped, open-mouthed again, while picturing the sway-backed, round-shouldered Mr. Marvin Abelson, with a face as ashy and wrinkled as an Egyptian mummy, Etta Ruth reached over to the red Radio Flyer, retrieved a small box, and dumped out a pile of letters.

"I found these behind paint cans in the garage. They are love letters from Old Man Abelson to Clarence! The last one is dated just days before Clarence dropped dead! No telling how many letters Clarence wrote to *him*!" Etta Ruth began to sob. "I'm gonna make a bonfire with them. Hand me those matches, Clara." She pointed to her purse at the far end of the wagon. "And then I will never set foot on this cheating old son of a bitch's grave again!"

Clara handed her the box of matches and then leaned close and guided Etta Ruth's trembling hand with the lighted match to the pile of letters. The smell of liquor on Etta Ruth's breath was eyelash-wilting.

"Another thing, Clara," she said. "A few days before Clarence's heart attack, he tried to kill me."

"Oh now, Etta Ruth," Clara began doubtfully.

"It's true! I woke one night because I felt something pressing into my leg. I saw Clarence sitting on my side of the bed, and he was pressing something into my shin!" She rubbed the area between her knee and ankle. "I opened one eye so I could catch him at whatever he was doing to me. He had one of those little box cutter knives. The blade was retracted, but he was pressing the butt of the sleeve *hard* into my leg... to make the spot numb, I guess, so he could give me a shot of poison with a hypodermic needle in that numb spot."

"Now, Etta Ruth," Clara said kindly, wanting to calm her and realizing that Etta Ruth's mind was even more fragile than was already common knowledge in the town.

Etta Ruth was not ready to be calmed. "I tell you, it's true! He had a hypodermic needle in his other hand! When I screamed and jumped out of bed, he ran into the bathroom and locked the door! I locked myself in the spare room with a butcher knife under my pillow and didn't sleep the rest of the night. The next morning, he knocked on the door and said I had a terrible nightmare during the night and ran out of our room screaming." She glared at Clara. "It was a damn lie! I don't have nightmares."

"Cousin Etta Ruth," Clara began and then hesitated a long moment before gathering her nerve. "I know this isn't a good time for you, but I think I can help you feel a tiny bit better."

"I doubt it," Etta Ruth sniffed, while stoking the flames with her trowel.

"Justine and I were speaking fondly of you just this morning, and we suddenly remembered how you have loved Hesterwine Place all your life. Why, you and your parents were there so much when Momma was alive, it seemed as if you were being raised there right alongside Justine and me, didn't it?"

"I always felt your mother should have left my mother a share of it, them being sisters and close as they were. When she was on her deathbed and dying, she should have instructed your father to do so."

"I know, and in light of your warm feelings for the place, and seeing that you are all alone now, with Clarence Jr. practicing law in Houston and Nancy Louise married again and moved to Louisiana, Justine and I have decided to offer you a third ownership for a very reasonable price." She drew another deep breath. "Of course, we know you won't want to leave your lovely home in town so close to shopping and all, but owning a third of Hesterwine Place means you will certainly be welcome to come out for a nice visit whenever you choose."

Etta Ruth stared at her a long moment, then surprised Clara by throwing down the trowel and slapping her dirty hands to her face. An instant later, she was bawling louder than ever.

*The woman is hysterical with gratitude!* Clara could scarcely contain her happy thoughts at the prospect of paying off Banker Prickett. With a wide smile stretching her lips, she settled back and watched Etta Ruth cry.

However, when Etta Ruth finally raised her head and stared at Clara from beneath heavy folds of papery eyelids, looking every bit her sun-damaged sixty-seven years and then some, Clara's relief, like Justine's sourdough dumplings, melted into mush.

"I am broke, Clara! Clarence Jr. has gotten Power of Attorney over everything I own! He convinced the judge that I am *senile*! He has my money now and gives me only a piddling allowance. He says if I don't behave, he'll put my house up for sale and move me to Houston so he won't have to be driving down here all the time to check on me. I know what he wants. He wants to lock me away in some *loony bin!*"

Clara's shoulders slumped as Etta Ruth continued blubbering.

"And that ingrate daughter of mine, Nancy Louise, agrees with him. She's divorced again, by the way. She and her new boyfriend showed up one night a few months ago, took my car, and haven't been back since! Clarence Jr. says I need looking after, but it's as plain on his face as that goofy-looking upper lip of his that he doesn't want to be bothered with me. I suspect he's already made my reservations at that loony bin in San Antone, and he and that fat wife of his are having a hell of a good time with my money!"

Clara's shoulders sagged even lower, and she could feel her cheeks doing the same. Klunk's Junk was suddenly back in the picture.

"I can't go to that nuthouse, Clara—it's for *crazy* people! I can't! I can't!" She reached for Clara's hand but then jerked it back, as if she'd just remembered that it wasn't something she'd normally do. "I think I'm just gonna lie here and try to die." She kicked away the lacy embers of her little bonfire, scooted down, stretched out on the grave, and laced her fingers atop her bulging midsection. Then, as if on second thought, she felt around for the thermos and stationed it upright on her bosom between praying hands, as if it were a bouquet.

Clara stared at her, dreading the words that she knew were about to come out of her mouth.

"You don't have to go to... San Antone, Cousin Etta Ruth. I'll talk to Clarence Jr. You can live with Justine and me."

## 8

CLARENCE MORLEY JR. GRINNED as if the governor of Texas had just handed him a reprieve from the electric chair. However, as he sat in the Hesterwines' parlor balancing a teacup on his wide knee, he must have felt it his duty as a lawyer to warn Clara and Justine that his mother was "a bit unstable."

Etta Ruth, carrying her huge gray cat, *Beelzebub*, under her arm, had gone straight upstairs the minute her son ushered her through the front door, and now he looked around to make sure she hadn't snuck back down and was lurking around a corner.

"I had to declare Momma mentally unfit to handle her finances when she told me my daddy once tried to murder her with the empty sleeve of a box cutter," he said, smiling grimly, then chuckling. "Just try to imagine *murdering* someone with a teensy-weensy *empty* sleeve of a little box cutter."

"Impossible," Justine agreed, while worriedly eyeing the delicate, gold-rimmed, porcelain teacup balanced precariously on Clarence's knee—an heirloom cup that, so far, had survived one hundred years of use without so much as a chip. She sighed with relief when Clara abruptly leaned from her chair, removed the tinkling cup and saucer from his knee, and placed them on the little tea table she had earlier set in front of him specifically for that purpose. He nodded as if she had done him a favor and then crossed his legs.

"Momma said she awoke one night to find Daddy pressing that empty box cutter sleeve into her leg and about to shoot her with a hypodermic needle." Clarence Jr. chuckled. "What an imagination! Momma's claims got crazier every time she told me that story."

Clara sipped her tea, wondering if Etta Ruth had told her son about his father's thirty-year affair with Mr. Abelson.

Clarence continued, "Nothing Momma said, though, topped that tale about Daddy trying to do her in."

*Good!* Clara thought. *She hasn't told him.* At least Etta Ruth wasn't so "unstable" that she didn't realize how pointless it would be to tell her son about his father's love life. As for *her*, she would take Etta Ruth's revelations to her grave. She smiled kindly at Clarence. "Your mother told me that outrageous story ... as well as other things not worth mentioning."

"Which proves she's just making up stuff as she goes along, Miss Clara. Dad was a doting and loving husband. I can't imagine why Momma would accuse him of something so rotten."

"Neither can I," Clara said, while easily imagining why—*the discovery of Clarence's "doting and loving" affair with Old Man Abelson had cracked an already leaky bucket!*

"She is losing her marbles, Miss Clara, sure as I'm sitting here." He sighed long and loud. "Anyway, just thought you ought to know you can't believe much of what Momma says. Otherwise, I'm sure she's harmless, and you'll all get along like loving sisters ... just like in the old days, Momma said on the way out here."

Justine sounded like she was choking and then looked at Clara, as if she expected her to set Clarence Jr. straight, but Clara only nodded at him—perhaps because she was preparing to ask the big question.

A few minutes later, Clarence Jr. politely refused to allow his mother to buy one-third of Hesterwine Place. "Really, Miss Clara, what good would it do Momma? It isn't as if she has an especially long future anymore and would get a lot out of it. It wouldn't be a good investment, since I'm not interested in owning this big, old hotel-sized reminder of an era long dead. Now, if this place was in Houston, I could make a pretty penny off it, but not in little ol' Hesterwine, Texas."

"I understand," Clara said, eyes blinking as she tried to hide her disappointment. Justine's groan made *her* despair obvious.

Clarence looked first at one and then the other. "Momma will of course keep getting her allowance, and"—he paused to put a finger to his protruding top lip and hummed, as if the sound was coming from his brain—"I'll tell you what I'll do. I'll pay for fixing the old elevator. I don't reckon it's worked for years, has it? I know it wasn't operating when I was a kid. It'll make life easier for all three of you."

"How kind of you, Clarence," Clara said.

"Okay, ladies, then that's that," he said, slapping his knees before rising to his feet. The women followed as he strolled into the foyer. "Why don't you all just buy Momma's house from me and move to town?" he asked, and chuckled. "Oh, well, I can tell by your faces *that* ain't gonna happen."

"No, it isn't," Clara said, and smiled sweetly at him.

"I got Meskins that's gonna move the rest of Momma's stuff out here tomorrow." He studied the double front doors. "Your doors look wide enough to squeeze that old Kimball Victorian parlor organ of hers through. Great! The blame thing won't have to be disassembled."

Justine glanced with concern at Clara. "Oh my, that old organ will be coming along?"

"Momma won't do without it. She likes to pump away at it occasionally. And it does *not* come with ear plugs," he added with a laugh. "Bye-bye, ladies. I gotta skedaddle on back to Houston now. Have fun with Momma," he said, chuckling as if he'd just said something funny. He slapped on his wide-brimmed Panama hat, pulled down the cuffs on the coat of his seersucker suit, pushed open the screen door, and called over his shoulder as he hurried across the porch and down the steps, "I'll send the elevator repairman around in a day or two."

"The attic was Grandfather's space. He spent a lot of time up here," Justine explained to Mary and Leeta as they made their way up the many stairs to the massive storeroom over the third floor to inventory items they would make available to Mr. Klunk at Klunk's Junk. Etta Ruth, looking disgusted, and still in the nightgown and chenille robe she'd rarely changed out of since arriving, tagged along.

"He considered the attic his museum," Clara added. "On top of everything else imaginable, it is full of stuffed animals from Africa, one of them a huge water buffalo, much larger even than Mr. Valentino."

Justine laughed. "He wanted to put that gigantic animal on display in the foyer, but it was too big to get through the front doors, so he had it sawed in two, brought it in, and sandwiched a big bookshelf between each half."

"It stood where Etta Ruth's organ now stands—his 'showpiece,' he called it," Clara added.

Justine giggled. "We once fooled the maid by putting a big pile of cow poop on the carpet beneath the buffalo's tail. Of course, we were only children."

"You don't get credit for that," Etta Ruth growled. "It was my idea."

"So it was," Clara said. "You only had Justine and me shovel up the manure and carry it into the house."

Justine sighed. "Grandfather loved that buffalo. He brought it back from a widely publicized African safari with two famous British hunters he'd met in England. Wonder what he'd say if we sold it to Mr. Klunk along with all those other stuffed creatures?"

Etta Ruth gave out a wry cackle. "The old son of a bitch is too busy begging for ice water to give a crap about that old water buffalo anymore."

Except for Justine, the others only glanced at her. After a week of Etta Ruth, they were accustomed to her outbursts *and* her expletives. Clara explained to Mary and Leeta soon after Etta Ruth's arrival: "Her foul language is a sign of her overwhelming unhappiness."

Justine glared sourly at Etta Ruth before turning to Mary and Leeta. "Our grandfather was an upstanding citizen. He didn't believe in that terrible war with the Yankees, but because he was such an honorable man and loyal to his region, he joined the Confederacy and, because he was a West Point man, immediately became General Andrew Ignacio Hesterwine."

Etta Ruth put up a finger and gazed pointedly at Leeta. "Oh, yes, before Justine forgets to tell you, Willie. *After* the war—and because he was so 'loyal to his region'—he became the Grand Dragon of Vander County's Order of the Ku Klux Klan."

"He did not!" Justine cried.

"Of course he didn't," Clara calmly added. "That was only gossip spread by a man he'd had arrested for stealing a fully loaded cotton trailer from him and selling it at a gin over in the next county."

Etta Ruth laughed. "Next you'll say there was never a Klan in Vander County."

"No, but they've not been heard of in ages."

"That's because they are a *secret* organization. That bastard, Clarence—my dead husband," Etta Ruth explained to Leeta, "was a member in good standing. He always wanted me to bake cookies for the sons of bitches. So, one time, I made them a special batch. Clarence came home mad as hell. Said after they ate my cookies, they spent half the night squatting behind the dunes."

They all laughed, even Justine.

Etta Ruth eyed Leeta and Mary. "My husband tried to kill me, you know. But it didn't have anything to do with the cookies."

Clara and Justine directed subtle wags of their heads at the girls, indicating they should disregard the remark.

At the attic stairway, Clara switched on the flashlight she carried and explained that the attic was the only place in the house that didn't have electricity. Justine handed out candles to all except Etta Ruth. "We only have the one flashlight because of war rationing of batteries," she said as Justine lit Mary's candle.

"I want a damn candle," Etta Ruth said. "Everybody else has one."

Clara patted her hand. "You stick close to me and the flashlight, Etta Ruth. We wouldn't want you to burn the ... yourself."

"To hell with you and your flashlight, Clara. I-want-a-goddamned-candle! If I ever decide to burn the damn house down I'll use something with more fire power than a piss-ant candle."

"Here, Miz Etta," said Leeta. "You can have mine." She handed Etta Ruth here unlit candle.

"Light the damn thing, Justine," Etta Ruth demanded.

Justine shook her head. "I don't have any more matches. You'll just have to carry it unlit."

Etta Ruth grabbed Mary's wrist to steady it as she lit her candle off Mary's candle. "I don't mind you all thinking I'm crazy, but it pisses me off that you think I'm stupid."

No one had a reply.

In the attic, they lit the kerosene lamps that hung on every wall and on tables stationed every few yards apart. As the brighter flames brought the warehouse-sized room to life, Mary was taken aback by the number of trunks, boxes, tables stacked high with books, paintings, lamps, candlesticks, dishes, linens, and dozens of other items, including an entire wall of wild animal heads. Resting against the wall beneath a pair of stuffed boa constrictors entwined in a deadly grip on each other was the north and south ends of the sawed-in-half water buffalo.

Mary and Leeta gazed stupefied at a long line of life-sized male and female mannequins fully clothed in stunning garments from eras long past, many of the fashions elaborate with laces, inlaid pearl, epaulets, and glittering sequins of costume jewelry sewn right into the fabrics. Racks of shoes and purses stood nearby. Elegant hats, plumed, feathered, or plush with silk flowers and of every size and material adorned each life-size form. The male figures were just as spectacular.

Etta Ruth snickered. "Clara and Justine had names for all these dummies when we were kids," she said, pointing. "There's *Daniel*, Justine. When you thought nobody was looking, you used to stand on a chair and kiss him so hard his face fell in."

"I did not!"

"Look at him! You deformed that poor old dummy with those kisses of yours. Or maybe you toppled him over and sat on his face, huh?"

Justine let out an enraged gasp.

Mary sang out louder than was necessary: "My goodness, you could open an antique store with all this wonderful stuff!"

"I never dreamed we'd be selling any of it," Clara said sadly. "There are priceless memories attached to almost everything up here."

Etta Ruth made a *har-har* sound. "*Priceless memories*? What use are they? Face it, Clara. You, Justine, and I are just three old broads who missed every boat that sailed into port. You two never snagged a husband, and the one I got wasn't worth killing. What kind of priceless memories are those? If somebody cut our throats they'd be doing us a favor."

"That is ridiculous!" Justine snapped. "We have all had a *life* and for that, Clara and I are thankful."

"*A life?* How long have you two been rattling around all *alone* in this old museum now getting on each other's nerves—and before that, told every day by your *Poppa* which way to hop? I think life has probably made *us all* candidates for the booby hatch, don't you?" She turned her back on them.

Before Clara or Justine could tell her to *speak for herself,* Etta Ruth whirled around to stare accusingly at Clara. "Have you told *them* about Clarence?"

"Of course not."

"Told them *what* about Clarence?" Justine asked.

"Nothing! Just that he was a son of a bitch." Etta Ruth flounced off across the room.

"You've been telling us *that* ever since you got here!" Justine called after her.

"Aw, shut up, floozy!" Etta Ruth yelled over her shoulder.

Justine waited until Etta Ruth was out of earshot before hissing, "I don't think I can take much more of her, Clara!"

Clara ignored her and whispered to the girls, "We mustn't mind what Etta Ruth says. She is angry. I'm told widows often stay mad at their dead husbands for a very long time, simply because they died."

"Oh, Clara," Justine blustered beneath her breath, "I wish you would stop defending her!" She glared across the room at Etta Ruth, who was now holding a whalebone corset around her middle and wiggling her hips. "You know as well as I do that the woman is just a mean old bi—" She bit her lip and fanned her hand in front of her face.

"She is *family,* Justine, and that should mean something to both of us, especially now that she is, well, sort of ill."

"*Ill*? She's nuttier than a Christmas fruitcake! And so are you for inviting her here!"

Clearly agitated, Clara motioned for Mary and Leeta to follow her past the mannequins to a section of the attic that contained row upon row of magnificent old furniture. Mary's eyes widened at the sight of it. She knew about antiques because her maternal grandfather had been a smalltime antique dealer in New Jersey. She had helped at his store every summer until he died and her grandmother sold the business. *If the Hesterwine ladies sold even half of this furniture, they would certainly get enough to pay Banker Prickett and have plenty left over.*

Clara called out from nearby. "Mary, Willie, I have something for you!" She jerked away a dusty sheet to reveal a big yellow bicycle built for two.

"It is beautiful!" Mary cried.

Justine bustled up beside Clara. "It's a gift from *me,* too, Clara. That bicycle was half mine, you know."

"Thank you both so very much," Mary said, gripping the handlebars.

"The tires need air," Justine said. "There's a pump in the barn."

Leeta gazed curiously at it. "I used to want one of these when I was a kid. Tomorrow, I'm gonna ride that thing to town and find myself a job."

"Willie, dear, are you absolutely certain you want to do that?" Clara asked. "We shall have money as soon as Mr. Klunk gets here next week. Then we shall help you get where you want to go."

"Just the same, Miss Clara, I'd like to look for a job. I learned a long time ago there ain't no guarantees 'bout nothing, no matter how much of a sure thing you might think it is."

"Clara and I guarantee Mr. Klunk will want our treasures," Justine said.

Leeta frowned. "Don't seem like to me there'd be a big deman—"

Mary touched Leeta's arm to keep her from expounding further. "If you don't mind, Willie, I will go to town with you."

Leeta shrugged. "I guess four legs pedaling is better than two."

Justine laughed. "How well we know, don't we, Clara?"

"I know I did most of the pedaling on those hot summer days and you did most of the coasting," Clara replied. Then she turned to the girls. "If you're going to pedal to town in this hot weather, you had better wear hats. Texas is famous for causing sunstroke."

Mary glanced over her shoulder at the beautiful vintage hats adorning the mannequins. "Did you wear one of those when you pedaled to town, Miss Clara?"

"I certainly did. I loved my hats. Young ladies today would never dream of wearing something as elaborate as Justine and I once wore."

"I would," Mary said. "I think they are beautiful. They would certainly keep the sun off."

"Then, by all means, dear, take any hat that pleases you. I'm sure Mr. Klunk will want our lovely millinery right along with the mannequins, so take your pick before he sees them." She gazed longingly at the hats and then sighed heavily as her eyes watered.

"Clara and I don't want to think about selling our treasures, though we know we must," Justine said.

The look on the elderly sisters' faces was suddenly so forlorn that Mary could not help but say what she was thinking.

"I know it is none of my business, but Aunt Lucy said Mr. Klunk has only a big, old, rundown warehouse full of nothing but scraps and garbage. This beautiful old furniture is not junk, nor is anything else up here, Miss Clara, Miss Justine. My grandfather was an antiques dealer, and I know there are very valuable pieces here. Isn't there a bona fide antiques dealer in town other than Mr. Klunk?"

"The only antique shop in Hesterwine went out of business last year when the owner joined the marines," Justine replied. "We could find one in Corpus Christi, but the police won't allow Mr. Valentino on the *bascule* bridge anymore."

Etta Ruth, with the corset hanging loosely around her middle, had joined them. She put up a hand. "I have a good idea! Why don't we all go jump off the *bascule* bridge?"

"Oh, *Etta Ruth*," Justine said heatedly.

"I suppose we shall have to rely on Mr. Klunk," Clara said. "I can't think of anything else to do, short of shooting Banker Prickett and hiding his body," she added jokingly.

Etta Ruth nudged Clara, her big eyes suddenly glinting with mischief. "That's what you should have done to Boyd Pendleton, Clara—or *did* you? No one's seen him since 1914, almost thirty years ago."

"*Ridiculous!*" cried Clara and Justine in unity, obviously extremely upset by the remark.

Mary and Leeta's inquisitive stares jerked from one woman's flaming face to the next and then back to Miz Etta Ruth—who was grinning like she'd just sunk her verbal pickaxe into a vein of gold. *Who was Boyd Pendleton?*

Etta Ruth continued, "No one's seen hide nor hair of Boyd since shortly before you ran off to Europe for that *second* six-month stay, Clara, and didn't come home until the Germans started World War I."

Mary's curiosity intensified. She watched Miss Justine quickly step to her sister's side. She was still as red in the face as if she'd spent the day digging in the flowerbed bareheaded. "Clara?" she said in a voice that clearly indicated she expected Clara to do something about Etta Ruth.

"Etta Ruth, if you mention that man's name in this house ever again, you will no longer be welcome here. As to my two vacation trips to Europe, you must stop your ridiculous insinuations! They had nothing to do with *him*." She managed to speak this last softly, despite her obvious distress.

Justine, looking only slightly appeased, jerked her chin at their grinning cousin.

"Oh, oh ..." Etta Ruth said, snickering as she glanced around the attic. "Where oh where is that Pandora's Box? I hope I didn't accidentally pop it open." Her black eyes, full of mischief, darted back and forth between Clara and Justine. "A love triangle between one man and two women is always a bad situation, but a love triangle between one man and two sisters is disastrous, isn't it, girls? Even if it is ancient history."

Justine appeared ready to leap on top of her. "Shut your mouth! Clara and I mean it, Etta Ruth! You will no longer be welcome in this house!"

Mary now knew the cause of the reoccurring hostility between these otherwise good-natured ladies—and his name was Boyd Pendleton.

Leeta jabbed Mary's ribs and whispered close to her ear, "Uh oh, looks like all hell is 'bout to break loose."

Etta Ruth surprised them. "I have naught to do but obey," she said. "I leave you now because I need a damn drink."

Justine still glared at her. "Good! Our life is so much better when *you* aren't around making *us all* a little crazy!"

"Well, Justine, when I get downstairs and have my cool refresher in hand, I shall drink a toast to 'us all.'" She raised a hand as if gripping a glass. *"Here's to women of every age and stage whom life has made a little crazy ... or a lot."* She eyed Justine and Clara a long moment. "As to yourselves, don't blame me, blame the Pendleton heir with the savoir faire."

The stony expression on Miss Clara and Miss Justine's faces, as they abruptly parted company to different parts of the room was further proof to Mary that—even though the Hesterwine sisters were neither a little crazy— nor a lot—a man named Boyd Pendleton had greatly affected their lives, namely their relationship with each other.

Leeta followed Miss Justine over to the furniture to help label it, and Mary followed Miss Clara to a table stacked high with books. As they sorted the books and packed them into boxes, Mary kept glancing at the silent woman. Miss Clara looked so deep in anguished thought that Mary dared not speak for fear of startling her. Every now and then, the pink-faced woman touched her cheek reflectively but then jerked her hand away, as if displeased. Watching Miss Clara's turmoil, Mary felt a swell of excitement mix with her pity for the woman, then marveled that she was actually beginning to feel as if she was part of this peculiar *family dimension*— something she had never felt in her father's house, 'odd' or otherwise.

Suddenly she wished she knew what memories concerning the mysterious Boyd Pendleton had so upset both sisters.

Clara stared absently at the book in her hand. *No one has spoken that man's name in this house since ...* Not even she and Justine spoke it when they frequently sniped at each other! That was the rule and they stuck to it. *That Etta Ruth! What does she think she knows?* No one, not even Poppa, on the day he died, knew the entire truth....

Clara could scarcely keep up with the kaleidoscope of events flashing across her mind as her memory raced back to that first time she and Boyd Pendleton, in their youth, had planned to announce their engagement. It was so long ago—forty-nine years, to be exact—but she'd forgotten none of it; unspeakable emotional pain does that to a person. Boyd was to come to a dinner party at Hesterwine Place. However, Boyd never showed up. She had sat in the parlor worrying that something terrible had happened to him—he did drive that buggy of his like a madman, and with a team of horses that were much too spirited. Justine, who had stayed upstairs out of sight the entire evening, slowly entered the room to stand trembling before her, nose red and dripping, her eyes swollen nearly shut from crying.

"I'm sorry, Clara! I am so sorry," she cried between hiccupped sobs. "I don't know what came over me! I was just so miserable! I just wanted him to know! And-and now he's gone!"

"You wanted *whom* to know what? Who is gone?"

Justine bit her lip. "Boyd! I-I confessed to him that I loved him!"

"You what?" She knew most of her friends had a crush on Boyd and Justine was no exception. The two of them had even joked about it when Justine giggled and said, "You'd better marry him, Clara, before I make him see how lovable I am."

"Get your own boyfriend," Clara always joked back, "because Boyd Pendleton is mine."

"He was very upset after I told him, Clara. I am so sorry!"

"I can imagine!" Clara cried, coming to her feet, intending to go and find him. "Poor Boyd! I will forgive you this, Justine, as I am certain Boyd will forgive you, but you must never voice that silly infatuation to him or *me* again! I will tell him that you have ceased that foolish notion."

"He is gone, Clara! He said he is not going to marry anybody because ... because he said he loves us both, and it would not be fair to either of us if he chose one over the other!"

Their father entered the parlor just in time to keep Clara's open hand from connecting with Justine's hopelessly contrite face.

The next week, Clara took her very first vacation trip to Europe, refusing to let the tearful Justine join her. It took six months before she felt she could return home and tolerate being on the same continent with Justine again. Sisterly love won out in the end.

Twenty years later, not long after she turned forty, as Etta Ruth had so cruelly reminded her, Boyd came back and begged her forgiveness. This time, they planned to elope. However, even before she had reached the bottom of the stairs that euphoric evening with suitcase in hand, she heard her father yelling up to her.

"They're gone!" he roared, so red in the face that she thought him about to collapse.

Clara's heart pounded as she remembered her reaction to her father's words that day. Her throat had frozen, and even as she croaked out, "Who?" she knew whom.

"Your sister, that's who! She left a note! She's run off with that sorry Boyd Pendleton of yours, the son of a bitch!"

Clara remembered standing on the porch, rigid and dry-eyed, and watching her father speed away to search for Justine and Boyd. Personally, she had never wanted to see either of them ever again.

She would have left the universe if she could have, but that being impossible, she settled for Europe again. Halfway there, she leaned far out over the ship's railing and dropped Boyd's second engagement ring into the ocean.

In England she had walked the stormy, wind-swept Yorkshire moorlands like some angry, lonely, heartbroken, misplaced heroine in a Bronte novel. However, even at that low point, misfortune had not finished with her... because walking those same craggy moors was broodingly handsome forty-one-year-old Fritz Von Heuvel, a doctor with a thriving practice in Aachen, a town in North Rhine-Westphalia, Germany, and a recent childless widower still mourning his dead wife. A spark lit, and flickering in that proverbial flame that discombobulated moths seek with no regard for the consequences ...was a promise of solace, and they flew into it.

The virginity she had struggled for years to keep Boyd Pendleton from wresting from her before they had said their I do's she relinquished to Fritz Von Heuvel the same day they met.

To this day, Clara still felt the sting of her foolishness. One would think that a forty-year-old woman would have attained enough dignity to withstand a bit of heartbreak without, immediately afterward, surrendering her virtue to the first man who smiled kindly at her!

Worse, she had lived in sin with Fritz for *six whole months* until Germany's Kaiser and the German establishment—in hopes that warfare would unite the public behind the Kaiser's monarchy—began warring with the rest of Europe. Being a doctor, and needed at the front lines to treat the wounded, Fritz immediately obeyed induction into the German Army, but not before he slipped an engagement ring on her finger and made her promise to marry him when he returned. The moment the door closed behind him, she lugged her suitcase down to the depot, boarded the train to Hamburg, and then sailed on the SS *Vaterland* for America, leaving most of her belongings behind, along with the little jewelry box containing his ring. She arrived at New York in late July 1914, just as World War I broke out.

She avoided any feelings of guilt at her abandonment of Fritz with the easy assumption that he had only asked her to marry him in the aftershock of discovering that he had destroyed forever a forty year-old spinster's claim to moral chastity ... by getting her so drunk on Bitburger that she relinquished her virginity to him without so much as a weakly whispered *no*.

She'd not expected to find Justine home at Hesterwine Place, but there she was, looking terrified, her big eyes batting tears as she mumbled like a broken record, "I'm sorry ... I'm sorry ... I'm sorry ... I'm—" Clara slapped her so hard that her own ears rang.

Later, their poppa said, "Be glad neither of you married the son of a bitch, Clara. He's a finagler and an idiot! Not long after you left, Justine called me from Del Rio to come get her. The son of a bitch said he was sailing to the African continent to work in the Egyptian oil fields. Your heartbroken sister said he'd changed his mind about her when she refused to put the wedding bed before the preacher."

That bit of news about Justine's moral fortitude only added another layer to her bitterness—she had always figured her more popular younger sister would be the one to end up prematurely despoiled.

The old mansion, being big enough to accommodate her rancor, gave her the luxury of not having to speak to Justine for two years ... until the day Poppa died, and they realized that they were all each other had. *That*, and the beautiful old home they had inherited equally and were now about to lose ....

Clara laid aside the book she had been squeezing and glanced across the room at Justine. Just as in childhood when they squabbled over things important and not so important, sisterly love had emerged to save the relationship. However, Justine's and Boyd's second betrayal had merged with the first to form a bitter aftertaste that had left *her—the betrayed one—* with an irrefutable sense of precaution. She became *a widow of disillusionment*, forever thereafter unwilling to chance any sort of relationship with another man. Her consolation over the years, and now, was that not Justine, nor anybody else on earth, would ever know about her six-month association, *of a most carnal nature*, with a German named Fritz Von Heuvel.

# 9

WEARING VINTAGE HATS FROM THE ATTIC, Mary and Leeta pedaled to the top of Windy Knoll, then stopped to rest. The little basket in front of Mary's handlebars brimmed with tomatoes from the garden. Leeta's basket, on the platform behind her seat, held fresh-dug potatoes, all of which Miss Clara had asked them to deliver to Mr. Ewald at the lumberyard.

"Whew! It's gonna be a lot easier pedaling *down*hill," Leeta said, wiping her brow and then blowing at the thick flounce of red ostrich feathers cascading from the wide, curled brim of her black felt hat.

Mary looked over her shoulder at her. "*The Three Musketeers* would love that hat, Leeta ... I mean, *Willie*. You look quite cavalier in it."

"All you look is *silly*," Leeta said. "Looks like you're wearing a big dishpan full of flowers on your head."

"Maybe so, but this lovely old hat once belonged to Miss Clara and Miss Justine's grandmother. I loved it the moment I saw the bright mixture of silk flowers that did not fade a bit all those years in the attic. We are most colorful today, you and I, *Willie Holloway*."

I'm taking mine off before we get to town. I got color already that attracts too much attention."

"I have a feeling we will be okay here in Hesterwine, Leeta."

"*I* got a feeling I'll be okay when I get my sweet ass to California."

As they sat balancing the bicycle beneath them at the top of Windy Knoll, Mary examined the pleasant countryside for a long moment and then gazed at Clara and Justine Hesterwine's massive old mansion in the distance.

"I cannot stop thinking of all that great stuff in the attic. I'm surprised Miss Clara and Miss Justine never thought to sell some of it long before now."

"You heard what they said. They don't wanna part with any of that stuff."

"I wonder why, since Miss Clara said they had not looked at any of it in ages before yesterday."

"'Cause they is *old*, that's why. Old people don't wanna part with nothing. I bet them old ladies got every pair of holey underdrawers they ever owned. They probably got 'em folded all neat in a box up there in that attic."

Mary laughed, then sobered. "I feel they would do much better if they left Klunk's Junk out of it and sold that beautiful old furniture themselves. Except they would have to advertise it in the paper, and that takes money."

"Girl, don't you know you don't need to run ads in a newspaper to sell something? When I worked at Mandingo Q. Mann's place in Chicago, I made flyers telling what was happening at the club every weekend and then I handed them out on the street. It worked just fine getting the crowds in. I reckon it'd do the same for selling that stuff in the attic. Just say in the flyer *where* and *when* it's gonna be sold."

"Why, Leeta! That is an excellent idea! We could haul the furniture down and line it up on the porch ... the mannequins, too. But first we will have to sell Miss Clara and Miss Justine on the idea."

"Me and my big mouth."

"Before we say a word, we will make a few flyers to show them. If we get two dollars for the tomatoes and potatoes, Miss Clara said we could split a dollar of it. I'm going to the Five and Dime and spend my share on supplies to make those flyers."

"And *I'm* going to the bus station and see how far out of town I can get on fifty cents!" Leeta cried, mimicking Mary's excitement.

Laughing, Mary stood up on the pedals, tore off her hat, and waved it high over her head. "Oh my gosh, Leeta! This is weird, but suddenly I feel just great, don't you?" Still laughing, she jerked the ribbon from her hair and allowed her locks to blow freely in the wind.

"No, I *don't* feel just great. I'm a long way from feeling just great. How many flyers you planning on making, and *who* gonna hand 'em out on the street? *I* ain't!"

"We will have to work fast, because we will need enough flyers to put in every store window and shop in town." She patted the handlebars. "We have transportation, and it does not require an ounce of gasoline." She slapped the hat back on her head and tied the ribbons beneath her chin.

In reply to Mary's exuberance, Leeta poked out her tongue and made a long *pufffft* sound at the red ostrich feather that suddenly dropped down to tickle her nose again, but she didn't say she wouldn't help with the flyers.

There was a part of Hesterwine, Texas, not visible to the main drag when gazing out the window of a Greyhound bus, and the girls had no idea, until they were pedaling to town on their two-seater, that Hesterwine was actually divided into three communities—the *white*, the *Negro*, and the *Mexican*. Today might not have been the day Mary and Leeta discovered the latter two neighborhoods had they not sighted a dark-green 1937 Packard with the word "SHERIFF" stenciled across the trunk in big white letters, sitting on the side of the road.

"That's gotta be that Sheriff Bloot," Leeta said.

Hoping he had not looked in his rearview mirror, they swerved off the highway and bumped across a railroad track onto a crumbling old road edged by weeds and clumps of garbage. Empty cotton fields bordered the narrow thoroughfare, scraps of cotton lying scattered between the rows and dirty, tire-rutted tufts of it sticking to the pavement. The girls swerved away from the shoulder to avoid crashing into the remnants of an old mattress; the soggy stuffing lay scattered about, dingy puffs of it dangling from tall weeds as if sprouting from them. In contrast, a rusty set of bedsprings somehow became a trellis for a blanket of velvety green grape vines, strangely adding a glimpse of bucolic prettiness to an otherwise unappealing scene.

"This must be a back road into Hesterwine," Leeta said. "Looks like some folks use it mostly for dumping their old shit, don't it?"

"Looks that way," Mary said, and held her nose as they neared the bloated carcass of a big, black dog surrounded by a gang of turkey vultures. "Buzzards are nasty birds. We could throw rocks at them, but they would just come right back."

"I chucked rocks at plenty of them stinking birds when I was a kid back in Mississippi," Leeta said. "That reminds me; why you think the sheriff sitting on the side of the road like that?"

"Maybe he is watching for speeding cars. Since war-rationing of tires and gasoline, it's against the law to drive faster than thirty-five miles an hour."

"Bet Rudolph Valentino could go *that* fast if somebody poked his rump with a sharp stick."

Mary grinned. "Not if he was pulling that old Buick. To his credit, though, he doesn't need to be filled up at the gas pump before he takes Miss Clara and Miss Justine to town."

"That's 'cause he got a big supply of his own, and so potent it could be a weapon of war if somebody could figure out a way to bottle it into a bomb," Leeta said, and they both laughed.

After several minutes of steady pedaling, Leeta broke the silence. "I was just thinking, Mary Kenny. I told you why I was on that bus, but you ain't told me why you was on it."

"I'll tell you tomorrow. I'm too out of breath today. We're pedaling against the wind."

"I got a hunch there was a man involved."

"Not much of one, I guess."

"Story of my life, too, girl."

"His name was Claxton Mitchell, and I thought he loved me. Anyway, he said he did."

"Just long enough to get in your drawers, eh? We *do* have a lot in common."

"We broke up. No. He dumped me. Soon after that, he was drafted into the army. Last I heard, he was ... missing in action," Mary said, unable to stop the tremble that came into her voice.

"Oh shit, girl. Don't love him like that."

"I don't."

"You don't even know it."

"You're mistaken."

"Uh-huh."

Somehow, Mary was ashamed to admit to Leeta that she loved Claxton. She kept remembering the times he stood her up and never offered an excuse, or the times he left her sitting alone at gatherings while he partied with his buddies across the room.

They rode in silence for a while, concentrating on pumping against the strong wind, but then Mary abruptly put on the brakes.

"Leeta, I had Claxton's baby. He was stillborn. My father hates me for shaming him, but I think he hated me even before that. I think I hate him, too. I will never go back there." She waited for Leeta's remarks, but only felt Leeta's effort to get the bike moving again. Finally, when they were rolling along, Leeta poked her shoulder.

"Feels good to tell somebody, don't it?"

"Yes," she replied and, actually feeling lighter, pointed up ahead. "Look, there is a bridge up there. I suppose it spans that same little river that crosses the main highway into town."

As they approached the long wooden bridge, they noticed that another narrow paved road, such as the one they were on, forked off just this side of the bridge and ran alongside the river. Riding onto the bridge, they saw yet another road on the opposite riverbank, and that forked off in the same direction as the first road. Oddly, both roads skirted the course of the water for perhaps a hundred yards until all three curved out of sight behind a heavy curtain of overhanging trees.

The girls rolled to a stop. Below them, two small Negro boys sat on the bank, long fishing poles dangling over the water. The boys looked up, and the smaller of the two proudly hefted a nice-sized catfish for them to see. The girls waved down to him.

"I'm having another feeling of déjà vu," Leeta said, her neck tensing and her eyes widening as she cocked an ear toward the river.

Mary smiled. "You have them often?"

"You hear it, too—or am I dreaming?"

Mary turned her ear to the faint sound coming from somewhere behind the curtain of trees, then nodded. "I hear music."

"Not just *music*," Leeta said, "but *blues* music! *Juking* Mississippi Delta blues music, and it ain't coming from no *jukebox*. If I didn't know better, I'd think I was home in Mississippi!"

Mary had never seen such a big smile on Leeta's pretty face.

"Come on!" Leeta cried. "Let's go down there and see what's going on."

"But which road?"

Leeta pointed. "*That* road."

"You're guessing."

"Hell, no, I ain't guessing. Them little colored boys is probably fishing from the same side of the river they live on, and I reckon that guitar-picking *Negro* lives there, too. Ain't no white man play blues guitar like that."

Ten minutes later, around the curve and past the curtain of trees, Mary and Leeta stood, feet on the ground while still astraddle their bike, and gazed at two ramshackle neighborhoods, one on the east side of the river, the other on the west. On the west side across the water, she saw a cross-topped bell tower of a church jutting up through a thick line of tall trees and heard the faint sounds of children speaking a language that she knew to be Spanish. Someone had a radio turned up, and lively Mexican music floated across the river to compete faintly with the Mississippi blues guitar.

Mary and Leeta, their legs stretched out to balance the bike beneath them, heard the guitar loud and clear now. A few yards distant and a block from the nearest street lined by shabby houses and tiny shacks stood a large, sun-bleached, blue building over which hung a long, white sign with dark-blue lettering—*BLUE CREEK LOUNGE.*

"No, *suh*," Leeta murmured, poking Mary's shoulder and slipping into a familiar dialect, as if to make a point. "That *sho* ain't no jukebox we hearing. That a Mississippi Delta man on that guitar if I ever heard one—and I heard plenty of 'em. Back home, when I was a kid, there was one blues man who could do *slide* guitar like that, and damn if he don't *sing* just like him, too." She poked Mary again. "Listen," she commanded, pointing at the Blue Creek Lounge as her neck and body began to move appreciatively to the sensual tempo of blues guitar and the growling, raspy male voice bawling out the thumping lyrics:

> *Get down, baby ... climb down off my back*
> *I said get down, baby ... climb down off my back*
> *You're a mean-mouthed woman ...*
> *Won't cut your man no slack*
> *Well, I love my baby ... love her all night long*
> *I love my baby ... love her all night long*
> *But when the sun come up,*
> *She turn that mean mouth on ...*
> *Lawd, she turn that mean mouth on ...*

Then, the guitar took over in its hugely emotional Delta blues style, and Leeta's excitement grew. Mary stared at her in surprise at first and then appreciatively, as deeply soulful humming sounds, masterful and mesmerizing in their intensity, came from somewhere inside Leeta Bulow to mate with the guitar sounds floating from inside the *Blue Creek Lounge*.

Leeta stepped off the bike, smoothed her borrowed skirt over her hips, and removed her hat. Although she wore a pair of Miss Justine's sturdy black lace-up oxfords with the one and one-half inch walking heels over a pair of Mary's pink socks, she moved toward the Blue Creek Lounge as if she were dressed for a ball. Mary watched agog as her bicycle partner slunk along like a graceful cat while swinging her ostrich plumed Musketeer hat jauntily at her side.

Pushing the weighty two-seater but keeping her distance, Mary followed. Then, as Leeta stepped up to the lounge's double screen doors with the faded metal Coca-Cola signs across them and strolled right in, Mary veered off to wait beneath the beckoning shade of a small umbrella-shaped tree nearby. She had a feeling that Sheriff Bloot would not like her being *here* anymore than he had liked Leeta being on the *white* side of the bus stop behind Goldrod's.

# 10

THE BLUE CREEK LOUNGE'S INTERIOR was exactly as Leeta imagined it would be—a big, wooden room naked of anything but wooden tables, wooden chairs, and a wooden bar off to one corner and lined with wooden stools—all, even the walls and floor, showing the hammer-shaped dents of homemade construction. Being that this ramshackle room was so like the Mississippi juke joint that she had fled seven years ago for Chicago, she puzzled over why the sight of it energized her almost as much as the guitar blues music that filled it.

Standing just inside the doorway, another feeling of déjà vu flickered in front of her eyes like a newsreel flash at the Bijou. Suddenly she saw herself, small and wide-eyed, squeezed between her four siblings at a corner table ... entranced, like everyone else in the room, as they watched their mother sing and sway on a little wooden stage nearby. From time to time, one of Adeline Bulow's slender hands dropped to the guitar man's shoulder to steady herself. Her other hand, gripping a bottle of bootleg whiskey, gently undulated in time to the sweet, throaty, sounds coming out of her—sounds that could stop everyone in the room from talking until the last note had passed from between her sensuous lips. Adeline had beautiful, shiny, straight hair, thanks to G. A. Morgan Hair Refining Cream and Madame C. K. Walker's ointments and heatable metal combs, all of which filled a shelf in their little shack. Leeta and her sisters dared not touch those expensive hair products because all were strictly the property of their stylish mother.

The same went for their mother's classy clothes and sets of nice, pastel-colored underwear.

As quickly as the memory passed, another began to creep into Leeta's mind, persistent and brooding, even as she tried to knock it away with a quick slap at the fake curls dangling over her left eye. Always, when she remembered that historic night at the Mississippi juke joint where her mother reigned, she thought uncomfortably of the stuttering child she had been at eleven; tall for her age, skinny, her legs like shapeless noodles, and her nappy hair in a dozen piccaninny braids all over her head. She'd had gaps on both sides of her front teeth because her incisors were slow in coming in. She used to cry and then get furious when her siblings and kids at school caller her "Rabbit." At that age, she had rarely smiled. Her clenched mouth, combined with her rounded, continuously questioning eyes, gave her a permanent look of comical angst, never more so than when her mother called her name that night.

"Leeta ... baby girl! Come on up here and show everybody what you got from your momma, girl!" Adeline waved her arm at the crowd of partying men and women. They yelled their encouragement, all eyes going to "Adeline's baby girl" as she melted farther back into her space between her brothers and sisters. Then, before she could get up enough nerve to run, her mother grabbed a shoulder strap of her faded new pinafore dress (picked from the ragbag behind the white folks' church) and was jerking her toward the little wooden stage. One end of the strap tore loose, and Leeta grabbed at the pinafore's sagging bib and held it to her flat chest as her mother, still clutching the other end, pulled her along like a dog on a leash.

"Okay, Leeta, baby, sing!" Adeline cried, the *leash* still clutched in her hand. She jerked it a couple of times as Leeta hovered, silent and trembling, holding her bib to her chest and staring at the expectant faces whose grins suddenly looked like Halloween masks.

Leeta's mouth opened wider and wider, her lips stretching farther and farther away from her rabbit teeth, her usually angst-ridden face no longer inert but alive with the panic one must feel when about to be shoved into an inferno filled with smirking devils. That little girl had never sung for anybody! She'd never sung a note outside that little river shack they all lived in, the sound of her voice always lost in the clamor of noisy siblings. She was too shy! She'd mess up, and then they would all laugh!

"I-I-I-I-I *can't,* Momma!"

*Slap!*

A brief murmur of protest rose from the crowd but Adeline, unable to do wrong in the eyes of her fans, was immediately forgiven.

Standing in the doorway of the Blue Creek Lounge, Leeta shuddered again, almost tasting the blood inside her lip as Adeline grinned at her adoring fans, wagging her three-quarters empty bottle at them.

"Tomorrow is Sunday, so my Leeta gonna sing 'Amazing Grace.' And she gonna sing it the *blues way* like I done heard her sing it at home when she think nobody listening."

Leeta sang, sniffling between the stanzas at first, then halfway through the old spiritual she belted it out with an angry passion that suddenly had the crowd staring silently at her the way they stared at Adeline when she sang.

After that, the club's owner gave Adeline an extra two dollars a week for Leeta's talent, and she took her turn onstage with her mother, sometimes the two of them in duets that stood the bootleg-boozing crowd on their feet. Leeta only got a glimpse of the money she earned as it passed from the owner's hand into her mother's brilliantly ringed fingers.

She sang on that little wooden stage until shortly after her thirteenth birthday, when one of the male customers followed her outside to the outhouse, waited until she emerged, slapped his big hand over her mouth, dragged her down to the riverbank, and raped her. To keep her from telling, she figured he might have killed her when he finished ... if not for Momma's guitar-picking blues man coming up from behind and grabbing him. She ran, hearing the struggle behind her, followed by a croaky groan, and then something heavy hit the river with a big splash. She hid behind the outhouse and watched the blues man stroll back inside the juke joint. A few seconds later, she heard him doing sweet bluesy runs on his guitar, and her mother started singing. Though battered, bleeding, and nearly naked, she stood hidden there a long time, swaying and humming to the sounds—sounds that were in her soul like God himself had put them there and wouldn't let her worship anything else.

Then, standing behind that outhouse sobbing and clutching the bloody remints of her torn dress to the injured part of her, she vented her years of pent-up rage at Adeline Bulow. She knew her condemnations were drowned out by the loud music coming from inside the juke joint and no one heard her, but she cried out anyway: "How come you let your chillren go hungry most time, Momma? How come you spend every dollar you got on all them fancy evening gowns and all that jewelry when your chillren ain't got no school clothes or shoes that fit or paper to do theys homework? How come you ain't looking out for your chillren like a momma is 'posed to? I just a kid, Momma, but I know a momma 'posed to look out for her child so bad stuff don't happen to her...like what happen tonight, Momma! You hear me, Momma?" This last came out in a whisper as, feeling empty and worthless, she turned away from the lights of the juke joint and walked home in the pitch-darkness.

The next day, she stole every dime and dollar from her mother's hiding place in the shack and, without good-byes to anyone, took the first bus out of town. Somehow, she wasn't as scared as she used to be—just fed up. Rolled up in her hand at the bus station was a magazine she'd found months ago in the garbage behind the Negro grocery store; inside was an article about the South Side of Chicago, with pictures of fancily dressed Chicago Negroes looking somber and important... the way she had always pictured she would be one of these days.

Unfortunately, when she got to Chicago, her feeling of worthlessness had made her perfect prey for Mandingo Q. Mann.

"You looking for somebody, miss?" The raspy voice brought the interior of the Blue Creek Lounge back into focus.

"I thought you was him when I heard you playing slide guitar and singing like you was, but you ain't him," she said to the slightly built man with the startling light-green eyes and understated features. If he hadn't been so black, he would have looked white. She guessed he must be sixty. He sat on a little stool next to the stage, his long hands draped over his guitar in a relaxed fashion as his pencil-thin lips smiled at her in a hospitable manner.

"We ain't open for business 'til noon, but if you want a Coke, they over there in the icebox." He nodded to a spot behind the bar. "Help you self; it's on the house for you and the young lady under the Chinaberry tree out yonder." He nodded toward the open window where Mary could be seen holding the bicycle upright and nervously gazing around.

Leeta took a Coke, opened it with the loose bottle opener that hung from the box by a string, and went to the window and called out to Mary. She laughed aloud as Mary paused to look left and right before she gently laid the bicycle down, ran over, took the Coke, then hurried back to the tree with it.

"Friend of yours?" the old man asked.

"That scaredy-cat little white girl?" Leeta scoffed and rolled her eyes. She laughed again and, after a moment, added, "I *guess* so."

The old man ran his fingers over the guitar strings before setting it aside and rising stiffly from the stool. "I reckon I'll get me one of them Cokes. Better get one for yourself. I reckon you must be mighty thirsty after pedaling that bicycle from ... where did you say you come from?"

Leeta beat him to the icebox, drew out two Cokes, opened them and handed him one. She took a big swallow from her bottle.

"Where did I come from *originally* ... or lately?" she asked.

"I know where you come from originally. You thought I was a Mississippi Delta blues man you used to know, so I reckon that's where you is from originally. I also got a feeling this ain't the first juke joint you been in, either."

"I got a love-hate feeling for joints like this."

He laughed. "Me, too. I been owning this place a long time. It be hard work, long, loud nights, and most my customers want credit 'til payday, if it ever come. Reckon I'm getting way too old for it. Just me and my ol' woman, Mozelle, mostly run the place now. Business is falling off more every week since the war."

Leeta's eyes lit up. She grabbed up his hand and shook it, speaking all the while. "What this place need is a *draw*, and *I'm* it. My name is *Willie Holloway*. I'm one hell of a singer, and I'm what you need to go along with that hot Delta blues guitar playing of yours. I'll do it weekdays, weekends, and holidays for ten dollars a night, and you can sit there on that stool and watch your business grow."

"Denton Maxwell," he said, still shaking her hand. "My friends call me Dink, and if I was to hire you, it'd be *six* dollars a night, six days a week, 'cept Sundays, when we ain't open."

Leeta's stubbornness showed in the way she tightened her lips. "Pick up that guitar and follow my lead. I'm gonna show you right now what that measly *eight dollars* a night gonna get you, Mr. Denton 'Dink' Maxwell."

Still smiling, he went over and picked up his guitar. "I guess I better hear what my *six dollars and fifty cents* a night gonna get me. If you ain't as good as you think you is, it likely gonna go down to *two* dollars."

Leeta had scarcely drawn a breath and opened her mouth to sing when the screen door slammed hard and they turned to see Sheriff Bloot shifting into his wide-legged stance of intimidation.

Leeta was suddenly scared. Back in Mississippi, she had seen good white sheriffs and bad white sheriffs—she had already learned that this one was a big, bloated advertisement for *bad*.

"Gal, why'd you bring that white girl out here to Rose Hill?" He pointed out the window at Mary. She was astraddle the bicycle again and staring worriedly at the building.

"We didn't come here on purpose. We was on the way to town and thought it was a shortcut." As calm as Leeta tried to be, she could not keep the fear out of her voice, while thinking, *I shoulda never got on that bicycle with her!* The only time black women and white women associated was when the black woman was the white woman's maid or mammy to her kids. *Even then, there wasn't never no bicycle rides took together!* There were laws against such associations, even though some of those laws were unwritten. In Mississippi, her momma, grandparents, and other kin had taught her those unwritten laws. Almost from birth, they told her, "Don't offer a handshake to a white person unless they offer their hand first. Don't challenge what they say, even if they be dead wrong. Don't talk back no matter what. And, for God's sake, don't make eye contact, because they take it as the worst kinda insult." Behind Goldrod's when she'd encountered Sherriff Bloot for the first time, she'd done all of those things—except offer to shake hands.

"You remember what I told you at the bus stop, gal? It still goes," said the sheriff.

"I'm staying out at the Hesterwine ladies' place," Leeta offered, clasping her hands behind her to keep them from trembling. As scared as she was, the rebellion in her kept her from staring at the floor as advised by her kin. Instead, she gazed steadily past him to a spot on the wall where a tiny sliver of sunlight filtered in through a crack.

He dismissed her explanation with a sneer. "Miss Clara and Miss Justine are getting too unthinking in their old age," he drawled. "You're a *vagrant*. You ain't got any folks here 'bouts, and you ain't got a job. I'm taking you to jail." He grabbed her arm.

Dink rose from his stool and laid his guitar aside. "She ain't no vagrant, Sheriff Bloot, suh," he said politely. "She my *niece* and she work for me." He took Leeta's other arm. "Go on in back, like I told you, and help your Auntie Mozelle skin them catfish. I done told you when I hired you, you gots to do more around the place than *sing* iffen you wanna earn that *five dollars twenty-five cents* a night," he added with a slight smile.

"Hold up there, gal," Sheriff Bloot ordered, throwing up an authoritative hand as Leeta turned to leave. He narrowed his eyes at Dink. "Now, Dink, you ain't lying to me now, are you, boy, just to keep one of your own kind outta my jail?"

"Come by tonight, Sheriff, like you always do on Saturday nights, and see for yourself. She gonna be here working, and working hard."

"You know I will. I gotta keep them trouble-making coloreds that come in here to drink your booze from cutting each other up."

"Ain't nobody been cut in my place in a long time, Sheriff. Folks just mostly come to eat catfish and listen to me play. Sometime we gets a little band of musicians together and some folks dance a little. No fighting in my place."

"Well, Dink, I know from experience history always repeats itself in these nigger joints, and your place ain't no different from the rest in the county."

Leeta had frozen on the spot when he told her to wait up, and now he turned to her in his threatening manner.

"I asked that Mary Kenny out there"—he pointed out the window at Mary, still clutching the bike's handlebars and staring at the building—"what in hell she was doing in nigger town, and she answered like a goddamn smart aleck and said, 'I'm having a Coke.'"

Leeta swallowed back a smile. "Miss Mary gave me a ride to work, that's all."

"Looks like she woulda said so when I asked."

"Maybe she was scared you might put her in jail for it."

"You being a smart ass, too, gal?"

"No, suh. I'm from Mississippi. I don't know all the rules in Texas."

He frowned deeply at her, and she could tell he didn't know whether she was being a smart ass or not. He had folded his arms across his chest, and now he dropped them menacingly to his sides.

"Get outta here before I decide to take you in anyhow. I got business to discuss with Dink." He jerked his thumb toward the window. "Then I'm gonna go back out there and educate your bicycle partner on the *law of the land* in these parts."

Leeta, glad that she now had a job and, for a second time, had escaped scrubbing floors in Sheriff Bloot's jail, hurried toward the back room to help "Auntie Mozelle" skin catfish. She'd discuss that five dollars and twenty-five cents with her new boss later, after he heard her sing. As she passed the window, she cast a glance out at Mary and hoped she had enough sense to pedal as fast as she could back to Clara and Justine Hesterwine!

# 11

MARY DREW UP STRAIGHTER ON THE BICYCLE SEAT at the sight of Sheriff Bloot exiting the Blue Creek Lounge. He paused briefly on the porch to shake his head at her, then clumped down the steps. Once beneath the umbrella-shaped tree, he tore off his hat and mopped at his sweaty face with a big handkerchief that had dangled from his hip pocket. His forehead, pasty from never seeing sunlight, showed a deeply imprinted slash of red where the hat rim had dug in. Standing there, he reminded Mary of her hulking father—big, pudgy-bellied, angry, and mean-eyed most of the time. It was not a pleasant recollection.

The sheriff stressed each word as he towered over her and the bicycle. "*Rose Hill,* better known as *nigger town,* ain't no place for a white girl," he said. "You got a lot to learn if you're gonna be in Vander County long, girl. Ain't no white women hang around Rose Hill unless they're trash that ain't never been taught the difference tween them and us." He tossed a thumb toward the Blue Creek Lounge. "That gal in yonder is trouble, and I intend to keep an eye on her—you, too, as long as you keep hanging with her. If I ever catch you in Rose Hill again, I'm gonna start wondering what you two might be up to."

"I am not a criminal, and you have no right to tell me where I can—" She snapped her mouth shut.

"Are you sassing me, girl? Don't you sass me, goddamn it!"

This time, Mary spoke barely loud enough for him to hear. "Willie and I are not up to anything, Sheriff." She pointed to the baskets. "Miss Clara sent us on an errand to deliver these vegetables to Mr. Ewald at the lumberyard."

"That colored gal said you were giving her a ride to work. Somebody's lying."

Mary stared at him a moment. "Both explanations are true, Sheriff Bloot. We planned on going to the lumberyard first, and then I was to drop Willie off at the cutoff and she was to walk the rest of the way here to her job, but ..." she paused, searching for her next words. "It was so hard pedaling against the wind, I wanted to take the shortcut to town. Willie said no, we absolutely should not come this way, but I insisted. When we got here, I was tired and thirsty, so she went inside and brought me out this Coke." She raised the half-full bottle as proof. "So you see, Sheriff, this is really all my fault," she finished, hoping the necessary lie would work.

Even though he still glared down at her, he nodded as though he believed her story. "Yep, Rose Hill is a tail-end shortcut to Hesterwine, all right. But next time, stay on the main highway."

"I will. I definitely will."

He eyed her a few seconds as if he had just noticed something. "Funny hat," he said. Then his scowl returned. "I reckon, if you weren't from up North, you'd know folks down here don't cotton to white women keeping company with coloreds, not even if it's another female."

She knew not to respond, and busied herself by leaning down and pulling grass burs from her shoestrings.

"I reckon the rules is different where you come from, but like they say, when in Rome, you better damn well do as the Romans do, or you're gonna wind up in a heap of trouble." He slapped his hat back on his head and stalked off to his 1937 green Packard with the big red light across the top, started the motor, then stuck his arm out the window and pointed. "Don't be wandering over the river into Meskin town, neither—*they* call it *La Villita*. Them Roman Papist's pepper-bellies ain't no better'n these Rose Hill niggers. They dance and get drunker'n skunks every Saturday night, and then on Sunday they pile into that church of theirs and get forgiveness from that flannel-mouthed greaser priest who thinks he's got the backing of Jesus Christ Almighty."

"I only want to deliver these tomatoes and potatoes to Mr. Ewald," she said, thinking that Sheriff Bloot, like her father, had a contemptuous description for just about everything and everybody who wasn't like him.

He motioned toward the shack-lined street up ahead. "Go straight that-a-ways. You'll be on the white side of Hesterwine in a couple miles."

It was then that a slightly built colored man came out onto the porch of the lounge and raised his hand as if to get her attention.

"What's your problem, Dink?" the sheriff growled.

"No problem, Sheriff," he said. Then he gave Mary a polite nod before addressing her. "Begging your pardon, Miss Mary, Willie want me to tell you she gonna be working mighty late tonight... a little bit past midnight maybe. So you just go on home without her, she say."

Mary immediately wondered how Leeta would get home. *I certainly cannot come get her on this bicycle after dark,* she thought, suddenly picturing Sheriff Bloot putting Leeta in handcuffs. Then another picture flashed across her mind... of *her* on the front seat of the old Buick, tugging on Mr. Valentino's reins in the dead of night and on their way to the Blue Creek Lounge. She groaned inwardly. *If I must, I must.* As she rode past the porch, she nodded amiably to the man the sheriff had called Dink and shouted out, hoping Leeta would hear her: "Tell Willie she is not to worry. I will make sure she gets home after work tonight."

Eager to find the lumberyard, deliver the tomatoes and potatoes to Mr. Ewald, buy the flyer supplies, then get back to Hesterwine Place, Mary pedaled as fast as she could through Rose Hill. Without Leeta pumping on the pedals behind her, the hot Gulf winds were more of a foe than ever. She gripped the sweaty handlebars so tightly her hands cramped. Hunched forward in a half-crouched, half-standing position, she forced her tired legs to grind away at the pedals as she made her way past the tiny shacks and larger houses along the way.

A group of children froze perfectly still to watch her come riding down their rubbing-board street, the tomatoes and potatoes bouncing so high they seemed about to leap right out of their baskets. Mary felt she was a comical sight to the children, for they suddenly laughed and pointed. However, moments later, they were waving energetically at her. She felt foolish in her frantic efforts to wave back and at the same time keep a tight grip on the vibrating handlebars. Finally, a few yards past the last house, she bumped onto the pavement, glad that all she had to do now was avoid the deep potholes.

She had pedaled less than ten minutes when, on the long stretch of road with nothing but farm fields on both sides, she glanced over her shoulder as the distant drone of an airplane interrupted the silence. Flying extremely low, a small, yellow aircraft with a single propeller drew nearer, flying so low and close that she could see the insignia on the side—a big blue circle with a bright-red propeller inside a white triangle. The airplane looked no more than seventy-five feet off the ground! Below the insignia was the word CAP. Mary knew CAP meant Civil Air Patrol, an organization of volunteer civilian pilots formed just days before the Japanese bombed Pearl Harbor. An article she had read in a magazine on the bus said that CAP pilots patrolled the United States coastlines looking for enemy submarines lurking just offshore.

She felt a surge of excitement at seeing a CAP plane up close. If not for the insignia, it would have looked like an ordinary private aircraft. Beneath the insignia was a picture of a stereotypical white-sheeted ghost with huge, staring, green eyes and the words *The Flying Ghost of the Briny Coast*.

Still pedaling, Mary watched the airplane swoop past, make a wide turn, and fly off in the direction from which it had come. She saw a blur of a face in the cockpit window. Had the pilot seen her? *How exciting!* Was this plane patrolling the coastal waters that lay only a mile or so from the Hesterwine sisters' home?

Just when she thought the aircraft was gone, she heard the low drone of the engine again. This time, it flew along at a slant-winged angle, so close that she saw the pilot's face close enough to see that he was *smiling at her!* Then, he swerved away.

The third time he buzzed her, she was so intent on trying to get another look at him that she took one hand off the handlebars to bend back the wide brim of her fancy hat, and then instantly regretted it. The front wheel dropped into a deep pothole and twisted completely sideways. The abrupt halt of the bike could not have occurred any quicker if it had hit a brick wall; it happened so fast, there was no time to scream. She catapulted over the handlebars and slid across the hard pavement on her belly—much like a runner sliding over home plate, but minus the skill.

With both knees and an elbow skinned and aching, she eased into a sitting position and rested there a moment, groaning as she wiped bits of dirt from her fiery wounds. Finally, she struggled to her feet.

*What an awful day,* she thought, not so much annoyed at the pilot whose curiosity had piqued her own, but at *herself.* First, she had gotten in trouble with that awful Sheriff Bloot by being in Rose Hill. Then, she'd had to leave Leeta behind and, as scared as she was, set out on her own. And now she was struggling to pedal *all alone* against the wind on probably the hottest day of the year on a road so mangled with choppy holes and pits that one could not possibly maneuver it without disaster! The tomatoes were ruined and the potatoes bruised. What would she tell Miss Clara and Miss Justine? *Worst of all, how will I ever get back to Hesterwine Place in this condition ... then get Leeta back there after midnight?*

She was limping painfully around, gathering up the scattered tomatoes and potatoes and depositing them in the sling of her skirt when she heard the plane returning. He swooshed past her lower than ever, but this time, instead of making a wide turn, he flew off straight ahead and did not return. Despite her pain in righting the bicycle with one hand so that she could relay the vegetables from her skirt to the baskets, she could not help but smile ever so slightly: His arm had been out the window, his palm upraised, his mouth forming the words *I'm sorry.*

# 12

**B**Y THE TIME MARY GOT TO EWALD'S LUMBERYARD, her swollen knee felt stiff. Outside the door she eased off the bike and raised her skirt to examine her wounds, until she saw Mr. Ewald looking out the window at her and shaking his head in sympathy. Minutes later, smiling kindly, he purchased the battered vegetables without comment. At least some good had come from her injuries, she thought as, exhausted and limping, she pushed the bike to the Five and Dime and spent forty cents of her fifty cents on materials for the flyers. Then, with her remaining dime, she pushed the heavy bike to Goldrod's to replenish her strength with a fountain Coke, all the while regretting the painful trip back to Hesterwine Place.

In Goldrod's, she wasn't aware that the nineteenth century, flower-filled, washtub of a hat was still on her head until she noticed the stares she was drawing. In one of the booths, four teenage girls whispered to one another and then giggled behind their hands. *Grandmother would say, "Stick your nose in the air and act like you don't give a darn."* With that, she forced her lips into a little smile, untied the bow from beneath her chin, carefully removed the hat, and then fluffed the profusion of silk flowers before daintily laying the hat on the counter. Aware that they were still watching, she slipped casually onto a stool and ordered a cherry Coke and a glass of water.

A while later, with the Coke sipped down to the ice, she glanced subtly over her shoulder to make sure she was no longer a curiosity to the girls in the booth. Satisfied, she dipped her handkerchief into the glass of cold water and pressed it to her scraped elbow, wishing she could lift her skirt and do the same to her burning knee.

"You're hurt, aren't you?"

Mary jumped. One of the girls from the booth was standing directly behind her.

"Wow, those are some ugly scrapes," the girl said. "What happened?"

"I-I fell off my bike. It's very nice of you to ask."

"Well, somebody needed to let you know that your blouse is ripped right down the back and your pink bra is showing," she said, and laughed in a friendly manner.

Red faced, Mary spun around on the stool so that her backside faced the counter rather than the booths.

The girl laughed again. "Last week I was jitterbugging up a storm with a good-looking sailor right out there on that dance floor when the button on my underwear popped off and my drawers fell down around my ankles. You can't possibly be as embarrassed as I was. I'll be glad when Uncle Sam and the War Department declares us gals can have elastic in our panties again, won't you?" She stuck out her hand. "I'm Linda Dunston."

Mary introduced herself. Linda Dunston was possibly the prettiest girl she had ever seen. She was *movie star* beautiful, with coal-black hair and crystal-clear green eyes.

Mary laughed. "What did you do when your underwear fell off?"

"I stepped out of them and kept right on dancing. One of my cousins, Janice, over there"—she pointed to the booth—"ran out and rescued them for me."

"I'm sure the buttons are popping off a lot of drawers since all the rubber in the country is going to the war effort," Mary said, smiling at the friendly girl as she stretched her arm around to tug at her torn blouse. "I guess, when I leave here, I will have to back out the door."

"No such thing." Linda Dunston swooped up the big hat, slapped it against Mary's shoulder blades, then tied the ribbons beneath her chin. "There, you're covered. That's the way Dale Evans wears her hat most of the time when she and Roy are loping along on Trigger and Buttermilk," she said jovially and then asked, "Aren't you the girl Miss Clara and Miss Justine took home with them?"

"How did you know that?"

"Nobody comes to Hesterwine and stays without the whole town knowing—especially not a girl traveling all alone. Besides, I saw you peeking through the window that day. Excuses me for saying so, but I thought you looked kinda lost."

Mary decided she would tell part of the truth to this nice girl. "I did feel a bit lost that day. I was living with my grandmother in New Jersey until she died a few weeks ago. My parents ... were gone a long time before that."

"Gee, I'm sorry. That's rough, I know. Both my parents died in an automobile accident five years ago. It's just me, my big brother, Jack, and our housekeeper. Of course, we have a slew of aunts and uncles. They pop in real regular bringing food to my brother and me as an excuse to boss me around. I'll be glad when I'm eighteen."

"I wish I had a large family like yours," Mary said, while thinking that if she'd had a "slew of aunts and uncles," someone among them would have cared enough about her to want her among them after her father disowned her and her grandmother died. She smiled at Linda Dunston. "You are lucky to have those relatives. After my grandmother passed away and I had no one in that part of the country anymore, I decided I would go to California and start a brand-new life."

"What about Miss Clara and Miss Justine? Everyone was surprised to find out they had a niece. I bet they want you to stay here."

"To tell the truth, Linda, Miss Clara and Miss Justine are sort of my *adopted* aunts."

Just then, the green door at the back of the room opened and in stepped a tall young man in an Army Air Corps uniform with a red CAP patch on his sleeve. The girls in the booth waved and called out their hellos, as did the soda jerk and everyone else in the room. He returned their greetings with an amiable flash of white teeth and a playful salute. Almost immediately his eyes locked on Mary, then swept over her in recognition.

As she stared back, he grinned, his mouth again forming the words *I'm sorry.*

Linda Dunson turned around on her stool. "Oh, my gosh, *Jack!* You're home! I was beginning to think you'd finally abandoned me to our relatives like you always threaten to do!" She ran to him, grabbed his arm, and pulled him along. "Mary, I want you to meet my big brother, Jack, *The Flying Ghost of the Briny Coast!*"

"We met on the road," Mary said, and could not help but smile at the apologetic way he was staring at her. He was like his sister in appearance—black hair, clear green eyes made even more startling by thick fringes of black lashes. He was well over six feet tall, she guessed.

"Met on the *road*? Umm," Linda mused, "that sounds interesting. Tell me about it, brother dear."

Jack ignored her. His eyes were still on Mary. "I knew someone interesting had to be under that hat ... and riding a bicycle built for *two* all by herself." He paused to grin good-naturedly. "I was right from a hundred feet up, and now, with my two feet firmly on the ground, I'm even surer."

Linda faked a swoon. "Oh, wow, Jack, I've never heard one of your lines before. That was good! What do you think, Mary?"

"I suppose it was okay." Despite her smarting elbow and knees, Mary was suddenly enjoying the fun moment. She couldn't remember the last time she had joked with friends.

He chuckled. "I can do better, but not on an empty stomach. Come on." He motioned to a booth. "The burgers are on me."

Soon, they were eating and chatting like chums. The thought of making new friends gave Mary a feeling of excitement that she had been without for a long time. Jack kept feeding the jukebox and saying that when her knee healed she would have to dance with him.

She had not planned to tell the pair about her dilemma, but after another quick glance at Jack's pleasant face—one of many such glances during the past hour—she blurted, "Actually, later tonight, I must pick up my friend, Willie Holloway, at the Blue Creek Lounge in Rose Hill, where she works. I dropped her off there earlier."

"You went to *Rose Hill?*" Linda cried. "Don't you know you could get into bad trouble going out there?"

"I found that out when your sheriff saw me. He said I was not to come back. Just the same, I am worried about Willie. I feel responsible for her."

"Is that the colored girl that got off the bus when you did?" Linda asked.

"Yes. Sheriff Bloot threatened to arrest her for vagrancy. That is why Miss Clara and Miss Justine gave her a place to stay."

Linda was quick to tell her about the sheriff. "He packs his jail with folks from Rose Hill and La Villita every weekend. Most of them haven't broken the law, but that doesn't stop him. The more people he arrests, the more money he gets from the county's Commissioner Court to run the jail, but it's said the jail never sees that money. Anyway, our cousin who works for the county clerk's office says the sheriff has a moneymaking scheme going with two of the commissioners. They always vote for him to get the extra money if the jail is full, then they split it with him. Judging by how many colored people and Mexicans are peering out the jailhouse windows every Sunday morning, I think it must be true."

"No one complains?" Mary asked.

"They don't dare. There are folks in Vander County who are trying to get Jack to run against Sheriff Bloot when he comes up for re-election," Linda said. "So far, though, he's not been convinced."

"That's because I couldn't win."

"How can you be sure?"

"Because, Mary, I would need the Negro and Mexican populations of the county to back me, and *they* don't vote."

"Why not?" Mary asked.

"They're scared. Years ago, the Klan used to assemble outside of Rose Hill and La Villita on Election Day for the sole purpose of keeping the residents out of town and away from the polls. Finally, those who had paid their poll tax, which made them eligible to vote, just quit paying it. With the Klan ready to stop them from voting, what was the use in spending their hard-earned money on a worthless poll tax?"

"Miss Clara and Miss Justine said the Klan has not been active in Vander County in years."

"Not like they once were, but they're still around. A few years ago, a couple of leaders sprang up among the Mexicans and pushed their people to vote. Soon afterward, their homes burned to the ground, and they and their families left the county. Fear is a mighty big weapon."

"Is Sheriff Bloot a Klan member?"

"I don't think he's ever put on the sheets, but he defers to them, and I'm sure many of them are more than passing acquaintances. Their members are drawn from all sectors of our society in Vander County—civic leaders, politicians, ordinary citizens, and just plain old ignorant white trash making up the bulk of them. Whatever their background, they have one thing in common—a deep-rooted hatred for anyone who isn't *white* and doesn't share their religion or their politics. The Klan sees themselves as the 'saviors of Christian moral authority,' but they are anything *but* Christ-like."

"Our mom used to say that evil often wears a saintly veil," Linda Dunston said, adding, "Boy, was she right about that—Sheriff Bloot prays louder than anybody in church every Sunday. Mom and Dad used to laugh at the irony of that when we got home after services."

"Whoever runs against Bloot will need to get the people of Rose Hill and La Villita to the polls on Election Day. But first, they've got to be talked out of their fear of the Klan," Jack said.

Mary eyed Jack Dunston with admiration. He was clearly a man who did not ascribe to inequality based on prejudice of any kind. He would make a great sheriff... someone *everyone* could trust. With that thought, she proceeded to tell him how she and Willie had wound up at Rose Hill, including all that had transpired afterward with Sheriff Bloot. She thought of telling him about Willie's fear of the horrible Mandingo Q. Mann, but did not. She knew Leeta would not like it if she did. "So, you see, Jack, I *must* go to Rose Hill tonight and get Willie... especially after finding out how the sheriff arrests folks out there every weekend."

Jack grinned. "On that bicycle? And after midnight? Or were you planning on hitching up Rudolph Valentino to that old Buick?"

"As a matter of fact, I was. I have been a farm girl all my life, raised on a dairy farm. I know how to handle animals. Besides, Mr. Valentino likes me."

Jack laughed as he took her elbow and urged her from the booth. "He likes you, eh? That means you haven't tried to lead him around by that ring in his nose yet. Don't ever do it. It's his sensitive spot. Come on. Since I'm responsible for temporarily laming you, it's only right I take you home." Outside, he loaded the bicycle built for two into the bed of his maroon Ford pickup truck. Linda waved good-bye as they drove away.

"Mr. Valentino is a lot gentler than some of those cows I milked," Mary insisted when they were riding along.

"I'll tell you what, Mary Kenny. Being as you're so worried about your friend, I'll pick you up at eleven thirty tonight and we'll drive to Rose Hill and see if we can get her home safe and sound. The sheriff won't say a word if you're with me. My friend, Hank Posey, who works cattle on Sheriff Bloot's ranch, lives out there. I've taken Hank home more than once when that old truck of his broke down." He paused to grin at her again, his green eyes twinkling in a way that unexpectedly made her smile. "Besides, Mr. Valentino's headlights don't work, and I doubt if his taillights do, either. You'd be a menace on the highway at night. Furthermore, if I know Miss

Clara and Miss Justine, they'd never let their old pet out on the road after dark."

Mary's smile widened. "You have convinced me. Besides, Jack Dunston, *Flying Ghost of the Briny Coast,* as sweet as Mr. Valentino is, you are much sweeter." No sooner were the words out of her mouth than she felt herself blush, shocked that she had actually *flirted* with him. *That tumble off the bicycle must have jarred my brain!*

"I have a question for you, Mary Kenny. Why have we been smiling so much at each other? I can't seem to stop."

She tried not to smile. "I don't know. You tell me."

"Soon as I figure it out. In the meanwhile, let's just keep doing it." He gave her a big, comical grin.

She did the same, and they both laughed. Jack Dunston was a lot of fun, she decided.

# 13

"Miss Mary and that Willie gal shoulda been back by now with that potato and tomato money," said Aunt Lucy as she stood at the sink washing dishes. "I don't trust that Willie for nothin' with that money."

Clara, sitting at the table rubbing leather-restoring cream onto her sturdy walking shoes, didn't look up from her chore. "Hot as it is, they are probably waiting 'til the day cools a bit before pedaling home, Aunt Lucy. They'll be along soon."

Justine sighed. "I wonder if we should be concerned."

"Oh, I don't think so," Clara replied.

"*I* think so," Justine insisted. "I'm concerned they've gotten lost."

"*Lost?* They are bright girls, Justine. I am not concerned."

"Obviously, you aren't concerned either about the damage your cousin is doing to our parlor this very minute."

"Etta Ruth is your cousin too, Justine. And I'm sure you are worried enough for both of us."

"It isn't fair, Clara. For years and years we've enjoyed our afternoon tea in the parlor, but now, because of her and her nasty pastime, we've been *exiled* to the kitchen; either that or choke to death on her smoke."

Aunt Lucy flared her nostrils. "I smell that smoke all the way in here, Miss Clara. It took me long nuff to get the stink of your poppa's cigars out'n the house after he died, and now Miz Etta Ruth's stinking it up again with them Pall Mall cigarettes."

"Perhaps she will abandon the practice soon, Aunt Lucy. She seldom sticks to any one thing for long."

"It a sorry sight watching her scooch up them lips like she do to blow that smoke out. Her mouth looks just like an old laying hen's back-hole."

"Now, Aunt Lucy, don't be unkind," said Clara, smiling.

"Don't be *unkind?*" Justine yelped. "My heavens, Clara, the woman is nothing but unkind to *us*. She hasn't said a decent word to me since she arrived, and she's rude to Aunt Lucy as well."

"I admit Etta Ruth's behavior is a problem in more ways than one, but we must take into consideration that she is terribly unhappy presently, and handle her accordingly."

"*You* invited her here, so you can '*handle her accordingly*' all by yourself." Justine turned aside to dry the delicate teacups Aunt Lucy had washed.

Feeling her blood pressure rise, Clara refrained from replying. *Isn't handling her all by myself exactly what I've been doing ... at her beck and call for her every need ... including getting down on my knees and clipping those petrified toenail of hers?*

Privately, Clara recognized that a strange sort of loyalty—though certainly unspoken by either of them—had developed between her and Etta Ruth that day in the cemetery, and she was now Etta Ruth's one and only confidant. It was a strange relationship; indeed, since the woman's sharp tongue stabbed *her* as often as anyone else in the house.

"Have you ever watched her smoke those nasty cigarettes?" Justine was saying, "She never inhales. She just blows smoke rings one on top of the other ... then, cold-eyed as an old snake, she stabs a forefinger through them like she's slaughtering some monster she dreamed up."

Clara, having kept secret Etta Ruth's shocking divulgences about Clarence in the cemetery that day, knew exactly *who* and *what* those smoke rings symbolized.

"And Clara, have you ever wondered how long she's been hiding the fact that she's an alcoholic? Or haven't you noticed that she's a 'rummy'—as Momma used to call people who drank demon rum to excess. Along with her drinking, smoking, and her abusive tongue, she's as nosy as a raccoon ... poking through every drawer and chifforobe in the house the way she does. Or aren't you aware of any of that?"

"I'm as much aware of it as you are, Justine," Clara said, thinking she could add her own complaints about Etta Ruth, but Justine would just say, "I told you so."

"Her behavior is extremely disturbing, Clara. I keep waiting for the day she does something so unnerving it will open even *your* eyes. Maybe then you will call Clarence Jr. to come get her."

Clara kept dabbing at her shoes, thinking, *Yes, indeed, Justine, Etta Ruth does do extremely disturbing things.* Much of it proving beyond a doubt that the woman is truly *losing her marbles*, just as Clarence Jr. and the whole town says she is—wearing her dead husband's clothes, pulling a little red wagon all over town, and constantly being a witch spelled with a *b*. Worse, soon after moving in she'd stepped up her drinking, and then started chain-smoking just to blow those smoke rings that she clearly enjoyed stabbing. She'd become even 'weirder' when she dragged a male mannequin down from the attic, dressed it in Clarence's clothes, and now spent hours sitting in her room mumbling to it. Aunt Lucy had been the first to witness *that* oddity, and then had summonsed her and Justine to Etta Ruth's keyhole. The three of them took turns witnessing her muttering incoherently to the thing. Aunt Lucy went into Etta Ruth's room one morning to collect the bed linens and found her and the mannequin under the covers, the mannequin wearing a pair of Clarence's pajamas and Etta Ruth sound asleep on its shoulder!

*Poor Etta Ruth,* Clara thought. After finding out about the mannequin, she wasn't so sure Etta Ruth hated Clarence as much as she professed. Regardless, Etta Ruth must be handled with compassion, not acrimony. Clara glanced at Justine and Aunt Lucy still at the sink; evidently, *she* was clearly the only one in the house willing to offer that benevolence, albeit the constant effort was definitely wearing her to a frazzle.

As to her loyalty to Etta Ruth in keeping mum about Clarence's and Old Man Abelson's thirty-year affair, she'd told Justine and Aunt Lucy only that Etta Ruth thought Clarence had cheated on her, but she said nothing about *with whom* he had cheated. When the two of them were alone, Etta Ruth insisted that, if Old Man Abelson wrote love letters to Clarence, it was only common sense to assume that Clarence had written love letters to him as well. "I want those letters, damn it, Clara! They need to burn on Clarence's grave just like I burned Abelson's letters!" she had cried. Moments later, Clara's sympathy had deepened considerably for her despondent cousin when Etta Ruth, turning red in the face, wailed, "I'll die of humiliation if people find out that that son of a bitch preferred Old Man Marvin Abelson to me!"

Clara looked up from applying the shoe restoring cream as Aunt Lucy interrupted her thoughts.

"There's cigarette holes burned in Miss Etta's bed linens. I wouldn't doubt she didn't do it on purpose just to be—"

"Hello, Etta Ruth!" Justine cried out in warning.

Etta Ruth, barefoot and wearing a thin cotton slip completely void of undergarments beneath it, stood slouched in the doorway. The heel of one hand was on her hip, a Pall Mall cigarette clamped between her fingers. The other hand rested high on the doorframe. Her below-the-shoulders hair was uncombed and a clump of it hung over one eye. Considering the way she kept resetting her hips, it occurred to Clara that in Etta Ruth's mind she might be playing in a scene from a Bette Davis movie. Her big eyes—the only indicators that Etta Ruth, Justine, and *herself* shared the family's big-eyed gene—popped as wide as she could get them as her mouth, slathered with bright-red lipstick, formed a snarl that she probably meant to be alluring but was instead asinine.

"Where is your robe, Etta Ruth?" Clara asked. "Shall I fetch it for you?"

"And your slippers?" Justine added.

"Don't use that sneaky force of your will on me, you two."

"No such thing," Justine insisted.

"I suppose, since Clarence is dead, you expect me to dress like a crow even when I go to bed. Well, go to hell!"

"We were only thinking of your comfort, Etta Ruth," Clara said.

"Ha! Remember, ladies, hypocrisy is the compliment that vice pays to virtue," Etta Ruth said, gazing suspiciously at them.

"What*ever* do you mean by *that*?" Justine asked, the huffy look she'd worn for the past hour still there. Clara instantly wished she had cautioned her sister to never asked Etta Ruth to explain anything she said or did.

"I *mean*, Justine Hesterwine, I heard you three talking about me, and now you're being hypocrites!"

"We commented on the hazards of your cigarettes, Etta Ruth, not about you," Clara said in a mollifying tone as she patted the chair alongside her. "Come, sit down. Have a cup of—" She jumped as Etta Ruth cut her off.

"No! I don't want any damn tea!" She padded into the pantry and emerged moments later with a bottle of rum and a Coke.

Justine rolled her eyes at Clara, as if expecting her to do something.

Clara ignored her. "Aunt Lucy, would you mind fetching Etta Ruth's Mason jar—the one with the handle—and filling it with ice? The trays should have re-frozen by now."

The three women watched silently as Etta Ruth poured rum over the ice, then, after sloshing in a bit of Coke, leaned against the sink and drank half of it down in one continuous swallow.

Clara went back to dabbing her shoes with the restoring cream.

Etta Ruth smirked. "You still take your shoes to that old son of a bitch Abelson, Clara?"

"He has the only shoe shop in town, Etta Ruth," Clara replied.

Etta Ruth tilted her head back and downed the rest of her rum and Coke, the ice clicking against her teeth. Scowling, she slammed the jar down on the countertop and, after a long moment of staring hard at Clara, she whirled and marched to the door. Once there, she grabbed the doorframe as if she needed it to stop the forward thrust of her body.

*Another Bette Davis maneuver,* Clara thought as Etta Ruth spun around to face them, her mouth working.

"None of you better ever be mean to me like that cheating son of a bitch Clarence Morley was! I mean it, now! I do mean it!" She hurried away, her bare feet padding on the wood floor like the short, rapid steps of a child.

Moments later, they heard the elevator grinding slowly upward. All three women remained mute until the clang of the elevator's wrought-iron gate told them Etta Ruth had reached the third floor.

"At least she ain't gonna play them spooky tunes on that old organ 'til bedtime, like she most always do," Aunt Lucy muttered.

"*Clara,*" Justine said, stressing Clara's name accusingly. "Etta Ruth sounded like she was threatening us!"

Clara gave a dismissive wave of her hand. "Pay no attention to what she says. She threatens that mannequin with those very same words and so far she hasn't laid a hand on him other than when she cuddles up to him in bed every night."

Justine sighed. "I don't know why she just can't give up all that bad talk about Clarence. After all, the poor man is dead and gone."

Aunt Lucy shook her head. "Miz Etta Ruth got it in her head Mista Clarence was cheatin' on her, so I reckon, to Miz Etta Ruth, Mista Clarence just ain't *dead* enough."

"I suppose that's it," Justine said and sighed again. "I wonder who the woman was."

"She was probably from out of town," Clara said.

"I wish you hadn't invited her into our home, Clara. I feel something terrible is going to happen. We've enough to worry about with Banker Prickett ready to throw us out onto the street." She fanned her face in frustration. Then, suddenly, as if pause had given her thought, she fumed, "I suppose she was just trying to sound *smart* with her insults when she said 'Hypocrisy is the compliment that vice pays to virtue.' I, personally, have never been a hypocrite."

"A big *ho-hum* to that," Clara said, dipping her fingers into the leather restoring cream.

"It's true!" She stared at Clara as if waiting for her to admit it.

"Ho-hum," Clara repeated.

Clearly flustered, Justine threw down her cup towel. "Anyway, like I said, I'm just waiting for the day something opens your eyes and you call Clarence Jr. to come get her. I hope it won't be too late!"

Just then, the sound of a vehicle coming down the road drew their attention. All three women went to the kitchen window to watch a maroon Ford pickup truck pull up to the gate.

"Why, that's that fine Mista Jack Dunston," Aunt Lucy said. "And look, there's Miss Mary. Mista Jack got wounded in the war, you know, but he look in pretty good shape, don't he?"

"He certainly does," Clara replied. "He was always a fine and brave young man, especially after his parents died in that horrible car crash and he took on the responsibility of his little sister, mostly all by himself."

"My cousin, Millie Mae, been the Dunston's housekeeper since long 'fore theys momma and daddy was kilt. She took good care of Miss Linda whilst Mista Jack was far away at war."

"I think Millie Mae looks just like Hattie McDaniel who played Mammy in *Gone with the Wind*," Justine said as she craned her neck to watch Jack come around the truck and open the door for Mary. "Does anybody ever tell her she looks like Hattie?"

"Yas'sum, they do. She don't like it. She say she 'bout forty pounds lighter than Hattie, but she ain't."

"I don't see Willie," Clara said. "I wonder why she isn't with them?"

"Cause she probably took off with the potato and tomato money," Aunt

Lucy replied. The three of them curiously watched the couple make their way to the house.

"Why, I think Mary is bringing him in to say hello," Justine said, suddenly excited. "Goody! Do you suppose he'd like a cup of coffee, Clara? I don't recall having a *real* war hero visit us since after the Great War, when we fed that homeless young man who lost an arm in France at the Battle of Château-Thierry, I think he said. Remember, Clara?"

"Of course I remember. Why would I not?" Clara snapped, repeating her favorite reply to Justine's countless "remember, Clara?" annotations.

They hurried from the kitchen, smiling enthusiastically at the prospect of greeting their admired guest. When scarcely halfway down the massive hall, loud thumping sounds, reverberating one on top of the other, drew their attention upward ... to Etta Ruth's life-like mannequin, dressed in Clarence's pajamas ... bouncing, head over heels, down the stairs.

Seconds later, Clara's and Justine's faces flamed with humiliation as Jack Dunston—looking as concerned as anyone would look after just seeing someone tumble down three flights of stairs—rushed across the enormous room to the prostrate dummy's aid ... as Etta Ruth cackled hilariously at him from the third-floor railing.

# 14

SHORTLY AFTER ELEVEN THIRTY THAT NIGHT, as Jack Dunston drove Mary to Rose Hill, she glanced sidelong at him and could not help but be curious. During their long conversation in the booth at Goldrod's earlier that day, she had learned from his sister that, up until a few months ago, this handsome Army Air Corps pilot was in the South Pacific flying long-distance missions against Japanese forces in the Solomon Islands. He received an early discharge, but neither he nor his sister had said *why*. Had he suffered injuries? If so, he showed no outward signs. He was now a CAP pilot for the civilian auxiliary of the Army Air Corps, flying his privately owned plane—a "Gullwing" Stinson Reliant—in search of German U-boats reported lurking off America's coastline. That small, lightweight airplane was capable of carrying a single, one-hundred-pound bomb that could destroy one of those enemy submarines, said his sister at Goldrod's today.

"No, Mary Kenny. I was not carrying the bomb when I buzzed you," Jack replied to her tongue-in-cheek question as they rode along.

"The way you kept coming back, I thought maybe you were going to land and offer to take me up for a ride."

"Would you have gone?"

"No. I don't accept rides with strangers."

"What about now? You're in my truck."

"If you were still a stranger, I would not be in your truck." Still smiling, she narrowed her eyes at him. "Don't you think you should watch the road instead of me?" Was she flirting again? Jack Dunston had the kind of looks and personality that made it difficult for a girl not to react to him. The girls in Goldrod's, those who were there when Jack entered the room and those who came in later, couldn't keep their eyes off him... just the way girls, young and old, used to ogle Claxton. However, unlike Claxton, Jack Dunston did not ogle back.

Mary rested her head against the window, wishing she had not thought of Claxton just now... while in the company of someone any girl would be thrilled to be riding cozily with down a moonlit country road. She wished things were different and she could go back to feeling *pretty and interesting,* the way she'd felt before Claxton dumped her.

"A bucket of pennies for your thoughts, Mary Kenny," he said quietly.

She straightened up. "They probably are not worth a penny, Jack Dunston... *Flying Ghost of the Briny Coast,*" she added in pretend gaiety.

"Try me."

"I was thinking how nice it was of you to carry Miz Etta Ruth's mannequin back upstairs to her after she so rudely yelled at you to do so. This, after first demanding you let him die," Mary said, grinning.

"Her language was a little more colorful than that," Jack said, and laughed. "Miss Clara and Miss Justine weren't too happy, but I think I convinced them not to be embarrassed—I've known Miz Etta since I was in first grade. She used to sit on her porch and wait for us kids to walk by her house. She'd yell out, 'Hot enough for you today?' If we said yes, she'd jump up and squirt us with her water hose. Sometimes, if the day was a real hot one, we'd let her give us a good soaking, then we'd yell thank you, ma'am! and run home."

Mary laughed again. "I was also thinking about those German U-boats your sister mentioned. Are they really coming into our waters? I suppose that is a silly question, since I already know that patrolling the Gulf in search of enemy submarines is what you do."

"I was wondering about something, too." He glanced at her bandaged elbow. "How's the arm and knee? I still feel awful for causing that spill."

"Well, don't. They are both fine. I see you are reluctant to talk about the U-boats. I understand. I guess you are not allowed to talk about them."

"Truth is, Mary, it's an unpleasant subject. Last year, a German U-Boat was sighted just off the coast of Port Aransas, a little town on Mustang Island not an hour's drive from here. The next day, a merchant ship from

Africa, carrying supplies and American passengers, was torpedoed and sunk by two German U-Boats off the Louisiana coast. Since the beginning of the war, losses of US and allied merchant ships in the Atlantic and Gulf of Mexico number in the hundreds, with more than five thousand lives lost."

Stunned, Mary stared at him. "Why have we not read about these terrible things in the papers, Jack? Obviously it is not a government secret, or you would not have told me about it."

"Every war has its anonymities, Mary. The US government isn't going out of its way to keep the U-boat raids secret, they're just not publicizing them. Too many folks might get panicked; but they shouldn't—our coast guard and navy are putting an end to those attacks.

"Then your job, hunting down those U-boats, and with only one little bomb, is a dangerous one, isn't it?"

He laughed. "I've yet to spot an enemy sub. I thought I did once, but it turned out to be a dead whale lying on the bottom about sixty feet down. I should have known a German sub wouldn't hover in a spot of ocean that was shallow and crystal clear. They'd be a lot deeper and in murky waters, where they couldn't be seen from a low-flying aircraft."

"I hope, if you see one of those nasty U-boats, you will not try to be a hero."

"I wouldn't mind being *your* hero, Mary Kenny." He was smiling again, like always when they were together.

"From the way all those girls greeted you when you walked into Goldrod's today, you *are* a hero. If I was your girl, I would have been quite jealous." No sooner had she spoken than she blushed, as she realized she was indeed flirting! She quickly changed the subject, describing to Jack all the great stuff she had seen in Miss Clara's and Miss Justine's attic, and that she and Willie planned to assist selling much of it from the old mansion's front porch. Jack immediately said he wanted to help.

As they approached the Blue Creek Lounge, Jack said that Dink Maxwell's place sometimes attracted a few of the colored military crowd from the bases nearby, but they never stuck around long. "Good as old Dink is with that guitar of his, the fellas apparently want more for their buck."

"With Willie singing here, they will surely get their money's worth," Mary said, remembering the impressive sounds that came from Leeta as the two of them sat on the bicycle outside the Blue Creek Lounge that morning listening to Dink Maxwell play.

"Oh yeah? She's that good?"

Mary nodded as they pulled up to the front door. "Just listen to that," she instructed as Leeta's distinctive voice, low and throaty at first and then rising in effortless emotional power, floated out to them. She looked at Jack and could tell he was as mesmerized as she was.

"What a set of pipes," he finally said. "If I've heard anyone better, I can't remember where or when." He cocked his ear toward the building, adding, "Dink must have thought so, too—I see he's added sax and piano to accompany her and his guitar playing. Business at the Blue Creek Lounge is bound to pick up." He got out of the truck. "I'll be right back."

No sooner had the screen door with the rusty Coca-Cola sign across it closed behind Jack than Dink Maxwell's guitar led Leeta into another song. Mary sat back to enjoy it while thinking that the combination of Leeta's voice and good looks must have made her the queen of entertainers at that terrible Mandingo Q. Mann's club in Chicago. Mary shuddered. *And now he wants to kill her!*

A shadow fell across the pickup truck's window; Mary scrunched down low in the seat as Sheriff Bloot walked past. She peeked over the window to see him clomp up the steps. Relieved that he hadn't noticed her, she watched him pause at the screen door to hoist his khaki pants up a fraction higher beneath his big belly, then adjust his crotch and his hat brim in one continuous movement. Mary almost grinned as he took another moment to arch his chest and bow an arm over the pistol strapped to his hip before he jerked the screen door open and strolled inside.

Leeta had just ended her song to loud applause and yells of appreciation, and when abrupt silence fell over the lounge, Mary knew all eyes had locked on Sheriff Bloot. *I hate bullies,* she thought, and straightened up on the seat, no longer caring that he might see her when he finished intimidating the small crowd inside the Blue Creek Lounge.

Five minutes later, Leeta was singing again. Jack walked out the door followed by Sheriff Bloot and the colored cowboy Leeta had cursed at behind Goldrod's. This time, the gangling cowboy called Posey wore a *clean* Hopalong-Cassidy-style black hat, starched jeans, and a paisley black, brown, and beige Western shirt. His shiny, high-heeled, knee-high boots looked as if they had never stepped in anything smellier than a mound of grass. All three men came to stand alongside the truck.

Jack addressed the sheriff. "I promised a friend I'd see Willie back to the Hesterwines' place, Sheriff. She won't get off work for another hour, so I intend to wait." He grinned at the cowboy. "Hank here offered, but she said no."

Sheriff Bloot snorted. "You're putting it too nice, Dunston. That ain't what the bitch said. She damn near yelled that wudn't no hick with horse shit for brains gonna drive her anywhere."

Jack nodded at the pickup window. "There's a lady present, Sheriff."

The sheriff noticed Mary. "Well, well. Lucky you're with Jack here, or I'd have to run you in for disobeying me."

"I came to get Willie, Sheriff. I feel responsible for her."

"That kinda thinking is plum ignorant. Like I told you before, you got a lot to learn if you plan on sticking around Hesterwine for long, girl. Ain't nobody owes these coloreds nothing. If they can't get where they're going on their own steam, that's their fault. Around here, we don't coddle our coloreds." He looked at Jack. "You was born and raised in Vander County, Dunston. You should have told her how *the cow eats the cabbage* around here," he said as he stepped away to talk with two of his deputies who had driven up and parked nearby. After a minute, he returned. "Take this girl home right now, Dunston. I got more deputies on the way, and things is gonna get lively around here when we start hauling some of these drunk niggers to jail before they decide to get into mischief."

"No!" Mary cried. "I have to wait for Willie. I told her I would be here to take her back to Hesterwine Place."

"I'll bring her home, miss," the cowboy said.

Jack slapped his shoulder. "Okay, Hank, I guess you're elected. Sure you can talk her into it?"

"Ain't no doubt about it," he said.

"I'm afraid Willie will not go with you," Mary said, remembering how Leeta had treated this man behind Goldrod's.

He turned politely to her. "I reckon I'll have *Willie Holloway* home 'fore she knows it, ma'am. Uh, that *is* her name, ain't it?"

Marys eyes widened at him, as the look on his face conveyed the message that he knew Leeta's real name—he had learned it from Leeta's own lips! Instantly, she recalled what Leeta had said to this man behind Goldrod's after they got off the bus: "*Ain't no shit-kicker like you big enough to make Leeta Bulow shut up ...!*"

Mary stuck her arm out the window and shook the cowboy's hand. "I am Mary Kenny. Thank you so much for bringing Willie home tonight."

"I'm Henry Posey, ma'am. Everybody calls me Hank. Don't worry 'bout Miss *Willie Holloway*. After I talk to her, she gonna let me take her home. I guarantee it."

"I got a place for her if she don't," said the sheriff, and stooped to the window to look at Mary. "Thought you might like to know ... my deputies just come back from the Hesterwine place. They was driving around out there making their rounds when they saw that crazy old Miz Etta Ruth Morley up the windmill. Them two old maids and their house help, old Nigga Lucy, was wringing their hands and a'begging her not to jump. 'Course, she didn't. She came down right quick when my deputies told her they was gonna call Clarence Jr. to come take her to the nut house in San Antone." The sheriff paused to laugh, shaking his head as if the situation was all too funny. "Clarence Jr. was gonna have her committed, you know, before the Hesterwine sisters volunteered to look after her. Told me so himself."

As Mary rolled up her window, he tapped on the glass.

"You two Yankee girls better watch out. Old Etta Ruth Morley just might go full-blown lunatic one night and hack you to pieces in your beds. It ain't for sure that old Miss Clara and Miss Justine ain't wacky as she is. They're cousins, you know. Blood's thicker'n water. Maybe they're *all* nuts." Mary rolled up the window even before he finished.

As they drove away, she looked over her shoulder at the sheriff and his deputies. She no longer tried to tame her feeling of dislike for the man. He was a bully, a man ruled by his prejudices. He hated Leeta because she was colored, and hated *her* who, though as white as he was, did not feel herself too good or too white to be Leeta's friend. He disparaged Miz Etta Ruth and the Hesterwine sisters because they were now elderly and perhaps no longer fit the mold into which he fit women worthy of his admiration. Because of his obvious mindset of male superiority, she doubted if he respected women of any age or race. He was like her father.

Jack reached over and patted her hand. "Don't worry. Hank will watch out for Willie—and Dink Maxwell is not about to let anything bad happen to his new *Queen of Song* at the *Blue Creek Lounge*."

Hank Posey, stooping a bit so that he stood nose to nose with Leeta in the darkened parking lot, was calm but firm. "I told your friends I was gonna see you to home, and that's what I aim on doing."

The hour was past one in the morning, and the deputy cars had pulled away loaded with their catch of the night—four or five Negroes per carload, and headed for jail. A group of slowly departing customers called out to Leeta in praise of her singing.

"I'll be back every night 'cept Sundays from now on," she yelled gaily at them between hostile glances at Hank Posey. "You all bring your friends." Then she concentrated on Hank again.

"What you mean you told my friends you gonna see me home? I ain't got no damn friends 'round this hickey little town, and if I did, they damn sure wouldn't be telling me who was or was not gonna take me home!"

"Miss Mary Kenny said so. She's you friend, ain't she? *She* thinks so. And Mr. Jack Dunston is friend enough to Mary Kenny to bring her out here to get you. Only now, because of the sheriff, the chore is mine."

"*Chore!* I ain't nobody's goddamn *chore*, you shit-kicking hick!"

"I told you before, you got a real dirty mouth, *Leeta Bulow*."

Suddenly frowning, she stared at him before her eyes darted away and then back. "That ain't my name. It's Willie Holloway."

He pushed up the brim of his black Hopalong-Cassidy-style hat and chuckled. "All right, if you insist. But if you want me to keep your *real* identity a secret, Leeta Bulow, you'll have to let me see you home, and be *peaceful* about it."

Dink Maxwell, carrying his guitar in a beat-up old case, called out to her from the steps. "I'll vouch for Hank, Willie. He ain't never murdered nobody yet that I know 'bout."

Leeta gave out an angry sigh. "Okay, where's that dirty, smelly, old truck of yours, shit-kicker?"

"Another thing we're getting straight, *Willie*. You ever call me anything but *Hank* or *Henry* again, the deal is off, and I won't feel bad if I let your real name slip out."

"Okay! Okay! Where's the truck, *Hank*? I'm tired."

"It's got a busted fuel pump, and I ain't had a chance to fix it 'cause I been herding Sheriff Bloot's cattle all day."

"So you work for a white man that calls you *nigger, ain't got no* respect for you, and fills his jail with colored folks every weekend even if they ain't broke the law. *Ain't that rich.*"

"A man's gotta work ... even if he got flat feet and can't go in the army," he said, and then put two fingers to his lips and whistled. Immediately, a big silvery white horse came trotting out of the darkness toward them.

Leeta screamed, grabbed Hank Posey's sleeve, and jumped behind him.

"Miss Willie Holloway, meet *Topper*, your ride home. He seats two real easy."

Leeta stared at horse and master. "I don't believe it! A *colored* Hopalong Cassidy with a white horse named *Topper!* I swear, I ain't met nothing but mostly crazy people since I got off that damn bus!"

Hank stepped into the saddle and extended a helping hand as he directed her to put her left foot into the stirrup. Grumbling, she did so, and he swung her up to plop behind him, astraddle. She locked her long arms tightly around his middle and braced her cheek against his back.

"I'm gonna call you *Hoppy* from now on, whether you like it or not."

"At least it ain't a dirty word."

"No, but *Hoppy* ain't what I'll be thinking."

"Long as you keep it to yourself."

"You'll know."

"Thinking it, ain't mouthing it."

"It is to me."

"Ain't to me."

She jerked her head away from his back. "How come we're just sitting here like we got something to say to each other?"

Even before the last word left her mouth, he gave Topper's flanks a sharp kick and the horse leapt into a wild sprint down the road. Leeta's piercing, uninterrupted shriek sounded like the air raid siren atop Hesterwine's old courthouse.

Jack Dunston felt oddly at ease sitting and conversing with Mary Kenney among the pillows on Clara and Justine Hesterwines' porch swing. Sometimes the two of them grew silent, simply to watch the moon slip in and out of the clouds. Behind their easy conversation, the distant hum of katydids floated from all directions, the musical cadence stilling only briefly as an owl hooted from the direction of the barn. Far off, the faint yipping of coyotes as they communicated with each other, either in claim to their territory or in answer to a mating call, added to the serenity of the night. Jack smiled to himself, thinking that a coyote's method of attracting a mate was covetable. If a male and female liked each other's barking and howling, the match was made, sight unseen, the rendezvous of love inevitable; not so, for him. He easily attracted the opposite sex, but the ones he could have actually fallen in love with had an aversion to what they sometimes tearfully confessed was his one and only flaw—an imperfection they could not live with on a long-term basis. They hadn't put it exactly that way, but he got the message. Maybe he shouldn't judge all women by the one who broke their engagement after he returned from overseas.

He glanced at Mary Kenny, admiring the pale glow of her skin in the moonlight, the moist sparkle of her eyes, the way her thick hair framed her face and fell across her shoulders—all the things that moonlight makes magical about a woman so as to cast a spell over a man. Several times tonight, this pretty girl from the northeast—who pronounced nearly every syllable of every word and wasn't embarrassed to wear a hat that looked like a big flower-filled dishpan—had stopped in the middle of a sentence to frown at him. He suddenly realized he'd been examining every inch of her face like a dermatologist looking for something life-threatening. He wanted to tell her that he wasn't searching that lovely external part of her for any reason other than to see beyond it into her mind. His searching had gotten him a glimpse of something forlorn beyond that sweetly calm exterior, but revealing his findings to her might have caused that frown to deepen when he couldn't give her a definitive description of what he saw. Whatever that sadness was, it remained there when she laughed, even when she glanced pleasantly around at her surroundings... the way she'd done at Goldrod's, and just as she was doing tonight. He liked her well enough to wonder what was on her mind, what was bothering her. Before he knew it, he had asked.

"My fiancé is missing in action," she replied.

"I'm sorry," he said, feeling strangely annoyed. *She's in love with somebody, Jack Dunston, not that you ever had a chance anyhow.*

"We ... sort of broke up before he left. But I am hoping, if he comes back, maybe we will...." She didn't finish.

He knew he was about to be unkind, but he did it anyway. "Good luck with that. Let's pretend he *wants* to rekindle an old flame that burned out. Are you still gonna want him if pieces of him were left behind on the battlefield ... or in some hospital garbage can?" he asked flatly, thinking she'd be mad at him now. He was surprised when, instead, she stared intently, but not angrily, into his eyes.

"Yes, I would want him even then, as long as he still loved me."

"I'm sorry I said that, Mary. I'm not usually so mean." He touched her cheek. "I hope he comes back, but if he doesn't, remember me, will you? I've been looking for a girl like you."

Her expression lightened and she smiled doubtfully at him. "*You?* Looking for a girl? Must I remind you again how every female who came into Goldrod's today couldn't keep their eyes off you, Jack Dunston?"

"They like what they see on the outside." He grabbed her hand and placed it below his left knee where the stump of his leg attached to the prosthesis he'd worn the past six months. "It's this *missing* part of me that gives them the heebie-jeebies when things start getting cozy," he said, thinking she'd jerk her hand away. But she surprised him again, and he watched her hand move down his artificial leg, feeling it as if it were a curiosity rather than a shock to her.

"Why, I would have never guessed." She leaned forward to look at the shoe on his metallic foot. "You hardly limp at all. When I first saw you at Goldrod's, I thought you might have sprained your ankle—and you actually *ran* to Miz Etta Ruth's mannequin when you thought it was a real person who had tumbled down the stairs," she said, grinning.

"Some days are better walking days than others," he said. "Today was a good day." He laughed. "I owe Miz Etta Ruth and her mannequin my thanks because, to tell you the truth, I didn't know I could run like that until I'd done it without thinking—the power of *mind over matter*, I guess, working in reverse."

"The loss of your leg is why you were released early from the Army Air Corps, isn't it?"

"Yes. My plane was shot up, and I wasn't too successful at crash landing it when I got back to the base."

"I say it was a very successful landing—you are alive."

He gently lifted her hand away. "I've adjusted to walking with it. I guess I'm lucky I still have the knee."

"Yes, you certainly are." She was still smiling. "You said you were going to dance with me. Did you mean it?"

"You bet. I do a great belly-rub, but you'll have to do your jitterbugging with somebody else, at least until I break in this new shoe."

"I don't like to jitterbug," she said. "I won't miss it at all."

They looked up at the same time to see Leeta and Hank Posey ride up on Hank's big white horse. Mary began to laugh.

Before either couple could call out a greeting, Aunt Lucy, wearing a yellow chenille robe, hustled out onto the porch and yelled at Hank.

"What you doing with that gal, Henry?"

"I ain't doing nothing with her, Auntie. I'm giving her a ride home!"

Aunt Lucy stuck her fists on her hips. "The preacher know 'bout this?"

"Didn't think to ask him if I could take a girl home, 'cause it ain't none of his business ... or yours, you sweet thing, you."

"The *preacher*?" Leeta fairly caterwauled. "You gotta ask a preacher if you can take a girl home?"

"The preacher is Aunt Lucy's brother and *my* poppa, and no, I don't have to ask him a blame thing."

"Jesus-Pete! That woman is your auntie?" Before Leeta could go back on her promise to stop cursing around him, Aunt Lucy called out again.

"Since you is here, Henry, and it gonna be breakfast time soon, I'll fix you some of your favorite hot cakes. You too, Miss Mary and Mista Jack." Then, as Leeta limped up the steps rubbing her sore buttocks, Aunt Lucy snapped, "You, too, I guess." Then she cautioned everybody, "We gots to be real quiet, though, 'cause we don't wanna wake Miss Clara and Miss Justine. We sure don't wanna wake Miz Etta Ruth! She was acting real crazy tonight out yonder at the windmill, but I ain't 'posed to talk 'bout it."

An hour later, stuffed with hot cakes, bacon, and eggs, Jack got into his pickup truck ... then nearly jumped out again as Etta Ruth Morley rose up, like a jack-in-the-box, on the passenger side. After he started breathing again, he turned the key in the ignition and switched on the overhead dome light. Immediately, she stuck a conspiratorial finger to her lips, her big eyes squinting at him like little spears of black fire.

"Drop me off at my old house, Jackie boy. I have errands in town... something I need to do."

Jack glanced at the glow-in-the-dark hands of his wristwatch. "It's three thirty, Miz Morley... the wee hours of Sunday morning. The stores will be closed."

"I know they're closed! I'm not stupid!" She straightened on the seat to stare out the windshield, a gesture obviously meant to indicate that she was ready to go.

Jack turned off the dome light and started the engine. From the look in Etta Ruth Morley's eyes, he chose not to argue the point.

# 15

SITTING AT A SEVENTEENTH CENTURY CHIPPENDALE tea table in the parlor, Mary watched Leeta draw perfect replicas of the attic mannequins and antique furniture along the edges of the flyers they were making. "Leeta Bulow, you are the most talented person I have ever met! Not only are you a marvelous singer, you are also a fine artist. Those illustrations look as if a professional did them. What other talents have you been hiding from us?"

"Nothing you'd wanna hear 'bout."

Mary poked her shoulder. "Stop pretending to be such a smart aleck."

"Smart aleck? Ain't that a sissy word for wise-ass?"

"Neither of which apply to you."

"You trying to flatter me into being a nice person?"

"You *are* a nice person. But you could stop using such bad language to describe a certain *other* nice person we know."

"I bet you're talking 'bout that shit-kicker, Hank Posey, ain't you?"

"After Aunt Lucy fed us breakfast, Hank tried to compliment you on your singing talent and how he thinks you are good enough to make records, and you told him to 'shut-up, you flinty-mouthed asshole.' That was not very nice, Leeta."

"Oh, yeah? What could I have called him other than flinty-mouthed asshole, 'cause that's what he is."

"You could have said ... well, you could have said, 'you flinty-mouthed *devil.*'"

"What! He woulda thought I was flirting with him!"

Mary laughed, then laughed even louder when Leeta, ducking her head to sketch another picture, mumbled, "Girl, your kinda cussing would get me in a lot worse trouble than my kinda cussing ever would."

"You will not know until you try."

"I don't wanna try. Besides, calling him a flinty-mouthed asshole was a slipup. When he brought me home on that damn horse, he made me promise not to call him those names anymore and I said I wouldn't. He's blackmailing me, saying he'll tell my real name if I call him stuff."

"He might do it."

"No, he won't, I can tell by the look in his eyes, the damn fool." She glanced at Mary, then busied herself with her drawing. "I felt sorry for him, so I told him I'd go fishing with him this evening. He's gonna pick me up in an hour."

Mary laughed. "I have a date, too. Jack is taking me to the movies."

"I ain't going on no damn date," Leeta insisted. "It's a *pity* venture I'm going on. I told you, I feel sorry for the idiot. He's gonna teach me how to 'gig for flounder,' whatever that means."

"A *gig* is a spear. You will wade along in the water and spear fish."

"Gawwwd!"

Just then, Clara and Justine, dressed for church, came into the parlor. They took one look at the sample flyer and agreed that selling a few of their treasures from their very own front porch rather than turning them over to Mr. Klunk was not only a grand idea, but also the sensible thing to do. "Even if it means we will be parting with so many of our sweet memories," Justine said, her eyes widening and then blinking rapidly.

Clara glanced at her. "Yes ... well, your sweet memories won't pay the piper, Justine, so we certainly won't cry about it. Practical minds find practical solutions."

"We will make more flyers this week," Mary said. "I am sure Jack Dunston will drive us around so we can put them out."

Clara suddenly frowned. "Oh, my child, you did not tell that young man about our dire straits, did you?"

"He only knows that you decided to clean out your attic." Mary smiled softly at her. Miss Clara's insistence on keeping her and Miss Justine's neediness private reminded her of her own grandmother's doggedness for privacy.

Justine clasped her hands together. "We shall call on Mr. Klunk at Klunk's Junk and tell him we've changed our minds again. I never thought a man with such dirty fingernails would fully appreciate our treasures anyway, though nice man that he is, of course."

Clara looked out the window as their yardman, Flaco Rosales, led Rudolph Valentino and the vintage Buick to the front gate. "We're off to church." She paused to straighten her hat, then glanced toward the elevator. "I thought Etta Ruth would be up by now, not that she cares to go to church anymore. Unfortunately, she's lost her religion, just like she's lost her ever-loving mi—" She looked at her watch. "Good. We shall just slip away before she can give me my chore list for the day," she added, then cried out in a voice that sounded very much like the person she mimicked: "Pluck my eyebrows, Clara! Put my hair in curlers, Clara! Clip my *petrified* toenails, Clara!"

Mary and Leeta looked at her in surprise. Obviously, Miss Clara was still upset by the mannequin incident in the foyer.

"You asked for it, Clara," Justine said as she lifted the watch on her white lace lapel and frowned at it. "Don't you think it's odd she hasn't made any noise this morning?"

"*Odd*? She's the *queen* of odd," Clara replied, turning to Mary and Leeta. "Would you girls mind keeping an eye on her when she gets up? Follow her about the house and make certain she doesn't burn the place down with those cigarettes of hers. Be very discreet about it, of course."

Justine continued to frown. "As mopey as she's been lately, she could be ill ... or *dead*. Maybe somebody should go upstairs and check on her."

"Or go look under the windmill," Clara quipped as she headed for the front door.

"Clara!"

"Whatever Etta Ruth's condition, I'm sure it will keep a bit longer. And if she's dead, we've got a couple of days before she gets ripe."

"Clara!" Justine cried again. "What a surprise! I can't believe you just said that. It isn't like you to be so blasé about Etta Ruth's welfare."

"And it isn't like *you* to be so concerned about her," Clara replied.

"Maybe not, but you always scold *me* for making remarks like that. Besides, it's Sunday, and one should never speak ill of *anyone* on Sunday—especially if they're on their way to church."

Clara waved a dismissive hand. "My remarks were a poor attempt at making a joke. I've never had much success at such things."

"A poor attempt, indeed," Justine huffed as she rushed to catch up to Clara, already at the door. "You should be ashamed of yourself, Clara."

"*Shame* is your department, Justine," Clara shot over her shoulder before she called out to Mary and Leeta, "Give us an hour head start, then go up and check on her, won't you?"

An hour later, just as they were about to check on Etta Ruth, the sound of a car coming down the road sent them to the window. Moments later, Leeta tensed at the unusual sight of a taxi pulling up to the gate.

Mary read her thoughts. "You need not worry, Leeta. Even if that Mandingo Q. Mann person discovered where you are—which he will not—I doubt he would arrive in a taxicab in broad daylight, and with the taxi driver as a witness."

"I guess not, but I ain't ever seen a cab come out here before. You think maybe Mr. Valentino finally ran out of gas?"

However, that notion dissolved as the taxi door pushed open and Etta Ruth, moving with unusual morbidity this morning, struggled out. She was wearing her dead husband's trousers and his big brown-and-white wing-tipped loafers. On the opposite side of the cab, the chubby driver successfully dislodged himself from beneath the steering wheel, went to the rear, opened the trunk, and lifted out a red wagon. After handing Etta Ruth a large decorative canister—the type in which one might store five pounds of flour or sugar—he extracted a collection of garden tools from the trunk and put them in the wagon. Etta Ruth handed him his fare. He tipped his hat, got in his cab, turned it around, and drove away.

"I don't guess we need to go up and check on her now," Leeta said. "She must have sneaked out long before daylight and walked to town."

"Maybe so. She is limping a little. Although, it is hard to believe someone her age would attempt to walk that far."

"Crazy people can do lots of things ... 'cause they is just crazy enough not to know they can't do it."

They watched Etta Ruth open the gate and pull the wagon through. When she was almost at the porch steps, Leeta nudged Mary. "What's that on her trousers and all over them men's shoes she's wearing? It looks like she dumped a box of powder on herself."

"It is white enough to be flour. Why ... it is in her hair, too," Mary said.

"It ain't too white for *her*. She powers up that ol' sour puss of hers like a ghost when she's primping in the mirror."

Suddenly, Etta Ruth stopped struggling in her attempt to pull the wagon up the steps and, seeing them watching her from the window, glared at them. "Got your eyes full yet?" she growled. "Then get your skinny asses out here and help me get my goddamn wagon on the porch where the sun can't ruin the goddamn paint! I need help!"

"Amen, you do," Leeta said under her breath.

"I'll go," Mary said, and immediately went out to Etta Ruth and pulled the wagon up on the porch.

"I suppose you're wondering why I've got flour all over me," Etta Ruth asked in her usual hostile tone.

"Yes, ma'am," Mary said honestly.

"I was making a cake and it didn't turn out the way I planned. I spilled the flour, slipped down in it, and hurt my damn hip. Believe me?"

"Yes, ma'am, of course I believe you. Why would I not?"

"Why would *anyone* not? Tell me *that*, Yankee girl."

"I ... I don't know, Miz Etta. *I* certainly believe you," Mary said a bit nervously—Miz Etta Ruth's eyes could be quite frightening when not in Bette Davis mode.

Just then, Hank Posey drove up. Leeta stepped out the door, maneuvered warily past the glowering woman, and dashed down the steps.

"Don't do anything I wouldn't do, Willie!" Etta Ruth yelled after her and laughed, but then suddenly turned grim-faced again when she looked at Mary. "Well? What are you waiting for? Put my damn wagon over there on the shady side of the damn porch!" With that she went into the house, slamming the screen door vehemently behind her.

Mary immediately decided that this might be a good time to leave Miz Etta Ruth to her privacy. After pulling the wagon into the shade, she retreated to the porch swing to wait for Jack.

Clara and Justine sat on their usual stools in Goldrod's waiting for Bobby to bring them their usual vanilla-laced root beer. The place was full of folks who enjoyed a sundae or malted after church.

"Have you heard about Mr. Abelson at the shoe shop?" Bobby asked as he arrived with their refreshments.

Clara's eyes widened briefly at him, the secret she was keeping about Clarence Morley and Old Man Abelson leaping to the front of her mind. *Was the scandalous secret out?* "I hope you are about to tell us he has finally lowered his prices," she said calmly. "Otherwise, if he has somehow managed to attract the town gossips, we don't want to hear it."

"He's attracted them, all right; he's *dead*. Miz Harlan Watson, wanting the shoes she'd left for repairs, went round to the alley to knock on his door early this morning—he lives in back of the shop, you know. Even though it's Sunday, she knew he would give her the shoes. He was good like that to folks," Bobby added with a sad nod. "Miz Watson found the door wide open and him naked as a jaybird and deader'n a doornail on his kitchen floor, *flour* scattered all over the place, and on him, too, I heard."

"Oh, my!" Justine cried. Clara was too stunned to gasp.

"Appears he was fixing to cook something in the *raw* when he had a heart attack," Bobby said, and then chuckled. "In the *raw*, get it? Ain't stuff always *raw* before you cook it?" Receiving only stares, he went frown-faced again. "Can't blame him, though, hot as it's been."

Not sure of what she'd been thinking, Clara released her breath. Justine was more animated:

"*Oh my GOD!*" Her hands slapped hard to her cheeks. "He was *naked*? One would think the man would have at least worn an *apron* when he cooked in the nude. Poor Vernell must still be in shock!"

"A heart attack?" Clara asked, still not sure of what she was thinking.

"Yes, ma'am, a heart attack. Sheriff Bloot and the chief of police were in here drinking coffee soon after the body was discovered, and that's what they said," Bobby replied, and then addressed Justine. "Miz Watson couldn't a been *too* shocked. The sheriff said she musta walked all around old Abelson's naked carcass because her big shoes left mighty big prints in all that flour."

"I never thought Vernell's feet were so big, Bobby," Justine said. "They couldn't be more than a seven. I know, because she and I have worn the same size shoe since we were in high school."

"I reckon the sheriff knows what he's talking about, Miss Justine. At any rate, poor Old Man Abelson's dead and gone ... sucked into the abyss of death *naked* as a jaybird, forever and ever, amen, to walk around that way."

"Oh, I don't believe that," Justine scoffed. "If that were the case, no one would ever take their clothes off for fear the grim reaper would catch them so embarrassingly exposed to God and everybody else up there."

"How sad," Clara said absently, while thinking that there was one person she knew who would not be a bit sad about Marvin Abelson's fatal heart attack. Even so, perhaps now Etta Ruth could relinquish her bitterness and, unless she was too far gone, miraculously regain a bit of her *compos mentis*.

With that thought, Clara's eyes rolled downward. Even if Etta Ruth *did* experience a phenomenal return to sanity, she doubted if Etta Ruth would ever be anything but *Etta Ruth,* unless she had a stroke and her prickly tongue suddenly went numb—*God forbid, of course.*

Despite feeling sorry for Mr. Abelson, Clara was eager to get home to tell Etta Ruth that her husband's lover was dead and gone. Perhaps now she would stop obsessing over *letters* that more than likely never existed. *Yes, Etta Ruth would be better now,* Clara decided.

However, there was that thunderstruck moment, upon arriving home and standing in the parlor doorway and seeing Etta Ruth slouched in Grandfather Hesterwine's big leather chair smoking a Pall Mall cigarette ... and seeing Clarence's *flour-speckled*, wing-tipped shoes propped up on the ottoman, that Clara felt she would faint for the very first time in all her sixty-nine years. Almost in that same instant, her eyes locked on the white splotches on Clarence's pinstriped trousers and then traveled up to the powdery patches in Etta Ruth's hair—even one of the woman's eyebrows was much lighter than the other was!

Justine, oblivious to Clara's discovery, went straight to the kitchen. A moment later, she marched past on her way to the elevator. "Since today is Aunt Lucy's day off, I'll start lunch as soon as I've changed, Clara. If I recall, it's my turn to cook and your turn to clean up." She turned briefly. "By the way, Etta Ruth made a cake."

Clara backed slowly away from the foyer doorway and made her way to the kitchen. As she pushed the door open, a relieved smile spread on her lips—the floor, kitchen table, and sink top were a mess ... splatters of *flour* everywhere! However, on a glass pedestal, in the middle of the table, stood a freshly baked three-layer cake with chocolate icing.

# 16

AT DAYBREAK ON THE MORNING OF THE BIG SALE, Jack Dunston, Hank Posey, two of Hank's brothers, and deaf and dumb Flaco lugged the furniture, mannequins (except for Etta Ruth's effigy of Clarence), and countless other items down from the attic and helped arrange them on the encircling porch. As advertised on the flyers, the sale would start at 8:00 a.m.

Everyone milled around outdoors except Etta Ruth, who had begun sleeping late most mornings. Mary and Leeta dusted and re-dusted the furniture as they kept an eye on the road in search of the first customers.

At seven thirty, a fast-moving dust cloud appeared at the top of Windy Knoll, and then Sheriff Bloot's green Packard, sirens blaring and red lights flashing, emerged from the swirling vortex. Before anyone could wonder aloud, the screaming vehicle was abreast the house, where the sheriff evidently floor-boarded the clutch and brakes because the rear end of the vehicle spun around with life-and-death urgency before coming to a rut-digging halt at the front gate. Almost before the car quit bouncing, he piled out and charged toward the house as if he'd just recognized a fugitive on an FBI's Most Wanted poster.

Sitting in the passenger seat of the sheriff's vehicle, Banker Prickett stared straight ahead.

"So *that's* him," Leeta said when Justine pointed him out. "He looks just like Bela Lugosi. You know, the guy who plays Count Dracula in all them scary movies."

Justine squinted at him. "My goodness, he certainly does, doesn't he?"

"Hold up there with that sale you're fixing to have!" the sheriff yelled, waving a paper over his head as he stomped up the porch steps.

"Miss Clara, Miss Justine, this is an order, signed by Judge Parkerwood, demanding y'all *cease and desist* with this sale. You ain't to sell none of that stuff off the place. It ain't legal."

"Wha-a-a-t?" Clara and Justine cried.

Cars were pulling up at the front gate, people coming into the yard, their eyes scanning the items they had come to buy.

Jack Dunston stepped forward. "May I, ladies?" he asked, as he took the paper from the sheriff's hands. Mary and Leeta read over Jack's shoulder.

"I see that Judge Parkerwood's brother-in-law, Banker Prickett—who is also *your* father-in-law—is with you today, Sheriff Bloot," Clara said, her soothsayer's eyes locked on Banker Prickett's profile; he had yet to look at any of them.

Ignoring her, Sheriff Bloot none-too-gently nudged Leeta out of his way as he stepped to Jack's side and pointed at the paper. "That there is a *Writ of Mandamus* that says—"

"A writ of *who*?" Leeta interrupted.

Sheriff Bloot glared at her for a long moment before he continued addressing Jack. "That there is a *Writ of Mandamus* stopping this sale 'cause it's against the law to sell anything that's bigger than a bread box out of a private residence unless you apply for a license to do so and get the sale approved by the Commissioner's Court of Vander County."

"Since when?" Jack asked. "My neighbor sold a garage full of furniture just last week. My housekeeper was there helping them out, and she said you and your wife bought an old trunk at that garage sale, Sheriff. You never said anything about a Writ of Mandamus *then*."

"Commissioner's Court held an emergency session last night and drew it up. You gotta have a permit. No ifs, ands, or buts about it."

Jack glanced at the sheriff's vehicle and Banker Prickett, who still stared straight ahead. "Does your father-in-law usually accompany you on missions like this, Sheriff... or only when he's personally involved with the outcome?"

Miss Clara's eyes widened, and Mary instantly knew she was thinking that she had gone back on her word and told Jack about the financial troubles at Hesterwine Place. "Miss Clara, when Mr. Klunk found out that you planned to sell the furniture without him, he told people why you were selling it. Jack overheard him. I am so sorry."

"I don't suppose Mr. Klunk meant any harm, Clara," Justine offered.

"Ain't no secrets kept in Hesterwine," Sheriff Bloot said with a dismissive wave of his big hand as he returned his attention to Jack. "As to my father-in-law being with me today, Dunston ...." He squinted in his usual threatening manner. "Well ... I wouldn't be making any insinuations, if I were you."

Jack turned to Clara. "I'll drive you to town to get that permit, Miss Clara. I'm sure folks will want this fine old furniture bad enough to wait here until we get back."

"Sure thing, we'll wait," said a man standing nearby. His wife had her hand possessively on an eighteenth century table with pedestal legs.

"I shall get my handbag," Clara replied, but before she could take a step, Sheriff Bloot spoke again.

"Sure, Miss Clara, you can go and apply for the permit, but this here *Writ of Mandamus* says there's a forty-five-day wait before it can come up before Commissioner's Court and get approved—*if* it gets approved."

Jack shook his head. "And by that time, Stanton B. Prickett's bank will have foreclosed on Hesterwine Place and he'll somehow end up the new owner. Are you proud of your part in this, Sheriff?"

"Don't you get smart with me, Dunston. I just follow orders and enforce the law, and this here writ is one of them laws, all signed and legal." He waved an arm at the crowd mingling among the antiques on the porch. "You folks, listen up! Ain't gonna be no sale, so you might as well head on outta here and don't come back ... or you'll be breaking the law!"

"*You* are the law," Leeta said. "The law oughta be on Miss Clara and Miss Justine's side, not helping some greedy crook steal their land!"

Sheriff Bloot turned slowly to stare menacingly at her again. "You're sure stepping outta your place, gal. You know that, gal?"

Like that first day in town behind Goldrod's, Leeta's glare locked with his.

He smirked. "No, you don't know it, do you? That's the problem with you *Yankeefied* coloreds. With that uppity, big-city attitude of yours, you could get to see my jail any old day now."

"You cannot arrest a person for what they believe, Sheriff," Mary said.

"Yes, he can. He can arrest me for nothing at all. Just ask any of them folks at Rose Hill."

"What's that you said, gal? You mouthing off again?"

"No, she isn't." Jack dropped his arms over both girls' shoulders. "I guess your business is finished here, isn't it, Sheriff?"

"As a matter of fact, it is. I got more important matters to tend to than serving *Writs of Mandamus* on people. We mor'n likely got a killer on the loose in Vander County. You folks is warned to be on the lookout."

"A killer? Somebody's been murdered?" Justine's eyes rounded.

"Yep. The coroner says there's something mighty fishy about Old Man Abelson's death, and says maybe something more'n a heart attack killed him. The body's been sent to Houston for an autopsy." He narrowed his eyes as he shook his head in affirmation of his next words. "I thought them big size ten shoeprints in all that flour round the body was mighty suspicious ... 'specially since Abelson wore a size eight, and Miz Watson, who discovered the body, is a size seven, I found out. Even if Abelson's feet had a been size tens, how could he make them prints after he was dead and *barefoot* on the floor?"

Clara's hand went slowly to her cheek, possibly because she had felt it suddenly go pale as she pictured Clarence's size ten shoes on Etta Ruth's feet. However, after a moment of rational thinking, she calmed. *Etta Ruth couldn't have killed Mr. Abelson, because she had not left Hesterwine Place since moving in. Thank goodness!*

"Even more suspicious," continued the sheriff, "there weren't any flour *under* the body, just on top and all around him, and it was messed up like the killer musta slipped down in it. My theory is them big shoeprints belong to the killer and was made *after* poor old Abelson hit the floor. That's why I'm betting that autopsy is gonna say it weren't no heart attack that killed him. But the only clue I got so far is that the killer wears size ten shoes."

"Well, that should give you something to go on," Justine said.

"Maybe, but until Abelson's murder is solved, the whole town is suspect."

Justine tittered. "The *whole* town? Do you really suppose there are that many *killers* in Hesterwine, Sheriff Bloot? Forgive me, but that notion is really too funny."

He wagged his big head. "Well, put *this* in your pipe and smoke it, Miss Justine. I think we got a homicidal maniac on the prowl in Hesterwine. How funny is *that*? They'd have to be a homicidal nut to kill a harmless old man like Abelson."

Justine's expression sobered.

Grinning, he squinted first at her and then at Clara. "Did either of you little ladies have it in for Old Man Abelson? Maybe he left a cobbler's tack in your shoe or something," he said, then guffawed at the shocked look on their faces. "Just joking, ladies! *Jesus!*" He laughed harder.

Justine and Clara stared down their noses at him. "That is not a bit amusing, Sheriff Bloot. However, just so you know, none of us, not a single soul living at Hesterwine Place, was in Hesterwine on the eve of Mr. Abelson's death," Clara said. "Justine and I only went to town the next morning to church, as usual... hours after the dreadful event took place, according to Bobby at Goldrod's, who gave us the news of the poor man's demise."

"I said I was just joking. You ain't suspects," he said, still laughing. Then he turned serious. "The Biddles boy, who cleaned up the shop for Abelson every few days, said the place had been ransacked. But, as far as he could tell, wudn't nothing missing except a big flour canister and a tall stack of letters he remembered seeing under the sink when he put away the cleaning supplies."

"Oh?" Clara said, but it sounded more like a croak as she tried not to look jolted. *Were they the letters Etta Ruth insisted Clarence had written to Mr. Abelson?*

The sheriff continued, "You'd think the killer woulda taken the money from the cash register or stole the old man's watch and wallet. But nope. All they took was that flour canister and them letters." He made a face. "It'd be interesting to know what was in them letters and who they was from."

Clara's mind whirled. But even if Mr. Abelson was indeed murdered, Etta Ruth could not have done it. *The woman is unbalanced, but she is not a homicidal maniac!* After a moment of heart-pounding deliberation, in which she reminded herself that Etta Ruth had not left the house since Clarence Jr. delivered her there, bag, baggage, and grouchy old cat, Beelzebub, Clara once again forced a calming breath. As to the woman's flour-splattered hair and clothes on the morning after Mr. Abelson died, the mess she had made of the kitchen while baking that three-layer cake was the perfect alibi.

Everyone watched silently as the sheriff and Banker Pricket drove away behind the long line of cars heading back to town, Prickett still looking straight ahead. Aunt Lucy, dropped off at the house moments earlier by Hank Posey, pushed the screen door open and motioned to Clara.

Even as Clara entered the foyer, Aunt Lucy was urgently pulling her inside as she whispered breathlessly, "My cousin that cleans up at the taxicab stand in town told me that Miz Etta Ruth took a cab out here Sunday morning... and she had *flour* all over her." Her eyes widened at Clara. "Miss Clara, my cousin said Miz Etta Ruth was wearing a pair of men's mighty *big* brown-and-white shoes, and them shoes had flour on 'em, too!"

Staring at Aunt Lucy, Clara stepped backward to bolster herself against the foyer wall, her mind once again reeling. If what Aunt Lucy's cousin said was true... *But how could that be?* Clara's hand went worriedly to her forehead. Could it be true? If so, the sheriff would eventually question that cab driver, and Etta Ruth would surely become the number one suspect. *Oh, my!* No Hesterwine or extended family member had ever been involved in scandal—not any of its *women,* anyway. Certainly, no one on the family tree was ever accused of *murder*!

What to do? Clara's eyes blinked rapidly as she searched for an answer. She would need to discuss this delicate family matter with Clarence Jr. *Perhaps he should follow his original plan and put his mother in that asylum before the sheriff could figure out who it was that kil—*

She stepped away from the wall to gaze steadily at Aunt Lucy. "Thank you for that information, Aunt Lucy. However, we shan't repeat it, not in this house or out of it, especially not to *Justine*. You know how upset she gets over any and every little thing. Besides, Etta Ruth could not have come home in a taxi that day because she was upstairs asleep when Justine and I left for church."

Aunt Lucy eyed her knowingly. "If you say so, Miss Clara."

Just then, Mary and Justine came inside, leaving Willie and Hank Posey standing in the yard conversing calmly for a change.

"Oh, my, it has been such a horrible day, Clara!" Justine cried. "I need a cup of strong black coffee! I'm going to the kitchen and make a pot, and I am actually tempted to dust off a bottle of Poppa's medicinal Schnapps and pour a tablespoon of it into my cup." She hurried away. Aunt Lucy followed. "I'll have a tablespoon in mine, too, Miss Justine!" she called out as she rushed to catch up. "Maybe *two* spoons."

"I am so sorry the furniture sale did not work out, Miss Clara," Mary said. "Aunt Lucy told me Flaco is selling the watermelons tomorrow. Willie and I would like to help him."

Clara tried to be cheerful. "Of course, dear, go right ahead. As pretty as you and Willie are, everyone who drives down the highway will surely stop and buy a melon."

Mary was about to go to the kitchen when Clara, hoping against hope that Aunt Lucy's cousin was mistaken, touched Mary's sleeve. "I forgot to ask what time Etta Ruth got out of bed after Justine and I went to church last Sunday," she said. "Sleeping so much isn't healthy, you know, but I suppose staying in bed half the day with that mannequin of hers is healthier than wandering aimlessly around town like she did before moving in with us."

"I agree," Mary said, then hesitated a moment. "I hope this does not mean anything, Miss Clara, but I heard what you told the sheriff about none of us being in town the day Mr. Abelson died." Mary paused again as she looked carefully around the room, especially toward the stairs and elevator, before continuing. "When Jack left here after Aunt Lucy fixed breakfast for us that morning, Miz Etta Ruth was hiding in his truck. Jack dropped her off at her house. The next morning, after you and Miss Justine went to church, a taxi brought her home. I should have told you this before, but I just didn't think it was important, and ..." she paused as if she didn't know what else to say, but then quickly finished, "... and I'm sure it isn't. I just thought you were already worried enough."

Clara's shoulders slumped.

"Are you all right, Miss Clara?"

"Yes, yes. Certainly, dear. I was just wondering how I will ever convince Cousin Etta Ruth to stop wandering around like that. She's going to get herself run over by a train ... or something," Clara said, not wanting to frighten this sweet girl by saying what she was really thinking. Besides, as much as she adored Mary, Etta Ruth was *family*.

"I imagine Miz Etta Ruth just wanted to get her red wagon and gardening tools," Mary said. "She must have tried to make a cake at her house before coming out here and making one, because when she got out of the taxi she was a flour-spattered mess. She also had a big flour canister with her ... which is probably how she got so covered with ..." She didn't finish. Her eyes rounded, and Clara knew Mary had suddenly made the connection between Mr. Abelson's missing flour canister and the one Etta Ruth had brought home.

Clara managed to sound unconcerned. "If we asked her why she went to town that night, she would have a hissy fit but would have a perfectly reasonable explanation, I'm sure. We won't ask, though, will we, my dear? We don't want to upset her."

"No, ma'am."

"Then, it's agreed. And another thing, Mary. We shan't say a word to *anyone* about Etta Ruth being away that night ... nor to Justine, either. She has a positively uncontrollable imagination, and she'd drive herself to distraction thinking all sorts of outrageous things and I'd never hear the end of it."

"I will not say a word to a soul," Mary said.

"We shall just wait and see what happens. I'm sure Sheriff Bloot will find the guilty party ... eventually." Then, still trying to sound casual, she added, "In the meanwhile, Mary, I think I shall call Clarence Jr. and ask him to come get his mother and take her home with him for a while. Or perhaps it would be better if he just took her to wherever he originally planned to take her in the first place. Etta Ruth being *family*, I really have no other choice than to see that she is safely put away... er, I mean ..." she trailed off. However, Mary's sudden compassionate nod quickly assured her that the sweet girl understood the need for confidentiality.

That night, when everyone was asleep, Clara called Clarence Jr. and, because the Hesterwines' phone was on a party line that allowed rural neighbors to eavesdrop on the conversation if they picked up their receivers, she simply told him he needed to visit Hesterwine Place as soon as humanly possible. *Yes ...* she thought as she climbed the stairs to her room instead of taking the noisy elevator, *perhaps Clarence Jr. should put his mother in that asylum after all, and right away!*

# 17

"Just don't expect me to stand on the side of the highway hawking these damned things," Leeta said to Mary as they struggled toward the Buick, their arms wrapped tightly around huge watermelons. "Miss Clara thinks folks is bound to stop and buy one when they see me and you. I look damn good, but I ain't ever stopped traffic before, have you?"

Mary laughed. "The sight of Mr. Valentino hitched to the old Buick will stop the traffic and sell the watermelons, not you and me. The only reason Miss Clara let us help Flaco today is because she knows how badly we want to be of use around the place."

"*Correction*," Leeta grunted as she struggled along with her watermelon. "It's how badly *you* want to be of use around the place, not me. That Aunt Lucy is having the time of her life bossing you around. I ain't letting her make me into no *housemaid*—'house nigger' is probably what ol' Grandpa Hesterwine called 'em back in the days he ran de ol' plantation," Leeta quipped, then looked at Flaco Rosales as he jabbed a crooked brown finger at them and then pointed at the next melons he wanted them to load. "And now we got a pint-sized, deaf-mute old Mexican running us all over this damn watermelon patch telling us which way to jump," she added. "Have you noticed his face, Mary? That scrappy little Mexican got so many battle scars he looks like he was used for a punching bag."

"Shusssh, Leeta. He is standing right there."

"So? The little squirt can't hear a damn thing I'm saying."

Mary glanced at Flaco's expressionless face and realized he was interested only in loading the watermelons. Despite the slightly forward bend of his spine and two missing fingers on his right hand, he had loaded five melons to every *one* melon they had managed to load.

"The poor man," Mary whispered. "Even with his many handicaps, he has done most of the work. Miss Clara said that for someone of his tiny stature and age he is as tough as they come."

"That's right. Which means he don't need our help."

"I like helping. It is absolutely the right thing to do," Mary said, bending to pick up another watermelon.

"Fine, but I wish you'd stop volunteering *me* for stuff." She hoisted a huge watermelon and staggered back with it a few steps before recovering. "I'll bet this sucker weighs fifty pounds!" She glowered at Flaco. "Hey, *you*, little tough guy, wanna take this one off my hands? Mary says you're tough as an old boot, even if you ain't no taller'n one. She says you smell like one, too."

"Leeta, I said no such thing!"

Leeta laughed playfully. "You sound like you're worried about hurting his feelings. I could cuss the little sourpuss up one side and down the other and he wouldn't hear a word I said."

After an hour of heavy lifting and lots of sweating, and with the old Buick's backseat, along with the trailer hitched to the back, filled with watermelons, they crowded onto the front seat next to Flaco, with Leeta in the middle. Mr. Valentino effortlessly pulled them down Hesterwine Road toward the highway. Flaco had also loaded onto the trailer a plank board table, a tarp, four long poles to hold up the tarp that would protect them from the sun, a scale to weigh the melons, and a sign advertising *Juicy, Sweet, Delicious Watermelons Only 2¢ Per Pound*.

They were almost to the main thoroughfare when Flaco reined Mr. Valentino off the narrow dirt road to let an oncoming car pass. Leeta craned her neck as a familiar 1941 cream-colored Chevy coupe rolled past.

"Ain't that Miz Etta Ruth's son, Clarence Jr.? Aunt Lucy said Miz Etta maybe done got herself in some bad trouble. Wonder what it could be, other than her always bugging the hell out of everybody."

Mary immediately knew why he was here, and it had everything to do with Miz Etta Ruth coming home covered with flour and, yesterday, Miss Clara saying she wanted Clarence Jr. to come get his mother. However, in keeping her promise to Miss Clara, Mary only shrugged.

"That Miz Etta Ruth got to be the second-toughest old woman I ever saw, and the scariest," Leeta said, and laughed. "First prize woulda gone to my grandma back in Mississippi."

"How so?" Mary smiled at Leeta's sudden cheerfulness.

"My grandma was a *funny* kinda mean. You know, the kinda woman who, when she did something most folks wouldn't do, everybody'd just shrug and say 'That's all right, Darcella, you was just doing what you had to do.' Her and my grandpa never argued much, but every once in a while he'd get mad at something and tell her that one of these days he might have to put a knot on her head. He never did it, though. But one day, when we was all out back barbecuing, he got drunk on corn liquor right out'n the jug and kept promising her that knot. We was all laughing at him and knowing it was all just talk, but then all of a sudden Grandma grabbed up a long barbecue fork and jabbed it into his butt right down to the bone. He screamed like she had cut his arm off."

Mary chuckled behind her hand. "I guess I should not laugh."

"All us kids laughed. Between yelps, he asked her why she done it, 'cause she oughta know by now that he wasn't never gonna hit her. Grandma jerked the fork out, waved it at him and said, 'No, you ain't ever hit me, and *now* you ain't ever again gonna *say* you is, is you?' And he never did again."

Mary laughed harder and as she did, became aware of Flaco. His mouth was wide open in a silent guffaw! He had read Leeta's lips, and had probably *heard* every word the two of them had uttered all day!

At the juncture where Hesterwine Road met the main highway, Mr. Valentino lumbered across and pulled the Buick well off the shoulder. Leeta and Mary watched Flaco reach inside his baggy white shirt, pull out a sign that explained, "I am deaf and dumb," and hang it around his neck.

"Now we'll find out just how many customers that damned old bull can attract," Leeta said.

Mary responded with a heavy sigh, "I hope enough to pay the electric bill. When I was cleaning the kitchen, I accidently knocked that old cigar box off the shelf over the stove, and a pile of bills fell out—grocery bills, utilities bills, phone bills, and others. Most all are four months overdue. The electric co-op wants twenty-five dollars and fifty cents. If we don't take in that much today, the electricity will be cut off day after tomorrow."

"Well ... that's too bad, but I already got a place for *my* money," Leeta said, her expression turning almost hostile. "I'd help out, but a few more weeks singing at the Blue Creek Lounge and I'll have enough dough to get to California, so don't ask me."

"I am not asking."

"Good! Don't ever. The answer will still be hell no."

They got busy unloading the table. "If only we could have sold that furniture yesterday," Mary murmured. Suddenly, as they carried the table to the spot Flaco pointed to, she felt yesterday's anger all over again, only worse this time. "*Damn* that Sheriff Bloot and his greedy father-in-law!" she cried.

Leeta widened her eyes at her. "Did I hear right? Did *little Miss Goody-Two-Shoes* actually *damn* somebody?"

"I am no goody-two-shoes, Leeta. Actually, if I have reason to, I can be quite the bitch."

Leeta clamped both hands over her heart. "Miss Goody-Two-Shoes saying *damn* and *bitch!* I can't take it!"

Mary laughed, then nodded toward an approaching car. "That could be our first customer."

"*Smile*, Mr. Valentino!" Leeta yelled as they stepped behind the table to stand next to Flaco. He had already unloaded half the watermelons, and now he jerked up the advertisement sign and held it high over his head.

Soon, cars were stopping on both sides of the road, the passengers getting out to cautiously pet Mr. Valentino before trailing over to the watermelons. Flaco used his pocketknife to cut a small one-inch plug through the rind, and then humbly offered the sample to the potential buyer. So far, every customer had found their plugged watermelon sweet and juicy, and bought it. Business was good, and they all three stayed busy.

Three hours later, fewer than two dozen watermelons remained.

"Sixty cents is too cheap for them thirty pounders. They oughta go for a dollar," Leeta said as she fanned herself with one of the rattan fans Miss Clara had urged them to take along.

"Miss Clara said the price has been two cents per pound for thirty years and she will not ask more in these times of war and ..." Mary trailed off as they both recognized Sheriff Bloot's green Packard coming slowly down the highway.

"Oh, Lordy," Leeta murmured.

"We are not doing anything wrong, Leeta."

"Since when does that matter? He's slowing down. He's gonna stop."

"Maybe he wants a watermelon," Mary said, then smiled with relief as he revved his motor and drove on past. "Good! I had quite enough of his company yesterday."

Her relief was short-lived. He made a U-turn in the middle of the highway and headed back toward them. Seeing the tension on Leeta's face intensified Mary's dislike for Vander County's small-minded sheriff. She stared coldly at him as his vehicle pulled well off the road and rolled to a stop no more than a few feet from them. He sat there squinting oddly at Leeta for a long moment before finally shifting his attention to Mary.

"Hello, sweet thang," he said. "I see you're still associating with the wrong people." He looked past them at the watermelons. Then, with his narrowed eyes back on Leeta, he shifted gears, revved the Packard's engine, and drove slowly away.

"I don't like it," Leeta said. "Did you see the way he was looking at us? He gave me the creeps."

"Me, too. But what could he say? Flaco has been selling watermelons from this spot for years."

"Yeah, but I don't trust him. He's planning something. He don't want Miss Clara and Miss Justine to be able to pay off that damn mortgage his father-in-law's holding over 'em. Maybe he went to get another one of them *Writ of Mandamus* things and ain't gonna let us sell these watermelons."

"He was trying to intimidate us, as usual, Leeta," Mary assured her, even though she could not shake the feeling that he was not finished with them.

An hour later, her hunch proved accurate when a brown pickup truck with three teenage boys on the front seat and three others standing on the pickup's bed behind the cab pulled off the road and parked in front of Mr. Valentino. The boys piled out of the truck and sauntered over to the table. Three of them carried baseball bats. One of them poked Flaco's arm with his bat, staggering him.

With his pocketknife still in his hand, Flaco recovered and, gazing blankly at the teen, pointed to the rows of watermelons.

"Sure, dummy, that's why we're here. We wanna buy a big one."

"That's right," another boy said. "But we ain't buying 'til we see if it's nice and sweet ... like *sweet thang* here," he added, using Sheriff's Bloot's favorite moniker for Mary as he reached out and caressed her cheek. She slapped his hand away, and then she and Leeta stepped behind the table to stand close to Flaco.

The boy motioned for Flaco to plug one of the melons. Flaco obeyed, then handed him the sample. He tasted it, made a sour face, and flung it away. "Move this bad melon, Joe, and set another one up here on the table," he said to one of his grinning companions.

Joe, a tall, heavyset, muscular teen, laid his bat aside, lifted the plugged melon, took a few steps backward, opened his arms, and let it fall. It burst open with a *splat* as it hit the ground.

After that, four more watermelons were plugged, tasted, refused, and then smashed in the same manner.

"Stop!" Mary cried. "Why are you doing this?"

"Because the sheriff told 'em to," Leeta said as she came around the table and tried to prevent Joe from placing another watermelon in front of the boy who waited, grinning, to reject it.

Mary joined her, stepping in front of Joe. "You had better leave now, or—"

"Or what?" He grabbed her arm and effortlessly slung her aside, then did the same to Leeta. Both girls instantly charged back to the table. Leeta got there first and grabbed Joe's arm as he hoisted another watermelon. He shook her loose, dropped the melon, cursed, and then, to Mary's shock, he grabbed Leeta by the front of her shirt and struck her in the jaw with his fist.

Mary screamed as he flung Leeta aside and she landed, unmoving, in the deep grass. Mary tried to run to her, but Joe grabbed one of her wrists and held her back. Enraged to the point of fearlessness, she fought him with her free fist. Then she saw Flaco charging to her rescue, his pocketknife poised in a threatening manner in front of him. But he and his small knife were no match for the muscular, six-foot teenager. Still holding onto Mary with one hand, Joe grabbed Flaco's hand and bent it back until Flaco's mouth opened in a silent cry of pain and he dropped the knife. If Joe thought Flaco would back away, he was wrong; Flaco flew at him like a belligerent bantam rooster, his small fist a blur of wildly aimed swings that never connected as Joe, laughing playfully, held him at bay with his long arm.

Knowing that Joe could hurt Flaco at any moment, Mary tried to get between them but Joe, still holding tightly to her wrist, jerked her aside. He then raised his foot and shoved Flaco hard in the stomach with it. Flaco landed on his back in the grass but jumped to his feet and charged at Joe again. This time as Joe reached for Flaco, the small Mexican ducked beneath Joe's long arm and sank his teeth into his thigh. Joe howled with pain.

"You goddamn greaser!" he yelled as he let go of Mary, jerked Flaco up by his collar, and shook him violently before smashing his huge fist into his face.

Mary screamed her rage at the hulking bully as he pounded and pummeled Flaco, her breath exploding from her in desperate cries, but nothing she did stopped him. He grunted with each cruel blow he struck, so intent on his brutal assault on Flaco that he seemed not to notice that she was even there. His cohorts pulled her off him and held her back, and now all she could do was cry out for him to stop, begging him to stop. "He is an old man! You will kill him!"

Sobbing helplessly, her eyes moved frantically between Flaco and Leeta. Flaco's head was now rolling insensibly with each blow, his face becoming bloodier by the second. Finally, his attacker executed a final horrendous jab before letting the comatose man drop to the ground. "Goddamn greaser," Joe repeated as he bent down, ripped the *I am deaf and dumb* sign from around Flaco's neck, and then wiped his knuckles on Flaco's shirt.

The boys released Mary and she ran to Flaco and dropped down on her knees to cradle his head. Still sobbing, she dabbed gently at his bloody face with her handkerchief. Leeta had regained consciousness and was slowly sitting up. When she saw Mary and Flaco, she crawled to them.

"I'm all right," she said, even before Mary could ask. "The son of a bitch knocked me out cold, that's all." She looked down at Flaco. "Jesus Pete! Looks like they tried to beat him to death! Is he breathing?"

Mary listened at Flaco's frail chest. "Yes, he is breathing."

Leeta glanced over her shoulder as the boys proceeded to destroy all the watermelons, slamming their bats into them, splattering them to the ground and then stomping them into squishy pools of red and green mush. "Don't say anything to them, Mary," Leeta cautioned. "Maybe they'll go away and leave us alone when they finish what Sheriff Bloot sent 'em to do."

The boy who had ordered Flaco to plug the melons came over and seemed intent on watching Mary tend Flaco's bleeding face with her handkerchief. "We already knew you're a *nigger* lover, but it looks like you're a damn *Meskin* lover too, ain't you, sweet thang?" He raised his foot and stomped on Flaco's straw hat that lay nearby, flattening it. "You know what a *Meskin* is, don't you, sweet thang?" he drawled.

Mary glanced up and down the highway, wishing a car would come along, but dusk was falling and, like all rural communities, most folks were off the roads and gathered around their supper tables by now.

"I asked you a question, sweet thang."

Mary glared up at him. "Yes, I know what a Mexican is, and a colored person as well. They are *people*, just like you and me—well, maybe not like *you*."

"You don't know *shit*. Where I come from, most folks reckon a Meskin ain't nothing but a nigger turned wrong side out."

His companions, taking a break from squashing the watermelons, roared. One of them yelled out, "My grandpa used to say that about the Irish."

"Hey! I'm *half*-Irish," said another, causing the others to laugh uproariously again as they resumed slamming their bats into the last watermelons.

Mary looked up as Joe, carrying his bat over his shoulder, sauntered over to them. "I almost forgot," he said. "I got orders to leave a message with your uppity *city* nigger friend here." Mary screamed as he raised his bat and poised it over Leeta's head. "Don't worry, sweet thang, I ain't gonna hit her hard enough to kill her ... just gonna give her the bruisin' she been cruisin' for." But then he jerked his head toward the road as a huge truck loaded with cattle came over the hill.

"Time to go, fellas!" he yelled, and the entire gang ran, stumbling over each other as they piled into the pickup truck, did a wheel-screeching U-turn, and sped back toward town.

Leeta had thrown her crossed arms up over her head to protect it when Mary screamed her warning, and now she dropped them to her sides and let out a long sigh of relief. "I never thought I'd love the sound of a bunch of cattle bawling like crazy. That cow poop don't smell all that bad, neither," she quipped as the truck pulled to a stop on the opposite side of the highway and the driver jumped down from the cab and ran over to them, nearly slipping down in the red mud made by the squashed watermelons. Like half the Vander County men Mary and Leeta had seen since arriving, he wore cowboy boots, dungarees, a big hat, and a red kerchief around his neck.

"*Jesus*, I saw them kids skedaddling like bats out of Hades. Did them little bastards make this mess and do that to the Mexican?"

"They sure did," Leeta replied. "And they was gonna do the same to the *colored* gal, too, if you hadn't showed up when you did."

"We can never thank you enough," Mary said.

The man kneeled down. "Looks like he's coming around. Got any water?"

Leeta went to the Buick and got the water jug. The truck driver doused Mary's handkerchief and then pressed it to the knots and cuts on Flaco's face and head. "I know this man. He's old Flaco Rosales from over at La Villita. He used to do yard work for my folks when I was a kid."

Flaco's eyes opened and he immediately tried to get up, but Mary and Leeta grabbed hold of him and slowly brought him to his feet. He waved them away, signaling that he was okay by brushing at his clothes and straightening his crumpled collar. Then he took up the water jug, leaned his head back, and poured water on his face, his white collar turning pink.

The truck driver laughed. "Read my lips, old fella. Your head must be hard as a coconut, but I think you oughta be checked over by a doctor."

Flaco waved his arms, plainly indicating he did not need a doctor. He picked up his demolished hat, poked his fist at the crushed bowl, slapped it on his head, and began dismantling the plank board table.

The truck driver helped load everything onto the trailer, then stood scratching Mr. Valentino between the ears as Mary thanked him. He glanced at Leeta and Flaco sitting in the Buick. "I'd advise y'all to file charges against them hooligans, but it wouldn't do any good. I live in Hesterwine, and I recognized that pickup truck. It belongs to one of the county commissioners, and I reckon that was his son driving it." He laughed cynically. "They should have named the town *Cahoots*... because every dern small-time politician and official in Varner County is in *cahoots*—deep into each other's hip pockets—and Lady Justice always tips the scales in their favor. No, sirree, Lady Justice ain't worn her blindfold in Vander County in many a year ... *blinders*, maybe, but no blindfold. The Mexican, old Flaco, ain't got a chance of getting any justice." He nodded toward Leeta. "That colored gal got even less a chance."

"She discovered *that* her first day in town when the sheriff threatened to throw her in jail for no real reason," Mary said.

"Stuff like that gives folks a bad impression of the town, don't it?" He shook his head. "I was born and raised in Hesterwine. Fact is, it's a fine little place. It just has some bad people running it right now. There's lots of people here that hates the way things are, but folks get *numbness of the brain* after a while if the bad guys keep winning. They get to where they don't even bother to vote anymore. My momma used to say Hesterwine, Texas, was a 'colorful little garden of a town with its mixed bed of flowers, but with an infestation of stinkweed that requires the sure hand an honest-to-goodness, weed-hating gardener."

"You need a new sheriff, that is for sure," Mary said.

"That'd be a start," he said, tipping his hat to her, then waved good-bye to Leeta and Flaco.

After he left, it dawned on Mary that they had not found the little tin box of money made from the watermelon sales before the gang of boys arrived. She started looking through the weeds. Flaco, his face grotesquely swollen now, got out of the Buick and came over to her. He held out his arms as if he was gripping a baseball bat, pointed down the road, and then doubled up his fist and made a motion as if striking himself in the chin.

"Those hooligans took the money, Flaco?"

He made a motion as if stuffing something under his shirt. Obviously, before he was knocked unconscious, he witnessed the box being stolen.

As she turned dejectedly aside and started toward the Buick, Flaco took up her hand and patted it in a tenderly, almost fatherly, manner. She didn't realize she was going to hug him until she had done it. He hesitated a moment, then hugged her back.

As Flaco turned Mr. Valentino onto Hesterwine Road and headed for home, Mary again fought back tears. "Miss Clara and Miss Justine would have been so pleased to at least be able to pay the utility bills, but now..." She ducked her head to wipe her cheek on the corner of her collar and noticed that Leeta was frowning intensely at her, as if in horrific pain.

"Oh, Leeta ... he hit you pretty hard, didn't he? Are you okay?"

"No! I'm not okay, I'm nuts! I'm probably as *nuts* as old Miz Etta Ruth Morley!" She jerked her hand from her pocket and shoved a roll of bills at Mary. "*Here*! This is my pay from the Blue Creek Lounge last weekend, plus my damn tips—forty-eight dollars in all. I was saving it to get the hell outta here, but ... give it to Miss Clara to pay the electric bill."

"Leeta, you are *wonderful*! I knew you were. I *always* knew it."

"Shut up ... or I'm taking my money back."

Clarence Morley Jr.'s cream-colored Chevy coupe sat parked near the gate.

Clara and Justine were alone in the parlor.

"Good news!" Leeta called out from the foyer. "We sold enough watermelons to pay the utility bills and then some. Give it to 'em, Mary. I'm gonna go take a nap." She rubbed her sore jaw as she headed for the stairs.

Mary smiled. She and Leeta had agreed not to tell Miss Clara and Miss Justine what happened today. Such news was sure to upset them, and the prospect of losing their home was worry enough. Flaco had nodded in agreement, then opened his mouth wide in silent laughter when Leeta teased him that she was going to tell everybody she heard that he had gotten into a drunken fight at the Mexican beer joint in La Villita and somebody had beat the crap out of him. He then made a motion as if he were drinking a beer. Judging by those older scars on his face, Leeta's story was not so farfetched.

The sisters certainly did not need more worries—especially not Miss Clara, who Mary had discovered handled the brunt of things in the household, from the tiniest problem to the largest. Tonight, when Jack came over, she would tell him what happened, although she doubted he could do anything about it since, like the truck driver stated, the little garden that was Hesterwine, Texas, was currently controlled by a powerful crop of *stinkweeds* and was in bad need of a weed-hating gardener.

Justine sighed. "I can't believe it is taking Clarence Jr. so long to convince Etta Ruth to go home with him. The way she ran out of here when he told her he'd come to get her, one would think he had just said he was going to take her out behind the barn and shoot her. Anyway, thank God, I am so glad she is not going to become a permanent fixture in our lives!"

Just then the elevator rattled downward and Clara, Justine, and Mary expected to see Etta Ruth and Clarence Jr., with his mother's suitcase in hand, pass through the foyer. However, only Clarence Jr. appeared.

He shrugged as he came into the room. "No use, Miss Clara. She's got her arms locked around the bedpost and won't budge. I reckon Momma's dug in for the duration."

"Oh, no," Justine groaned, clearly upset.

"She's just gonna have to handle that situation you and I talked about the best she can, Miss Clara," Clarence Jr. said. "I'll do what I can on the other end, but I don't know what influence I'll have, considering... uh... well, the thing we talked about."

Justine looked suspiciously from him to her sister. "What *situation*? And *considering* what? What have you been talking about?"

"Momma's excessive drinking. What else? She's become a boozer of the worst degree. It's a bad situation, a bad situation," Clarence Jr. repeated as he whipped out his handkerchief and clamped it to his temple in pretense of wiping at perspiration, when he was actually hiding the collaborating wink he directed at Clara.

Justine did not look convinced, but if she was about to say so, Etta Ruth's yelling from the top of the stairs stopped her. The acoustics in the massive and lofty hall were like those in a grand opera house and her voice carried to every corner.

"Go home, Clarence, you ungrateful bastard! I know what you're up to ... and I am not *crazy*! Quit discussing me with those nosy old maids! You got all my money now, so go spend it on that fat harpy you married. Go have a good time! I'm staying right here!"

Clarence Jr. headed for the exit. "I better get going before she busts a gasket. Sorry, Miss Clara, I did my best." He looked at his wristwatch. "I shoulda been back in Houston an hour ago. Wilma's gonna accuse me of every dern thing in the book." He turned at the screen door. "Uh, by the way, do y'all know Momma's got a dern *mannequin* in her room?" He paused as if he wanted to say more, but instead pushed the screen door open and hurried away.

Mary went to Miss Clara's side. The poor woman looked as if the weight of the planet had just dropped onto her shoulders, and Mary knew why— Miz Etta Ruth was dead set on being that 'permanent fixture' that Justine dreaded so.

# 18

Like thousands of towns across America in those times of war, Hesterwine's patriotism shone in its war bond rallies, longer church sermons, and victory gardens growing in nearly every yard and vacant lot, even on the courthouse lawn. Rationing, enforced by government allowances of coupons and tokens to purchase meat, butter, cheese, eggs, sugar, milk, tea, coffee, cooking oil, chocolate, tires, fuel, rubber, shoes, clothing, and many other supplies, was accepted without complaint in the historic little hamlet that once considered *change* of any kind an ominous threat to Southern-style traditions.

One such tradition—as deep-rooted as the giant, centuries-old oak tree that grew on the vacant lot behind Howell's Gas Station—was the loathing of the "Yankee" that started long before the South lost the Civil War to the North over a hundred and twenty year before. Albeit, the spleen did intensify almost beyond reason the moment news reached Hesterwine that Lee had surrendered to Grant. After that, Hesterwinians looked upon anyone not born south of the Mason-Dixon Line as transgressors, nothing less than *"birds of ill omen come to feather their nests on Southern soil."* The recent war with Germany and Japan modified those attitudes. Somewhat.

With the influx of thousands of military men and women from all over America into the navy bases surrounding Hesterwine, *non-southerners* were now as welcome as rain after a ten-year drought—as long as they were there in service to their county via the military. To some in Vander County, like

Sheriff Bloot and those of his segregationist ideology, the uniformed men were welcome as long as they were *white*, Protestant, and non-Jewish. In that regard, Hesterwine, Texas, was like other racially segregated towns. Uniformed *brown* men were welcomed with directions to La Villita, referred to by Bloot and his fellow racists as "Meskin Town." *Colored* military were pointed toward Rose Hill, referred to by Bloot and his sort as "Nigger Town." To the town's credit, there were Hesterwinians who had no use for such vulgar terms.

Lately, due to the lure of Willie Holloway's enchanting talent, more and more colored military from the area's navy bases (two of which were less than twenty miles from Hesterwine) were making Rose Hill's Blue Creek Lounge their favorite hangout. Dink Maxwell's Mississippi blues guitar playing was an added bonus, as was the cooking talents of Dink's wife. Mozelle's fried catfish, slaw, potato salad, pinto beans, corn on the cob, and spicy bread pudding were devoured by the platters-full by the homesick patrons. Also available was beer, wine, and shots of under-the-table whiskey, the latter of which Sheriff Bloot received a fifty-fifty cut on; this, because Dink only had a license to sell beer and wine and not hard liquor, nor was he supposed to allow hard liquor on his premises. Sheriff Bloot had the same deal with all the bars and dancehalls in the county. Those who didn't go along with his demands didn't stay in business long.

On this Friday night, a few days after the stymied antique sale, the Blue Creek Lounge was packed to the walls with new clientele, their neat uniforms almost luminous against the drab interior. Leeta finished her song to loud applause and cries for more. After promising she'd be back in five minutes, she motioned Dink to follow her outside via the back door. He set his guitar aside and obeyed.

"Dink, we are losing money as fast as we make it." She peeked around the corner at the military men milling around in front of the building as they waited for someone to leave so they could get inside. More stood crowded around the open windows.

"Girl, you got to be kidding me! I'm making more folding green than this joint *ever* made before. Hiring you was the best thing I ever done. Them boys never come to my place before you come. A few showed up now and then, but when they see wasn't nothing happening, they up and split."

"That's right, but now they are coming, and every time somebody walks away 'cause he can't get in, we are losing money. Your juke joint is too little, Dink."

"Can't nothing be done 'bout that, Willie. I'm making money, but not enough to build onto the place." He paused to laugh. "The church is the biggest building in Rose Hill, but I don't reckon the pastor gonna let us turn it into a weekend juke joint, do you?" He laughed again.

"I know a place as big as a barn. That's 'cause it *is* a barn. And first thing in the morning, I'm gonna ask the owners if we can use it."

Dink laughed so hard he began to cough. Recovering, he shook his head. "A body sure can tell you ain't from 'round here, Willie, gal. You talking 'bout them old white ladies you live with, ain't you?" He laughed again. "They ain't about to let a bunch of jukin' *niggers* on they place 'less they coming to pick cotton."

"They ain't got no cotton to pick. 'Sides that, you don't know Miss Clara and Miss Justine well as you think you do. They don't talk like that and they don't think like that. They took *me* in, and I'm blacker than you are," she said with a grin as she squinted into his pale greenish-gray eyes. "From the looks of you, I'm more *pure*-blooded than you are, too."

"What you talking 'bout, gal? Don't you know it don't take but a dram of black to make you a bona fide *Negro*? That make me pure as you, I reckon," he said, grinning back.

Leeta waved a dismissive hand at him. "You got to keep this under your hat, but Miss Clara and Miss Justine ain't got but three weeks left to come up with six hundred dollars to pay off their mortgage to the bank. If they don't, they gonna lose the place to that snake, Prickett." She paused. "You ever notice how he looks just like Count Dracula?"

"No, but that's probably all I'm gonna be thinking 'bout now 'til I get another gander at him."

"Anyway, I bet Miss Clara and Miss Justine gonna say yes to us making that money for 'em so they can keep their grandpappy's old plantation. If that don't soften your heart up, you need to consider we'd be making plenty of dough for our own selves, too."

"That's a shame them old ladies might lose the place," he said, suddenly reflective. He rubbed his long, guitar-picking fingers across his thin lip and then his chin. Finally, he nodded. "Go ahead and ask 'em, but I ain't gonna hold my breath." He turned to go back inside but stopped, still rubbing his chin. "I do remember a day, though, when old General Andrew Ignacio Hesterwine went over to the next county and got my grandpap outta jail. My poppa told me 'bout it. This was right after them slave Negroes was set free, my grandpap being one of 'em. The law sayed Grandpap had been going over there to the next county just to stir up the cotton pickers... telling 'em they was getting cheated out'n their rightful pay. Sheriff Bloot's great-grandpappy was the judge over the whole district back then—the 'hanging judge' theys all called him... 'cause he just as soon hang a Negro as look at him. Well anyhow, the general told the judge that my grandpap couldn't be stirring anybody up 'cause he been working for *him* for weeks and hadn't left off the place."

"So, old Hesterwine told the truth. That don't make him no hero in my book."

"He lied through his teeth and didn't blink an eye doing it. Grandpap was getting over to that next county every chance he got and raising the rabble, just like they accused him of doing. After the general testify that day, he told my grandpap he ain't seen a nigger yet that needed hanging or jailing just 'cause he was trying to help his own kind from being cheated out'n their hard-earned twenty-five cents. That old white man had a soft spot in his heart for Negroes, that for sure."

"Ha! Miss Justine said the old fart owned a dozen slaves and their families before the war, and afterward, belonged to the Klan, or so said Miz Etta Ruth. I don't see him as having a soft spot for Negroes."

"All I know is, Grandpap said when the slaves got freed, the old general paid to have all them *colored* drinking fountains put in town so the colored folks could have water and not have to beg a cup."

"Well, wasn't that *white* of the old poop," she chortled. "You ever stop to think he paid for them colored fountains because he didn't want them freed Negroes drinking out of the *white* fountains?"

"You too suspicious for your own good, Willie."

"And you're too *Uncle Tom* for yours, *Uncle* Dink," she said, smiling as he pretended to slap her.

The crowd inside the Blue Creek Lounge began calling out her name. Dink took her arm and headed back inside. "Girl, I see our new steady customer, Hank Posey, must be having a good influence on you when he take you home every night the way he been doing."

Leeta again waved a dismissive hand at him. "What you talking 'bout, man?"

"Number one, you want to help them old ladies. Number two, you called the general an old poop, but I knowed a time when you woulda called him a lot worse just as natural as if you was breathing."

"Oh yeah? Well, *you* are an old poop, *too*." She paused at the back door to sweep out her arm and motion him to enter ahead of her. "Get your skinny old bones on that guitar stool, old poop ... and tell that fine crowd to give your star attraction a big hand."

At breakfast, Clara and Justine sat with elbows on the table, their hands clamped firmly to their delicately powdered and lightly rouged cheeks. Mary and Leeta, watching the pair intensely, hoped they were about to do the unthinkable for ladies of their standing in the community ... and allow their rambling old barn to be temporarily turned into a *"colored juke joint."* The girls grew even tenser when one of Clara's hands slid around to her mouth and a finger began tapping at her upper lip.

"But, Willie, dear, you keep saying *juke joint*, but don't you think we should call our barn a *canteen?*"

Wide grins enlivened the girls' faces as Justine added, "After all, the larger cities have gathering places for military men and women, and they call them *canteens*. Goldrod's is one, of a sort, when the buses and trains stop over and those fine young men dance with our town girls to the tunes on that beautiful old Wurlitzer."

"Goldrod's is a *whites only* canteen, Miss Justine," Leeta said. "*Your* canteen gonna have a real live *blues* band, not no jukebox—and *lots* of color ... nothing *but* color."

"Yes, we know, dear. However, we do not feel right about you telling Dink Maxwell that renting the barn will cost him six hundred dollars. It seems to me a disproportionate figure."

"It ain't enough?"

"It is far too much, even if it is the exact amount we need to pay Banker Prickett," Justine said.

Clara nodded. "Yes. Well, apparently Mr. Maxwell doesn't think it's too much to pay, and if he insists, I suppose we shall have to accept the six hundred."

Justine frowned. "But what if the military folks don't show up? After all, it is *still* just an old barn five miles from town."

"They'll come." Leeta pulled a flyer from her pocket. "Me and Mary gonna make a bunch of these, and Mr. Jack gonna fly 'em to the bases. Some of 'em fellas done know what a great band me and Dink got, and since we now gonna have room, the word's gonna spread. Then colored fellas and their dates will be here by the carload."

Justine's frown deepened. "But what if Sheriff Bloot finds out?"

"So what if he does," Clara replied. "It's none of his business if we want to have a private party for folks who are in service to our country—a private party for *colored only*."

Leeta grinned. "Me and Dink was thinking 'bout charging two dollars at the door. What you think, Miss Clara?"

"I don't think it's too much. After all, it isn't as if Justine and I will be accepting *charity*. We will be providing a much-desired service to those young folks in uniform."

"Good," Mary said. "With the cover charge, food, and beer sales, you will earn more than enough to pay Banker Pricket, even after expenses. I am so excited!"

"*Beer*?" Clara looked surprised. "The only alcohol Poppa ever allowed on the place—other than his private collection he kept locked away—was Grandfather's special recipe, and then it was mostly only used on holidays and was our only beverage for toasting special occasions."

Justine laughed. "Oh, my, what memories the mention of that special recipe conjures up! One time, when Clara was ten and Etta Ruth and I were eight, the three of us snuck into the smokehouse where Grandfather kept all those barrels of it and had our fill." She giggled at the memory. "Actually, it was Etta Ruth who dared us to do it—just as she always dared us to do things that got us in trouble. It tasted just like delicious Delaware Punch. We drank so much that we became quite ill."

"*Drunk*, I believe is the correct word," Clara said stiffly. "And we were each punished with a tablespoon of castor oil and no supper—except Etta Ruth, of course. Her mother put a cold rag on her head and gave her peach ice cream."

"I suppose that little lesson in life made teetotalers out of us both, Clara. However, as to having *beer* at Hesterwine Place, Poppa would surely have something to say about *that* if he were here. I can hear him yelling at us now and—"

"You can?" Clara interrupted. "Then tell him to butt out. And while you're at it, tell him that if it weren't for him, there would be no need for us to come up with six hundred dollars in less than three weeks so that we won't be thrown out on the street." She turned to Leeta. "Beer it is."

"Yes, beer it is! That is exactly what I was going to say, Clara, if you had let me finish," Justine cried, as if she'd just been cheated out of her say.

"Goodness, we are finally agreeing on something," Clara quipped.

"On *something*, but not *everything*, Clara. You are mistaken about us only toasting holidays and special occasions with Grandfather's recipe. We toasted with *champagne* on *truly* special occasions."

"I don't think so," Clara said.

"Yes, we did. Don't you remember the night you were to announce your engagement to—" Justine suddenly looked shocked by her own words. Her big eyes were like those of an ailing puppy dog as she stared pleadingly at Clara. However, it was too late; Clara's chest was heaving in anger.

"He is always on your mind, isn't he!" Her owlish eyes fairly bulged at her sister, and she turned to Mary and Leeta. "Justine is correct. I was to announce my engagement to be married that night and indeed we were to drink a toast to my happiness from an especially fine bottle of *champagne* ... *not* Grandfather's recipe." She turned with slow deliberation back to Justine even as she continued to speak to Mary and Leeta. "But lo and behold, Mary, Willie, I came downstairs to find that, *for the second* time in my life, my *sister* had absconded with that fine bottle of champagne ... *and my fiancé!*"

*And his name was Boyd Pendleton,* Mary instantly thought, remembering that day in the attic when Etta Ruth opened that Pandora's box. Suddenly, the frequent flare-ups of hostility between the elderly sisters were no longer a mystery. Mary glanced at Leeta and knew she was thinking the same thing. More than once they'd suspected that the *past* weighed larger in Clara and Justine Hesterwine's daily consciousness than the present, and now they were sure of it.

A distant howl coming from somewhere outside interrupted whatever was going to happen next:

"Bombs away! Bombs away!" cried a familiar voice.

Justine's shame-faced expression abruptly altered to one of relief. She edged her way to the back door. "You go ahead and finish your breakfast, Clara. I shall coax Etta Ruth down from the windmill this time." Her eyes were on Clara as if she was edging her way around a coiled rattlesnake. "I still don't see how she can climb up there, at her age," she added nervously, as if that had been the topic of the conversation all the while.

"She's got legs like a lumberjack, that's how," Clara growled.

Mary and Leeta, wide-eyed at the horrifying thought of Etta Ruth Morley having again climbed to the very top of the rickety old windmill, shot out the back door behind Justine.

"Oh my goodness!" Justine cried over her shoulder. "The wind is blowing ferociously today! I do hope she hasn't been blown right off that platform!"

Hurrying down the worn trail that led to the windmill, they could hear the frantic squeaks of the blades whirling in the hellacious wind. Clutching her skirt against the blustery assault, and almost disbelieving that Etta Ruth would be there, Mary rounded the corner of the house and looked up. Sure enough, Etta Ruth, in her usual state of nakedness beneath her flimsy slip and robe, sat straddle-legged on the platform's edge, her chunky legs swinging back and forth, her red silk robe billowing straight out behind her like a set of flaming wings. As they stared, the wind curled the robe over Etta Ruth's head and she punched and jabbed it away as if sparring with an assailant.

Justine called up to her. "No! No! No! Don't do that, Etta Ruth! You might fall!"

Etta Ruth leaned precariously forward to look down at them. All three gasped, thinking she would surely tumble over the edge.

Justine twisted her hands in her apron. "Won't you come down now? Your breakfast is ready. Please, dear cousin ... come down! You are scaring us half to death!"

Silent, Etta Ruth leaned out yet further, and then spat. The wind carried the saliva away before it could land on target. Even so, Justine jumped aside and shook a finger at Etta Ruth before addressing the girls.

"This is the fourth time it has happened that we know about. She climbs up there sometime during the night. We have never seen her go up and would not have known she was doing it if Flaco hadn't banged on the back door one day and motioned for us to follow him out here. She usually makes us plead an hour or so before she climbs down, but then she tells us to leave *first*. You can imagine what nervous wrecks we are until we see her come in the house acting like she's just been out for a stroll."

"How terrible for you and Miss Clara," Mary said, gazing up at Etta Ruth. "Why didn't you tell Willie and me? Perhaps we could have talked her out of going up there at all."

Justine rolled her eyes helplessly. "I don't know; I suppose Clara and I were embarrassed for anyone to know that we had a relative who would be so craz—uh, who would be so *adventurous* at her age. We were relieved that you hadn't seen her sitting up there like the Queen of Sheba. It was bad enough that two sheriff's deputies saw her once when they drove by on their rounds. I think we convinced them that she'd been crawling up there lately to oil those screeching blades because their awful racket kept her awake at night. They had to threaten her with Clarence Jr. before she would come down. I asked the deputies not to tell anybody about it because folks may not understand about the squeaking windmill blades needing to be oiled, you know, and they said they wouldn't breathe a word of it."

"Neither will Willie and I, Miss Justine," Mary assured the distraught woman.

"Oh, thank you, dear. You are such a blessing to Clara and me, which surely makes you *family*, as far and Clara and I are concerned."

"I am flattered that you feel that way, and I know Willie is, too," Mary said, with an eye still on Etta Ruth.

Obviously delighted, Justine looked to Leeta for affirmation.

Leeta's head did a slight bobble, a gesture that could be taken as a yes, but she dodged verbal confirmation by shading her eyes against the sun's glare and squinting up at Etta Ruth. "Is that all she do, just sit up there swinging her legs like that?"

"Well, she spits a lot," Justine replied.

"Maybe she's trying to make up her mind to jump."

Justine was genuinely surprised at Willie's remark. "Oh, no, dear. I think that was just a threat she made to aggravate Clara and me. Why would she want to kill herself? From the day she was born, she never had a care in the world, other than a cheating husband, but many women have those. I know of quite a few in our church group alone, and they don't make up a fraction of the town's population of fornicators. Still, I have yet to hear of a wife committing suicide over a husband's dalliances, especially not if she's been married as long as Etta Ruth and Clarence were married. Nor do they commit suicide when their husbands die. Vernell Watson told me that when she caught her husband, Harlan, cheating, she just got even by spending lots of money. To this day she keeps up the practice, just in case he's still doing it." With that, she grasped Mary's hand. "Try and coax her down, won't you, Mary? She is fonder of you than she is of anyone else in the house. I've never heard her swear at you the way she does the rest of us, telling us to do that awful thing to ourselves."

Mary, after first clearing her throat in an effort to compete with the screeching windmill and the whistling wind, cupped her hands around her mouth, leaned her head far back and yelled, "I will meet you halfway on the ladder, Miz Etta, if you start down now. Please?"

Etta Ruth's reply, a deep croak that rose clearly over all other decibels of racket, likely carried all the way up to the house.

"Piss off, Yankee!"

Jack Dunston, Hank Posey, Flaco Rosales, and a dozen of Hank's friends and relatives from Rose Hill cleaned out the rambling old barn and painted it azure blue inside and out. "As azure blue as Mary Kenny's eyes," Jack said. Mr. Valentino did the work of dragging away the heavy stall timbers. Once the barn became an empty blue hull, the men laid a smooth plank floor in the barn's vast middle, courtesy of Ewald's Lumber. In asking for the flooring, Jack simply told Mr. Ewald that the kindly Hesterwine sisters were volunteering their barn for a special entertainment event for the colored military who had no place to go when they came to Hesterwine. The generous man, a Fourth-Degree Knight of the Knights of Columbus, was almost gleeful in his desire to help. He'd had a fondness for Clara and Justine that stretched as far back as grammar school.

"However," he said to Jack, "in high school, I made the mistake of saying I liked them both *equally*, and that innocent disclosure soured them on me real quick." He scratched his head. "Now that I think about it, I actually liked Clara better, but that Justine was always bigger than life, you know."

All was going well at the barn until Dink suddenly remembered that his license to sell beer was legal *only* at the Blue Creek Lounge.

"Most them military boys like a little alcohol refreshment with their music, Miss Clara," Dink said as the two stood gazing at the prepared barn. "I'm sure sorry I didn't think 'bout my beer license being no good out here."

Clara was not discouraged. "We shall proceed Saturday night as planned, Mr. Maxwell. I am sure those young folks will not mind quenching their thirst on Grandfather's old recipe. We have *five* fifty-five gallon barrels of it in the smokehouse, and just as many in the basement."

Dink's eyes lit up. "I tasted your Poppa's *recipe* plenty times, Miss Clara, when I used to help your poppa come hog killin' time. Them boys gonna like it just fine."

"I am certain they will, Mr. Maxwell. It tastes just like delicious Delaware Punch."

Dink hesitated. "But ... I ain't so sure we don't need a license to sell that there Delaware Punch, Miss Clara, the same as I needs a license to sell beer."

"Oh no, Mr. Maxwell, we would never dream of *selling* Poppa's special recipe. We shall put a donation basket atop the keg, and if those generous young men want to donate a quarter or two each time they draw a cup, that will be *their* business and none of ours."

Dink chuckled. "You use your head just like your grandpappy always did, Miss Clara. My pappy told me the old general was a saint ... always thinking a mile ahead of everybody else."

"Grandfather was no saint," Clara said, and scoffed lightly. "Fact is, he could be quite the devil."

Dink nodded politely again. "Well, you know what they say, Miss Clara, 'The devil most always in the details.'"

# 19

SATURDAY MORNING BEFORE THE NIGHT OF THE DANCE, "the devil and his *details*" converged on Leeta as she sat in Hank Posey's pickup truck in front of Christ Emmanuel Baptist Church, waiting for him to open the door for her. She looked around at the empty cars in the grassy parking lot. *I must have been crazy to let him talk me into coming here on baptizing day just 'cause his two little sisters gonna be baptized. Besides that, we're late!* Shuddering, she realized that the pews must be full of Rose Hill's "holier-than-thou" by now—the ones who'd just as soon wrestle Lucifer himself than step inside the Blue Creek Lounge to hear her sing.

Hank had gotten out of the truck a good five minutes ago and caught up to two middle-aged men. *What the hell are they talking about so long?* She could have sworn Hank jerked his head toward her once as he spoke, and both men turned to stare at her. She gave them a dirty look. *Ain't much telling what he telling them two! Well, it's a damn lie! I ain't give him anything to talk about ... yet.*

Finally he strolled up, grinning, and opened the door with great ceremony—something he'd insisted on doing ever since he made himself her only source of transportation to and from work. As sort of a lark, she was okay with Hank's attention and door-opening chivalry. She also considered it a lark that she had agreed to come with him today. "After the way he been so nice to me, how could I refuse?" That's what she had said to Mary as his old pickup truck pulled up in front of the house that morning.

Now, here she was, and it was too late to back out.

"I don't know 'bout this, Hank," she said as he escorted her across the parking lot toward the church. She craned her neck sideways to look beyond the trees at the river running placidly behind the little white clapboard church. "Ain't we supposed to be going to the river to watch your sisters get baptized?"

"Yeah, but my poppa always does a little Saturday preaching first to get everybody in the right frame of mind."

"You didn't tell me *that*." She gave him a piercing look.

"The walls ain't gonna fall in on you, *Willie*. I promise."

She recoiled slightly as he pushed the wide church door open and she looked inside. This was one time she didn't want to make a grand entrance with all eyes turning to her, but they were late, and the church was full.

She slowed her step despite Hank's tugging and tried to remember the last time she'd been in a church. Suddenly, the memory was there. She was nine... around the time her mother's drinking and late hours of entertaining at the Mississippi juke joint left her too hungover to get out of bed and set her little brood of young'uns on the righteous path to Faithful in Christ Baptist Church a mile down the road from their shack. She, Leeta, was supposed to be baptized that Sunday, along with her brothers and sisters, but none of them made it. Later that day, the preacher came to see why they hadn't shown up. Momma, still hungover, made him wait at the door while she fixed her hair and put on her lipstick. Then, she went outside and cussed him right off the front porch. After that, Leeta didn't know if it was embarrassment or fear that kept her away from the preacher and his congregation, but she never went back—not to any church.

She shuddered, wondering why she had let Hank talk her into coming here. *He was too damn convincing last night, that's why, and it scared me. I don't need to get crazy about anybody!* To her shock, he had suggested that *she* get baptized alongside his sisters, of all things! She had screeched an emphatic "NO!" Finally, they struck a compromise. She'd go to the baptism if he'd stop asking her to go to church with him on Sundays. The compromise, however, did not stop him from trying to convince her that she needed baptizing.

"Even if you decide never to go back to church again, Leeta, you still need to be baptized—for your own protection."

"You think if I got baptized that it gonna keep the devil from getting me?" she'd laughed, even while thinking that the only devil she'd ever feared was that Chicago devil, Mandingo Q. Mann. She hadn't told Hank about him. The more she saw of this clean-living, calmly down-to-earth, Hopalong-Cassidy-style cowboy, the more she doubted she ever would tell him about her past. He'd probably jump on that white horse of his and head for the hills so fast all she'd see was his dust—not that she cared.

The previous night as he drove her home, Hank looked at his watch and said, "Yes, ma'am, Leeta Bulow, my stubborn gal, I think being baptized might help keep the devil off man, woman, or child. I ain't as religious as my preacher-man daddy, but I believe most everything he preaches. And I believe, at ten thirty in the morning, exactly eight hours from now, you need to be baptized in the river behind Christ Emmanuel Baptist Church. What could it hurt?"

"No! And hell no! So shut up about it."

Shaking his head, Hank had shut up, and she relaxed. Later, after he walked her to the front door of the old mansion and told her good night, she lay in bed staring out the window at the star-filled sky, wondering if maybe she really should be among the baptized of the world. The state of being baptized might be reassuring, even if not redeeming. Besides, Hank wanted it for her. She and this Hopalong-Cassidy-style cowboy had evolved from the arguing stage to the hugging and kissing stage, and she could see her and Hank Posey actually *doing it* some night real soon. She rather liked the idea of him becoming a more intimate part of her life—at least until she saved enough money to leave Hesterwine, Texas, and him, behind. But get baptized for him? Uh-uh.

Hank ushered her all the way down to the front row. Nervous, and looking neither left nor right at the dozens of eyes she knew were skimming her from head to toe, she watched only the tall, portly man with no neck and a shiny bald spot standing behind the pulpit with his back to them. She wondered if Hank's father was as sweet as his son. Hank said he was. She sat down, folded her hands in her lap, and waited for him to turn around.

When the Reverend Henry Posey Sr. finally faced the congregation, it was hard to determine which happened first—*his* eyes bulging at *her* in shocked recognition ... or *her* eyes bulging at *him*.

"*Pee pants!*" Too late, her hand slapped to her mouth.

A censorious murmur rose in the room as the Reverend Henry Posey Sr.'s stare crawled furiously from the top of her head down to her shoes and then back again ... just as had happened on the bus. The look on his pudgy face was as readable as the big "*We Save Souls*" sign on the wall behind him. The sparks of flashback shooting from his protruding eyes said he was not seeing the demure black-and-white polka-dot dress and sweet little hat she had picked from the attic especially for this occasion. Nor was he seeing the sensible, flat-heeled, black patent leather shoes she wore. Instead, he was seeing the three-inch, fake leopard-skin platform heels, the tight, short skirt, and the filmy peek-a-boo blouse she had worn on the bus.

Finally, he fixed his son with a perplexed stare that all but screamed his disapproval. Then, he stepped behind the pulpit, tossed aside his notes, and slammed his fist down hard on the Bible. Everyone in the room, including Leeta and Hank, jumped. Somewhere behind them, a child's rift of giggles ended with a slap.

"The *WORD* of the LORD," rumbled the Reverend Henry Posey Sr. "The word of the Lord fills me this very minute, and as much as I want to ignore it, I cannot! I cannot close my ears to it, even should I cover them!" He clamped his big hands to his ears and then dropped his arms. Silent, he stared ferociously at Leeta, the congregation straining their necks to get a better look at her.

At last, while still staring daggers, he raised one arm, jerking it spasmodically, making a big show of struggling with the effort to raise it as if an invisible power was holding it down. "I cannot *slap* the word of the Lord away! I cannot *raise* my foot and kick it away!" He struggled to raise his foot the same as he had struggled with his arm. His eyes bugged at Leeta. "*Why* can I not follow every urge of my being, every caution in my soul, every twist in my gut, and send this *Salome*, this seductress daughter of Herod, *away* from this holy place?" He boomed the question, emphasizing each word with a trembling vibrato that filled the clapboard interior.

An unnatural silence prevailed in the room as each man, woman, and child waited to know *why*—all except Leeta. She had launched into her Joe Lewis attitude, chin and chest up and out, her narrowing eyes locked with his, her breath coming and going in loud puffs. She felt Hank's hand close over hers, but his touch did nothing to sever her heated connection with his father.

"Why?" continued the reverend. "Because our Lord, Jesus Christ, speaketh unto me through the Gospel of Matthew, that's why!"

Suddenly, he extended an open hand, and Leeta thought he pointed it at her. He picked up his Bible with the other hand and held it over his head. "The Pharisees asked the Lord's disciple Matthew why his teacher sat down at the table and ate with tax collectors and sinners." The reverend made a wide sweep of his arm to indicate the entire room, ending with a pointed finger aimed, unmistakably this time, at Leeta. "When Jesus heard it, he said to them, *Those who are healthy have no need for a physician, but those who are sick, do.*' Then the Lord said to them, *'But you go and learn what this means.'* The preacher paused a long moment to study his congregation.

Leeta angrily waited for his condemnation... ready to tell him—she wasn't sure what she would tell him, but she'd try to keep from adding any dirty words—*after all, this is a da— a church.*

"What do you suppose the Lord meant when he told Matthew to go and learn what that means?" Reverend Posey continued. "Do you think he meant that, at that point in Matthew's training as a disciple of our Lord Jesus Christ, Matthew had not yet learned what Christ meant when he commanded—yes, *commanded*—that we love the *sinner* as well as the saint? That we love our fellow man as we love ourselves... even if that sorry sinner is sure enough bound for the fires of Satan?"

Leeta, slightly calmed by this last pronouncement but still bristling, watched the preacher gaze meaningfully at his congregation, taking his time doing it, before staring at her again. The only thing that kept her from leaping to her feet and bolting to the door, which at this point looked a mile away, was the feel of Hank's firm but gentle hand holding hers on the pew.

She jumped, like everyone else, when the preacher slammed his fist on the Bible again and roared, "I desire mercy, and not sacrifice, said the Lord to Matthew that day among the tax collectors and sinners, 'for I came not to call the righteous, but the *sinners.*'"

A murmur of "amen!" and "hallelujah!" and "yes, Jesus Lord!" rolled over Leeta's head in undulating waves of enthusiasm. With that, Reverend Posey closed his Bible. Then, after reciting from memory several passages from The book of Hosea on the sins of "whoredom" and "prostitution," he did his entire sermon—an hour and fifteen minutes of growls and roars and diminutive whispers—on the Lord's demand for forgiveness of sins, *"even those sins of the fallen Jezebels of this world."*

At last he made a beckoning motion, and Leeta looked over her shoulder at the sound of shuffling feet to see four young women and two small boys come trotting up the aisle. When they were abreast the front row, two of the girls, who looked a lot like Hank, left the others and stepped over to her, grabbed her arms, and attempted to pull her from the pew.

"Come on. We got to change clothes and go get dunked in the river," said one of the girls.

Leeta stiffened up like a fossilized mummy, leaning so far back that she would have dropped on her head if the girls had released her arms. Panicking, she whispered to Hank, "You lied to me, Hank Posey! I told you, I ain't about to let myself get dunked in no river!"

The girls were tugging on her and the preacher was eyeing her up and down again, looking as if he was ready to backslide from his Christian teachings and forget about loving the *sinner* as well as the saint. He jabbed a finger in her direction, scowling so hard that his face resembled a giant pitted prune.

"Come with me and be cleansed of sin through baptism, girl. Come humble and ashamed into that river. Wade through the murkiness and muddiness of your sinful life!" He threw up his hands and spread his arms wide. "I feel the Spirit of the Lord, people! You feel it? You feel it? Pass it on!"

The congregation began jumping and bouncing, shouting with "the Spirit of the Lord." The wood floor creaked and vibrated beneath Leeta's feet as the two girls holding onto her jumped up and down, joggling her stiff body between them.

"Go ahead, honey!" Hank yelled over the noise. "Do it for your own self, and if that ain't good enough, do it for me!"

She stared at him, trying to break free so she could kick him where it hurt. When the girls finally let loose, she straightened her clothes and lopsided hat, then glowered at him.

"All right! I'll do it! But I'm doing it for the *hell of it*, Hank Posey, and *just* for the hell of it, not for me, you, or nobody else!" She blew at the fake curls that dangled over her left eye from beneath the pert little hat and allowed the girls to lead her away.

Barefoot, and with her polka-dot dress, hat, and pocketbook hanging on a nail in the back room of Christ Emmanuel Baptist Church, and wearing two heavy layers of white "holy robes" that turned out to be bed sheets with round holes cut in the center to get her head through, she tripped down to the river behind the others.

The crowd along the bank slowly waved their arms above their heads as they sang "All God's Children Got Wings."

As they sang, two pious-faced men escorted the four young women and two little boys, one by one, into the water. The preacher prayed over them, and then dunked them. Leeta watched, wanting to run, but Hank held her to the spot. All too soon, Reverend Posey wiggled a beckoning finger at her. Her panic rose. She hated water deeper than could be held in a number two galvanized washtub, which was how she and her siblings bathed when she was a kid—one tub of bathwater to wash all. They had drawn straws to see who got first water, and by the time the last kid got their bath, the water was brown with Mississippi dirt and peed in by one or more of the younger ones. This river was the color of that old bath water ... and much deeper!

Fear of drowning constricted Leeta's throat so tightly that she froze, unable to move or to scream. Hank stepped aside, and the two men who had escorted the others grasped each stiffened arm and pulled her dead weight through the water to the reverend, as if they were dragging a waterlogged stump. He recited biblical words that she was too terrified to hear. Then, as if in a nightmare, she felt his big hand grip the back of her neck and saw the other monstrous hand, with thick fingers spread like claws, coming over her face. She screamed, but it was too late. All in the same instant, he clamped her nose and tried to drown her.

Then she popped upright again, sputtering for breath, her sopping hairpiece plastered over her eyes like octopus tendrils, blinding her. With a shriek she jerked it off her head and, not waiting for her deacon escort, plowed her way back to shore, fighting the clinging sheets every step of the way. Suddenly Hank was beside her in the water, keeping her upright.

"Calm down, honey. You're fine. You did it. You should be feeling mighty good 'bout yourself right now."

The way he was grinning enraged her even more. Jerking loose, she gathered up the anchoring sheets and stomped the rest of the way to the shore while continually pushing his hands away. The hymn singing had stopped, and every member of Christ Emmanuel Baptist Church was gawking silently at her again, most of them frowning—except the children; *they* were giggling behind their hands. *The little shits,* she thought, glaring at them. Hank stayed abreast, arms ready to catch her.

"Damn you and that old fart daddy of yours, Hank Posey! He almost drowned me! And don't tell me it wasn't on purpose!"

"He didn't hold you under any longer than he did the others, Leeta. He dunked you real fast. I reckon it wasn't no more than three seconds. You just got panicked, that's all."

"He damn sure did it a lot longer than three seconds! I oughta know how long I had to hold my breath!"

Out of the water, she whirled to face him. "I wish to hell you'd stop trying to make me something I ain't!" She stormed away.

Hank threw up his hands. "I guess getting baptized was a big waste of your time, Leeta!" he called after her.

"No!" she shot over her shoulder. "It wasn't a total waste of my time—I *peed* while I was in there!"

# 20

ETTA RUTH TURNED UP HER MASON JAR and drained it. Then, as if in morose contemplation of what to do next, she dragged herself out of the big leather chair in the parlor and headed to the kitchen for a refill, but then detoured to the front door at the sound of a car pulling up out front. She watched Willie get out of her "lover-boy's" old truck, slam the door, then bang the gate just as hard. Suddenly, the cloud engulfing Etta Ruth's face lifted. *Someone besides me is having a bad day,* she thought, and tittered. She plastered herself behind the door like a Mata Hari spy as Willie, clutching her fake hairpiece in her hand, stormed past and headed straight for the stairs. Etta Ruth followed.

Upstairs, Willie knocked loudly on Mary's door before barging in. "We'll Meet Again" played on the old phonograph in Mary's room.

Etta Ruth looked disgusted. *I'm gonna celebrate when that damn record finally wears out,* she thought as she tiptoed across the hall to get a chair so she could stand on it and peer over the transom. *I'm a visual person. I like to see what I'm hearing.*

Leeta glared at the phonograph. "Girl, I can't believe you carried that damned record in that beat-up old suitcase all the way from New Jersey. I know who you're thinking of every time you play the damn thing. When you gonna stop being stupid?" She slammed her wet hairpiece over the bedpost.

Etta Ruth nodded. *Yep, Willie must be real upset, picking on the Yankee like that.*

Mary glanced at the wig. "Looks like Hank took you fishing again."

"No, he ain't took me fishing again! I got baptized in the goddamn river! Jesus Pete! Your eyes are all puffy! You been crying over that damn Claxton Mitchell, ain't you? I thought you were getting over him. Stop playing that damn record!"

*Who is Claxton Mitchell?* Etta Ruth wondered.

"Gee, Leeta, getting baptized sure put you in a bad mood."

*Leeta? Who in the hell is Leeta?* Etta Ruth saw only Mary and *Willie Holloway* in the room.

"We ain't talking 'bout me just now. We're talking 'bout you still pining after a sorry bastard that treated you like dog crap."

"I can't help how I feel, Leeta. But to tell the truth, I am getting a little confused over—"

"You *can* help it, dammit! Just keep reminding yourself that he dumped you. Maybe you being so upset over that asshole caused your baby to be born dead, you ever think of that?"

*Hummm,* Etta Ruth thought. *Little Miss Innocence has a past after all.*

"That was a cruel thing to say, Leeta." Mary went over and lifted the needle from the record.

"Maybe so, but it makes me boil just knowing if that jerk came back from the dead and snapped his fingers at you, you'd jump right into his arms. But he ain't coming back. He's dead."

"He was reported 'missing in action and *presumed* dead'—which means he could still be alive. He could be a prisoner somewhere. If that is true, then he never got my letters. Never knew I was going to have his baby."

"If he knew, he probably woulda made you get rid of it, like Mandingo Q. Mann did me."

*What the hell?* Etta Ruth wondered.

"Leeta ... oh my God! I always thought you simply miscarried!"

"I did, but it weren't simple. Mandingo gave me such a beating when I told him he was gonna be a father ..." She turned away from Mary's shocked stare.

Outside the door, Etta Ruth, looking furious, pushed her uncombed hair away from her face. *He did it on purpose! The son of a bitch!*

"I am so sorry," Mary barely whispered.

"Yeah, me too," Leeta muttered, then turned around to gaze intently at Mary. "That asshole Claxton wasn't good enough for you, Mary." She sounded almost pleading. "Hell, he wouldn't a been good enough for *me*, even on my sorriest day back in Chicago."

*Ah-ha*, Etta Ruth thought. *Aunt Lucy knows what she's talking about, after all.* She watched the girl she had known as *Willie* pick up a handkerchief and hand it to teary-eyed Mary.

"I hope the bastard is dead and you find it out real soon so you'll forget about him."

"It is not right to wish someone dead, Leeta."

"I wish Mandingo Q. Mann was dead. If he was dead, he wouldn't be looking for me so he can kill me. I gotta be on the move soon."

Etta Ruth's eyes widened. *Whaaat? Somebody's looking to kill sassy-face?*

"I truly believe you are safe here, Leeta. I wish you would stay."

"I can't take that chance. And, Mary, when I'm gone, I'd like to think you ain't still fooling yourself about that ex-boyfriend of yours."

"I ... there is something I have not told you, Leeta. A few days after I decided to stay in Hesterwine, I wrote to my father's girlfriend and told her that if by some miracle Claxton comes home and asks for me, she is to give him this address."

"You left your address for that bastard? I can't believe it! Let's say he's alive and wants to make up; you'd be making the mistake of your life to take him back."

"Before you say anything else, I admit I wish I had waited a while longer before sending that letter because ... because even though I still have unfinished feelings for Claxton, I think Jack Dunston and I are ... becoming close. He says he cares for me, and I like him very much. But ... Oh! I am so confused!" She jumped up and crossed the room to stare out the window.

"Whoa!" Leeta yelped. "These country boys work fast, don't they? Hopalong Hank Posey got that same notion. He ain't said the love word out loud yet, but it's as plain on his face as the horse poop on his boots."

Mary came back to the bed and sat down next to Leeta. "I think if Hank pops the question, you should accept. He is a real gentleman—exactly what you once told me you wanted in a man. I would not be surprised if he got down on his knees when he asks."

"He wasn't no 'real gentleman' today," Leeta huffed. "He almost got me drowned in the damn river by his old man." She jerked her hairpiece off the bedpost and started fluffing it with her fingers. "If he gets down on his knees to propose, he can just crawl on off into the sunset. I ain't about to marry nobody. I'm gonna be a big-time singer when I get to California. Hank Posey or nobody else is gonna tie me to a cook stove all day and squeaky bedsprings all night. I got a dream, and I'm gonna stick with it 'til it comes true."

"My dream about Claxton was that strong, but I think I am discovering that dreams can change."

"That ain't no *dream* you have of Claxton, it's a damn nightmare." Leeta made a face. "*Claxton.* What kinda name is that, anyhow? Sound like a damn venereal disease," she said, and then hooted. "Whooee! Poor Mary Kenny's got *Claxton,* and now she gonna need a lifetime supply of penicillin!"

Watching the two girls laugh, Etta Ruth tittered behind her hand. *That Leeta's got a way of trying to change somebody's mind,* she thought as she rested her chin on top of the transom in plain sight if the girls happened to look up. If so, they might invite her to join them, and she could add her two cents to the conversation.

"When I've earned enough dough to get to California, I'd sure feel better knowing you were married to Jack Dunston, rather than mooning after old *Claxton.*"

Mary reached over and touched Leeta's hand. "You are the best friend I ever had, Leeta. I am going to miss you."

"If it weren't for Mandingo Q. Mann looking to cut my throat, I could make a name for myself singing and still have a hometown like Hesterwine, Texas, to come back to every now and then."

*Dummy!* Etta Ruth thought. *If you make a name for yourself singing, he's gonna find you.*

"If he finds me in California," Leeta continued, "maybe I *will* have made a name for myself and got too rich to kill. He'd want a part of the action. I'd give it to him. I'd just have to accept it. I was making him lots of dough singing at his club. That's what he misses, the money. He thinks he owns me ... he swore nobody else ever would."

"You said he is crazy mean. He may kill you anyway, no matter how successful you are. What if we tell the authorities about him, Leeta, and ask for protection?"

"The *authorities*? I know you ain't forgot that the authorities around here is none other than Sheriff Bloot. You really think *he's* gonna give a damn if I get my throat cut? If Mandingo finds me here, he's gonna kill me ... maybe Hank, too, and anybody who gets in his way."

The sound of the elevator grinding slowly up the shaft, accompanied by a familiar husky voice singing "Swing Low, Sweet Chariot," wrested Etta Ruth away from her ringside intrusion into the girls' pasts. She scooted the chair back to its spot, then leaned against the wall to await the slow ascent of the elevator. *Clara and Justine are back from that damn twice-monthly Hesterwine Medallion's meeting and are sending Aunt Lucy up to spy on me*, she thought ... *just like everyone else spies on me—the grocer, the soda jerk, strangers on the street, even the schoolkids....* She laughed aloud, thinking that her two cousins would croak if they knew how many times she had peeked over their bedroom transoms to spy on *them*.

Her passion for spying had greatly improved her knowledge. For instance, she'd learned that Clara still took several spoons of Lydia Pinkham every night, although she'd passed menopause decades ago, and she greased her face with so much Palm's Cold Cream before climbing into bed that a ghost would think she was one of them. She and Justine both primped in front of their mirrors most every night, lifting and poking at their cheeks as if trying to put everything back to where it once was. They reminded her of the two old peacocks that pranced among the other fowl in the chicken pen out back. The two birds fought each other to stand before a little mirror someone had hung on the fence, their heads twisting and bobbing while they stared curiously at themselves. Clara shelled and ate peanuts in bed. In one of Justine's bureaus drawers, there was an old 1902 Hamilton Beach electric vibrator. *Ha!*

*One indeed could learn a lot peeking over the transom*, she thought. Just moments ago, she'd learned enough about those annoying Yankee girls to fill half her journal—the white one capable of loving only a lout, and the colored one incapable of loving anything but a dream of fame.

The elevator ground to a stop and Aunt Lucy stepped out carrying a fresh stack of bed linens.

"You can have the lift all to you'self, Miz Etta. This where I gets off."

"It ain't a *lift*. It's an elevator."

"Miss Clara call it a lift."

"It's a lift in England, in America it's a goddamned elevator. You're in America."

"I knows where I is," Aunt Lucy said, giving her a cross look.

"Clara calls it a lift because she's a showoff. She wants to remind us all she's been to England and we haven't. No telling what the hell she did over there."

"Miss Clara ain't got a showoff bone in her body, and she ain't done nothing over there 'cept see all them sights they got."

"That's all you know," Etta Ruth mumbled as she slammed shut the elevator's ornate wrought-iron gate and pulled the lever.

Alone again, she immediately fell into her usual bad mood, annoyed that Aunt Lucy had shown up. There wasn't any telling how much more she might have learned about those two if she could have hung over the transom a bit longer. *Obviously, both girls are almost too damn needy to survive on their own.*

She exited the elevator and saw old Rube still lying at the front door, which meant Clara and Justine were not home yet. Shrugging, she slouched along to the kitchen to refill her Mason jar, her bare feet slapping the floor with the same lackluster sloppiness as her mood. *Matters of an urgent nature are definitely piling up around here,* she thought. *Clara and Justine's unpaid mortgage, weepy little Mary's stupid confusion over a jerk named Claxton, and Willie—or Leeta, or whoever she is—very likely to end up murdered if that Mandingo Q. Mann finds her.*

"Not that I give a rinky-dink about any of their damn problems," she mumbled aloud. For a long time now, she hadn't been able to get interested in anything for more than the few minutes it took for discovery. She'd be in a heck of a mess mentally if she didn't have the habits she'd adopted lately—*the cigarettes, spying over the transoms, the drinking ... the windmill.*

An hour later, on her third trip from the parlor to the kitchen to refill her Mason jar, Etta Ruth stopped at the front door to watch Rudolph Valentino lumber to a halt at the front gate. She snickered, thinking that Justine and Clara were sitting up there on the front seat of that old rattletrap Buick as if it were a grand limousine and they were still the socialite belles of Varner County.

Unexpectedly, her attention, as well as Clara's and Justine's, suddenly turned to a big Allied van coming down the road. A shiny black Pontiac followed, its only passengers the male driver and a big German shepherd dog with his head stuck out the passenger window. The van and the Pontiac slowed to maneuver carefully past Mr. Valentino and the Buick, the occupants of both vehicles doing a double take at the massive, dangerous-looking bull hitched to what they surely recognized as a transportation relic of the past. Etta Ruth tittered again, thinking that they also appeared to notice the *two relics staring curiously back at them from the front seat. Bet they've never seen a sight like them and that old bull before.* She laughed aloud this time.

As Clara and Justine reached the porch, Etta Ruth joined them to watch the van back up to the ramshackle vacant house down the road. Two men got out and started unloading furniture.

"It appears Banker Prickett has a renter," Clara said.

Justine made a scoffing sound. "Can you imagine anyone wanting to live in that old shack? It's about to fall down, and the roof is bound to leak like a sieve."

When the man and the dog got out of the Pontiac, Etta Ruth raised her binoculars, her big eyes growing wider. An unusually shaped black eye patch covered the man's left eye and curved downward to cover part of his cheek. *Must be a nasty scar under there,* she thought as she adjusted the lens for a closer look and discovered that he was not a young man. Suddenly, he took off his brown felt Homburg hat and seemed to be staring right at her ... or was he looking at Clara and Justine? The two of them stood at the edge of the porch, their open hands shading their eyes from the sun.

Etta Ruth turned her binoculars back to the villainous-looking new neighbor and laughed before calling out, "Hey, Justine, I don't see a woman with him, which means he might be available. Wanna size him up through my binoculars?"

"Of course not! And put those things away! What will he think?"

"I don't give a damn what he thinks. Only you and Clara keep your butt muscles in a knot over crap like that."

"They are only in a knot when we're around *you*," Justine shot back.

Etta Ruth laughed louder and then, like her curious cousins, resumed watching their new neighbor.

Behind them, Rube nudged the screen door open, sniffed the air, and then tore off down the steps and out the gate.

"Uh-oh," Justine said. "Rube's smelled a strange dog in his territory."

At the farmhouse, the German shepherd barked and dashed out into the road. Rube did the same, and the two huge dogs lunged toward each other.

"Rube! Rube! Come back here!" cried Clara and Justine.

"Snitzel! *Verhalten! Verhalten!*" the man called out in a heavy German accent as, despite a limp, he swiftly reached the growling dogs, gripped Snitzel's collar, and led him away. Rube returned, took a light scolding from Clara and Justine, and then followed them into the house.

Etta Ruth remained on the porch, the man and his oddly shaped eye patch no longer a curiosity, as her binoculars moved to other sights—the sky, the ground, a leaf, a bird, a line of tiny ants crawling along a tree trunk. Earlier that day, she'd thought about digging up the canister in the garden, but she wasn't interested in the letters anymore now that she had them. Maybe she would get interested again at some point and burn them on Clarence's grave, maybe not. She adjusted the lens again and peered off across the road—up and down, along a fence, a patch of weeds... a telephone pole.

Finally, she dropped the binoculars to her chest and went inside to refill her Mason jar. In the kitchen, she glanced at the calendar on the wall. She had lost track of the month, as well as the date. For her, life consisted of one boring week after another—boring except for her panacea-filled Mason jars, one of which would help her to make that final climb up the windmill one day.

# 21

BY NINE IN THE EVENING, the barn was over half-full of military men and their dates, *colored* and *white*, the latter unexpected ... since Dink and Leeta had assumed that the event would appeal only to *colored* military. However, as the night progressed and the crowd became a mixture of white and colored patrons wearing a variety of military uniforms, it was plain to see that appreciation of a phenomenal musical talent like Willie Holloway knew no racial boundaries.

In addition to the white military personnel showing up, no one responsible for the dance thought that the town's youth, consisting of high school-aged boys and girls and students home from college, would show up after exiting the Rialto, having hamburgers at Goldrod's or the Toot & Get Drive-In, then heading for Lovers Lane, officially known as Hesterwine Road, would make the detour to Hesterwine Place. Hearing live music and seeing cars lined up on both sides of the road adjacent to the massive old barn was clealy a curiosity not to be ignored.

Soon, more than a dozen white teenage couples stood outside the big blue structure listening to Willie sing to the bluesy notes of the Blue Creek Trotliners—a four-piece group consisting of Dink Maxwell on guitar, Hank Posey on sax, and two of Dink's nephews on piano and drums.

When the band took a short break, Clara and Justine tried to assure Dink that there was nothing to worry about when he said, "Seem like we done cooked up a big pot of Worry Stew, Miss Clara, Miss Justine. I didn't have no idea them white folks was gonna come out here and start dancing right alongside them coloreds. I'm getting kinda worried 'cause I knowed them old Jim Crow laws ain't skipped over Varner County... even if ain't nobody heard much 'bout 'em in a few years round here."

"My goodness, what's the harm?" Justine said. "I never heard of a law that said folks couldn't go to a dance if they wanted to."

"I'm sure Mr. Maxwell is referring to an unwritten law, Justine—a Jim Crow law *de jure*—that attempts to frighten people into celebrating among their own kind instead of...." Clara motioned toward the dancing couples.

Rubbing his chin, Dink nodded. "Leastwise, *I* sure ain't gonna ask nobody to leave."

"Absolutely not," Clara said.

"Anyhow, I reckon them white military folks got a right to enjoy Willie's singing just as well as the colored folks do." He glanced outside. "And I don't reckon them young folks standing round out there is gonna be a problem as long as they stays outside and nobody hands 'em any 'freshments from your grandpappy's barrel."

"Oh my goodness, no!" Jusine said. "Grandfather's recipe is certainly not for anyone that young. We'll have to keep an eye on them, Clara."

Dink rejoined his band, and Clara and Justine resumed watching the dancers and listening to Willie sing. Nearby, Mary and Jack collected the two-dollar cover charge. By ten thirty, the crowd inside the barn numbered over three hundred, and the energetic crowd of youths outside was increasing.

Clara shifted from one aching foot to the other. She hadn't stood so long in one spell since waiting in line at the Rialto in '39 to see *Gone with the Wind*. She lifted the little watch pinned to her prim collar and then glanced at the large straw basket atop the refreshment barrel; it was brimming with what Dink called *"folding money."* More barrels of special Deleware Punch recipe were stationed at intervals inside the barn, the baskets atop them filled with folding money as well.

Justine nudged Clara. "Good Lord, look who's coming."

Etta Ruth, brandishing a long silver cigarette holder in one hand and her Mason jar in the other, traipsed toward the barn amid stares and grins from the outside crowd. Wearing an off-the-shoulder pink evening gown that she had draped with an old fox stole despite the summer heat, she slunk along the path like a seductress. Her binoculars dangled from her neck, the straps wound with fluffy lengths of tulle and tiny silk flowers. She nearly stumbled and then laughed as she lifted her Mason jar high over her head as if to protect it.

"My God, Clara, she's dyed her hair *black*, and she's got *bangs!*" Justine scarcely drew another breath before she gasped again. "Good grief, she's wearing more eyeliner than Theda Bara!"

"Close your mouth and stop staring at her like that, Justine. We don't want to upset her," Clara said, finding it almost impossible to stop her own staring. The extremes that had ruled Etta Ruth since Clarence's death were getting worse—the chain-smoking, the drinking, wearing Clarence's clothes and shoes, her usual state of undress beneath her flimsy red robe, the mannequin, and now *this*, the hair dye and the hideous makeup.

More disturbing, Etta Ruth's windmill episodes were happening with alarming frequency. The deputies had talked, and now she was jokingly referred to around town as "the windmill sitter," of all things! "How's the windmill sitter, Miss Clara?" Harlan Watson had asked with a chuckle when she and Justine were in Piggly Wiggly's the other day. His wife, Vernell, had poked him, but she'd had a big grin on her face.

Watching Etta Ruth, Clara suddenly felt overwhelmed by the situation that was Etta Ruth Morley. Marvin Abelson's autopsy report was still not back from the coroner, and according to the grapevine, Sheriff Bloot was busy rounding up potential suspects and questioning them... just in case the autopsy proved him correct in suspecting murder.

For the hundredth time, Clara wished that Clarence Jr. had succeeded in luring Etta Ruth away to that asylum in San Antonio. With the sheriff's investigation going on, Etta Ruth would fare much better tucked away somewhere...uh... where she wouldn't be so free to roam. Not that she wanted Etta Ruth to get away with anything—*certainly not—although the stigma of having a family member put away because she's "cracked" would be far less humiliating than having a convicted murderer in the family.*

Clara shifted uncomfortably on her aching feet, trying to dispel her guilt at wanting to protect Etta Ruth for all the wrong reasons.

Justine poked Clara's elbow. "I'm going to help Mary and Jack. If I stay here, Etta Ruth will say something insulting to me, like always."

As Etta Ruth drew closer, she flippantly peered at Clara through the binoculars. Clara noticed right away that one of the lenses was missing. *Etta Ruth probably isn't even aware it's gone*, she thought as she studied Etta

Ruth's heavily powdered and rouged face and tried to determine her mood. She decided the woman looked almost sociable tonight... although obviously inebriated. Was that the face of someone who could kill without conscience? No. Etta Ruth was *strange;* that's all. Many people had eyes that looked as if they were always plotting something sinister. *Being odd does not a murderess make*—even if she did despise Mr. Abelson and had disappeared from Hesterwine Place on the day he died... and had come home doused with flour... and was carrying a canister exactly like the one missing from Mr. Abelson's place and which no one had seen since.

Clara forced a smile as Etta Ruth came to a halt beside her, executing that hip swiveling thing she always did when in Bette Davis mode. "You look very nice tonight, Etta Ruth," Clara offered.

Etta Ruth took a long puff from the cigarette holder and blew the smoke at Clara. "Where did Justine run off to? You two squabbling again over you-how-who?" She took another long puff, this time expelling the smoke through her nose as she narrowed her eyes at Clara. "Me oh my, Clara, you and Justine must have thought *Boyd* was the *crème de la crème* of the male species... the way he keeps popping up between you two, even though he hasn't shown his face to either of you in... how long has it been now?" She tapped her cheek. "Why, I do believe it's been over a quarter of a century."

Clara controlled herself. Apparently, the warning in the attic had gone in one ear and out the other. However, this was not the time or place to remind Etta Ruth of it. *A piddling lot of good it would do, anyway.*

"Look at Willie, Etta Ruth," Clara said, and pointed at the stage where Leeta could be seen over the heads of the dancers and the large crowd gathered around the foot of the stage. "Doesn't she look stunning in that sparkly red lamé dress? We found that fabric in the attic, and Willie designed and sewed the gown herself. She looks like a movie star, doesn't she? Let's listen to her sing."

"She's gonna get us all killed, Clara."

*"What?* What on earth are you talking about?"

"You mean I'm the only one who knows about Mandingo Q. Mann?"

"*Who?*"

"You don't know much, do you, Clara?"

"Why don't you tell me, Etta Ruth?" Clearly, Etta Ruth was more confused than ever tonight and required careful handling.

"Just joking. Forget it." Etta Ruth laughed and gazed around at the crowd before again eyeing Clara, an amused grin stretching her well-greased red lips. "You *do* know, though, that old green-eyed Dink Maxwell's ancestors belonged to your green-eyed granddaddy, General Andrew Ignacio Hesterwine, don't you, Clara?"

"Of course, I know," Clara said, dropping the kindly look, since she knew exactly where Etta Ruth was going with that remark. "However, Cousin Etta, *that* was *then* and *this* is now. I am certain those folks do not blame Justine and me for Grandfather's participation in the South's adherence to slavery back then any more than Clarence Jr. blames his father for his upper lip." "Oh, but Clarence Jr. does blame his father for his upper lip, Clara—*and* for his cowlick."

Clara managed to soften her tone. "I am profoundly sorry I mentioned Clarence's upper lip, Etta Ruth. It was a poor comparison."

Etta Ruth was no longer listening. She shoved her Mason jar into Clara's hands, slung her fox stole around Clara's neck, grabbed the arm of a young marine passing by, and ordered him to dance with her. Though at first looking shocked and then uncomfortable, he was obviously too much of a gentleman to refuse.

Clara, peering through the wide barn doors, watched Etta Ruth pull the marine toward the dance area, where she slung her binoculars around so that they dangled down her back, snuggled up to him, and then pressed her head against his shoulder. *That poor young man*, Clara thought. Perhaps she could talk Jack into cutting in so the marine could escape. No, that would be a terrible thing to do to Jack. She watched Etta Ruth grasp her shy dance partner by the back of his neck and force his cheek against hers. *Oh, Lord*, Clara thought, reconsidering. An instant later, she had taken only a couple of steps in Jack's direction when someone cried: "Fire!"

"*Fire! Fire! Fire!*" reverberated outside the barn and then from inside.

The hair on the back of Clara's head went prickly. Her first frantic thought was that Etta Ruth had left a cigarette burning and the house was on fire! She spun around, and what she saw sent a chill through her that almost made her wish it had been the house.

In the field across the road, a giant cross writhed in flames from top to bottom, red and orange tongues licking angrily at the sky. Below the torched cross, one hundred or more hooded, white-robed Ku Klux Klansmen stood in formation, their ghostly images creating an octagon beneath the cross... their swords, rifles, knives, and pistols pointed symbolically toward the barn. The servicemen piled out the wide exit, the rage on their faces illuminated by the fire as they ran across the road to station themselves along the fence, shoulder to shoulder, not twenty-five yards from the Klansmen.

"Go home, niggers!" The Klansman who yelled pumped his rifle in the air and then aimed it at the uniformed men. "Hell gonna be unleashed on you goddamn niggers and nigger lovers if you don't get moving outta here! We ain't fooling now!"

"Go away!" Clara cried. "You have no right to trespass on this land!"

"What them *niggers* doing on your place, Clara Hesterwine?" he yelled back. "You know it ain't right! *We*, the guardians of the sanctity and purity of the white race, are sworn to prevent this decadence—this blatant integrating of Negroes with whites!" He threw up both arms and turned to the horde of Klansmen behind him, then screeched, "Segregation today, tomorrow, and forever!" His one hundred or more cohorts roared out the phrase, repeating it twice more before he lowered his arms and turned back around.

"Daddy, is that you?" cried one of the teenage girls who had crowded into the road to watch. "What are you doing over there, Daddy?"

A shot rang out, stirring the dirt at the man's feet.

Jack Dunston, standing on the bumper of his truck, kept his rifle pointed. "Go home, like your daughter said, Mr. Setler... all of you, or the next shot will take off somebody's toe." He aimed the rifle from one man to the next, then back to Setler.

"This ain't none of your business, Dunston!" another Klansman yelled in a raspy voice, as if he had a summer cold, and then he coughed before adding, "What are you, a damn *nigger lover*?"

"I told you this morning at your gas station, Mr. Howell, you should get that cold looked after before it turns into summer pneumonia," Jack said.

Clara, feeling Mary's arm go around her shoulders, looked out over the sea of pointed hoods that concealed faces of men from families she and Justine had likely known all their lives, their white robes whipping in the wind. She, too, recognized Mr. Setler's and Mr. Howell's voices. She would likely recognize most all their voices if they spoke.

"You fellas really want to declare war on men in service to the United States of America?" Jack yelled, and pointed at the overwhelming crowd of angry military men pressing against the fence and filling the road. "You're outnumbered by your betters, so go home before you get hurt!"

"It's them niggers that better get moving, Dunston!" A loud rumble of agreement traveled through the rows of Klansmen.

Jack yelled over them. "Go home!" He pulled off another shot just short of Howell's feet and then fired again, the dirt fluttering inches from Setler's shoe. "The next shot is gonna shorten somebody's foot! If you don't believe me, just stand there another five seconds!"

Half the Klansmen backed away a few yards and then hesitantly began peeling off from their formation. Jack fired again, just missing Setler's foot. Setler cursed and hopped sideways. The rest of the Klansmen took off toward their vehicles parked at the back of the field. Setler barked for them to stay put, but when he turned and saw Howell on his way to catching up with the others, he threw up his hands, cursed again, and followed. "This ain't over!" he yelled. "Mark my words! Somebody's gonna reap the whirlwind for this!"

"We'll know who to look for then, won't we, Setler?" Jack yelled back.

The crowd in the road and around the barn cheered. When The Blue Creek Trotliners struck up a bluesy run of piano and guitar and when Leeta, after handing Hank Posey his saxophone, began singing "Why Don't You Do Right?" half the white youths outside crowded into the barn and onto the dance floor.

Etta Ruth came over to Clara, stripped her fox stole from around her neck, then snatched her Mason jar from Clara's hand. "There goes your grandpa's old alma mater, Clara," she said, tittering as she nodded toward the Klansmens' cars retreating across the bumpy field, their headlights bouncing in the dark like disorientated fireflies.

Clara ignored her. Justine, having abandoned the chaotic scene for the front porch of the old mansion, returned. She reached Clara's side, panting. "Thank God they're gone! I thought we were all going to be tarred and feathered! I wouldn't be surprised if that Banker Prickett was behind this. That man will do absolutely anything to get Hesterwine Place!"

Etta Ruth gave them both a disgusted look. "And Prickett *will* get his hands on it sooner or later, since you two have no idea how to solve the problem."

"And I suppose *you* do, Etta Ruth Morley," Justine said with her usual crabbiness when dealing with Etta Ruth.

Etta Ruth took a drink from her Mason jar. "He needs the right kind of talking to, that's all."

"We *have* talked to him," Justine snapped. "It did no good!"

Etta Ruth stuck her face close to Justine's face. "You didn't say the right words."

"Indeed? Well, if you think you can do any better, be our guest!"

"I could ... if I wanted to. Prickett needs a comeuppance to end all comeuppances, and I know just how to deliver it to him." She flipped the tail of her fox stole at Justine's face. "Well, back to the party. Bye, floozy." She flounced off toward the barn, nearly tripping again. "Where's that big, chocolate-covered marine of mine?"

"Bitch!" Justine said beneath her breath.

Clara called out to Etta Ruth: "My goodness, Etta Ruth, it is almost midnight. Don't you want to go home? I'll go with you if you like."

Etta Ruth didn't bother turning around. "Clara, sometimes I think you are as *cracked* as everybody says I am. Why in hell would I wanna go sit all alone in that dreary old museum when all the fun is happening in the goddamned barn?"

The party was again in full swing an hour later when Justine nudged Clara and pointed toward the shadows alongside the fencerow.

"Look, Clara, it's that German with the eye patch who moved into Prickett's rental house today ... and he's coming right toward us! What do you suppose he wants? Oh, my! I didn't think of it before, but maybe he's working for Prickett and will try to *frighten* us away!"

Clara watched him curiously. Despite his limp, he was moving swiftly toward them, as if with purpose. However, he never reached them, for the sudden wail of sirens caused every head to jerk toward the sound, and when Clara next looked in the stranger's direction, he had turned around and was retreating the same way he came.

Clara had no time to ponder the man's intention. A headlight-lit cloud of illuminated dust marked Hesterwine Road like the long tail of a speeding comet, as what appeared to be every sheriff's vehicle, police car, and State Highway Patrol car in Vander County barreled toward Hesterwine Place as if the world was under attack and they were hell-bent on rescuing it. In a matter of seconds, the vehicles had surrounded the barn and blocked off every car trying to leave, red lights flashing and sirens belching ominous warnings at anything that moved.

Justine clutched at Clara as half the law enforcement troops leveled their weapons over their open car doors and the other half swarmed into the barn. Sheriff Bloot, scowling, got out of his car, hitched up his khaki pants, and directed a censuring wag of his head at Clara and Justine as he stomped past. He paused just inside the barn to stare at one of the servicemen.

"What the hell you doing in that Marine Corps uniform, boy?"

"President Roosevelt put me in it this past June, sir, when he say us Negroes can wear it now same as anyone else."

"I don't know what this goddamn country's coming to," muttered the sheriff as he looked around. "You military, colored and white, take your gals and get on outta here. And thank your lucky stars I ain't gonna arrest every last one of y'all. Get on back to your bases, and don't be coming back to Hesterwine looking for a place to raise hell like you been doing tonight."

"We been dancing and enjoying the music, Sheriff!" a sailor yelled out over the murmuring crowd. "Ain't no *hell-raising* in that!"

Sheriff Bloot's face, already bloated with superiority, puffed up even more. "You back-talk me again, boy, and you gonna be the first to wear these bracelets." He loosened the handcuffs from his belt and then looked from face to face among the white uniformed men. "You fellas could be arrested, too. I don't know where in hell you come from, but it's against the law for whites and coloreds to fraternize in these parts." He dangled the handcuffs in the air and shook his head in disgust at Etta Ruth, who had both her arms wrapped around the arm of the young colored marine she had commandeered to dance with her. With a final sneer at the pair, he turned his attention to Clara.

"What are you and Miss Justine doing out here among these coloreds, Miss Clara?" Before she could reply, he continued, "What's more mystifying is what them *coloreds* is doing out here on *your* land and in *your* barn?"

"This is private property, Sheriff Bloot," Clara said. "We can invite whomever we choose onto it. With the help of Mr. Maxwell, we are hosting a dance with entertainment and refreshments for the colored troops who have no other place to go in Hesterwine. Our harmless event was proceeding very nicely until now."

"My, my, *Mr.* Maxwell, you say?" He grinned at Dink, still on the bandstand, and then yelled out to him: "You come up in the world since I last seen you, Dink, *boy*," he said, snickering as he turned his back to Clara. "A party for the *troops*, is it? I see that some of 'em is *troops*, but other than those white fellas over there, all I see is a bunch of uniformed cooks, mess attendants, and maybe some truck drivers and stevedores, but no troops."

One of the colored men yelled out, "I was at Pearl Harbor, and that's my leg you hear me knocking on! The flesh and bone part is still back there at Pearl!"

Another in the crowd said, "I'm training for *artillery*."

"Me, too—same battalion!" said another. Then the loudest of all yelled, "You are damn right I'm a cook! An army travels on its belly, or ain't you heard!" With that, the crowd cheered.

Grinning cynically, Sheriff Bloot squinted at Clara and Justine. "Now, you ladies already know it's illegal in Vander County to hold a public event without a permit. Ain't we done been through all that the day you tried to sell all that old junk from your front porch? Now, here you are again—breaking the law."

Clara looked down her nose at him. "I repeat. This is a private party, not a public event."

"Miss Clara, you really take me for that much of a dumb ass?"

Justine grabbed Clara's arm. "Please don't answer that, Clara. We're in enough trouble as it is." A rumble of laughter came from the crowd and Sheriff Bloot whirled around.

"As for you all, it ain't only illegal for whites and coloreds to mix socially like this, it's a *crime* punishable by arrest and possible prison sentence."

"You got a copy of that law with you, Sheriff?" Jack said. "I'd like to read it."

"Now, Jack, I don't have to show you no written paper. You know the law. We got separate washrooms. We got separate eating-places. We got separate schools. We got separate churches. We got separate railroad cars when we travel. We got separate everything, Jack. The list goes on and on. *Separate* means *kept apart*. Hell, even after we're dead and gone we got separate cemeteries. I shouldn't have to explain to you or anybody else that gatherings like this here one tonight ain't supposed to happen!" He took a cup from the table, filled it from one of the barrels, and drank it down. "Now, y'all hit the road, goddamn it, before I change my mind and run you in! All of you; but *not* the band," he added, pointing at the stage. "Y'all stay put right where you're standing."

When the barn was empty except for Clara, Justine, Mary, Jack, Leeta, and the band members, the sheriff turned to his deputies. "Arrest Dink and his band ... the gal, too." He grinned at Leeta, who silently watched him from the stage. "I told you you'd be seeing my jail sooner or later, didn't I?"

Jack spoke. "Sheriff, can we talk outside? I'd like a chance to appeal to your better nature."

"My better nature, eh? Hell, Jack, I'm a reasonable man. Let's talk about it out back." He was grinning.

As they stepped outside, Clara and Justine rushed over to peek at them through cracks in the barn wall, but then immediately jerked their heads back as the sheriff unbuttoned his khaki pants and began to pee. They closed their eyes and pressed their ears to the wall.

"I'll save us both some time, Jack," the sheriff was saying. "I know why Dink and his band are here. Y'all are trying to get enough money together to pay the old ladies' mortgage." He looked down as if to examine his pee stream. "Trouble is, this whole damn shebang was illegal from the get-go. I ain't just talking 'bout the dance. I'm talking about fraternizing with *Negroes*. Jesus! What the hell was y'all thinking?"

"Sheriff, I don't believe you give a damn about colored military coming out here any more than you'd care if they were at the Blue Creek Lounge tonight instead. I think you're here on orders from your father-in-law, Prickett. He wants to keep Miss Clara and Miss Justine from paying their debt to him because he wants this property. Don't you have any qualms about taking part in that kind of low scheming?"

"I ain't gonna take you to jail for that, Jack, on account of you being a wounded vet and a member of the Civil Air Patrol, but watch yourself. After tonight, there's some folks in Vander County that ain't gonna like you as much as I do. Guess I'm done out here." He buttoned his pants. "Nice talking to you, Jack."

Jack stepped in front of him. "Prove me wrong, Sheriff. I'd truly like to think you're a better man than one who'd arrest folks because they were trying to keep two fine ladies from losing their home."

The sheriff hitched his khakis a bit higher. "I tell you what, Jack. If somebody can come up with the band's bail money, let's say twenty-five dollars a head, I'll turn 'em loose tonight after they're booked." He paused to grin. "But I don't reckon a damn one of 'em's got five bucks to their name, much less twenty-five." He paused again to grin at Jack. "And just so you'll know, I could also arrest those two old maids if I wanted to, 'cause the stuff in those kegs they been selling by the cupful is about eighty proof, and they damn sure ain't got a liquor license any more than they had a license to sell them antiques from their front porch."

"They weren't selling their wine, they were giving it away," Jack said.

"I guess you think I'm a dumb ass, too, don't you, Dunston." He hiked up his gun belt, spat, and sauntered off, but then turned on his heel. "By the way, I'm confiscating them baskets of cash, for evidence ... every last dollar." He grinned wider. "Too bad. Looks like it might have been enough for them old gals to pay off every penny of their debt to my father-in-law ... and then have a tidy little sum left over for incidentals."

# 22

AFTER THE SHERIFF DROVE AWAY with his prisoners and the money baskets, Clara, Justine, and Mary walked slowly to the house, their faces so sad that a laureate would have written a poem about them.

Rather than going inside, they eased into the rattan chairs on the porch and sat there wordlessly for a long time, each apparently occupied with her own thoughts and too dejected to talk about the obvious: The last chance to save their ancestral home had failed. The deadline to pay the mortgage was nine o'clock next Tuesday morning and, unless a miracle happened within the next few days, Banker Prickett would soon own Hesterwine Place and everything in it and on it, including the animals.

Finally, Mary broke the silence. "Jack said he was going to try his best to get everybody out of jail tonight."

Clara, still with a detached look in her eyes, put a hand to her cheek and patted absently at it. Although she worried about Leeta and the others being in jail ... and worried as well over losing the recipe money, she dared not tell her two companions what else preyed on her mind—*Etta Ruth's absence.* Finally, she said, "Etta Ruth got a ride to town with one of the teenage couples. Said she had something to do at her house. I can't imagine what that could be at this late hour."

"Who cares?" Justine snapped, the mention of Etta Ruth apparently jarring her out of her melancholy mood.

"I do," Clara replied. "I'd surely feel better if I knew what she was up—" She stopped herself. "Anyway, she could get snake bit walking into that weedy yard of hers at night."

"I'm sure the snake would die immediately," Justine muttered.

"I'm worried about Willie," Mary said. "She has never been in jail before ... I don't think."

"Surely not," Clara said, then added, "Although, knowing Sheriff Bloot's history when it comes to colored folks, I'm not so sure about Dink Maxwell and his band members."

They grew silent again, still no one daring to say aloud what all three were thinking—*their last chance to save Hesterwine Place was gone.* Tuesday after next, they would move to the crowded boarding house in town ... where the rooms were small, the stairs were steep, and meals not of their choice were served in a noisy, communal dining room.

Clara finally voiced the obvious. "I suppose we should start packing our personal belongings tomorrow, Justine."

Justine sighed. "Do we even have the energy, Clara? Besides, it *is* tomorrow ... the sun will be up soon."

Mary, sitting between them, grasped their hands and all three fell silent again and stayed that way until half an hour later, when headlights appeared on the road.

"The sheriff has come back for us!" Justine cried, locking her arms around the armrest of her chair. "He will just have to drag me, chair and all, to his old jail!"

Mary leaned forward for a better look, then jumped to her feet. "It's Jack!" She hurried to the gate to meet him, Clara and Justine close behind her.

"Glad to see you folks are still up!" Jack called from his truck. "I got the bail bond money for the band. There's a hitch, though. The sheriff seems to have forgotten his word to let them go if they make bond. Before he frees them, he wants five individuals to sign pledges saying they'll be responsible for bringing all five '*defendants*' into court Monday morning. I'll sign for one of them. Reverend Henry Posey is waiting at the jail ready to sign for another. Guess the sheriff figured I wouldn't find anybody among Hesterwine's citizens to sign at this hour. How about you three ladies? Care to sign for the other three?"

The sheriff's office was on the second floor of the historic old courthouse, the jail on the top third floor. A long bench resembling a church pew hugged the wall directly across the hall from the sheriff's door, and that was where Clara, Justine, Mary, Jack, and Reverend Henry Posey Sr. sat waiting for the sheriff. At the sound of the elevator coming up the shaft, Clara looked at the watch on her collar. They had been sitting there since 4:00 a.m. and it was now past seven.

Sheriff Bloot and one of his deputies exited the elevator and stood whispering for several minutes before the sheriff ambled over and halted in front of the long bench where they all five sat, his eyes hard on Reverend Posey.

"Now, Henry, what you doing sitting there? You know better than that. You supposed to be down yonder in the colored section." He pointed to a bench at the far end of the hall, over which hung a sign that said *Colored*.

"I come to sign that there pledge for to hab them band folks in court when de judge says they 'posed to be," Reverend Posey said, causing the others on the bench to stare at him in surprise. Moments earlier, before the sheriff arrived, Reverend Posey had conversed with them in the vernacular of a highly educated man.

Clara stared at him, wondering what on earth suddenly possessed him. He sounded like someone who had never seen the inside of a schoolhouse, much less graduated from "*Wiley*, the oldest Negro college west of the Mississippi... on a scholarship just 'cause he was the smartest kid in the family." Aunt Lucy had bragged many times about her brother while standing at the sink in the kitchen.

Suddenly, it dawned on Clara that Reverend Posey was playing a role. Somewhere in his life, he had learned how to survive when dealing with men like Sheriff Bloot—men who, through the ignorance of their bigotry, considered an educated Negro a threat.

"You know you can't sign for nobody, Henry," the sheriff was saying.

"Why not?"

"Cause you ain't *legal* to sign. You ain't registered, that's why not. Now get on outta here before I chuck you in there with them other troublemakers."

"I can't sign 'cause I ain't registered *where, suh?*"

"You ever voted in Vander County, Henry?"

"You knowed I ain't, suh. Them Klu Kluxers done make sure long time ago that us coloreds don't come to town on 'lection day."

"That's a damn lie and you know it!" Sheriff Bloot fairly shouted.

"I pretty sure it wuz Kluxers hiding under dem white sheets, suh."

"You being damn disrespectful, boy!"

Jack stood and touched Reverend Posey's arm, as if to help him up from the bench. "It's okay, Reverend. Go on home. I'll get somebody to sign, and I'll see that everybody gets to Rose Hill."

"Thanking you just the same, Mr. Jack, but my son, Henry Jr., up there in dat jail. I'll just go wait on dat bench like the sheriff say."

Sheriff Bloot shrugged. "Suit yourself, but you ain't legal to sign no paper." He looked at his watch and then at Jack. "I'll give you fifteen minutes to find another signer. After that, the deal's off."

"I vill sign za paper," said a voice next to the elevator.

"Heavens to Betsy," Justine whispered to Clara. "It's that German who moved in next door. He was coming right toward us at the dance until the sheriff and half the law enforcement in Vander County showed up and scared him away. Remember, Clara?"

Clara did not answer. Experiencing that same peculiar curiosity she'd felt upon seeing him from her porch, she leaned forward trying to see past the black patch to the good side of his face, but he stood at an angle to her. *Who is he? Why had he moved into that dilapidated old shell of a house? More importantly, why is he here now ... offering to help?* She leaned back on the bench. *Perhaps he came to the courthouse on business, overheard the situation, and, out of kindness, decided to be a Good Samaritan.*

"Who in the hell are *you*?" Sheriff Bloot asked.

"I am ..." he paused, as if he had to think. "I am Gustave Herrmann. I am new citizen in Hesterwine."

Justine leaned close again to whisper to Clara, "Seems like he almost forgot his name. Do you think he could be one of those German spies they say are sneaking in from across the Mexican border and the Gulf waters?"

Clara put a shushing finger to her lips, intent on listening to the conversation between the German and the sheriff.

"You wanna sign for some colored you don't even know?" the sheriff was saying. "Why? Besides, I don't generally accept a signature from a man I don't know. If I do, he has to have a local bank account that shows me he's got enough in it to be accountable."

Gustave Herrmann pulled something from his pocket, limped over to the sheriff, and handed it to him.

"Yeah, I see it's a bankbook. That don't mean a thing. I doubt if I'll have ten dollars left in my own bank account after my wife goes shopping in Corpus Christi Monday."

Justine poked Clara and muttered beneath her breath, "What do you want to bet she will be shopping with *our* Delaware Punch money!"

Gustave Herrmann jerked the bankbook from the sheriff's hand, flipped it open, and tapped at a page, then shoved it back at him.

The sheriff looked. "Okay, I get it. You've got dough. You're also dressed like a damned foreigner just off the boat—heavy tweed and leather elbow patches. It could have been a damned *U-boat* for all I know. For sure, you ain't been in the country long enough to Americanize any of that German accent you got. Just how long you been away from your Nazi relatives, *Herr Herrmann?*"

"I am recent American citizen. I have za papers."

"Oh, yeah? There's lots of them forged papers going 'round these days."

Clara cleared her throat. "Sheriff, there is no need to insult this man. If you suspected every person with a German accent of being a Nazi spy, you would have to include almost every farmer in South Texas, including your own grandparents."

If Gustave Herrmann's expression altered in any way, it was too fleeting to notice. Even so, his one eye, emotionless as it was, was clearly now on Clara.

"I sign now," he said again to the sheriff. "I vill also pay za bail and za fines for all of zem."

"That's damned white of you, Herrmann," the sheriff said flatly, "but Jack Dunston here gave me his own personal check for the bail. The fines, though, won't be leveled until the jailbirds stand before the judge Monday morning."

"Zen I vill pay za fines Monday."

Clara didn't know why she rose from the bench, other than there was something about this man that suddenly made her uneasy now that she saw the rest of his face. There was a harshness about that unscarred side, as if he had experienced life *more* than most men, and then had permanently absorbed the severest of those experiences into every crease. She forced herself to make eye contact with him again. Possibly, her discomfort came from the way he looked at her with that one eye.

"We shan't allow you to do that, Mr. Herrmann," she said. "It is our debt to pay—mine and my sister's. It is our fault they are in jail."

"You have za money, zen?"

"No, but—"

"Zen I will pay." He turned his back and limped to the sheriff's office door, but before going through it he paused and, without turning to look at her, said in a tone oddly soft, "I vill write eet in my book."

Clara swayed. Justine grabbed her arm. "My God, Clara, you've turned as white as a ghost! Sit down before you fall down."

Mary rushed to her side. "Miss Clara, you do look quite ill."

Clara slowly straightened her shoulders. "I've been up all night. I'm not used to it."

She sounded calm, but she was anything but tranquil. Playing in her head were the two words missing from that stunningly familiar sentence— "I vill write eet in my book, *mein liebchen,*" and spoken to her time and time again many years ago in Aachen, North Rhine-Westphalia, Germany, when Gustave Herrmann was Fritz Von Heuvel—her long deserted fiancé!

*"I vill write eet in my book, my love,"* he had said, speaking to her in his native language each time she had professed affection for him.

Sitting back down on the bench and staring at the sheriff's empty doorway, Clara's trembling hands twisted the handle of her black purse, her thoughts buzzing in her head like disrupted bees. *Why was he here* now, *after all these years?* Surely, he had not come to Hesterwine to see *her*! Naturally, since they had lived together for six months back in Germany before he joined the Kaiser's army, she had described Hesterwine Place to him many times and had shown him exactly where it was on a Texas map. That being so, it would be quite fanciful to assume he had randomly chosen Hesterwine, Texas, to settle down in, and then unknowingly rented a house mere yards down the road from her. No, his presence in Hesterwine was no coincidence. What were his intentions? Only the sheriff's arrival last night had stopped him from walking right up to her! What would he have said to her? What would she have said to him?

The sheriff's rough voice jerked her back and she looked up to see Willie, Hank, Dink Maxwell, and Dink's two nephews following the sheriff out of his office. Off to the side and looking neither left nor right, Fritz Von

Heuvel—alias Gustave Herrmann—was getting into the elevator. Clara breathed a sigh of relief; he would not expose her in front of witnesses. Doctor Fritz Von Heuvel was still the gentleman she remembered him being.

"All right, folks," said the sheriff, waving a clipboard at everyone on the bench. "The German's signed his pledge. Now, y'all gotta sign yours. Remember now, there ain't gonna be no more events out at Hesterwine Place." He stopped along the bench to have each of them sign. Then, when standing in front of Clara, he forced his puffy face into an expression of sympathy.

"Why don't you ladies give up on trying to raise that money? Y'all ain't got but 'til next Tuesday after next to do it, and you know it ain't gonna happen—especially with nothing but a buncha dirt-poor niggers helping you." He leaned down to look sternly into Clara's face. "I wanna hear you say you understand there ain't to be no more gatherings in your barn or anywhere else on your place."

"There will be no gatherings at Hesterwine Place," Clara said quietly.

"We certainly do not want to go to jail," Justine huffed at him.

Dink Maxwell spoke up. "Do that mean I can't run my Blue Creek Lounge at Rose Hill, as usual, Sheriff?"

"I ain't closing you down this time, Dink, but me and the fire marshal better not come out there and find more'n thirty or so of them uniformed niggers in your joint, or we'll nail that place up tighter'n a drum."

The Reverend Henry Posey Sr. had left the colored bench at the far end of the hall and now stood next to Leeta and Hank. He cleared his throat to speak, and when he did, everyone turned to stare at him once again. He was standing tall, his head up, and Clara had a feeling he had dropped his role playing.

"Those *uniformed niggers* will be coming to *my* place next Friday and Saturday nights, Sheriff, not the Blue Creek Lounge that is much too small for the crowd I'm expecting."

The sheriff glowered at him a long moment. Then he snickered. "What the hell you talking about, Henry? You ain't got a place."

"Before we built Christ Emmanuel Baptist Church, we used a tent for our services. I still have that tent, Sheriff, and come Friday night, it will be raised and ready. It's a very large tent, plenty of room for folks that want to hear the Blue Creek Trotliners' playing and Miss Willie Holloway's fine singing." He nodded politely to Clara and Justine before again facing the sheriff. "Us buncha dirt-poor niggers are not finished helping Miss Clara and Miss Justine just yet."

Willie squealed her delight and hugged his neck, but let go almost as quickly as she had grabbed him.

He turned back to Clara and Justine. "And it isn't *charity*, Miss Clara and Miss Justine, it's called *payback*. Seventy-five years ago, your daddy bought that tent so the faithful of Rose Hill could pray in the shade and out of the rain, and then he paid for building the church, paid every dollar of it down to the last penny. So don't you go thinking you'll be taking charity. You'll just be letting Rose Hill finally show its appreciation."

Clara and Justine smiled for the first time in hours. "Poppa never told us," Clara said.

"Poppa never told us anything, Clara. Remember?"

The sheriff cleared his surprised expression, and then laughed. "A *preacher* putting on a dance? Ain't that a sin in your book? It's sin for sure, the way I was taught."

"The Lord loves the sinner, Sheriff, just like he loves everybody else. He won't mind me doing what I can for the sake of two fine ladies that need protection from the evil schemers of this world."

"Evil schemers, eh? You ain't saying what I think you're saying, are you, boy?" He squinted in his usual intimidating manner.

Reverend Posey smiled amiably at him. "Why don't you and Miz Bloot come on out to Rose Hill and enjoy the music, Sheriff... you will be most welcome. For that matter, the whole town is invited."

The look on Sheriff Bloot's face as he stared at Reverend Posey left no doubt that he felt himself unbelievably insulted by the invitation.

# 23

Home from the courthouse, Clara, though thirsty, hungry, and exhausted, kept vigil at the parlor window rather than accompany Mary, Jack, Justine, Willie, and Hank to the kitchen to eat the meal Aunt Lucy had prepared for them. The thought that she would soon be staring into the eye of the fiancé she had jilted almost twenty-nine years ago made her so nervous that her left eye began to twitch. She rubbed at it and tried to regain her usual calm. What would he say to her? *But, oh, my! Even more frightening was her complete ignorance of what she would say to him!*

Finally, Gustave Herrmann's Pontiac came over the hill. She held her breath, staying well behind the draperies and practically wrapping herself in their heavy folds. Should she remain in the parlor and let someone else answer the door? With that thought, she peeked out again ... only to see him looking straight ahead as he drove past the house.

She released the deep breath she had been holding, its weighty expulsion indistinguishable from either relief or disappointment, her thoughts coming a bit slower this time. So he had decided against seeing her—which was as it should be. Clearly, in passing her by, Fritz Von Heuvel's judgement had silently merged with her own. He, too, had decided that their six-month affair and brief engagement all those years ago should remain buried in Germany where they had both left it—*either that, or he had taken one close-up look at her in the courthouse and decided he didn't want to regress that far into his past after all.*

She touched both hands to her face. *How dare he compare me to that youthful forty-year-old woman I was back then! True, I've aged, but, my Lord, what about him! At least, I don't have to cover half my face with a black patch!*

Feeling foolish, she rubbed her forehead. What a terrible turn her life had taken! After years of a relatively calm existence, she was suddenly swamped with worry. Worry over losing the house. Worry over how she and Justine would manage afterward. Least of all, worry over the strong possibility that Etta Ruth was a hair away from bringing disgrace to the family name by being charged with the murder of Marvin Abelson! Worry on top of worry.

And now, with Fritz Von Heuvel's arrival, there was the worrisome possibility that her twenty-nine-year-old secret of unrestrained foolishness in a cozy little flat above the picturesque Wurm River canal in Aachen, Germany, could soon became public knowledge. If he talked, *she*, like Etta Ruth, could be on the brink of bringing her brand of disgrace to the family name!

Had he talked already? He'd certainly had the opportunity to do so. After they left the courthouse and went to Goldrod's for coffee, Jack saw him enter the café across the street and, after excusing himself and saying he'd be right back, went over to thank him for signing the sheriff's pledge. "Right back" turned into more than an hour! Jack was apologetic when he returned but said nothing about their conversation. *What had they talked about so long?*

Looking more worried than ever, Clara went into the foyer, pausing to retrieve Etta Ruth's old fox stole from the floor where she had obviously dropped it when she came home. She looked up as Mary came downstairs.

"I thought you were having breakfast with the others, Mary, dear."

"I wasn't hungry. I knew you would be worried about Miz Etta Ruth, so I went up to check on her. She is in bed with the mannequin, and they are both sound asleep," Mary said, and grinned. "Strange, but she is now wearing a *pale-blue* evening gown instead of the pink one she left in last night. She is also wearing her husband's trousers beneath the blue gown, and his *muddy shoes* are on the floor. I thought it odd that there was mud on the shoes, Miss Clara, since it has not rained once since I arrived in Hesterwine."

"Dry as it's been, I fear we are in the early stages of a drought," Clara said absently, and then frowned. "Mud on Clarence's shoes? First, *flour* on them, and now *mud.* I wonder what the woman's been up to *this* time."

"Oh, Miss Clara, I did not mean to worry you. Miz Etta Ruth was probably watering her yard in town. I know that her shoes get quite muddy when she waters the rose garden here at Hesterwine Place."

"They do at that," Clara said, deciding to accept that explanation, and unwilling to allow Etta Ruth to be the warden of her thoughts just now. Fritz Von Heuvel had claimed *that* territory in the courthouse this morning the moment he uttered those words that almost made her faint! Her curiosity about the conversation between him and Jack had to be sated, and quickly, or she would never be able to get a good night's sleep again!

She waited until Justine went up to bed, and Hank and Willie drove to the bay to jig for flounder. As soon as the door closed behind them, she joined Mary and Jack in the parlor.

"That was very nice of Mr. Gustave Herrmann to sign the pledge and then offer to pay all the fines, wasn't it, Jack?"

"Yes, ma'am, it sure was."

"It was quite surprising, though, him being a complete stranger and having only arrived in Hesterwine the day before."

"I thought so, too, Miss Clara," Mary said, and Jack agreed.

Clara decided to get right to the point. "May I ask if Mr. Herrmann shed any light on why he chose to live in Hesterwine, and then rented that dilapidated old farmhouse down the road? One would think that a man like him—obviously able to afford better—would want the convenience of a boarding house where he wouldn't have to clean up after himself or cook his own meals," she added, then laughed lightly, hoping she hadn't sounded overly curious. "Anyway, I suppose he has a legal right to go anywhere he wants, since, as I recall, he told the sheriff he was an American citizen and had the papers to prove it."

"Yes, ma'am, a *recent* American citizen, and given a ride across the ocean on a US Army hospital ship, passage arranged by the British government. The sheriff touched on something when he made those German spy remarks. Gustave Herrmann was a spy, all right, but he spied for the British during the First World War, not Germany."

Clara managed to keep her astonishment internal as Jack continued.

"Early in the war, the Russians overran his post and arrested everybody in a German uniform, including him. When he told them he was with the

German troops because he was spying for the British, they didn't believe him and threw him in prison."

"How terrible," Clara whispered, trying not to appear stunned.

"He was almost killed when they captured him. After months in a prison hospital, he ended up in Siberia with other German POWs. Soon afterward, a drunken Russian guard stabbed him and tried to strangle him. He pulled the knife from his ribs and stabbed his assailant with it, killing him."

"Oh!"

"The Russians tried him for murder and sentenced him to life in a civilian prison this time, and that's where he slaved, in a frozen Siberian lumber camp, seven days a week, sixteen hours a day, for the next twenty-five years. They would have sentenced him to death by firing squad if they hadn't needed strong men to labor in the inhuman conditions of those camps."

Clara gasped, her shock deepening. "Dear God, what the poor man must have gone through," she said, barely audible this time.

"Yes, ma'am, the winters there are long and bitterly cold. There were no luxuries ... sometimes not enough food or warm clothes. Many prisoners didn't live through the first winter."

Suddenly, Clara felt glad that she hadn't known about Fritz's misery until now. She could not have borne knowing he was suffering so. "My goodness," she murmured. "I have a cinder in my eye." She turned aside with her handkerchief raised to wipe at the sudden stinging. *Was it possible that Fritz Von Heuvel never knew that she had abandoned him ... never knew that she had sailed home to America immediately after he went into the German Army?*

"A sympathetic guard finally helped him get word to England. They got him released, and after a year of recovering in a British hospital, he later worked there for three years—he didn't say in what capacity."

*As a doctor,* Clara's silent inner voice replied, remembering the many evenings Doctor Fritz Von Heuvel hurried away from dinner or their bed in the middle of the night to attend an ailing patient.

"He told the British authorities he wanted to come to the United States to live," Jack was saying. "He must have been a hero to England after what he'd suffered while in service to them. They immediately pulled strings with the US government and got him American citizenship, and passage on that hospital ship."

"But Hesterwine is such an out-of-the-way place, Jack. It seems odd to me that he came here, considering all the places he could have gone."

"True, Miss Clara. He said that a long time ago, he befriended a vacationing American who painted an alluring picture in his mind of a shady country road outside Hesterwine, Texas, which led to a grand manor sitting amid beautiful gardens and lush farmlands. He said his relentless dream of those beautiful gardens and lush farmlands were all that kept him alive those twenty-five years." Jack smiled. "I guess a man feeling that strongly about a place is reason enough to want to live there."

"Oh, Jack, that is so sad," Mary said. "But thank God he had something to cling to all those years in that prison. I wonder if he has found his American friend. Surely, the person must have lived in Hesterwine at one time or another to have described this place so accurately to him."

For a long time after Jack left and Mary went upstairs to rest, Clara stood on the porch gazing down the road at the old house. She knew now that Fritz had come to Hesterwine because he thought she had waited in Germany for him after he went to war. Perhaps he thought she had waited until she finally concluded he was dead and never coming back to her. Or maybe he thought that *she* thought he had changed his mind about their engagement and then *he* had abandoned *her*... and being the gentleman he was, he had come to Hesterwine to assure her that *that* had not been the case.

She went into the house. Perhaps he would come knocking at her door one day soon—that is, if all that was holding him back was fear of facing her. He would explain why he never returned to her in Germany and she would tell him... what? Tell him that it didn't matter because she had left almost immediately after his troop train pulled out of the station? Or tell him that while he had dreamed about *her,* yearned for *her*—not Hesterwine, Texas,—all those miserable years in that frozen Russian prison camp, *she* had thought only of Boyd Pendleton.

Feeling unusually low, she went to the kitchen for a glass of water and opened the refrigerator, her eyes moving from the water jug to the tall pitcher of Grandfather Hesterwine's *recipe* that Etta Ruth had syphoned from one of the barrels brought up from the basement for the party. After a moment, she carried the pitcher to the table, grabbing a coffee cup from the cabinet as she went, sat down, and then filled it to the brim. She gazed a long time at the pretty purple liquid before finally taking a sip. "It still tastes like delicious Delaware Punch," she said, then downed it just the way she downed a cold glass of water after a hot day of working in the garden. She picked up the pitcher, intending to refill the cup, but instead jumped as Mary came into the kitchen.

"Oh, my dear, awake so soon? I hope you won't think badly of me." She indicated the pitcher in her hand. "I am really not a drinking woman, you know, but...."

"I know, and it's all right, Miss Clara. You need not worry about what I think. Is that your grandfather's famous recipe? May I have a taste?" She took a cup from the cabinet and sat down at the table.

Clara filled both cups. "This is my second, and I may have a third."

"I can see why you would. It is such a pretty color," Mary said, and paused a moment before saying, "I hope you will not mind my saying so, but I saw at the courthouse how upset you got when Mr. Herrmann showed up, and I watched your face tonight when Jack told us about him. Who *was* that man, Miss Clara? You know him, don't you?"

Clara avoided Mary's eyes. "Yes, dear, I know him. I met him nearly twenty-nine long years ago on a cold, blustery February day in England—the last of my two vacation trips abroad that Etta Ruth keeps attaching so much *mystery* to." She waited for Mary to respond, but Mary seemed to be waiting for her to continue, so she did. "You are the first person I have ever spoken to about this, Mary...." She hesitated again, feeling herself flush with embarrassment, yet determined to go on, even though she could not fathom why she suddenly felt the urge to tell someone about her and Fritz. "It was shortly after my fiancé, Boyd Pendleton, and Justine ran off together for the second time." She chuckled dryly. "I lost my temper one day and blurted that out to you and Willie, didn't I?"

"Yes, ma'am."

"To make a long story short, my dear, Fritz Von Heuvel and I were lovers for six months in Germany until he joined the Kaiser's army."

Mary's eyes grew huge.

"We were engaged to be married, but I broke our engagement by taking the first boat home as soon as he was out of sight, and I never saw him again ... until today."

"Whoa, *Miss Clara*...."

"Yes, dear. '*Whoa, Miss Clara*'! That's exactly what I should have said the day he and I literally crossed paths while strolling the English countryside. He was on holiday, as was I." She drained her cup, then raised it almost to her nose and peered inside it. "I am definitely beginning to feel the *punch* in Grandfather's Delaware Punsssch," she said, slurring several words.

"Me, too," Mary said. "Want another? It really is very tasty. It could not possibly have much alcohol."

"Only eighty proof, I've been told."

"Is that a lot?"

"I don't think so."

"Then I guess we can have more." Mary refilled both cups until they threatened to run over.

Clara nodded her thanks. "He is Fritz Von Heuvel, not Gustave Herrmann. He gave the sheriff that false name because he took one look at me sitting there on that bench looking old and frumpy and decided he didn't want to contact me after all."

"Oh, that is not true, Miss Clara! You have preserved quite handsomely for a woman your age—Miss Justine, too."

"Yes, *preserved,* like two old pickles in a jar!" she cried, holding up her cup as if making a toast. "Here's to preserved old pickles in a jar ... or old pickles *in* a pickle, for that matter." They both giggled.

"Miss Clara, he will knock on your door one day soon. I will bet you *that.*"

"I certainly hope not! What would be the point?"

"Yes, that is the question, isn't it? How many years ago did you say you two parted?"

"Twenty-nine, going on thirty. I feel horrible that he was in that Russian prison most all that time, but I am glad he didn't show up *here* twenty-nine years ago when Poppa was still alive. How would I have ever explained him to Poppa and Justine?"

"Forgive me for saying so, Miss Clara, and I truly adore Miss Justine, but it seems to me you never owed her an explanation ... her running off *twice* with your fiancé, Boyd Pendleton, like she did. That being so, have you ever considered how lucky you were in finding out what a two-timing heel old Boyd was, and finding out in time to keep from marrying him? *Hic!*" She slapped her hand over her mouth too late to silence the hiccup.

Clara felt her face flush again. "I've thought of that *heel* all these years, never able to get him out of my heart—it's been a distressing situation," she said sadly, and then slowly drained her third cup before pushing it toward Mary, now in charge of the pouring. "Justine feels the same way, and it makes me furious that she still has the gall to harbor those old feelings we had for Boyd back then. I imagine it's been a distressing situation for us both. However, I have always contended that, after what she did, she should have raced, uh, *e-rased*, him from her mind, if only out of guilt ... *exspooned* him from any thought *whas-so-effer*. She owes me that much, wouldn't you say?"

"I would say." Mary reached across the table and patted her hand. "Okay, Miss Clara, my turn. I had a heel in my life, too. His name was Claxton Mitchell. He dumped me, but I think I still care for him a little. I also think I love Jack Dunston. *That* is *my* distressing situation."

"Forget Kaaxton Misssle, Mary dear. Marry Jack. Thaz's my advice."

"My point is, Miss Clara, could it be possible that *you* love both sorry old Boyd Pendleton *and* Frizzz what's-his-name?"

"*Von Heuvel. Frizzz* Von Heuvel."

"Yes, Fritzzz *Von Heuvel.* I do not see you living with a man in a foreign country for six months without loving him. You are just not that kind of girl, Miss Clara."

"*Jussstine*, maybe, but not me," Clara slurred. They both giggled again. Clara blinked repeatedly, clearly feeling the effect the recipe was having on the loosening of her tongue. "Just between us girls, Mary, Fritzzz was quite the lover."

"Ooh?"

"Yes, and although I'd had no former sssperiences of that nature to which I could have compared him, the obvious could not be denied. We made mad love right up to the hour before he left to join the Kaiser's war. Not an hour after *that*, I snuck off for home without even leaving a note." She raised a finger. "I *did* leave his engagement ring behind and a little box of his deceased wife's jewelry he gave me—that would have been terrrrble of me to take *them*." Suddenly looking quite bleary-eyed, she grabbed Mary's hand. "There were moments when I thought I loved him and I told him so. His reply was always '*I vill write eet in my book, mein liebchen.*"

"Ah-ha!" Mary cried. "That is exactly what he said at the courthooch that almost made you faint! Now that I think of it, it wasss bootiful ... like something outta uh movie."

"Mary, dear, I think you've had enough Delaware Pooch—you are slurring your words."

"So are you."

"Oh, well, I understand what I'm saying, don't you?"

"Yes, I understand what both of us are saying, I just feel a little dizzy, that's all. *Hic!*"

"I have wondered over the years if perhaps I might have stayed in Germany ... if Fritzzz hadn't given me the opportunity to leave when he put on that German uniform and *he* left."

"Maybe you should have stayed, and then made him stay home instead of going off to spy, and then you two could have lived happily ever after, Miss Clara." Mary abruptly rose from her chair, slapped her hand over her mouth, and spoke through her fingers. "Excuse me, Miss Clara, but I think I have to—" She did a staggering run to the back door, losing most of her not-so-delicious-anymore eighty-proof Delaware Punch recipe on the back porch before she reached the yard.

Moments later, Clara came carefully down the steps sideways while holding tightly to the porch railing with one hand and extending a dripping-wet dishtowel from the other. "Mary, dear, put this to the back of your neck—that's what Poppa used to do and it always made him feel better." With that, she sank down on the steps and haphazardly slung the dishtowel around her own neck.

Mary helped her to her feet and, holding onto each other, they went inside and made their way to the elevator, giggling sporadically as they went, and then loudly shushing each other. Clara was ready to sleep now. She didn't know whether to credit the eighty-proof Delaware Punch for her wiliness to close her eye ... or credit it to finally getting her twenty-nine-year-old secret off her chest. Whatever the reason, she doubted if she'd be able to stay awake long enough to shell even one peanut.

At 4:00 a. m., Mary awoke to the sound of the wind blowing harder than usual and banging the interior shutters. Drowsy and with her head throbbing, she rolled out of bed thinking to close the windows. As she reached for the shutter, she glanced out into the pre-dawn darkness and suddenly came wide-awake. In the distance, close to where the town of Hesterwine would be, a flickering orange glow licked at an otherwise pitch-black sky.

She scrambled into her robe and shoes and ran down the hall to bang on Clara's and Justine's doors. Behind her, the elevator was grinding down from the third floor. It rattled to a halt and Etta Ruth—still in the pale-blue gown she had changed into, and now wearing a pair of her own shoes instead of the muddy ones belonging to her dead husband—stood leaning against the elevator's inner wall, her arms folded over her chest. Suddenly dropping her arms, she grabbed up her dangling binoculars and playfully examined Mary.

"You know about the fire, Miz Etta?"

"I didn't set it, if that's what you're thinking."

"I would not dream of thinking such a thing, Miz Etta."

"I'm not one of those *firebugs* we read so much about in the papers, you know—although I did set an old lady's outhouse on fire once when I was a sweet little girl, but it was Halloween."

Clara and Justine came hurrying toward the elevator, Clara still fully dressed, and looking as if she might also have a headache. Mary stepped aside to make room for them.

"Want a ride in my *lift?*" Etta Ruth asked flippantly, raising her binoculars again. "Jesus Christ, Clara, you look like red-eyed crap." She leaned close and sniffed. "If I didn't know better, I'd think I smelled your grandpa's old recipe on your breath. Phew!"

Clara ignored her. "I'm afraid, in this dry weather and high winds, the fire is going to spread. What's worse, it looks to be dangerously close to Hesterwine."

Justine stared at her. "Hesterwine is burning, Clara? Oh, my God! Oh, my God! Oh, my Go—" Etta Ruth gave her arm a twisting pinch.

"Stop that, you mean thing!" Justine screeched, rubbing her injury. "Don't you care that our town could burn to smithereens?"

Etta Ruth now examined *her* with the binoculars.

*Miss Clara was right,* Mary thought as the elevator slowly descended. *That fire could spread far and wide in this drought.* During the past few weeks, the grass had turned brown and fairly crackled when one walked on it. A single spark could set acres afire, as well as the moisture-starved wooden homes and businesses in Hesterwine ... and tonight the wind was blowing like a mini-hurricane!

Outside on the porch, Etta Ruth went jauntily down the steps, the wind violently whipping her pale-blue evening gown in first one direction and then the other. "I'm gonna climb up the windmill and watch the fire. Any of you like to join me?" She looked at Justine. "How about you, floozy, wanna climb up there with me? I won't let you fall off... I promise."

Justine gave her a look. "What happened to your *pink* evening gown? Spill your Mason jar on it?"

"Not that it's any of your beeswax, floozy, but I burned it."

Justine rolled her eyes. "Good grief, you burned that perfectly good dress? I could have put it in the poor basket at church—someone who couldn't afford an evening dress could have used it. But that would have been an act of kindness on your part, wouldn't it?"

"I was in the middle of an 'act of kindness' when the goddamn thing got ruined."

"Ha! I'd like to know what *act of kindness* you—"

The sound of a vehicle speeding down Hesterwine Road from the direction of the bay captured everyone's attention, and they watched it sail past the house at a reckless speed. Mere seconds later, a second vehicle sped into view from the same direction. But rather than sailing past, it slid to a halt at the gate... just long enough for Leeta to lean out the window of Hank Posey's pickup truck, and yell: *"It's Rose Hill!* Jack's brother came to the bay where we was fishing and said the Klu Klux Klan done set fire to it!"

## 24

A LONE FIRE TRUCK FROM HESTERWINE got to Rose Hill the same time as Hank and Leeta. The fire truck was too late. The church and an entire row of houses southwest of the church stood engulfed in a solid wall of flames, the blustery forty-five-mile-an-hour winds swirling sparks and blazing debris from house to house. Rose Hill's vintage, 1920s fire truck with the barrel-type water wagon hitched to it was empty long before a second fire truck arrived. Rose Hill's residents, their faces contorted by heat and panic, battled the flames with water hoses stretched from their yards.

Hank left Leeta in a huddled crowd of women and children onlookers and joined a water brigade led by his father, alongside Jack and other white men from town. "Stay there," Hank commanded.

*He need not worry*, Leeta thought as she looked around at the anguished faces reflected in the eerie orange light.

A little girl with half a dozen braids all over her head—much like her own at that age—tugged at Leeta's hand. "Them spooks in white sheets was here. Momma say they is the *Klu Klux Klan*. Momma say they hate all the coloreds on earth worse than the devil hates God." She pointed at the roaring wall of fire. "My house is down there. It was burning up when Momma got us out."

The girl's mother glanced at Leeta, her soot-covered face streaked by dried tears and sweat. Leeta did not miss the hostility in the woman's eyes.

"You that singer, ain't you? We ain't had no trouble from the Klan in a long time 'til you got here."

Instead of flaring up in anger, as would be the normal thing for her to do, Leeta remained silent. The woman was right. If she hadn't sung at the Blue Creek Lounge, if she hadn't talked Dink and the Hesterwine ladies into having that dance for the colored military, none of this would have happened.

After a while, she wiped hard at her cheeks and wondered angrily what was wrong with her. Leeta Bulow wasn't supposed to let other people's problems affect her like this! She had learned long ago that it did no good to hurt for anything or anybody, but she was hurting now. *Damn that Hank Posey and them silly old ladies ... 'specially that damn Mary Kenny!*

A flashbulb popped, temporarily blinding her. Several white men with fancy cameras, like the ones newspaper reporters used, snapped pictures of the fire and the illuminated faces of the crowd watching it. One man had a movie camera mounted on his shoulder, humming away at first one scene and then another. The hostile woman with the talkative little girl turned to Leeta as if she had suddenly decided to be friendly.

"Them white men is reporters," she said, pointing at the one with the movie camera. "That one said he from Houston. Him and them others was touring the new navy base in Corpus Christi and was on their way home when they spotted the fire. They been asking lots of questions. We told 'em it was the Klan what done it, and we told 'em *why* they done it. They done it 'cause a colored gal from up North and two old white ladies wanted to have a dance in their barn for the colored boys from the military bases nearby here." She leaned close and fairly shouted in Leeta's face. "And that's what brung all hell and the devil down on us!"

Leeta, batting her burning eyes, again did the unlikely—she walked away.

Soon after the church and five houses on the block, including the Blue Creek Lounge, burned to the ground, fire trucks from surrounding communities arrived in time to save the rest of the community. By sunrise the wind had died down, although weightless flecks of ash and soot continued to float on the trenchant air, sticking to everything. The Reverend Posey's tent lay smoldering alongside the river, its poles charred, its canvas a flaking lump ready to disintegrate into blackened powder at a touch.

Leeta, seeing a hugely pregnant woman and two little boys dragging a mattress from a partially burned shack, went to help them. She carried out everything that was salvageable and stacked it wherever the exhausted woman pointed. Afterward, she held a young couple's baby and corralled their two-year-old while the couple sorted through their water-soaked belongings.

Finally, by mid-afternoon, she searched for Hank. She found him and Jack farther down the street, both barely recognizable beneath the soot and grime that covered them from head to shoes. Exhausted, and wiping at her eyes to clear them of the flecks of soot the filled the air like pesky gnats, she watched as they carried a rolled-up carpet from a small shack. Drawing closer, she halted suddenly, her raw eyes blinking in horror as she saw that the carpet was actually a thick blanket with an old woman rolled up inside it, her gray head sticking out the end, her eyes shut. Leeta's legs suddenly refused to hold her and she collapsed to her knees. *She* had caused that old woman's death! *Were there others?* She heard a long, dismal wail followed by someone screaming, "She's dead! She's dead!" She didn't realize it was she who cried out until she heard Hank yelling at her.

"Willie! Willie! She ain't dead! She is just wet and cold!" She looked up to see Jack gently set the old woman in a chair under a tree.

She was aware of Hank pulling her into his arms and trying to comfort her, but she was having none of it. She had seen too much misery and destruction today to be comforted. The coldness that had been in the pit of her stomach for as long a she could remember was writhing its way upward, almost choking her as it tried to burst free. When it did, splattering the ground around her, as well as Hank's boots, she wiped her mouth on the handkerchief Hank pressed into her hands and cried as she had not cried since that life-changing night by the river when she was thirteen and smothering beneath the weight and stench of her rapist. She had changed then, and not for the better. What was this strange shift of emotions she now felt? Whatever it was, it was as if she was *earth,* and she had felt it move.

After a while, she became aware of Hank's father standing nearby and smiling at her. She wiped her eyes and smiled back.

"This isn't your fault, girl," the reverend said. "It's mine. I should have known better than to invite the sheriff out to Rose Hill for the dance. It didn't take long for word to spread that *'a uppity nigger from Rose Hill'* had the audacity to invite white folks to fraternize socially with *Negroes*—and *that's* why the Klan did this."

Jack patted her shoulder. "The reverend's right, Willie. This isn't your fault; nor is it yours, Reverend Posey. And I am gonna do my darnedest to make certain something like this never happens again in Vander County."

Hank gave out a whoop. "Does that mean you finally made up your mind to run for sheriff?"

"Yeah." Jack looked around at the smoldering ruins. "But I'll need all the communities like Rose Hill and La Villita in Vander County to help me. They'll have to go to the polls and vote—every last one of them that's old enough."

"That might be a problem, Jack," Hank said. "Coloreds and Mexicans around here don't vote because of that old Jim Crow law that says they got to pay a poll tax beforehand. Most are too poor to pay it. In the past, some managed. Even so, they didn't get to vote, but not because they didn't try." He glanced meaningfully at his father. "I know a man that tried, but the Klan got him before he could get up the courthouse steps. I was just a kid, but I remember. They gave him a beating that almost killed him, and shot the mule he rode to town on. Then they tied that mule's bloody head to his back... and dumped you off on our doorstep, didn't they, Poppa? That wasn't but twenty years ago, when I was six, but I can still see it like it just happened."

Leeta stared at Hank and his father, feeling the need to tell Reverend Posey she was sorry for what happened to him. Nevertheless, she held back, thinking, *I'll tell him when I know him better.* Suddenly, she looked away. *What is wrong with me! I ain't gonna be around here long enough to know him better!*

"My dad told me what happened to you, Reverend," Jack was saying. "He and others suspected several men around town, but could never prove it. One of them is a county commissioner now. Men like him are why we need to organize the Mexicans and the coloreds into a coalition that can join other fair-minded voters in the county to win elections for the right people. I've got a plan but I'll need all the help I can get to put it into action."

Reverend Posey shook Jack's hand. "I'll make sure Rose Hill folks that are old enough to vote pays that poll tax, even if I have to give them the money out of the Sunday collection basket to do it. You've got my word on it."

"We'll need volunteers to spread out over the county from dawn to dusk, going into Negro and Mexican homes... talking about what needs to change in Vander County if they ever expect to get fair treatment."

"I'll talk to the Catholic priest over at La Villita. I think he'll get his people to join us," said Reverend Posey.

"I know him. He'll be all for it," Jack said. "After we've organized, we'll march *en masse* to the courthouse, pay the poll tax, and register to vote. On Election Day, we'll march again, this time, to vote."

Hank spoke up. "I agree it's a good plan, Jack, but Mexicans and Negroes suddenly paying their poll tax after generations of *not* paying it is sure to draw notice from the wrong people—the people who set this fire. They'll try to stop us, and I wouldn't be surprised if Sheriff Bloot will help them."

"Let them try. There's safety in numbers, Hank. As to Sheriff Bloot, his political savvy will keep him from openly opposing people registering to vote. He'll be hoping the Klan does that for him, like they did tonight and in the past. But if we've formed that coalition and we stick together, we'll outnumber them at every turn—on the street, and at the polls."

"I wanna help," Leeta said. "I feel like I owe it. I'm good at talking people into things," she added almost cynically, still feeling that if not for her, the fire would not have happened.

Hank cocked his head to one side and narrowed his twinkling eyes at her. "I thought you said you were *leaving* Hesterwine."

"I *am* leaving. I guess I should have said I'll help... if it don't take too long." She quickly shifted her eyes away from him as the pleased expression on his face melted and he looked like a little boy who'd just been told he didn't make the team. *Damn you, Hank Posey, I ain't got no choice!*

The next morning, news of the fire at Rose Hill was overshadowed in area newspapers—especially Hesterwine's evening edition of the *Vander County Picayune:*

BODY OF LOCAL BANKER, STANTON B. PRICKETT, FOUND MURDERED IN PARKING LOT BEHIND BANK.

> *The second death this month has Hesterwine law enforcement scratching their heads. The first to die was Marvin Abelson, owner of Abelson's Shoe Shop. The*

*coroner's report is pending on Abelson's death, but the Sheriff's Department reports he died under suspicious circumstances and was likely a murder victim. In Stanton B. Prickett's case, muddy shoe prints (not his) led directly to Prickett's body from the freshly watered flowerbed adjoining the bank's parking lot. Investigators believe he was slain by whoever left those prints. Is there a serial killer on the prowl in our once peaceful little community?*

The shocking news of Banker Prickett's murder made Clara feel as if she was in the path of a tornado and had no time to escape. She was worried enough already that Etta Ruth was on the verge of arrest for killing Mr. Abelson, and now...! Etta Ruth had said at the dance: *"Prickett needs a comeuppance to end all comeuppances, and I know just how to deliver it to him."* Had she delivered it to him?

*What to do?* Mary had seen mud on Clarence's shoes beside Etta Ruth's bed, and now there was no doubt in Clara's mind of where Clarence's shoes, with Etta Ruth's feet in them, had been the night Banker Prickett died. Just as suspicious, why had Etta Ruth burned the pink evening gown she'd worn that night? She had quipped to Justine that she was 'in the middle of an act of kindness' when it got ruined. An act of *kindness*? It would be just like Etta Ruth to consider Mr. Pricket's death an *act of kindness* in that he was no longer a threat to Hesterwine Place! Oh, Lordy!

*What to do?* Clara fell to rubbing her temples, as if that would miraculously produce an answer. Even though she was Etta Ruth's confidant and protector, did she not have a moral obligation to be on the side of law and order and therefore tell Sheriff Bloot all she knew? She shuddered; the mention of *Sheriff Bloot* and *law and order* in the same sentence was an oxymoron if she'd ever heard one! However, what was more important, her loyalty to family... or helping Sheriff Bloot solve his murder case?

Wearier than ever, Clara squeezed her eyes shut, then took a deep, deciding breath. *Perhaps we shall let sleeping dogs lie, continue to wait... let Sheriff Bloot find his own route to solving those murders.* Suddenly, Clara pictured Clarence Jr. rushing out the front door the day she asked him to take Etta Ruth elsewhere. *Why oh why didn't I demand he hogtie that woman and drag her away to that asylum!*

# 25

Shortly after Banker Prickett's funeral on Tuesday, which Clara, Justine, Mary, and *Etta Ruth* attended, the sheriff hand-delivered a surprising letter from the bank, extending the closure date on the mortgage thirty days, signed by *Betty Prickett*.

"Yep," drawled the sheriff after Clara read the letter aloud. "The bank gave my mother-in-law her husband's old position. She's giving y'all another chance. That way, the town won't look too unkindly on her when she takes possession." He looked around, smiling as he examined the room. "Me and the wife and kids is probably gonna move in here with her now that she's all alone. If I was you, I'd just go ahead and start moving out now. You ain't never gonna be allowed to operate a bakery out here again. Without an income to add to your old age pensions, you can't survive out here no more'n a monkey can survive without a tail."

"We have not applied for *old age pensions*," Clara snapped.

"It's the same as accepting charity, as far as Clara and I are concerned," Justine added.

Mary spoke up. "So why don't you give your advice to someone who wants it, Sheriff."

"You're mouthing off at me just when I was beginning to think you were a real sweetie pie," he said. "Looks like you're picking up some bad habits from that colored friend of yours."

"Mary *is* a sweetie pie," Justine retorted. "And so is Willie."

Mary nodded. "Yes, we are, and Willie has no bad habits."

Sheriff Bloot rolled his eyes. "Getting back to what I was saying, the *powers that be* in Vander County sure ain't gonna allow you no permit for a bakery, or any other venture y'all might cook up. They ain't happy about all that bad newspaper publicity you brung down on the community by having that dance for the *coloreds*. If it hadn't been for that, that fire at Rose Hill wouldn't never have happened. So, you see, it all boils down to *you*, Miss Clara and Miss Justine, causing the whole mess."

Mary could not contain her anger at his ridiculous remark and, although standing in Sheriff Bloot's hulking shadow still made her nervous, she glared up at him. "How dare you say such a thing! Miss Clara and Miss Justine are not to blame for that fire, but you know who is, don't you? Rose Hill residents told you what they saw and *who* they saw tossing those firebombs."

Justine nodded. "Everyone knows it was that awful Klu Klux Klan!"

"I wouldn't be talking like that where anybody can hear you, Miss Justine. You oughta know it ain't right to take the word of coloreds over white folks."

"We certainly *do* take them at their word, and that you *don't* is only a small part of the problem in Varner County," Clara said.

After rolling his eyes again, Sheriff Bloot continued. "Anyhow, some of them fellers on the Board of Commissioners that does the deciding for the county ain't happy with the notoriety. All that bad publicity for Hesterwine and Vander County ain't good for *nobody*. So don't expect to get that permit to sell your attic junk or anything else you scrounge up." He reached around to his hip pocket. "That's because I got a brand-new *Writ of Mandamus* saying you can't sell nothing off the place for a year. Y'all gonna be gone outta here long before then."

Clara laid the Writ of Mandamus on the table. "I am ashamed to think such men hold positions of power in Vander County, Sheriff Bloot. You should be investigating *them* instead of doing their dirty work."

"My house is *wood* through and through, Miss Clara, and it would burn *real* easy."

Mary could not resist. "I hear there is an election in Varner County soon, Sheriff. Maybe those commissioners will no longer be in office afterward—*or you*," she said, remembering Jack's words three days ago when he told her and the Hesterwine ladies that he was running for sheriff. He was not to announce his candidacy publically until he had filed his intentions with the county and had gathered other candidates to run against the current commissioners.

"Why, yes. There is an election coming up, isn't there," Justine said as she, Clara, and Mary exchanged secretive smiles. "Mary is right; someone could run against you this time, you know."

Sheriff Bloot narrowed his eyes at them and then laughed. "That's been tried before. I ain't worried." With that, he screwed his hat on his head and left.

As he drove away, Justine turned to Clara. "Did you hear what he said about us being as helpless as a monkey without a tail? That old monkey we saw in '29 at the Breckenridge Park Zoo in San Antonio was missing not only his *tail* but an arm as well, and he was surviving just fine ... the poor little thing."

"Too bad we aren't him," Clara said. "*We'd* have a cage to crawl into thirty days from now when Betty Prickett takes ownership of our home."

Mary's heart ached for the pair as she followed them into the kitchen. When they weren't looking, she sneaked another *anonymous* donation into the empty sugar bowl—Leeta's last pay from the Blue Creek Lounge before it burned. This time, there was enough cash for flour, coffee, tea, and the utility bills for the next thirty days ... before they all had to move out of this big, beautiful old ancestral mansion so dear to Miss Clara's and Miss Justine's hearts. The extension from Betty Prickett was almost cruel, she thought. Unless a miracle happened, it was just thirty more days of Miss Clara and Miss Justine being miserable.

That evening, Jack came to Hesterwine Place and said a fellow CAP pilot had called him from Portland, Maine, saying there was a big Associated Press article in a newspaper there, pictures and interviews with witnesses about the fire at Rose Hill, and saying the Klan was responsible.

"Good!" Miss Clara said. "The whole world now knows what happened here."

"Now, Jack, all we need is to get you elected sheriff of Vander County," said Miss Justine.

Jack smiled. "Like I said earlier, I'll need all the help I can get. But right now, I've got news that I know will put big smiles on your faces. Early this morning, trucks full of men and lumber from area navy bases arrived at Rose Hill to rebuild everything that burned. The US Navy and Marine Corps came in like gangbusters, tooting their horns, handing out food, clothes, and loads of toys and candy to the kids."

Up until now, Aunt Lucy had been at the sink quietly washing dishes, and now she cried out, "Praise the Lord and pass the ammunition!" For the first time since before the fire, Clara and Justine laughed in earnest.

"The church frame is up, as well as the house frames," Jack said. "All that many carpenters working on one project are a sight to behold. As soon as the homes are rebuilt, they said they are paying special attention to rebuilding the Blue Creek Lounge, and building it large enough to hold a crowd befitting Willie Holloway and the Blue Creek Trotliners."

Justine jumped up from her chair. "I'm going upstairs to tell Willie!" She laughed but then looked agitated. "Someone else can tell Etta Ruth. I looked through her keyhole this morning to make sure one of her cigarettes wasn't about to burn *us* down. She's got that mannequin dressed in Clarence's pajamas again, Clara. He's setting up in bed and she's mumbling away to him like he's her best friend—which he no doubt is."

"*Justine!*" Clara scolded as she glanced at Jack and then back to her sister.

"Oh, Clara, Jack knows about the mannequin. Didn't he pick him up off the floor when Etta Ruth threw him down the stairs? Like everybody else, Jack knows Etta Ruth is *cracked*, don't you, Jack?" She departed with a dismissive wave of her hand at Clara.

Although Mary was perplexed about her feelings for Jack and Claxton, there was one thing she was not confused about—Jack Dunston was a terrific person; thoughtful, kind, and fearless of challenges. He would be a wonderful sheriff if he could beat Sheriff Bloot. Before returning to Rose Hill to help out, he said he had talked several good men into running against the current powers that be. If he won his race, they were sure to win right along with him. Decent men would at last take over the important business of running the city and the county.

Jack proved his generous nature twice today when, together, they picked Miss Clara and Miss Justine up from their Hesterwine Medallion gathering at Vernell Watson's house and drove them home. Afterward, she and Jack had planned an all-day excursion to the amusement park at North Beach. The last time they were there, they'd won an entire roll of tickets, and today eagerly anticipated riding every ride and playing every game. However, upon seeing the glum expressions on the sisters' faces, Jack insisted they come along. He did not take no for an answer.

His second unselfish act occurred moments after they pulled into the parking lot at the amusement park and he told Miss Clara and Miss Justine that he wanted to borrow six hundred dollars from his bank and lend it to them to pay Betty Prickett and the First Loan & Trust Bank. Naturally, the offer drew appreciative cries prior to their emphatic refusal.

"We never borrow that which we are not certain we can pay back. That was *Poppa's* department," Justine said bitterly. "You know, Jack, don't you, that he indebted Clara and me to the bank without our knowledge."

"Justine ..." Clara warned, and Mary knew the conversation was about to turn unpleasant if Justine persisted in divulging the family's private business.

"That is a lovely hat you are wearing today, Miss Justine," Mary said, hoping to entice the woman into a less volatile subject.

Justine jerked out a handkerchief and dabbed her cheek, even though her eyes were dry. "Thank you, dear. We couldn't even pay our Hesterwine Medallion dues when our names were called this morning. It was the most humiliating moment of my life!" This time, her eyes did water.

Clara stared at her. "Dear God in heaven, Justine, are you serious? I can think of at least *two* moments in your life that should have been more humiliating than being behind on our *Medallion* dues!"

*Uh-oh,* Mary thought. *Now is no time for Boyd Pendleton to rear his two-timing head.* Thinking to distract the sisters from their age-old quarrel, she held up her and Jack's fat roll of free tickets. "Guess what! Jack and I are treating you two to every ride and amusement this place has to offer!"

Jack glanced at her and then laughed. "That's right, ladies, but you'll have to ditch those glum faces." Jack was being diplomatic; their faces were not glum, they were *combative*.

Later, Mary watched anxiously as they rode separate bumper cars, both hunched over their steering wheels like stock car racers, their unsmiling faces comically serious as they concentrated on ramming each other.

"Tell me if I'm wrong, Mary, but I'm beginning to suspect the Hesterwine sisters have some sort of feud going."

"A serious feud of very long standing, I'm afraid. I cannot tell you about it because it would be disloyal of me."

Jack grinned at her as he took her hands. "Sometimes, I think you're too good to be true, Mary Kenny."

Mary felt her face redden. "I probably am too good to be true, Jack," she said, trying to sound lighthearted. A hundred times these past two weeks she had wanted to tell him everything, but was afraid. What if those green eyes suddenly stopped looking at her the way they were this very moment. She was still confused. If she still had feelings for Claxton, why should the way Jack looked at her matter? Miz Etta Ruth was right in her remarks yesterday when eavesdropping again over the transom. "Did somebody drop you on your head when you were a baby, Mary Kenny?" she had growled. "Anyone with half a brain should be able to figure out the difference between Jack Dunston and that heel, Claxton Mitchell. From what I've learned about him from your own mouth, he's maybe only a shade better than Willie's old boyfriend, *Mandingo Q. Mann.*"

The remark had so annoyed her that she had not bothered to hunt Etta Ruth down in the big old mansion and invite her to the amusement park. Halfway there, however, she had reconsidered and wished she had looked for her: She knew Miss Clara didn't like leaving Miz Etta Ruth alone in the house for fear she would get into "mischief." And she *would* be alone all day, since Aunt Lucy was at Rose Hill helping with the cleanup and Leeta, seeing that Hank was tired and needed a rest, talked him into going fishing. Oh, but what *mischief* could Miz Etta Ruth do while alone in the house that she would not do when everybody was around? All she did lately was just mope from one room to the next, or play that spooky funeral music on her organ. She had sworn off cigarettes again, so was not likely to burn the house down. Everyone was greatly pleased with that decision ... until she fed an entire pack of her Pall Malls to the peacocks. The male made those angry ear-splitting noises for hours afterward and Aunt Lucy tried to help him by throwing cracked ice at him.

Those had been Mary's hesitant thoughts earlier as they left the house and until they pulled into the parking lot at the amusement park and saw the frolicking crowd. *Yes, of course she will be just fine. I am worrying over nothing,* was her final thought of Etta Ruth as the four of them joined the fun taking place on the breezy oceanfront. *What else could Etta Ruth do, other than pester the peacocks ... or maybe throw her mannequin down the stairs again—naughty, but harmless little things like that.*

# 26

ETTA RUTH, LOOKING DISGRUNTLED as usual, dropped her purse to the floor beside her old Kimball Victorian parlor organ, flipped the tail of her red silk robe behind her like a maestro about to begin his concert, plopped down, and began to hammer and pump away. After a few blasts, she squeaked around on the stool to stare dully at nothing. What was the point of playing *Chopin's Funeral March* again today if there was no one around to annoy with it?

"No invitation for *you*, Etta Ruth Morley," she mumbled. "Not that I give a damn ... too much sand and too many people at North Beach, half of them the worst part of the human population—*teenagers.*" *Maybe I'm prejudiced*, she thought—she hadn't liked teenagers ever since she'd raised a pair. "No invitation for you, Etta Ruth Morley," she repeated.

She stretched her back, then yawned from boredom rather than a need for sleep. *The hell with the four of them!* They had ridden off crammed onto the front seat of that pickup truck like a bunch of silly high schoolers, and Jack Dunston looking like he didn't mind at all having them two old biddies sitting between him and his smooching partner. *Not one of them, not even Clara, bothered to look over their shoulders at me in my bedroom window ... mooning after them like a miserable little waif in a Dickens novel. Anyway, it was a fine performance on my part. Too bad they missed it.*

She stared all around, examining the vastness of the foyer. "This damn old museum is so quiet I can almost hear it breathing," she muttered. Sassy-face Willie and her string bean cowboy pedaled off to the bay on the two-seater, fishing poles sticking up like flags and Rube trotting along behind. *Not even the damn dog wanted to stay home with me today!* Willie claimed they were gonna *gig* for flounder again. *Ha! They did an awful lot of gigging lately.* One of these days she'd have to warn her about men who fished a lot ... especially if her cowboy stopped asking her to go along with him. Clarence had been an angler, using the excuse of weekend fishing trips to cheat on her. She had suspicioned he was up to more than fishing, and it had galled the hell out of her every time he came home late Sunday nights, threw his smelly, wet, fishing clothes on top of the washing machine for her to wash, and dumped a little fish or two in the kitchen sink for her to clean.

She figured he was buying the fish somewhere and too cheap to buy bigger ones. He was smart, that Clarence, but she finally figured out a way to catch him. He always wore the same fishing pants ... so one Friday before he came home from work and packed his bag to leave, she sewed the legs of his fishing pants loosely closed at the cuffs. If he truly intended to fish all weekend and tried to jam his legs into those pants, the threads holding the cuffs closed would break.

She thought the weekend would never end, but of course, it did. Late that Sunday night he came in the back door and went through his usual routine—wet pants on the washing machine, fish in the sink. "My goodness, Clarence," she said. "Your fishing pants are dripping salt water all over the floor."

"I waded out pretty far this time," he said, then scolded, "Instead of complaining about my dripping fishing pants, you might thank me for that nice flounder I hooked for you. He was a fighting little sucker ... liked to have worn me out," he added as he headed for the bathroom. As soon as he was out of sight, she ran her fist down the wet pants legs. Lo and behold, just as she expected, not a thread had been broken in either cuff! *All those months, he'd been soaking his empty fishing trousers in salty bay water and then buying fish from a seaside market on his way home.*

"The son of a bitch!" Etta Ruth cried, her voice echoing in the vast room. The fish story had happened years ago when they were both young. She had forgiven him after about six months; but, at the time, she thought his cheating partner was a *woman ... someone she'd be able to compete with, and win. Ha!*

She snatched up her purse and dug in it for a stick of gum, but came up with a prayer card that Clara had handed her after returning from the holier-than-thou Hesterwine Medallions' prayer meeting at pooch-lipped Vernell Watson's house this morning. She sailed the card across the room and watched it ride the air until it finally slid across the floor. She knew what Clara and Justine had prayed for at that Medallion prayer meeting—*money*. They'd invited her to go along, but she knew they only asked because she was a Hesterwine Medallion and the entire damn group was probably lying in wait to chastise her about some un-medallion-like thing they thought she'd done. How many times did she have to remind Clara that she no longer cared to attend those damned sessions with a bunch of silly old women who dressed up like nineteenth century high school majorettes three times a year and paraded around town beating that old bass drum like they were doing something important? *And everyone thought* she *was crazy!*

Anyway, she was glad she hadn't been invited to the amusement park. A few hours alone, without having to look at her gloomy cousins, was most welcome. All they talked about lately was how "different" it would be living at grouchy Old Lady Harvey's boarding house in town, and they still hadn't figured out where they'd get the money to pay the monthly rent. That silly Justine had said a mouthful at breakfast this morning: "With no income, we shall never know *where* we will be living from one day to the next." To which *she* had yelled, "Apply for your goddamn old age pensions like everybody else has, dummies, and then you'll know where you'll be living from one rotten day to the next!"

They had only stared at her as if she had asked them to strip naked and do a jig under the traffic light in the middle of Main Street. Luckily, *she* didn't have Clara and Justine's problem. She *knew* where she'd be, and it wasn't gonna cost her a damn thing.

Etta Ruth hooked her purse containing her allowance money from Clarence Jr. over her arm and headed for the kitchen, slowly putting one bare foot in front of the other and moving along like a tranquil cat despite the frenzied voices rushing through her head. Upon waking this morning, one of those voices had cautioned her that since Clara and Justine were in such dire straits for cash, she shouldn't leave her purse unattended anymore.

The voices in her head didn't always give her such good advice as that, but she couldn't silence their annoying rants any more than that rusty old windmill could fend off assaults from the wind. She could only sit up there on that platform and wait for the screeching of the blades to drown out the voices... and if that pesky Mary and that nervy Willie kept trying to coax her down before the voices finally shut up, she was gonna tell Clara and Justine all that juicy stuff about them. Etta Ruth's greasy red lips stretched into a salacious grin: *The things one can find out about people while peeking over the transom!*

In the kitchen, she poked a sharp finger at the bread dough rising on the back of the stove then watched it go flat. "Oops!" she snickered, then went to the pantry where she kept her supply of liquor. Moments later, with her Mason jar filled to the brim with ice, rum, and Coca-Cola, she headed for the parlor.

Halfway across the wide foyer, she glanced out the front door and saw a strange, sinister-looking, black limousine roll slowly up to the gate—sinister in that black curtains covered the passenger windows, front and back. Whoever was inside seemed in no hurry to get out.

Several minutes passed before the driver's door swung open and the largest Negro she had ever seen gradually emerged, growing taller and taller as he separated himself from the vehicle and stood gazing at the house. She knew immediately who he was.

She was at the door and smiling pleasantly when Mandingo Q. Mann raised a beefy fist to knock.

Peering through the screen down at her, he reached beneath his fancy yellow jacket with the dark-brown topstitching, produced a newspaper, unrolled it, and held it up to the screen for her to see.

"I am a friend of a gal I was told live out here." He had a deep, growling voice, and Etta Ruth judged the look on his face to mean that he was incapable of being a "friend" to anybody.

"She a gal what call herself Willie Holloway. Is this her?" He pointed at a face among a crowd of other stricken black faces watching a fire. The headline on the Chicago newspaper said, "*Klan Burns Negro Church and Homes in Segregated Section of Small Texas Town.*"

"Why, yes. Willie lives here. She should be home in a half-hour or so."

"Where she gone?"

"I have no idea, but she said she'd be back around four." She pointed at the grandfather clock. "It's almost that time now."

He looked around. "Ain't nobody here but you?" He kept his eyes tight, as if trying to figure out why this barefooted old white woman, wearing nothing but a gaping red robe and a slip, was holding open the screen door as if she wanted him to come in.

"Just little ol' me is home today," Etta Ruth replied as she looked past him to the curtained limousine. "I've never seen curtains in a car before. Do you have traveling companions waiting for you in that fancy Cadillac?"

"No. I'm driving myself this time."

She raised her Mason jar. "I'm having a cool drink with a kick in it. Would you like a kick while you wait for Willie?" Etta Ruth's mind was on the bottle of sleeping pills in her purse in the kitchen. She'd give him a drink that would knock him out cold, then she'd call the sheriff and say that a monstrous-looking colored man forced his way into the house, got drunk on her liquor, and tried to molest her. The sheriff would lock him up and soon afterward, Vander County would try him and send him to Huntsville prison for the next hundred years. After that, *Willie* could do as she damn pleased without worry. *I don't have to be a goddamn Hesterwine Medallion to do a good deed.*

"I'll just wait in my car for *Willie*."

"Oh, come on in the parlor and have a drink. What's the matter, you 'fraid I'm gonna bite? It's hot out there. I got cracked ice to put in that drink." She opened the screen door wider and motioned for him to come in. After a few seconds, he stepped inside.

"I am Miz Morley. You must be Mr. *Mandingo Q. Mann* that Willie told me about."

His heavy-lidded eyes narrowed. "*Willie* tell you 'bout me? What she say?" Both questions sounded like a threat, and she suddenly pictured him beating Willie so badly that she lost her baby. She also pictured him cutting Willie's throat when she got home—maybe *hers*, too. She smiled at him.

"Willie never says much about anything ... just that she worked for you in Chicago." She swept her arm out toward the big leather chair. "You sit yourself right down and get comfortable, Mr. Mann. I'll be right back with that drink."

In the kitchen, she dumped her purse out on the table and grabbed up the bottle of sleeping pills, hurried to the sink and crushed six of them, then dumped the powdery substance into a tall glass. *Damn! No more rum!* She dashed into the pantry to look over her supplies. *What to fix? What to fix?* She decided on something sweet to mask the taste of the pills and she grabbed a bottle of gin. She'd make a pitcher of Singapore Sling—gin, cherry brandy, orange, lime, and pineapple juice over cracked ice. She scooped the cans of juice into the crook of her arm, then cursed as she remembered that she had used all her Blue Stamp rationing on the fruit juices this month and had been saving them for her Sunday fixings. "Oh, well, I'll figure out a way for Willie to pay me back," she said as she looked for her bottle of cherry brandy but didn't find it.

"Damn that Aunt Lucy! She must have moved my cherry brandy. I wouldn't doubt if she hasn't been drinking it," she muttered, then grunted as she stretched on her tiptoes to feel on the top shelf for her missing cherry brandy. "Ah-ha!" Her hand closed around the dusty bottle.

Scant minutes later, she had an entire pitcher full of colorful concoction—enough for her to enjoy later when he was gone. With Mandingo Q. Mann's tall glass of Singapore Sling in hand containing the six crushed sleeping pills, she hurried back to the parlor. *The damned ass is bigger than an ox, but six pills ought to do it*, she thought.

Sitting in the big leather chair, he was still glowering as if he was someone used to asking questions and getting answers.

"What else Willie tell you 'bout me?"

"Nothing else." She handed him the drink. "I hope you like Singapore Slings, Mr. Mann."

"I don't care, just so it's strong."

"Oh, it's quite strong. I wouldn't be surprised if you felt its effects almost immediately," she added, smiling, as she watched him turn the glass up and swill it down exactly as she expected. "My! You must have been thirsty! Was it to your taste?"

"Umm, it was mighty tasty. That liquor sure got a bite to it. Sweeter'n most Slings I ever had. You add something different to it?"

"Oh, no ... just the usual gin and cherry brandy, mixed with a bit of this and a bit of that."

"Got any more?"

"Certainly. I'll be right back with the pitcher." *Good!* she thought. *By the time I get back, he'll be sleeping like a baby and I can call the sheriff.*

In the kitchen, she grabbed up the pitcher and was about to leave when something odd about the bottle of cherry brandy caught her eye. She paused to wipe at the layer of dust covering the label, her eyes widening as she read, "RAT POISON." Below that, *"Veneno para rata"*... Spanish for rat poison!

Etta Ruth slapped a hand to her open mouth as she continued to stare at the bottle that was the same size, shape, and green color as her cherry brandy bottle. In the semi-darkness of the pantry, she'd not seen the label beneath all that dust! Besides, she wasn't wearing her glasses today. Actually, she never wore them anymore. Mandingo Q. Mann would not be asleep when she returned to the parlor—he'd *be dead* ... or close to it! She hurried back to the parlor, unaware that the pitcher was still in her hand.

However, a stunned expression crossed her face as she saw him resting easily in the chair and smiling like a relaxed gargoyle.

He laughed and shook his big head, obviously now accepting her hospitality as he held out his glass for a refill. She glanced at the pitcher in her hand, surprised to see it there.

"Oh, no, Mr. Mann! I think you've had quite enough." She motioned for him to get up. "Time to go."

He ignored her frantic gesturing and, placing his big hand over hers on the pitcher's handle, effortlessly forced her to refill his glass.

"I wouldn't drink that if I were you," she said, slowly stepping back to watch him drink. If he drank more, she'd never be able to get him out of the house and on his way before he collapsed!

"Sit down, lady. I got to know what you put in this here drink," he said, indicating the glass. "It pretty good stuff. I reckon I got me a sweet tooth," he said, then laughed.

*Oh, great,* she thought, hesitantly sinking onto a chair across from him. *Now he wants the damned recipe!* "It has the usual ingredients, is all. Do you speak Spanish, Mr. Mann?"

"No."

"I only speak a little of it—*un poco*," she said, squeezing a thumb and forefinger together. "The label on one of the liquors I used says *veneno para ratas.* I suppose it could be Spanish for the 'last drink you will ever want.'"

"Maybe so." He took another drink and then smacked his lips.

She stared worriedly at him. He didn't seem a bit affected by the poison *or* the sleeping pills. The damned Yankee must have the constitution of a damned elephant! *But what if he doesn't have such a great constitution, Etta Ruth?* asked one of the voices in her head. *If he dies here, they will find out he was poisoned and they'll know you did it. And if he's gonna die before you can get him on his way, wouldn't you rather him be in the yard when it happened, close to the rose garden where the ground is soft enough to dig a hole for him?*

Etta Ruth nodded. Yesterday, she'd hauled several wagonloads of bull, cow, and donkey manure from the barn to the garden, and it still lay there in a big, soft pile waiting to be spread around the roses. That pile of manure would make a grand temporary cover for Mandingo Q. Mann until dark, when she could dig that hole and plant him properly. *What else can I do? No one would ever believe I didn't poison the son of a bitch on purpose!*

Mandingo Q. Mann interrupted her contemplations. "Lady... I sure feeling funny." His eyes blinked rapidly at her, then rolled from side to side.

She jumped to her feet and tried to pull him from the chair, but he resisted. She had to think of something fast!

"Oh my! You must forgive an old lady for her lapse of memory, Mr. Mann. I plum forgot that Willie is working at the Farmer's Market today. You'd better run along and catch her before she leaves work and takes off somewhere with one of those boyfriends of hers."

"*Boyfriends!*" He came unsteadily to his feet.

"Oh, yes, Willie has a number of gentleman friends. I lost count a long time ago. They are in and out of her room night and day... like a bunch of rutting bucks in heat," she grunted as she pulled him toward the foyer and then out the front door. "Come along now, Mr. Mann, you are moving much too slowly to catch Willie." She was in front of him now, gripping the massive forefingers on each of his baseball-mitt-sized hands and guiding him down the steps.

Once they reached the bottom step, she got around behind him, pressed her palms to his back, and pushed him toward the garden, then cursed when he abruptly swerved toward the gate.

There was no stopping him, so she stepped back and waited, hoping he'd reach his car and get in it before he died. Then she'd call the sheriff and tell him she came outside and found this strange *dead* Negro parked in front of the house.

However, Mandingo Q. Mann dropped to his knees just outside the gate. *Crap! I'll have to roll the damn elephant back to where he belongs. No, he's too heavy for me!* She cast a stealthy glance toward the barn. *But he's not too heavy for that damn old bull.*

Etta Ruth headed for the barn, all the while looking up and down the road. What if a car came along before she moved him and got him covered with the manure? Their German neighbor had driven off toward town early that morning and hadn't returned. If he came home and saw Mandingo Q. Mann laying in the yard, she'd say he got out of the car asking for a doctor and then dropped dead. *Better hurry.*

She snapped the harness on Mr. Valentino in record time, then peeked around the barn door to make sure the coast was clear before she and the big bull trotted the seventy-five yards to the gate.

Mandingo Q. Mann was still on his knees, his hulking frame doubled over and his cheek pressed to the ground, much like a baby asleep in his crib. Etta Ruth snapped the end of the lead straps to the belt loops on the back of his pants, then stepped in front of Mr. Valentino and beckoned him to follow her. He emitted a noise that sounded like an elongated growl but did not move. Etta Ruth stuck her fists on her hips and stared him in the eyes.

"Clara is not the only one who can handle you, you spoiled rotten bull." Forgetting that the big brass ring in Mr. Valentino's nose was off limits to human hands, she stuck two fingers through it and pulled.

Mr. Valentino bellowed and tossed his big head around in a circle to rid himself of her grip. If she hadn't immediately let go, she would have been flung asunder, but she only staggered backward as he took off toward the barn, with Mandingo Q. Mann bumping and bouncing lifelessly behind him, his long arms and legs, like limp appendages on a gargantuan rag doll, flopping this way and that.

Mr. Valentino was already in the barn before Etta Ruth—wide-eyed and slightly limping—caught up. "Son of a bitch," she mumbled, standing outside the open doors and wondering if it was safe to go in. She needed to hide that body, and quick! Maybe she'd leave him in the barn, pile some hay on him until everybody was asleep tonight.

She peered again into the shadowy interior. Mandingo Q. Mann was getting to be more trouble to her dead than alive. She decided that since it was sassy little Willie's ass that was getting saved, Willie and her friend Mary could dig the hole after dark, then roll that damn elephant into it. After all, she'd done the important part—unwittingly, but done it, just the same.

She stepped testily into the barn, then stood there waiting to see what Mr. Valentino would do. She'd never known the big bull to charge anybody, but then again, she'd never known anyone to tether a Mandingo Q. Mann to him. To her relief, he glanced at her then nuzzled a nearby hay bale as if scratching his nose. "Good bull." She'd just unsnap his load, cover it with hay, and then wait until dark.

With her foot raised to take a forward step, she could only stare dumbfounded as the sprawled body of Mandingo Q. Mann moved and then slowly straightened until his hulking frame stood tall but wobbly while shaking his scraped, manure-crusted head.

Etta Ruth, strangely excited in a terrified sort of way, took a backward step as Mandingo's murderous, red eyes locked on her and his big hands curled into weapons.

However, he was able to take only two giant steps in her direction before he heard a noise behind him, turned and saw the bull... and, in that same instant, discovered himself tethered to the massive, evil-looking animal by his belt loops. His shrill scream could have shattered glass.

Etta Ruth doubted if any man had ever shucked his shoes and leaped out of his pants any faster, his blue-and-white striped underdrawers flying through the air alongside his trousers.

She stepped back and plastered herself against the barn door as naked-from-the-waist-down Mandingo Q. Mann zoomed past her and streaked to his car. As she watched, he leaped into the driver's seat of his limousine, revved the engine, and was gone. The Cadillac's tires peeled up dirt and grass as he roared off down the road toward the bay, evidently unaware of his direction.

*Holy Moses! What if Willie and her cowboy are pedaling home on the two-seater and he sees them? I can't let that happen!*

She was on her way to the telephone to ring up the sheriff and tell him to get out here right away because a crazy colored man had forced his way into the house and exposed himself to her, *and she had his pants, shoes, and underdrawers to prove it!*

On the porch she took a parting glance toward the receding Cadillac, and squinted with renewed interest as the car suddenly veered off the road, tore through a fence, and sped off across the field, bouncing and pitching over the uneven ground. *THUD!* It hit a massive oak tree at what must have been seventy or eighty miles an hour! *The sleeping pills and the Singapore Sling had been the right combination after all.*

Etta Ruth strolled to the end of the porch, shaded her eyes against the sun, and peered at the wreckage ... while wishing she hadn't lost her trusty binoculars. As best she could tell, the front of the Cadillac—all the way past the windshield and front seat—sat wrapped around the tree trunk as tightly as a fat wiener in a bun. After a brief silence, a hissing noise and then a popping sound, like a neon light spewing its last energy, enlivened the otherwise silent countryside. Seconds later, the entire automobile exploded into a Cadillac-sized ball of red-and-blue flames.

In the kitchen, Etta Ruth put the cherry brandy *look-alike* bottle back on the top shelf, making sure to push it to a dark corner where she wouldn't make the mistake of grabbing it again. She poured the pitcher of Singapore Sling down the sink, washed Mandingo Q. Mann's glass, dropped the empty bottle of sleeping pills back into her purse, dumped the watery rum and Coke from her Mason jar, refilled it with gin, and then took a big, long drink. Ignoring the sticky mess she'd made on the countertop with the fruit juices, she went outside and settled into the porch swing to watch the fire. Occasionally, she glanced down the road to see if anyone traveled on it. Nope, still not a witness in sight who could say she'd had a visitor.

Two hours later, after the fire had burned itself out and all that remained was the Cadillac's blackened hull and, likely, the charred, *unidentifiable* skeletal frame of its driver, she went into the house, called the sheriff, and reported an accident on Hesterwine Road.

As she watched the sheriff's car and a couple of Texas Department of Safety patrol vehicles bump slowly across the field to the smoldering wreckage, she felt her interest slowly begin to wane. She thought of the windmill. *Nope, not today*, she decided. She raised her Mason jar. "Over the lips and past the gums, look out stomach, here it comes...."

## 27

Back from North Beach, Jack stayed for supper. Everyone was in the kitchen, including Etta Ruth. Rather than sit down with the others, she stood leaning against the sink eating a sandwich and sipping at her Mason jar. After a while, her eyes shifted back and forth between Clara and Justine, and everyone knew it wouldn't be long before she said something.

"I've had a busy day keeping things in order around here while you two gallivanted around North Beach all day celebrating Banker Prickett's demise."

Justine snorted with disgust at the remark, then eyed the cluttered sink. "You were keeping things in order, Etta Ruth? Indeed? Where? In your dreams? You haven't put your empty fruit juice cans in the garbage or wiped up the sticky mess you made of the sink and countertop. Your *empty* rum bottle is sitting right there where you left it, as well as the empty Coke bottle." She tipped her spectacles up and gazed from beneath them. "As I see it, you have made a mess of the kitchen while we were gone. Where is the order in that?"

"Hush, Justine," Clara said quietly.

Justine waved off Clara's request. "The Coke bottle belongs in a bag with the others so we can return the lot of them for the deposit—*your* meager contribution to the running of this house."

While waiting for the profane reply Etta Ruth would surely give, everyone except Justine kept their eyes averted to their plates. However, Etta Ruth only shrugged and pointed her Mason jar at them. "I'm going to bed. When Willie gets home, tell her she owes me a favor." She took a bite of her sandwich, chewed a few times while staring at Justine, then dropped the sandwich into the sink. "Tell your floozy sister to go to hell, Clara," she said, and left.

"Go to hell yourself!" Justine shouted after her.

"Don't antagonize her, Justine," Clara said, and Mary thought she sounded almost pleading. "Try to consider all that Etta Ruth has been through," Clara continued. "She's alone in the world except for us. Her daughter came to see her only once in five years, and that was only to steal her car. Her son—who is clearly glad to be rid of her, by the way—had her declared incompetent. I imagine that would be quite a shock to a mother."

"Have you lost your senses, Clara? She *is* incompetent, and a lot worse! She was mean as a viper long before any of those things happened, and I am tired of tiptoeing on eggshells around her. From now on, she's going to *get* as good as she *gives*! I have a right to defend myself! What could she possibly do to me that she hasn't done already, call me more nasty names?"

Clara stared at Justine as if she had an important answer to that question, but then she knitted her eyebrows and looked elsewhere.

*Wow,* Mary thought, *Miss Clara was almost tempted that time to let Miss Justine in on her suspicions about Miz Etta Ruth.* Lately, the more Mary thought about the situation, the more she realized that Miss Clara actually believed that Miz Etta Ruth was capable of terrible things. Clearly, moments ago, she feared that Miss Justine might 'antagonize' their cousin into ... doing what, murdering them in their beds one night? On the other hand, could it be that Miz Etta Ruth was *all bluster and blow but no go*? Mary thought, remembering what her grandmother in New Jersey said about a ranting neighbor in her apartment building who had everybody afraid of her. Even though Miz Etta Ruth was awfully scary at times, Mary sometimes got a gut feeling that there was more to pity about Miz Etta Ruth than there was to fear. She had mixed feelings about that *gut feeling,* since her grandmother also said, *Trust your gut feelings until you discover you can't, but be careful ... because by the time you discover you can't trust them, it might be too late.*

Out in the foyer, the elevator gate opened, then clanged shut, and Etta Ruth yelled out, "Shut up, Clara! I don't need *you* to defend me to the floozy!"

Justine turned to Jack. "See what a horrible old thing she is, Jack? Has Mary told you that every few days Etta Ruth has a taxi bring a fresh supply of intoxicating liquor out here? The driver carries it right into the pantry and puts it on the shelf. I'm sure she spends her entire allowance from Clarence

Jr. on hard liquor and taxi fares, and Clara does not ask her to pay a dime of it for her room and board."

Jack kept his head down as he ate. Justine turned to Clara.

"You should not have invited her into this house, Clara. And what about when we move? Is she planning on going with us to that tiny set of rooms at the boarding house? I will not abide it! I won't!"

"Maybe she'll be elsewhere by then," Clara said, not looking at her.

"*Elsewhere*? Just where is elsewhere? She acts as if she is a permanent part of our family now. I tell you, she does not plan on *ever* leaving us because she's having too much fun making us miserable!"

Clara waved her hands in a way that clearly showed her frustration. "Just stop antagonizing her, Justine ... please." She glanced apologetically at Jack. "What will you think of us, Jack, having such a discussion? Forgive our bad manners. Perhaps we are just tired after such a busy day."

"Speak for yourself," Justine snapped. "I'm more mad than tired!"

"Well, put your glad hat on and be quiet!" Clara snapped back.

Mary immediately saw another opportunity to avert an argument. "I insist you both go up to bed right now. Jack and I will do the dishes and clean up Miz Etta's mess."

"How sweet of you, dear." Clara laid her napkin aside and rose. Justine did the same. After thanking Jack for a wonderful day, Clara and Justine, ignoring each other, marched off to bed.

"Mary the peacemaker," Jack said, coming up behind her. "That's just one of the things I love about you." Before she knew it, he had turned her around and was kissing her. She surprised herself by putting her arms around his neck and kissing him back.

"That's encouraging," he said long moments later.

"I think I meant it to be encouraging."

He reared his head back to smile at her. "You *think* you meant it to be encouraging. When will you know for sure?"

"I-I have been confused, Jack, for a long time ... about things that happened before I met you." She turned and picked up a plate to wash. "I'm not sure this is a good time to talk about this."

He took the plate from her, laid it aside, led her away from the sink, and then gently entrapped her by flattening both his hands to the wall on either side of her head. "I'd like to clear away some of that confusion. You told me about Claxton Mitchell ... said he broke off your relationship, was drafted, and is now missing in action. That's too bad for the poor guy. I hope he's all right, but whether he is or not, I get the feeling you care about me, Mary."

She ducked from under his outstretched arms. "I didn't tell you everything, Jack. You may not want me to care about you when you know the rest."

"Unless you tell me you're married, or engaged, or promised, there's nothing else I need to know, especially if it's something that's over and done with. I've been hurt like you were hurt, so much that I swore I'd never set myself up for a broken heart again. But, Mary, I love you." He looked hard into her eyes. "And if you tell me you need to know for certain what happened to Claxton Mitchell before we can move ahead, I'll be the lovesick fool that waits... even while knowing you might break my heart, Mary Kenny," he said, but then smiled.

Something in his eyes touched her so profoundly that tears filled her own. "I don't want to break your heart, Jack. I want to make you happy. I don't think of Claxton anymore when I am with you, but there are still things about me you need to know."

"You're not gonna feel right until you tell me, are you? Then go ahead. Tell me your deepest, darkest secrets right now." He led her to the kitchen table and sat down across from her.

She was stammering, trying to figure out how to begin telling him things that could change his feelings for her, when loud knocking on the front door brought her gratefully to her feet. "That must be Willie. I guess our talk will have to wait, Jack. I ...I am sorry."

As she hurried from the kitchen, she felt a twinge of guilt for not being sorry at all for the interruption; even so, at the very moment of that knock on the door, she had decided she could not tell him about her past. Could *never* tell him. If he proposed marriage someday, she would turn him down rather than tell him about herself because her sudden gut feeling told her that he would walk away. At that heartbreaking moment, she knew she had to break off their relationship before it got to that point. She wiped hard at the sudden tear that spilled down her cheek.

In the foyer she switched on the porch light, expecting to see Leeta standing there with Hank Posey. Lately, Hank escorted her all the way to the front door, and more often than not, she gave him a quick peck on the cheek before she backed over the threshold, demurely waving him away.

Mary found the screen unlatched and, as she opened her mouth to ask Leeta why she just didn't come in, she drew back in shock, almost not believing her eyes. *Claxton Mitchell!*

He had not changed much. He was still tall and tan, his sandy colored hair still thick and wavy—nor had the cross look on his face changed from the last time she has seen him. He stood staring intensely at her through the screen. "You haven't changed much," he finally said.

"I ... I am glad you are all right, Claxton."

"I got something for you, Mary." He spoke now in that same terse voice she remembered from when he broke up with her. He jerked open the screen door and dropped a small bag at her feet, and then whirled around and went back down the steps, walking so fast he was at his car and opening the door before she could collect her senses long enough to wonder why she was only stunned to see him rather than jumping for joy.

She looked down at the bag. What possessions did he have of hers that would induce him to drive all this way to *Texas* to deliver them? She could think of nothing. She called out to him.

"I am very glad you are alive, Claxton, and ... goodbye." She raised a hand to wave.

"Oh, no you don't!" he yelled, and in the shadowy dark, out of reach of the porch light, she saw him lunge back through the gate carrying something else he obviously planned to dump at her feet.

"You and your father thought you were pulling one over on me, didn't you, when he shoved him off on my parents."

She had heard a sound that did not come from Claxton Mitchell, and she was on the porch and reaching for the bundle as Claxton shoved it into her open arms. With her heart pounding so fast that she thought she would faint, she began to weep, her cries mixing with the baby's fretting noises. What she had believed was a dream the day her baby was born was not a dream! The distorted sight of her father holding a tightly wrapped bundle as he stood over her, his mouth moving on indistinguishable words that sounded like garbled explosions... before he turned away with the bundle and disappeared through the door, had been real! "You are *real! You are real!*" she whispered joyously to the baby boy in her arms.

Claxton was glowering at her. "It wasn't very nice of you, Mary, to have your old man push that kid off on my parents. They are too old to raise a kid.

They were damn near too old when they had me. They didn't want him any more than *you* did."

She didn't bother denying his false statement; her enchanted eyes, and thoughts, were occupied with her child.

"They only kept him this long because they thought I would want him when I got home. That was the dumbest thing they ever did! I wasn't ready to settle down with a wife and kid back then, and I'm still not!"

"No ... No, of course not," she murmured, now only half-aware that he was even there.

"Jessie gave my mom your address. Dad died three weeks ago, and when I got home, Mom and I drove straight to her sister's house in Houston. She's going to live there now that Dad's gone. Mom said you should be the one responsible for your kid since he was your idea in the first place, not mine."

"I am sorry about your father, Claxton," Mary said, unable to stop smiling, intent only on cuddling her baby, touching his fingers and toes, and then examining his chubby little face as if she'd never seen a baby before. "Please thank you mother for me."

"If you thought he'd get the Mitchell name, you thought wrong. He's got *your* name, not mine. *Bub Kenny*—that's what my mom called him. He's not her problem anymore, or mine, he's all yours."

Mary's smile widened. "Yes, you are right, Claxton. He is not your problem. Not your problem at all," she said softly, and then, "*Bub*? What kind of name was that for a beautiful baby boy?" She spoke more to her baby than to Claxton. "We will have to fix *that*, won't we?" She was suddenly so happy that even though under Claxton's hostile stare, she felt not a drop of anger.

"There's no birth certificate. You do the hell what you want about that, but don't go putting my name on it."

"I won't." The baby had stopped fretting, and his big blue eyes were gazing up at her. His soft ringlets of hair were reddish brown like hers. He didn't look a bit like Claxton, she decided, and was glad.

"The point is, Mary, you should have done something about being pregnant. Going through with it sure as hell wouldn't have been *my* choice. You aren't going to hold me up for any support money, are you? I don't even know for sure if it's mine. My mom always said you were a slut the way you chased after me, and then wrote all those pathetic letters almost begging me to come home and mar–"

Before Mary knew what was happening, Jack was out the door, his fists moving so swiftly she only saw the results: Claxton flying backward off the porch and landing in a semiconscious heap in the yard.

Then, from the corner of her eye, Mary saw Etta Ruth come charging out of the darkness from the direction of the garden, water hose in hand. By the time Claxton managed to stand up and stumble out the gate, he was soaking wet, and Etta Ruth was chasing after him. A mouthful of water curtailed his swearing, as he scrambled into his car and drove off. Without a word, Etta Ruth went back to the garden.

The elevator rattled downward, and then Clara and Justine rushed toward them, as Jack held the screen door open for her and her baby.

Apprehensive but smiling, Mary looked from face to face of her audience. "This ... this is *my* baby," she said, hugging him to her. "He ... he is nine months, three weeks, six days, and"—she paused as if counting, then blurted—"twelve hours old. This is the first time I have ever seen him." Tears filled her eyes, and she closed them, her heart suddenly pounding with fear that, for the first time, she would see condemnation in Clara and Justine Hesterwine's eyes. For a long moment, she actually trembled with dread ... until she heard laughter and opened her eyes to see Miss Clara and Miss Justine fairly beaming at her! Instantly, the love she felt for the generous-hearted women who had given her a home and so much more, and who were now eagerly participating in her joy, intensified.

"I owe all of you an explanation," she finally said, her glance encompassing each of them but avoiding Jack.

She walked into the parlor and sat down; they followed expectantly and pulled their chairs close, except for Jack. He sat on the sofa close beside her and, when the reddish-haired baby, with blue eyes like his mother's, began to fret, he dangled his key chain at him, and then took him on his lap.

# 28

EARLY THE NEXT MORNING, little "Bub Kenny" sat at the head of the breakfast table in an antique highchair that Clara had Flaco bring down from the attic.

A baby in the house seemed to cheer the entire household; even Etta Ruth seemed in a good mood, for she tapped lightly at Bub's chubby cheeks and asked him, "What's your real name, huh?" She glanced at Mary. "He needs a real name." She turned back to Bub, who was cramming a handful of scrambled eggs into his mouth. "You want Cousin Etta Ruth to think of a good name for you, huh?" She looked at Mary again. "When Jack was smooching you goodnight last night, I heard him say he was going to adopt little Bub as soon as you get married. So, I think you should name him *Jack*."

"That is not for you to decide, Etta Ruth," Justine said.

Etta Ruth snickered. "You probably want her to name the poor kid *Boyd*, after '*the Pendleton heir with the savior faire*,' as we called him."

Before words could fly, Mary did what she was getting used to doing at the mention of Boyd Pendleton—she averted them elsewhere. "I have already decided his name will be *James Jackson Dunston*—*James* after my grandfather, and *Jackson* after Jack, since that is actually Jack's name."

Just then Bub, obviously finished with his eggs and squishing his leftovers between his fingers, let them fly. Etta Ruth gasped as they struck her cheek and the collar of her red silk robe. Justine yelped with pleasure.

Mary jumped up and began dabbing the mess away with a napkin. "I am so sorry, Miz Etta! I hope it does not stain. I have been meaning to tell you, this is the prettiest red silk robe I have ever seen," she said as she worked on scraping away the egg.

"You think so? Every time I wear it I remember how mad Clarence got when I bought it ... the son of a bitch."

Letta hurried around the table and clamped her hands over little Bub's ears. "*Jesus Pete*, Miz Etta Ruth ...!" She gave Etta Ruth a scolding glance.

"Well, then, to put it nicely," Etta Ruth drawled, "the cheater was a *cheap SOB* to beat all cheap *SOBs*, and being a dead *SOB* does not change that memorable detail about the *SOB*."

Justine, still in the dark about with *whom* Clarence had cheated, commented absently, "My goodness, that's a bit strong, isn't it? Besides, I always thought Clarence bought you everything your heart desired."

"Ha! He was so tight, when he blinked, his little wee-wee bonked him in the chin."

As usual, when Etta Ruth's speech turned crass, loud exhalations of disapproval came from Clara, Justine, and Aunt Lucy. Mary and Leeta, being of a less shockable generation, exchanged subtle grins.

They ate in silence for a while until Justine wondered aloud about when the sheriff would get the results of Mr. Abelson's autopsy.

Glancing at Etta Ruth's narrowing eyes, Clara attempted to discourage Justine from further ponderings. However, Justine ignored Clara's wiggling eyebrows and grimaces and kept talking.

"I still haven't gotten over the shock of Mr. Abelson's death, and *now*, Banker Prickett has actually been *murdered*. Terrible! But at least *he* had clothes on when he died; not so poor Mr. Abelson. I imagine being found dead while *nude* would be humiliating beyond words, poor man."

Etta Ruth plopped a large bite of omelet into her mouth. "Being dead as he was, Justine, the little SOB didn't feel a thing when Vernell Watson got a bird's-eye view of his shriveled up old what-nots."

Justine's hostile eyes skimmed over her. "As usual, you just can't help but be vulgarly unkind toward him, can you, Etta Ruth? The poor man is gone forever from this earth, and I am sure he will be greatly missed by the entire town. I often enjoyed conversing with him."

Etta Ruth swallowed her mouthful, then took another bite. "You enjoyed conversing with him?" she asked, rolling the words over the food in her mouth. "I always thought the little bastard was suspiciously closed-mouthed around women."

Clara still had not managed to attract Justine's attention, so Justine continued, "Well, he wasn't closed-mouthed toward me. I thought he was interesting, and it is a terrible shame that he's gone."

Surprisingly, Etta Ruth did not respond, and everyone ate in silence. A few moments later, Etta Ruth wiped her mouth on her napkin and, after a final slurp of coffee, pushed away from the table, stood, and stared almost reflectively at Justine.

"I always thought the little runt was a snob. I don't recall the old bastard ever looking me in the eye all those years I took our shoes to him; mine, and Clarence's." She paused, shifting her eyes to the side as if reliving some angry thought. "Never trust a man who can't look you in the eye. Nine times out of ten, he's after your husband."

"What on earth do you me—"

Clara interrupted Justine's question with a garish chain of high-pitched cackles that instantly switched everyone's stupefied attention from Etta Ruth and Justine to *her*. "Etta Ruth Morley, you have a positively naughty sense of humor, don't you?" Clara crowed, in a tone too shrill to be *Clara*. "I didn't know you had it in you to be so funny ... and, really, Cousin Etta, I am quite entertained!" She continued laughing as if she'd just heard the funniest joke ever told.

Justine stared at her. "My God, Clara, you sound positively demented!"

Mary and Leeta exchanged looks. Did they now know that Mr. Abelson had been more than the town cobbler to Clarence Morley? *Nooo!* But then again, Miss Clara had certainly done her best to stop Miz Etta Ruth from remarking further on Mr. Abelson's reason for never being able to look her in the eye.

Etta Ruth, eyeing Clara with a disgusted tightening of her cheeks, stuck a Pall Mall between her lips, drew a lengthy kitchen match from her pocket, and slashed it hard across the table, causing a tiny explosion that filled the air with the choking stench of sulfur. Holding her stare on Clara until the match had burned well down, she lit up, puffed, and then spewed out a long stream of smoke before flipping the smoldering black stem into the air. She headed for the door, her sudden boredom with everyone evident in the slouchy slapping of her bare feet against the linoleum. "Yeah, Clara, I'm a real goddamn comic, aren't I," she muttered as she exited the kitchen.

"We're gonna have to get earplugs for little Bub," Leeta said.

"I thought she gave all those nasty cigarettes to the peacocks," Justine mumbled.

As usual lately, Mary's heart swelled with pity for Miss Clara. She knew what her elderly friend was thinking, and *she* was thinking the same thing. Suddenly, Mary pictured Miz Etta Ruth wearing her husband's shoes and standing in the flour that was scattered around Mr. Abelson's naked and dead body on his kitchen floor. Then, recalling the newspaper article reporting Stanton B. Prickett's death, she pictured Etta Ruth making those muddy shoe prints around *his* body as he lay murdered in the bank's parking lot. After a brief pause to let a cold shiver pass through her, she reached over and patted Miss Clara's shoulder. One thing was certain; Miss Clara had decided to protect her cousin at all costs. Therefore, s*he* would put those disturbing pictures of Miz Etta Ruth and the murdered men from her mind, and would never do or say *anything* that would add to Miss Clara's worries—just like she would never utter a word about Miss Clara's six-month affair and engagement to Fritz Von Heuvel while "on the rebound" from Miss Justine running off with *her* fiancé.

Miss Clara had not mentioned Fritz Von Heuvel since that day they'd shared cup after cup of Grandfather Hesterwine's eighty-proof recipe. No doubt Miss Clara regretted how the recipe had loosened her tongue as the two of them sat giggling at each other across the kitchen table. Smiling at the memory, Mary cast a warm glance at Miss Clara. Her long-ago lover had yet to call at Hesterwine Place, and Mary was beginning to wonder if he ever would. She tried to imagine what he and Miss Clara would say to each other if he did decide to call. Considering Miss Clara's professed abhorrence of such a meeting and her heatedly professed regret that Fritz Von Heuvel had chosen to come to the United states, Mary suddenly felt sad for them both.

Mary ran to her bedroom window as the *Flying Ghost of the Briney Coast* swooped past the house. Jack tipped the wings of his CAP plane as he made a wide turn, then flew past again before flying away to begin his shift of patrolling the Gulf of Mexico for enemy U-Boats. He would be back before sundown.

They would be married two days from now, standing next to the grand staircase and with her new family and friends surrounding them—Miss Clara, Miss Justine, Jack's sister, Linda, Leeta and Hank, Aunt Lucy, Flaco ... and Etta Ruth.

Jack, and the miracle of her son alive and returned to her, made her almost giddy with joy. Her face ached from smiling. How lucky she was to have ended up in Hesterwine, Texas, and then immediately taken under the wings of the town's two most compassionate Hesterwine Medallions, and then, on a bumpy bicycle ride down a deserted country road, found true love smiling at her from the cockpit of a bright-yellow airplane.

Mary turned from the window to watch Leeta rocking little James to sleep; she felt a friendly twinge of jealousy. She could not get enough of holding him, kissing every curl on his head, all the while feeling that there were so many lost months she needed to make up for to her child.

"I think you should marry Hank and get your own baby, Leeta," Mary grinned. "You look like a mother waiting to happen."

"I gotta keep moving, and you know why."

"Mandingo Q. Mann has not found you yet, and he never will."

"Yes, he will. I've had the strangest feeling about him lately and I can't shake it. I asked Hank to go to California with me, and he said no. He's always asking me *why* I gotta leave ... telling me I *love* him."

"Well, don't you? It's written all over your face every time you mention his name."

"Maybe it's shock you're seeing. Shock that I would even think of giving up my dream of being a singer for that shit-kicking cowboy." She looked up at the transom. "What do *you* say, Miz Morley? You see any love on my face when I look at Hank Posey?"

Etta Ruth, elbows braced on the transom and cupping her jaws in her hands, stared blandly down at her. "All you colored women look alike to me. I don't see nothing but smartass *sass* on your face." She twisted her mouth as if disgusted. "As to love and marriage, the day a woman marries a damn man it's a countdown to sorrow." She looked at the baby. "Jimmy Jack's a fast crawler. He'll be walking soon and able to catch my cat. Beelzebub does not like kids pulling his tail."

Mary smiled. "I won't let *James* pull Beelzebub's tail, Miz Etta."

"You can call him *James* all you want, but I'll guarantee you folks is gonna call him *Jimmy Jack*—it's a Texas thing." Etta Ruth shifted her gaze back to

Leeta. "You ever think that strange feeling you get about Mandingo Q. Mann just might mean you don't have a thing to worry about anymore? If I were you, I'd stop fretting about that son of a bitch showing up here and cutting your throat. *I, myself,* have a 'strange feeling' it *ain't* gonna happen."

"I guess I'll worry 'bout him finding me 'til I'm gray as old Rudolph Valentino out there in the barn," Leeta said.

Suddenly, Etta Ruth was laughing so hard that Mary and Leeta were taken aback. They stared up at her, wondering if she intended to stop.

Finally she quieted and Leeta quipped, "Did I say something funny?"

"You don't know how to be funny, sassy face. I was just remembering something that old bull did last week when a stanger came by and had a couple of drinks with me." She paused, as if thinking over her next words, and then added, "The sight of Mr. Valentino scared that stranger *halfway* to death." She tittered again, then gave Leeta one of her *I'm-sizing-you-up* looks. "You may not be a damn bit funny, sassy face, but you do know how to sing. Tell you what; I'll give you a nice present if you accompany me on the organ right now."

As Leeta made a face, Mary reached for her baby. "That is a wonderful idea, Leeta. Go ahead."

Leeta held onto little James. "Why don't *you* accompany her, Mary. I hear you singing all the time lately."

"The gift is not for her, it's for *you,*" Etta Ruth growled.

"Okay! Okay! I'll be down soon as I change clothes. I gotta get ready for work. What kinda songs you like? How 'bout 'Three Blind Mice'?"

"Careful, sassy face, you just may smart-mouth your way out of the best damn gift anyone ever gave you in your whole damn life," Etta Ruth said as she disappeared from the transom, then yelled from behind the door, "Hurry up, damnit, while I'm still in a good mood!"

# 29

By the time Leeta got downstairs, Etta Ruth was sitting at her old Kimball Victorian organ, a stack of sheet music beside her on the bench. Leeta shuddered, thinking of the morbid funeral march Etta Ruth always played to get everybody's mood to match her own. She eyed the stack of sheet music and wondered what gloomy tune this crazy old white woman was gonna make her sing. Shaking her head, she looked the organ over, coming to the conclusion that it and Etta Ruth Morley were two of a kind—old, loud, and scary-looking. "You got any blues notes in that thing?" she quipped, totally unprepared for what happened next.

Etta Ruth shoved several sheets of lyrics into Leeta's hands and then, even before Leeta could look through them, performed a C-note blues run on the keys that made Leeta's eyes pop in unison with her dropped jaw.

"Well? Are you gonna sing or not? I got the songs in the order I wanna hear them, so don't go switching them around." Etta Ruth repeated the bluesy C-note run and nodded for Leeta to start singing.

After the first two lines of "Hard Hearted Hannah," the entire household came hurrying into the foyer, as well as Mary from upstairs, carrying little James. Leeta's mesmerizing voice and Etta Ruth's shocking dexterity on the old Kimball were not to be ignored, and their smiling audience bounced and swayed to the tune—even Aunt Lucy did a hip-swinging maneuver that no one would have ever guessed she was capable of executing. "Hard Hearted Hannah" was immediately followed by "Cry Me A River," "Ain't She

Sweet," "Pennies Form Heaven," "Stormy Weather," and finally a rollicking "What A Friend We Have In Jesus," with all hands clapping in time to the bluesy style in which Etta Ruth played it and Leeta delivered it.

Even little James was clapping his hands just as he saw the others do, and he giggled when his mother danced around with him, spinning this way and that until she came to a sudden halt, the smile leaving her face.

Sheriff Bloot, with two of his deputies behind him, stood in the open doorway, his handcuffs dangling from one hand and the other resting on his holster. He was not smiling, nor was he bouncing to the music.

Leeta stopped singing the moment she saw him and edged toward her protectors, Clara and Justine, who had yet to realize he was there.

"Hey! Where you going, Willie?" Etta Ruth cried. "The song isn't over yet! You won't get that gift if you don't..." She turned as she spoke and her fingers froze on the keys, sending out a screeching note so loud and so long that Justine rushed over and removed her hands from the keyboard. Etta Ruth immediately began playing *Chopin's Funeral March.*

"Etta Ruth Morley, you are under arrest for the murder of Stanton B. Prickett!" Sheriff Bloot yelled above the morose tune.

"*WHAT?*" Justine was likely the only one in the room who cried out in dumbfounded surprise.

Etta Ruth turned around on the stool and stuck out her wrists. "Didn't you forget somebody? Last I heard, you were telling everybody in town that I murdered the merry little shoemaker, too."

He stomped over and snapped a handcuff on one of her extended wrists. "We know you was in his apartment. Lucky for you, the coroner's report came in and it said Abelson died of a heart attack. What'd you do, scare him to death? We figure it was *you* that ransacked the place. Only thing missing, though, were some letters. Why in hell would you want those?"

"Yes. Why in hell would I? Ask me another dumb question."

"Anyhow, you're under arrest for Stanton B. Prickett's murder."

Clara rushed to Etta Ruth, her eyes searching her face. "Etta Ruth, I have to know for certain if..." she trailed off, unable to finish the nagging question. She glanced at the sheriff, then leaned close to Etta Ruth and whispered, "You can just whisper it in my ear."

Etta Ruth worked her mouth in that agitated way that was so familiar now to her observers at Hesterwine Place. "What do *you* think, Clara?"

"I-I don't know. You must tell me."

Etta Ruth stared at her. Then, after a cagey glance at the sheriff, she leaned close to Clara's ear exactly as Clara had done to her seconds earlier and hissed as loudly as possible without yelling, "Go to hell, Clara!"

Sheriff Bloot snapped the cuffs on her.

Clara hesitantly put up a hand. "Sheriff Bloot, is it really necessary to put her in jail? Can't she just remain here with us until the trial? She isn't going to go anywhere."

Etta Ruth scowled at her. "Now, how in hell do you know that, *Miss Benedict Arnold*? I just might take off for Mexico, or hop a freight train to New York City and lose myself in the swarming masses."

"Oh, Etta Ruth, this is no joking matter," Clara said, still looking pleadingly at the sheriff, but he shook his head.

"Come on, Miz Morley. The judge may or may not set bail, all depending on whether or not he thinks you can be trusted not to set out for Mexico or New York City."

"Well, I guess I'll just have to turn on the charm for the old bastard, won't I?" Tittering, she fluffed her hair, then stuck her free hand to her hip and wiggled into her familiar Bette Davis pose.

Sheriff Bloot rolled his eyes. "Like Miss Clara said, this ain't no joking matter, Miz Morley."

The stunned look had not left Justine's face. "I can't believe this! Although, heaven knows, I suppose I shouldn't be the least bit surprised!"

Mary spoke up. "Don't you need evidence before making an arrest, Sheriff? What proof do you have that Miz Morley killed Banker Prickett?"

"I got evidence, sweet thang." He motioned to one of his deputies who stood nearby holding a small black briefcase. "Show them our evidence, Deputy." Everyone, including Aunt Lucy, crowded around to look inside the case at a pair of binoculars with a missing lens.

Justine gave Clara a look that said *I told you so*, then eyed Etta Ruth. "So that's why you haven't worn your binoculars lately. We might have known there was something sneaky going on with you and those binoc—" Clara gave her a pinch that stopped her in mid-word. Justine tried to pinch her back, but Clara moved her arm, then addressed the sheriff.

"Apparently, Etta Ruth lost her binoculars, Sheriff, and you found them. I certainly do not see that as evidence against her."

"This ain't no simple case of lost and found, Miss Clara. These binoculars were hanging on an oleander bush behind the bank right close to where Stanton B. Prickett's dead body was found lying next to his car."

"I refuse to believe that Etta Ruth is capable of such a thing."

"Oh *really*, Clara?" Etta Ruth drawled in a tone that said she knew better.

Sheriff Bloot grunted. "She wouldn't be the first woman to become a homicidal maniac while fooling everybody into thinking she was just peculiar. Look at Lizzie Borden. Y'all remember what they wrote about *her*?" He proceeded to recite: *"Lizzie Borden took an axe and gave her mother forty whacks. When she saw what she had done, she gave her father forty-one."*

Leeta stepped to Etta Ruth's side. "Miz Etta ain't no *Lizzie Borden*, she's just ... well, anyway, don't talk about her like that while she's standing right here. It ain't nice. What you think, she ain't got no feelings?"

Etta Ruth grinned at her. "Why thank you, *Willie*."

"Butt out, gal, or I'll take you in with her." He patted the extra set of handcuffs dangling from his belt.

Clara stepped to Leeta's side. "Lizzie Borden was acquitted of all charges, Sheriff. There was no real evidence to prove she killed her parents."

"She got away with murder, but that ain't gonna happen here." He turned to Etta Ruth. "Forget denying that these binoculars are yours, Miz Morley. There's witnesses in town—along with *me*—who know better ... 'cause they was always hanging 'round your neck in plain sight and they had a missing lens. Unless you can show me an exact pair, I'm gonna assume these are them."

"They're mine all right, and I want them back. Where you found them doesn't mean a damn thing. Prickett had more enemies than Japan's Tojo ... and *Prickett* didn't order the attack on Pearl Harbor like Tojo did. Lots of people probably wanted to knock him in the head, but not me."

Sheriff Bloot squinted at her. "Knock him in the head, eh? How did you know what killed him? I never said how he died and it ain't been let out to the general public yet."

"I was just generally speaking, Sheriff."

"Oh, yeah? He squinted harder at her, his mouth going down at the corners and his big head doing a judicial wag. If looks could convict, the trial would have been over then and there.

Etta Ruth tittered. "What happened to Prickett was a holy bolt from the blue. And if all the evidence you have against me is that my binoculars were hanging in the oleander bush near his dead body, you might be surprised to discover there are other reasons for them being there."

He grimaced as if he were concentrating. "Now, let me see. We done got evidence that a pair of clodhoppers like the ones that belonged to your late husband, and which *you* often wear, made those shoeprints in all that flour around *Abelson's* body. We also got evidence that my father-in-law's killer was wearing similar shoes and tracked mud from the flowerbed to all over the place." He cocked his head to the side. "You still got your husband's shoes, Miz Morley? I'd like to compare the soles to some pictures of shoeprints we took at Abelson's place and then at the murder scene behind the bank."

"I certainly do have Clarence's shoes," Etta Ruth crowed. "They are the exact same shoes worn by several dozen men in town. I recall seeing Banker Prickett wear a pair many times, as I am certain you saw, too, you being his son-in-law." She paused, putting a finger to her temple. "I believe I did walk through that muddy flowerbed behind the bank while wearing Clarence's shoes when on my way to the taxi stand that day—it's a short-cut, you know. I hate messy shoes, so I cleaned them with Rinso soap, bleach, and a toothbrush as soon as I got home."

"I'm sure you did. A witness said you were wearing a pink evening gown a little after daylight that morning. Whoever knocked Prickett in the head musta got some blood spattered on their clothes—there was a bunch of it squirted all around. I'd like to see that pink evening dress."

"I burned it. Mud from the flower bed ruined it."

All four women—Leeta, Mary, Miss Clara, and Miss Justine—were suddenly wide-eyed, and glanced briefly at each other before trying to look ignorant again.

Sheriff Bloot chuckled. "You burned it, eh? Why ain't I a bit surprised?" He turned to Miss Clara. "I guess you're gonna call it nothing but a coincidence that she was at the murder scene, eh, Miss Clara?" He put a finger to his jaw and eyed Etta Ruth again. "Oh, yes, there's something else I been wondering about. It's that call you made to the sheriff's office when you reported that automobile accident down the road last week. It happened no more than five hundred yards from this house. I'd say close enough to hear the loud noise it musta made hitting that tree. Then it musta burned at least two or three hours before you called in to report it. You still saying you didn't hear it hit that tree, or smelled it burning?"

"I didn't hear a thing. Like I said when I called, I didn't know it happened until I walked out on the porch and saw the smoking hull."

"Another thing I didn't ask; I'm wondering if maybe that car mighta stopped by here before it wrecked, and you just didn't recognize it later when you saw it all burned up? Maybe a stranger asking for directions?"

"*I* haven't had a visitor except for that asshole son of mine who showed up one day and tried to kidnap me."

Leeta stared at her, recalling Etta Ruth laughing earlier and telling her and Mary that she was laughing at "*something that old bull had done to a stranger*" who'd had a couple of drinks with her *last week*—a visitor that '*Mr. Valentino* had "*scared halfway to death.*' Leeta looked at Mary and saw that they were both thinking the same thing.

"You sure about that?"

"Wouldn't I have told you something as important as that, Sheriff?"

"I'm not sure what you'd do, Miz Morley. That's the mystery here."

Etta Ruth wiggled her hips and fluffed her hair. "I shall take that as a compliment."

"We still ain't found out nothing about that burned-up body, except he was big as a barn, maybe six foot seven or eight, and he wasn't wearing no shoes, which means he musta been from Arkansas," he joked, before continuing in a more serious tone. "Wasn't a bit of identification on him or in the car, as far as we could tell. That fire was a hot one. Everything in that vehicle was just metal and ashes, except for him—he was a giant stick of charcoal."

"Oh, how horrible!" gasped Justine.

"The license plate checked out to a woman in Dallas who said they were stolen off her car a few days ago."

"Hmm, he stole somebody's license plates?" Etta Ruth mused. "That means a smart man like you has already figured out that he was a crook ... maybe a dangerous criminal up to no good and, luckily, that tree stopped him."

"Maybe. Are you *sure* you didn't see anybody drive by here?"

"I repeat, nope. I was asleep. I am a very sound sleeper."

Leeta watched the sheriff lead Etta Ruth away, but then Etta Ruth suddenly pulled back from him and turned around.

"Hey, Willie, your gift is in a paper bag under your bed. I put it there a week ago, but I guess you never clean your room or you would have found it by now, wouldn't you? Don't run up there and open it until we're gone. I don't want you running back downstairs like an idiot and getting all mushy and thanking me over and over and over again for giving you the best damn gift anyone ever gave you in your whole damn life."

Etta Ruth continued chuckling as the sheriff guided her down the steps.

Still staring at Etta Ruth as if she were seeing her first horror film, Leeta followed everyone out onto the porch. Once sitting on the vehicle's back seat, Etta Ruth leaned forward and, it seemed to Leeta, looked her straight in the eyes again. Grinning, she gave her the kind of sly wink one would direct at a co-conspirator. Flummoxed by it, Leeta frowned.

"It will be interesting to see what she gave you," Justine said after the sheriff's car had driven away. "Bet it's some of her old costume jewelry. She has a ton of it. Her clothes would be much too large; but not for Clara."

Clara gave her a look. "You and I wear the same size, Justine, and have done so for the past twenty years, a healthy size fourteen."

"I am a size twelve, Clara."

"No, you are not." She turned to Mary and Leeta. "I'm sorry about all of this with Etta Ruth. We did suspect that she would be arrested for Mr. Abelson's demise but, as it turned out, it was Banker Prickett. We were hoping our imaginations were running away with us, but unfortunately.... Anyway, in retrospect, I suppose we should have alerted the sheriff early on, but we just couldn't." Clara was clearly depressed.

Justine tapped her shoulder. "Correction, Clara. Who is this 'we' you were talking about? *You* suspected Etta Ruth, not I. *I* just never *liked* her. You never told *me* anything, so how could I suspect her? I never had a clue until today."

"You've been clueless, that's for sure."

Justine missed the sarcasm. "What are we going to say to people, Clara? It's going to be terribly embarrassing having a homicidal killer in the family, and her a Hesterwine Medallion as well, sworn to do good for all."

"In Etta Ruth's mind, she thought she was doing exactly that," Clara said, and walked back into the house.

"That would explain it, I suppose," Justine said absently as she scanned Clara's backside as if calculating her measurements. "I think you are correct in saying you wear a size fourteen, Clara, but why on earth would you imagine I do?"

"Because you *do*."

"*My* dress patterns are size twelves, Clara."

"Yes, but you always cut them out three or four inches larger when sewing your dresses."

"I do not!"

Leeta and Mary had been standing politely by, and as Clara and Justine argued, Leeta whispered to Mary, "I knew Miz Etta Ruth was strange, but I never dreamed she would commit murder, did you?"

"One never knows about people," Mary said.

Leeta shrugged. "All I know is, she can make that old pipe organ come alive, and I got a new respect for her even if she did conk that crook on the head." She pinched little James' cheek. "I gotta go upstairs and get my purse and go to work." Then, as she and Mary climbed the stairs, she glanced over her shoulder at Miss Clara and Miss Justine on their way into the parlor. "I hope that argument over their dress size don't end up being all about that *Boyd Pendleton* again. Do you ever wonder what happened to him? He musta been some kinda Romeo to have them still fighting over him since away back in the Dark Ages. What was it that Miz Etta Ruth called him, '*the Pendleton heir with the savoir faire*'?"

"Yes. He sounds intriguing, doesn't he? Miz Etta Ruth sure knows how to push Miss Clara and Miss Justine's buttons saying stuff like that."

"She won't be doing it anymore though, if Sheriff Bloot is right about her being one of them Lizzie Borden types."

"Do *you* think she is capable of killing another human being, Leeta?"

"Another human being? Nope. But who knows how she figures out which is which. She's pretty scary."

"And yet, she was nice enough to give you a gift. Don't forget to look under your bed," Mary said as Leeta went into her room.

# 30

LEETA GOT DOWN ON HER HANDS AND KNEES and felt around under the bed for *"the best damn gift anyone ever gave you in your whole damn life"*... then there had been that wink. There was a message in that wink that she had not been able to decipher, but somehow knew the answer was in the large brown paper bag that her fingers now discovered.

Etta Ruth had rolled the bag tightly shut at the top, possibly to keep it airtight because when Leeta opened it she got a whiff of something familiarly unpleasant. *Did that crazy old woman give me a bag of cow manure?* There was something else in the bag, but she couldn't tell what it was; she started to lift it out but jerked her hand back. *Etta Ruth mighta put a damn spider in there just to scare the hell outta me.* Looking around, she found some newspapers and spread them on the floor. Turning her head aside to protect her nose from the foul stench, she dumped the contents onto the newspaper.

When she turned to look down, she wasn't surprised to see that the joke was on her, and *"the best damn gift anyone ever gave you in your whole damn life"* was a manure-encrusted pair of men's trousers, a belt, fancy suspenders, blue-and-white striped men's underwear, and a pair of humongous shoes. Leeta sighed. *That crazy old white woman musta got some sort of weird kick out of giving away a bag full of her dead husband's dirty stuff.*

Grimacing, she picked up the shoes, intending to toss them back in the bag, but paused to look closely at them. They were cream-colored, pointed-toed snakeskin loafers with metal taps on the heels. Almost as a reflex, she opened her hands and let the shoes drop heavily to the floor, her face going pale. She stared at the trousers a long time—knowing whose pants they were even before she lifted them by their belt loops and saw the thin silver belt buckle engraved with *MQM*.

Leeta staggered back, her knees going weak. *Mandingo Q. Mann* was the stranger Etta Ruth said had a couple of drinks with her ... *him*, that Mr. Valentino had "scared *halfway* to death" ... *him*, that was that *"long stick of charcoal"* the sheriff said was in that burned-out Cadillac limo!

Looking wildly around the room as if she expected him to jump out at her, she flung the pants away. Mandingo's wallet landed at her feet. She stood with her hands to her mouth a long time before she picked it up. There was no money inside, but his driver's license, social security card, and gas coupons were there ... and a folded piece of paper, addressed to *Leeta Bulow!*

> *Sassy face, when you get all the good you possibly can get out of my gift (which should not take but a few seconds if you have a normal amount of brain cells), burn everything that is in the bag, especially the wallet and everything in it until nothing is left but ashes. I kept the money in the wallet for incidentals; cab fare and such. So, keep your mouth shut, and thank God for Etta Ruth Morley, who freed you up to do as you damn please in this world.*
> *Yours truly,*
> *Etta Ruth Morley*
> *P.S. I suggest you eat this note.*

Leeta crammed the note into her mouth, her mind racing as she chewed. Etta Ruth Morley had somehow caused Mandingo Q. Mann to wrap his car around a tree! She shook her head violently, as if trying to unscramble her thoughts, and then abruptly dropped to her knees and began stuffing *the gift* back into the bag. She didn't even want to think about what had happened or how it had happened!

Through the open window, she saw Hank's pickup pull up at the gate. She clamped the paper bag securely under her arm, dashed from her room and ran down the stairs. After closing time tonight, she'd drop Etta Ruth's gift into the fire barrel out back where Dink burned garbage. She'd guard the inferno until everything was ashes, even if she had to sit there 'til daylight.

Miss Justine called to her from the parlor and wanted to know what Etta Ruth gave her.

"Just some old clothes I can't use, but it's the thought that counts." She poked her head around the parlor door. "By the way, I think it's a good day to tell you my name is Leeta Bulow."

"We know, dear. Aunt Lucy came across your social security card the first day you were here," Clara said.

"She came across it in my *pocketbook,* is where she came across it!" Try as she may, she could not stop grinning.

Mary and little James were on the porch swing, and Leeta yelled over her shoulder as she skipped down the steps: "You still holding that big boy on you lap? I ain't gonna spoil my kids like that."

"*Your* kids?" Mary called after her, smiling. "I thought you said you were not interested in having a family."

Leeta laughed and, as she reached Hank's truck, she shouted, "I love the way you always believe everything I say, Mary Kenny!" She hopped onto the seat, slid over to Hank, and kissed him in a way she had never kissed him before.

After a while, he pulled his head back. "That was no hi-Hank-take-me-to-work kiss."

Leeta slapped her hands firmly to both sides of his face and narrowed her eyes at him.

"You still wanna marry me, cowboy?"

That night as Mary, Clara, and Justine sat in the kitchen having their tea, Justine, looking furious, bit at her thumbnail. Suddenly, she slammed her open hands on the table and blurted, "I always knew Etta Ruth would blacken the family name someday! What are we going to do about it, Clara?"

"We are going to polish the silver and lay out grandmother's best china and crystal in the formal dining room."

"What? But Clara—"

"Aside from Etta Ruth's behavior, there has arisen an even greater threat to our good name, Justine."

"Losing our property will not ruin our good name, Clara."

Mary spoke up. "Nothing could ever ruin your good names, Miss Clara, Miss Justine."

"I'm afraid there is something that could, my dear." Clara pulled an envelope from her apron pocket. "The mailman delivered this note this morning. It's from Vernell Watson, and signed by the entire body of Hesterwine Medallions. Because of our involvement with Etta Ruth and her arrest for murder, you and I, Justine, *and* Etta Ruth, are being called before a tribunal of our peers. They will decide if we are still worthy of being members, or if we should be ostracized ... struck from all Medallion records, as if we had never been born."

"What? But why? It's Etta Ruth they should be calling before that tribunal, not us!"

"Vernell feels we are culpable in Etta Ruth's actions."

"But we are not!"

"Yes, we are; or rather, *I* am. Vernell believes that, because of Etta Ruth's *'extreme behavior'* and our willingness to take her into our home, even though it was obvious to everyone in town that she belonged in a mental institution, we are indeed responsible. I rang up Vernell after I got the note and she said it was against the rules to discuss the matter until the inquest, and then she hung up on me."

"Oh, Clara!" Justine bit harder at her thumbnail.

"That is not fair," Mary said. "Let any one of *them* try to stop Miz Etta Ruth from doing exactly as she pleases. As I see it, you were actually doing your duty as Hesterwine Medallions in taking Miz Morley into your home when her own son and daughter did not want her. I hope you tell them so."

Justine nodded emphatically. "Why, yes, Mary is right. We were doing our Medallion duty, Clara."

Clara sighed. "We can only hope that the tribunal committee has not been overly influenced by the gossip that Sheriff Bloot is spreading around town that Etta Ruth was in Mr. Abelson's apartment—possibly when he died—and ransacked it while he lay naked and dead on his kitchen floor." She heaved another despondent sigh. "However, it doesn't look good, Justine. Before Vernell hung up on me, she said Etta Ruth's arrest for Banker

Prickett's murder was such a shock to the Medallions that half of them nearly had a stroke."

"A sudden noise could do that," Justine muttered.

"Because of Sheriff Bloot's very public accusations against Etta Ruth, I'm worried that Vernell and the others now believe she had something to do with Mr. Abelson's death as well, although it's been proven that he died of a heart attack. I admit, I also struggled with that conclusion."

Justine frowned, then looked suspiciously at Clara. "Sheriff Bloot said he had proof that she ransacked Mr. Abelson's apartment and all that was missing were some letters. Was she looking for letters, Clara? You know, don't you? You might as well tell me. I'm sure it's all going to come out in the wash sooner than later."

Clara heaved her shoulders as if surrendering. "She was looking for thirty years' worth of letters that she suspected Clarence wrote to Mr. Abelson."

"What? Why in the world would she think such letters existed? Oh, don't tell me, I know why. She's *cracked!*"

"She had reason other than that. She was poking around in her garage one day shortly before she moved in with us and found a rather large stack of letters Mr. Abelson had written to Clarence over a period of thirty years, and right up until a few days before Clarence died. The day I went to the cemetery to ask her to buy a third of Hesterwine Place, I watched her burn those letters on Clarence's grave." Clara sighed heavily again. "I don't recall ever seeing Etta Ruth as devastated as she was in the cemetery that day, or crying as hard."

Justine snorted. "I don't recall her ever crying about anything, not even when we were children."

"She made quite a show of it in the cemetery."

"But why would Clarence and Mr. Abelson exchange so many letters, Clara? They had coffee *together* at *Beetle's Donuts* every morning of their lives. Seems to me they could have had all the contact they needed with each other over coffee at Beetle's."

"Maybe not."

"I would think writing a steady stream of letters like that is something one would expect sweethearts to do, not two grown men. But then again, Clarence and Mr. Abelson always were more thoughtful than most when dealing with folks."

Clara gave her a long, studied look, widening her eyes and nodding slightly, as if waiting for Justine to comprehend.

Justine frowned at her for an equally long period, then finally blurted, "Are you saying that Clarence and Mr. Abelson were...? Clara!"

"Yes, and it isn't something Etta Ruth wants the Hesterwine Medallions or anybody else to know about. It is nobody's business. It's a *family* affair, and Etta Ruth is absolutely correct to think so, as am I. And when I refuse to reveal Etta Ruth's and Clarence's personal situation to Vernell and the others, you and I will be drummed, literally *drummed*, right out of the Hesterwine Medallions."

"Oh, Lordy," Justine wailed, and turned to Mary. "If they carry that big bass drum into the house, we will surely know what's in store for us." She turned back to Clara. "What else is going to happen? We are not only losing our home, but also our fellowship among our peers. Next, the county will send us to the poorhouse work farm and stick us behind a plow!" She looked about to cry.

"Don't be ridiculous. The last work farm in Vander County closed down in thirty-five," Clara said, her face going as sad as Justine's was.

Mary frowned with concern for them. "I wish you would let Jack borrow those six hundred dollars from his bank. You can pay him back when things get better after the war, or whenever you can. Jack said so again just the other day."

It was as if she hadn't spoken. "Mary, dear, will you attend the tribunal with us? The rule is that anyone brought before a tribunal has a right to bring along a witness, as long as that witness is female and takes the Medallion secrecy oath, swearing *never, ever* to reveal anything they see or hear during the meeting—not to family, law enforcement, *God*, or anybody else—even upon their deathbed. Will you be our witness?"

"Of course I will, Miss Clara.

As darkness fell and they went off to bed, Mary glanced at the grandfather clock in the foyer; it was after nine, and Jack still had not called. One other time he had been late in telephoning because he had stayed at the hangar to help his mechanic work on his airplane and when he tried to call, the telephone line on Hesterwine Road had been down because of high winds. In the hallway upstairs, she picked up the phone receiver and heard the buzz that told her the line was working. She told herself that he was so tired after his patrol over the Gulf of Mexico he went home and went right to bed. He would call first thing in the morning.

The call came at 8:00 a.m. from Jack's tearful sister, Linda. Jack's plane was missing somewhere in the vast Gulf of Mexico. Mary was determined not to cry. Crying would mean she thought the worst. Questions went unanswered when she called Jack's CAP base of operations in Corpus Christi. "All I can tell you, ma'am, is we're searching," said the man on the phone. Had a Nazi U-boat shot him down? Had wreckage been spotted? These questions nagged her, but she did not ask them.

Despite Linda's upsetting message, she did exactly as she had done almost every day since she and Jack met—she watched the sky outside her bedroom window. She told herself he was fine. His plane would appear out of the clouds, the sun glinting off the bright-yellow wings as he dipped them at her. *I will not cry because there is no need,* she told herself. "You had better get yourself home and be quick about it, Jack Dunston ... or I just may not marr—!" After two days of constant vigil, she sank to her knees beside the window and cried.

Jack had been missing four days when the entire body of the Hesterwine Medallions, nineteen somber-faced, extremely elderly or moderately ageing females, arrived at Hesterwine Place in full ceremonial dress to bring Clara and Justine before their board of inquiry. Etta Ruth, of course, was in jail, and *her* tribunal would be by proxy, with Clara and Justine ordered to answer for her as well as themselves.

Mary and Leeta determined earlier that membership in the Hesterwine Medallion league of women was as important to Clara and Justine as breathing air. To get into the club, one had to have ancestors who played well-documented roles in Texas history, whether fighting wars, building cattle empires, or simply being early settlers who fought the Indians and the Mexicans. To be kicked out of the organization for *any* reason brought disgrace not only to one's self, but also to the worthy ancestors who had made it possible for them to become Hesterwine Medallions in the first place.

Mary and Leeta stood at the second-floor railing watching Clara and Justine welcome the assembly into the formal dining room off the foyer and across from the parlor. The immense, rarely used, elegantly furnished dining room looked out on the front of the house as well as the side, the windmill visible in the distance, its rusty blades squeaking and screeching in the wind.

"Ain't it a shame," Leeta said. "Miss Clara and Miss Justine got enough on their plate knowing they gotta turn this fantastic old place over to the bank in four days without having to kowtow to them weird-looking old ladies in their funny getup. Miss Justine told me she and Miss Clara got orders not to wear their Medallion clothes today... not until that damn tribunal decides whether or not they are worthy of wearing it."

"They were both pretty upset about that," Mary said.

"They ought not be. Miss Clara and Miss Justine is the only ones who don't look ridiculous." Leeta pointed at the women coming through the door. "If I wasn't so mad, I'd be laughing my head off at them silly-looking Hesterwine Medallion outfits."

Unlike Leeta, Mary gazed with interest at the women in their heavy white silk, nineteenth-century, mid-calf-length, drum major-style uniforms consisting of tight jackets adorned with fringed and braided red epaulets and tall, short-billed hats with downy red plumes jutting up in front. Each skirt had a flap hanging down the middle across the groin area, much like a Scottish highlander's *sporran* or *kilt* and with a shimmering, gold-threaded medallion embroidered in the center.

Leeta snickered. "Those flaps hanging over their hoo-hoos sort of make the outfit, don't they?"

Mary fought back a smile. "Stop trying to make me laugh, Leeta. I think those dear elderly ladies are adorable."

The women, of every size, shape, and physical condition, limped, strolled, or hobbled past Clara and Justine, their collective noses in the air, their white, flat-heeled boots with red tassels making all sorts of sounds on the polished hardwood floor. Clara and Justine aimed nervous but welcoming smiles at each of them. One elderly woman, whom Clara addressed as Evangeline, walked bent over at the waist, as if her spine had frozen in an eighty-degree angle. With arms stretched out in front of her, she gripped short canes in each fist, as if they were all that kept her from toppling over onto her face.

Leeta nudged Mary. "That must be 'the sand crab' Etta Ruth talked about—the only one among them that Miz Etta seemed to like."

As they watched the unfortunately bent woman she inched along, her tall, white hat with the red plume well on the back of her head so that it stood upright even though she did not, the canes tapping in cadence with her tiny booted feet. Then Leeta yelped at sight of the last woman that Miss Clara and Miss Justine welcomed through the door—a woman of enormous girth, and balancing a huge bass drum against her massive middle.

"I reckon Miss Clara meant it when she said they could be *drummed* out of them Medallions. If I was Miss Clara and Miss Justine, I'd tell all them ol' biddies to kiss my ... well, I'd tell 'em *something*."

"Being members of the Hesterwine Medallions is important to them, Leeta. Miss Clara said they do much for society, like help the poor, defend those who can't defend themselves ... all sorts of things."

"I can't see them defending anybody. Some of 'em can't hardly *move*."

"I am sure they defend *financially*, rather than physically," Mary said, giving in to a smile.

Leeta hiked the strap of her purse over her shoulder. "I gotta go. Hank will be here any minute. I gotta help get things lined up for the march into Hesterwine tomorrow. The Catholic priest from La Villita got over five hundred Mexicans from all over the county ready to march, and we got about that many coloreds from all 'round—every one of 'em ready to pay their poll tax and register to vote. Boy, are *the powers that be* in Hesterwine gonna be surprised to see what's coming down the road!"

Tears suddenly welled in Mary's eyes. "Jack and I were going to march into town with them."

"Don't give up, Mary. So he didn't make it back when he was supposed to. So what? Hank told me Jack crash-landed in the Louisiana swamp last summer when something happened to his engine, and nobody knew where he was 'til he walked out three days later with only a few scratches and lots of mosquito bites."

"I'm scared, Leeta—" She was going to say more, but it was all she could do to hold back more tears.

Leeta grabbed her hand. "You shouldn't be alone today, Mary. I'll tell Hank I can't go. I can help with the baby."

"No, go on. Aunt Lucy is watching over James. I've been asked to be a witness at the tribunal."

"Lucky you," Leeta quipped as she started down the stairs, but then halted, hesitated a moment, and then turned around and came back. She squinted at Mary. "I wasn't gonna tell you just yet, but maybe it'll cheer you up. Just don't ask me any questions, okay?" She didn't wait for an answer. "It was Mandingo Q. Mann that burned up in that car down the road. I got it from a very reliable source and ... uh ... the *person* gave me his clothes to prove it. I burned them."

Mary could only stare at her. Suddenly she knew what Etta Ruth's gift to Leeta was! Grinning, Leeta nodded as if she had read her mind.

"I gotta go. Don't let those old hornets get too rough with Miss Clara and Miss Justine now."

Mary was not listening. She was trying to convince herself that Miz Etta Ruth could not have possibly done anything to Mandingo Q. Mann that would cause him to crash his car into a tree! But ... if she did nothing to him, how did she end up with his clothes?

Mary's thoughts abruptly turned to Mr. Abelson and Banker Prickett. As she acknowledged yet another instance where her gut feeling had been wrong—she was immediately relieved that Etta Ruth was in jail.

# 31

TALL, SKELETAL VERNELL WATSON called the meeting to order, waved Mary forward, and instructed her to put her left hand on her heart and her right hand on Vernell's shoulder. Vernell did the same—left hand on her heart, right hand on Mary's shoulder.

"Do you swear to take to your grave all that you hear or see in this meeting of the Hesterwine Medallions?"

Mary said, "I do." Then, after nodding reassuringly to Miss Clara and Miss Justine, she hurriedly took a seat next to the big bass drum near the dining room's closed double doors.

Vernell bypassed further parliamentary procedure in order to "get down to the nitty-gritty." All said: "Aye!"

As instructed to do, Clara and Justine sat side by side at the head of the table; obviously, so that the body of women lined up in the plush seventeenth century King James II and King William-style chairs on either side of the banquet-sized table could stare directly at the indicted pair.

"As you know, Clara and Justine," began Vernell Watson, "a fellow member, *Etta Ruth Morley*, who lives in this very house, is accused of murdering Stanton B. Prickett. In addition, there is a lesser charge of ransacking Marvin Abelson's home while he lay naked and dead on the floor from a heart attack... or so said the autopsy. We Medallions have leveled the *ransacking* charge, since the Grand Jury did not see fit to do so." She waved a hand at the others and they all nodded in agreement. "We feel that poking through a dead man's property while he's dead and naked on the floor shows a wicked lack of character."

"Amen to that," Justine whispered to Clara.

"*And now*, Clara and Justine Hesterwine, it has come to our attention that the two of you had prior knowledge of your cousin's activities, and aided and abetted her in keeping them secret."

"Not true!" Justine cried, jumping to her feet.

Clara stood up. "I will handle this, Justine. Sit down." She looked up and down the row of women. "I want to make it perfectly clear that Justine knew absolutely nothing about any of this until the sheriff came out here and arrested Etta Ruth. I, on the other hand, suspected a time or two that Etta Ruth was involved in the things of which she is accused. However, I chose not to believe it." She paused and drew a deep breath. "No, that is not true. The truth is I said nothing because I was worried about our good name ... the heretofore-unscathed reputations of Hesterwines and their kin. Am I guilty of harboring information that would have helped the sheriff arrest Etta Ruth sooner? Yes, I am. Therefore, I and Etta Ruth should be your only victi—er, your only focus during this meeting."

Justine stood. "*You* sit down, Clara. I want to speak to our fair-minded body of peers about something they must never lose sight of, and that is our Medallion pledge." She placed her hand over her heart and said in a whispery but commanding voice, "*Honor, charity, fortitude, loyalty to our own and, above all, defenders of the defenseless.*"

Vernell Watson looked agitated. "What's your point, Justine?"

"My point is that Clara, in keeping quiet about her suspicions, was following our sacred vow to the fullest degree. Was she not being exceptionally '*honorable*' and '*charitable*' in containing her unproven inklings? Did it not take great '*fortitude*' to give someone like *Etta Ruth Morley* the benefit of a doubt in a situation that was utterly '*defenseless*'?" She paused a moment before adding as she sat down: "You know I'm right."

Even Mary, like everyone else in the room, appeared confounded by Justine's statement. Mary had no time to ponder the confusing testimonial because something lightly struck the back of her head, then fell to the floor—*a spitball the size of a sugar cube!* She glanced over her shoulder and up to the transom. *Etta Ruth*!

Etta Ruth grinned impishly down at her as she beckoned with a wave of her hand before disappearing from sight. Mary spun around on the chair to stare straight ahead. *Oh no! How did she get out of jail?* After a moment, Mary slipped out the door. Etta Ruth, tapping her bare foot and looking disheveled in her white slip and gaping red silk robe, was waiting. She had braided her long, uncombed hair into *little-girl* braids and was chewing impatiently on one of them.

"Oh, Miz Etta Ruth, I hope you did not escape. Things will go so much worse for you if you did!"

Etta Ruth flung the braid over her shoulder. "Clarence Jr. got me out. Politics, you know. Ain't they the shits? He dropped me off last night. I've been in my room all this time and not a damn one of you knew it." She laughed, then hurriedly began to unbraid her hair and run her fingers through the crinkled strands.

Mary nodded toward the dining room door. "Miss Clara and Miss Justine are in trouble with the Hesterwine Medallions."

"Leave it to Justine to confuse the hell out of them, but I'm about to give the whole damn bunch the nitty-gritty they came for." Both braids were undone now and she meticulously spread her wildly flowing mop around her shoulders.

"Miz Etta, don't you want to get dressed first, at least put on your underthings?"

"Hell, no! Now, go in there and say loud as you can, 'Ladies, I give you your fellow Hesterwine Medallion, the infamous *Etta Ruth Morley!*'"

"Oh, but Miz Etta—"

"Do it! You owe me for saving Willie, or Leeta, or whoever she is, from that damn elephant, Mr. Mandingo Q. Mann—accident that it was, of course. Or hasn't Willie told you about the crispy critter found in that burned-out car down the road?" She waited for Mary's hesitant nod, then grinned. "Good! It involves us all now, doesn't it? But I won't tell if you don't. Now get in there and say what I told you to say."

Mary did as told, and before the startled women had a chance to respond, Etta Ruth strolled in, one hand on a hip and the other holding a Pall Mall cigarette next to her cocked head. Mary feared at any moment the cigarette would set her hair on fire.

Clara and Justine could only stare like the others as she wriggled into her Bette Davis pose. Vernell rose slowly to her feet.

"Etta Ruth Morley, have you come to confess ransacking Marvin Abelson's apartment while he lay naked and dead on the floor, and then later killing Stanton B. Prickett?"

Ignoring her, Etta Ruth gazed at Clara. "You said you had your suspicions, Clara. Repeat them word for word, and I will answer."

"Etta Ruth ... I really don't want ..."

"Do it! And none of your namby-pamby whitewashing, either, or I might get mad!" She looked around as if searching for a weapon. A frightened murmur went up all around the table.

Clara drew a deep breath. "I'm sorry, but I thought you murdered them both—Mr. Abelson because of... well, you know, but then the coroner's report proved he had a heart attack, thank God."

Etta Ruth raised a hand. "Back up. Tell them why you think I might have murdered old fart Abelson."

"Etta Ruth, I really don't want—"

"Do it, dammit!"

"Because of ... him and Clarence."

"What about him and Clarence, Clara?" Etta Ruth prodded.

Justine jumped up. "Don't say it, Clara! You said yourself it was a family affair!"

"Do it, dammit!" Etta Ruth repeated.

"Oh, for God's sake, Etta Ruth, I thought you didn't want it spread all over the county!" She looked at the rows of enrapt women. "It-it was because they were having an affair."

A collective gasp went up as the women began to whisper frantically to one another, their tall hats going askew on their heads.

"Shut up!" Etta Ruth cried, and they did. "Continue, Clara."

"I suspected you killed Banker Prickett to keep him from taking Hesterwine Place, but, Etta Ruth, that was no way to go about it."

Etta Ruth threw her head back and laughed. "Sorry to disappoint you, Clara, but I didn't kill Prickett any more than I killed old man Abelson."

"You don't have to deny it to *us*, Etta Ruth. We are not Sheriff Bloot; we are Hesterwine Medallions." Clara paused to glare meaningfully around the table at the galvanized faces. "We are sworn to secrecy, and nothing you say will leave this room. As for Justine and me, we shall stand beside you no matter what."

Justine frowned. "I wouldn't go so far as that, Clara."

"Shut up, floozy."

Justine's eyes snapped. "Stop calling me that! I am not a floozy!"

"Not anymore you aren't. You're too old." Etta Ruth returned her attention to Clara. "I *did not* kill Prickett. I went to the bank to tell him that if he didn't leave you alone about that mortgage, I was going to tell his wife about that carhop, Melba, who works at the Toot & Get, and who he's been bonking for the past five years—paying her rent and buying her clothes. I wouldn't doubt if he didn't pay for that Chevy coupe she's been driving since thirty-nine."

Another collective gasp went up.

"I was only going to threaten him with ruin, that's all, but I never got the chance."

Clara almost collapsed with relief. "Thank God, I am so glad! So glad!"

"I saw him die, though," Etta Ruth said, grinning, as if she knew the disturbance her words would cause, and they did. Clara looked too jolted to speak.

Mary could not keep quiet. "You *saw* Mr. Prickett die?"

Vernell Watson glared at her. "Young lady, you are not a member of the Medallions. Restrain yourself, *please*."

"Yes, ma'am."

"Oh, yes, Mary. I saw the entire drama from start to finish, which was maybe a split-second—the dying part, anyway. It was an accident, and there was nothing anyone could have done to stop it." She looked over her shoulder at the huge silver coffee urn, cookies, cups, and saucers on a corner table, and went over and poured herself a cup of coffee. She eyed Clara. "I suppose you used all our coffee rations for this little gathering, and our sugar stamps for the cookies, didn't you? A lot of thanks you'll get from this bunch."

"We certainly are thankful for the coffee, Etta Ruth, *and* the cookies; if you'll pass them around," Vernell snapped.

Mary watched Etta Ruth take her time slinking to the table with the cookie platter. Before sliding it down the table to waiting hands, she meticulously picked out a handful for herself. With the women's eyes snapping impatiently at her, she sat down to sample them one by one between blowing her coffee and taking sips.

Vernell Watson waved her hands. "Well, is that all you've got to say, 'it was an *accident*'? The sheriff and police chief said Mr. Prickett was struck a hard blow to the forehead, Etta Ruth. How can that be an accident? Someone had to strike that blow. Maybe you just forgot what you did?"

"I did not kill the damn old fornicator, damn it! If those dumbass cops and deputies will look in the bushes next to where his car was parked—which is near where his body was found beside his *flat* front tire—they'd find the goddamn weapon. It's a red car jack, and it's stuck in those thick oleanders shrubs."

"You used a *car jack?*"

"Vernell, you're pissing me off. Watch my lips, I-did-not-kill-the-son-of-a-bitch!"

"We don't mean to upset you, Etta Ruth, but we just don't understand," Clara said.

"You're getting as dense as your sister, Clara. I went to the bank before sunup, knowing he usually came to work hours before banking hours, probably to go through the files and see who else was late on their payments so he could screw them out of their property. His car was beneath the carport near the bank's back door. I hid behind the oleanders and waited for him to come out. I hung my binoculars on the oleander bush while I waited—I didn't want them banging against my necklace and alerting him I was there. When I left, I forgot all about them, and that's why the sheriff found them at the so-called 'murder scene,' and chucked my innocent ass in jail." She extended her coffee cup to Mary. "I need a refill."

*More caffeine is all she needs*, Mary thought as she went to the coffee urn with Etta Ruth's cup.

"I was going to speak to Prickett when he came out of the bank, tell him I knew all about tight-pants Melba at the Toot & Get Drive-In. You can imagine my surprise when a pickup truck full of men screeched into the parking lot and Prickett got out with his Klan robe rolled up under his arm. Seems they'd all been out at Rose Hill throwing Molotov cocktails."

"I swear," uttered Vernell. "Who would have suspected Mr. Prickett was a member of the Klan, him being so big in the church and all."

"You are so damn naive, Vernell, it makes me sick," Etta Ruth growled. "Prickett got in his car and started the motor. '*Damn*,' I said to myself, 'why didn't the pickup leave sooner and give me a chance to chat with him?' But guess what? The truck left and Prickett started backing out, but then he stopped and turned off the motor. He got out and came around to look at the right front tire not five feet away from me in the bushes. It was flatter than a fritter."

Vernell Watson jumped up as if eagerly answering a quiz question. "You had let the air out!"

"No, I did not let the goddamn air out! How come you think every little thing that happens is my doing, Vernell? Sometimes, it's just pure luck, is all."

Mary could not help but blurt, "He got the jack out of the trunk, and you took it away from him!" She covered her mouth as Vernell fixed her with a warning stare.

"How many times do I have to say I did not kill the crooked bastard? I went over and said I wanted to talk to him. He knew I was living at Hesterwine Place and said he knew what I wanted but I could forget it, because he was foreclosing on Hesterwine Place this coming Tuesday. Then, he said if I didn't leave he would call Clarence Jr. in Houston and tell him I'd become a damn menace to the town and he'd better come get me and put me away somewhere where I couldn't bother anybody. He got the jack out of the trunk, stuck it under the car, and started pumping. I started talking. Told him I knew all about him and tight-pants Melba and I would tell his wife, Betty, the whole sordid story if he didn't stop trying to squeeze blood out of a couple of old turnips. I guess he forgot to put the car's emergency brake on, because suddenly the jack flew up like a red streak of lightning and hit him square in the forehead. *Crack!* That damn jack almost hit me as it bounced off him and into the oleanders. I couldn't believe what happened until I got a closer look at Prickett's split forehead. Blood was squirting out of him like a busted faucet."

"Oh, the poor man," Clara murmured.

"My pink evening gown got splattered all down the front and I had to burn the damn thing."

"What were *you* doing in a pink evening gown, Etta?" asked one of the women.

"I was modeling for the Boy Scouts of America, Lois—what the hell do you think I was doing?"

Clara was shaking her head. "I didn't like him, but I never wished him harmed in any way. I feel terrible." Justine nodded her agreement.

Etta Ruth tapped at her chin. "It *is* too bad he had to die. If he'd lived, I could hold Melba over his head and he'd forget all about foreclosing. But now, without Prickett to stop them, the bank's sure to do it." She bit into a cookie. "Anyway, Clara, you should at least get some satisfaction knowing the greedy bastard won't be moving into your home like he planned."

"Ha! Guess you haven't heard," Justine said. "*Sheriff Bloot* will be moving into Hesterwine Place with his widowed mother-in-law, *Betty* Prickett. I would have preferred Stanton B. Pickett rather than *him!*"

Clara sighed. "Nevertheless, it's sad that Banker Prickett died, sad for his family, sad for anyone else who cared about him."

Etta Ruth nodded. "You're right, Clara. Tight-pants Melba is probably beside herself with sadness wondering how she's going to pay her rent."

"But what about Mr. Abelson, Etta Ruth?" Vernell wanted to know. "Sheriff Bloot says you were in his apartment. You must have been furious with him after finding out about him and Clarence."

"You reckon, Vernell?" Etta Ruth tittered as if Vernell had just uttered a ridiculously obvious truth. "At first, I wanted to boil his ass in oil. Then, after I resumed rational thought"—all the women at the table glanced at each other—"all I wanted was to burn the letters I knew Clarence must have written to him." She paused, looking more furious than ever. "If those two idiots hadn't put it all in writing, Clarence would have gone directly from the closet to the grave and no one would have ever been the wiser! I would have preferred not knowing!" She took a deep breath. "Anyhow, the door was unlocked and I walked right in. He was prancing around naked, fixing to make a cake—he wasn't even wearing his frilly little apron. When I told the old bastard I knew about him and Clarence because I'd read his love letters he turned blue, coughed a couple of times, and dropped to the floor, simple as that. I never laid a hand on him ... other than douse him with flour as he lay there—like I said, Vernell, I was furious with the son of a bitch. He stole my husband! You of all people ought to know how I felt! When your Harlan cheated on you with Florence 'big tits' Berzanski, you jerked out half her hair coming out of church one Sunday right in front of God and everybody. I didn't touch a hair on Abelson's head. *I* only doused the old bastard with that flour. I didn't know he was dead. I thought he had fainted."

As Vernell turned beet red, her fellow Medallions nodded at her in affirmation of old news.

Just then, a loud pounding on the front door caused all heads to jerk toward it. Justine went to the window that faced the front of the house.

"The sheriff's car is out front and—oh, my! There are three men in white coats getting out of an ambulance, and Clarence Jr. is with them!"

Etta Ruth was already raising the floor-length window that looked out on the side yard. She stepped out the window, and was gone.

The wind picked up. The old windmill groaned and screeched like a tortured soul, as if pleading with the anguished woman standing, straddled-legged on its lofty platform. One of her hands gripped the center pipe while the other seemed to test the wind by letting it ripple through her spread fingers as she leaned far out, like a child clinging to a maypole.

Below, Mary, the sheriff, the three men in white coats, Clarence Jr., and the entire body of Hesterwine Medallions stared up at her.

"She's gonna jump," one of the women whispered, and a distraught noise burst from her fellow Medallions.

"Etta Ruth, dear cousin, please come down!" Clara cried, her voice trembling as it had not trembled before when Etta Ruth ascended her perch...because this time, there was purpose in Etta Ruth's lunacy, and Clara somehow knew it.

"Don't do it, Momma! Don't do it!" Clarence Jr. yelled up at her.

"Look out! She's gonna spit!" Justine's warning moved everyone back a few steps, but Etta Ruth only glanced downward for an instant before continuing to ignore them.

Clara turned to Sheriff Bloot and Clarence Jr. "I wish you had phoned before coming out here and scaring her like that, Sheriff. Perhaps we could have talked her into letting us bring her to you. And why on earth did you bring those burly men along—they frighten even *me*!"

Sheriff Bloot shrugged. "The white coats were the judge's idea. I didn't have no say in the matter. Clarence Jr. here pulled more strings and, rather than try her for murder, the judge signed an order committing her to the state hospital in San Antone instead. That done, he revoked her bond and ordered me to keep her in jail until she's transported to the loony bin tomorrow morning."

"I told you I was gonna do what I could, Miss Clara," Clarence Jr. said, then jerked out his handkerchief and mopped at the sweat pouring down his rosy face. "It's a dern sight better than Momma being in jail."

"But she hasn't murdered *anyone,*" Clara cried. "She is innocent!"

"That's what they all say," Sheriff Bloot said as the crowd of Medallions let out a collective gasp upon seeing Etta Ruth let go of the pipe and stand with her bare toes sticking over the edge of the platform. The wind whipped her red robe, almost tearing it from her as her thin white slip billowed up around her hips.

Vernell Watson drew a loud, indignant breath, cupped her hands around her mouth and screeched, "Etta Ruth Morley, we can see everything you've got! You come down here right now and put some clothes on!"

"Come on down, Momma. It ain't a decent sight you're presenting!" Clarence Jr. yelled.

The Crab, Evangeline, unable to straighten her body and look up, moved frantically among the Medallions asking one and then the other, "What's going on? What's going on?"

Vernell's indignation continued. "Get down here this instant, Etta Ruth! Have you no shame?"

"Leave her alone!" Mary cried, but it was too late.

"I'll be right there, Vernell ... Clarence. *Bombs away!*"

It happened so fast that after the initial horrified scream that tore from every mouth, they stared at the ground in shocked silence ... at Etta Ruth lying atop *Sheriff Bloot*. Even more astonishing was that this infamous bully of long standing had bravely attempted to break Etta Ruth's fall, and succeeded, but not without great harm to himself.

Etta Ruth rolled off him. "Asshole!" she screamed at the sheriff, tears rolling down her face as she pushed Clarence Jr.'s hands aside.

Two of the white-coated attendants dropped to the sheriff's side, while the other fetched a stretcher from the ambulance.

"He's dead!" Justine could not contain herself and began to wail, as did half the Medallions.

"No, he ain't, but he's out cold," said one of the attendants as he got busy feeling the sheriff's prostrate body from neck to boots. "Looks like he's got a broken shoulder ... a broken arm, too, and maybe a concussion."

Etta Ruth sat on the ground nearby, sobbing heavily, crying harder than on that day at the cemetery when she'd chopped at Clarence Sr.'s grave with her trowel as if she were killing garden snails. Clarence Jr., kneeling beside her but keeping his hands to himself, looked helpless.

"It serves him right," Etta Ruth blubbered, scooting closer to Sheriff Bloot and staring down at him. "He shouldn't have stopped me, goddammit!" She sniffed, then mumbled, "He's big as an ox. Can't anything hurt a damn ox like him." She motioned for Clara to lean down. "I had an *epiphany* while up there on the windmill this time, Clara. Remember what I told you about Clarence trying to do me in with that box cutter sleeve and hypodermic needle? Well, it was only a nightmare I had, like Clarence said it was."

"Knowing should make you feel much better about Clarence—no matter what else he did," Clara whispered to her, patting her shoulder.

"It doesn't," Etta Ruth growled.

The sheriff moaned and regained consciousness as they strapped him to the stretcher and lifted him from the ground. He reached a hand out to Etta Ruth. "You're coming with me, Etta Ruth Morley," he said weakly. "After this, the judge may change his mind and try you for murder."

"Okay," she replied, and allowed Clara and Mary to help her to her feet. Passively, she let them and Clarence Jr. hug her. Even Justine stepped up and reluctantly patted her on the back.

"You'll be fine, Etta Ruth," Clara whispered to her. "We will make certain the authorities know the truth. Until then, Justine and I will visit you ... wherever you are."

"You will?"

"Yes, of course we will."

"So will Willie and I," Mary said.

Etta Ruth grabbed Mary's hand. "Make sure she does what I told her to do with that gift I gave her. I can't afford to get in any more trouble."

"Yes, ma'am. I believe it has been ... taken care of."

The ambulance, with Sheriff Bloot and Etta Ruth lying opposite each other, left. One of the white-coated men drove Sheriff Bloot's car back to town. Before Vernell and the Hesterwine Medallions departed, Vernell assured Clara and Justine that they and Etta Ruth would remain Medallions in good standing. "Etta Ruth is *troubled*"—Vernell made a circling motion at her temple with her long forefinger—"but she is not a liar. If they attempt to try her on that ridiculous murder charge, we shall all be in court to testify in her defense. Clarence Jr. will naturally get a couple of his big-shot attorney friends in Houston to defend her and she'll be free as bird before we know it." Vernell paused. "I'm not sure we can keep her out of *you-know-where* in San Antonio, though."

Standing at the gate, Clara, Justine, and Mary waved good-bye to the carloads of shaken women. Clara turned to Mary. "What on earth did Etta Ruth mean, Mary? How could giving Willie a gift cause her more trouble?"

"Miss Clara, I am sorry, but that is the last thing you need to know right now, and ... and I cannot say, unless Miz Etta Ruth gives me permission. I hope you don't mind."

"No, I don't mind, dear. I admire your integrity. Besides, we've ingested enough information for the present. All that has happened today, along with the knowledge that in less than forty-eight hours our property will belong to Betty Prickett and the First Loan & Trust Bank, is enough to digest for now."

Justine's round face grew ghostly sad. "We are allowed to take our clothes and other personal items when we leave Tuesday, but absolutely nothing else."

"I am so sorry," Mary said, wanting so to help them and frustrated that she could not.

Justine gave Mary a peck on the cheek, as did Clara. "I'm glad you are going to the boarding house in town with us, Mary, at least until after the wed—" Justine didn't finish, but glanced apologetically at her.

"Until after your wedding," Clara finished Justine's sentence. "And if Jack doesn't make it back in time for the voter registration march tomorrow, we shall march in his place—us, and Mr. Valentino, of course," she said airily.

Mary nodded, unable to speak for fear of crying. Silent, they stood on the porch watching the last of the Hesterwine Medallion motorcade disappear over Windy Knoll. Miss Clara and Miss Justine's arms suddenly tightened around her with an urgency she understood—they were thinking of Jack, just as she was, and not at all as positive about his return as they pretended.

Just before the three of them went into the house, the familiar black Pontiac passed by on its way to the shack, as usual. Mary noted that Miss Clara's face remained expressionless as she cast a quick glance at it just as she would glance at any car passing her house. Obviously, Fritz Von Heuvel, alias Gustave Herrmann, had not at all been trying to build up enough nerve to call at Hesterwine Place; furthermore, it seemed not to matter a bit to Miss Clara.

# 32

THE SUN HAD NOT CLEARED THE HORIZON when men and women from Rose Hill, La Villita, and other such communities from all over Vander County met at the fork in the backroad into Hesterwine and moved steadily toward town, their destination the Vander County Courthouse to pay their poll tax and register to vote in the upcoming election for sheriff. The absence of their candidate for sheriff was not reason enough to call off the march. "We got several fish to fry in that election, not just getting Sheriff Bloot out of office," said Hank. "Jack would be the first to say so."

Leading the throng was the Catholic priest from La Villita and Reverend Henry Posey from Rose Hill, along with Hank. Newspaper reporters from the *Vander County Picayune* and several other newspapers in the area accompanied the more than a thousand marchers, cameras ready. Behind the leaders and setting the pace lumbered Rudolph Valentino, pulling the freshly waxed and shined old Buick, with *Future Voters For Justice* signs on the grill, doors, and rear of the vehicle. Clara and Justine sat stalwart on the front seat, Rube between them. Mary, Leeta, and Aunt Lucy occupied the back seat, their eyes never leaving the road ahead. Jack's sister, Linda, and two of her girlfriends were at Hesterwine Place babysitting little James.

The air was full of excitement and more than a bit of tension, for no one knew how the townsfolk and the powers that be would accept into their midst this early Monday morning an insurgence of heretofore invisible Negro and Mexican minorities of the county. For generations, both groups had stayed away from the polls due to threats of violence from the Klan, and today's marchers were on the lookout for trouble. Even though extremist hate organizations had become increasingly fragmented across the state over the past twenty years and were now mostly located in East Texas, their appearance at Hesterwine Place the night of the military dance and then the firebombing of Rose Hill reminded everyone that a diehard pocket of them still existed in Vander County. Like everywhere else in the South, Anglo-Saxon racism and militant Protestantism drove Vander County's Klan, and today, everything the Klan loathed was on the move toward the county seat in a bid for at least a semblance of equality, if only through the right to vote without fear.

Mary was glad that Sheriff Bloot's injuries, though not life-threatening, kept him hospitalized. Jack had said Bloot would not consider it politically advantageous to interfere today, but Mary could not help but wonder what the sheriff's reaction would be if he had somehow found out that the Negroes and Mexicans that he mindlessly belittled and disrespected daily were marching *en masse*... intending to vote him out of office come the next election.

Before Jack left, he also told Mary that he had advised the Texas Rangers of the march. "I'm hoping there'll be a few of them along the route," he had said. Mary hoped so, but so far, the marchers were alone on the road.

Somewhere in the multitude, a Mexican *conjunto* band riding on a flatbed truck began to play. Jack had explained *Tejano conjunto* to her one day when they stopped on the shortcut to town and heard music and the sound of a celebrating crowd coming from La Villita. The throbbing beat of the distinct South Texas *música norteña* produced by button accordion and the strong, lower-pitched rhythm of the *bajo sexto* set the entire crowd to yipping, some of them now dancing along the route instead of walking. If the marchers expected trouble, they hid it well. Mary and Leeta turned around on the seat to watch and listen.

Not until the leaders reached the top of the hill just outside Hesterwine's city limits did anyone see the white-robed figures, afoot and on horseback, blocking the way into town.

Reverend Posey turned and raised his arms. "Looks like there is well over three hundred of them down there. If they don't get out of our way, we are just going to stand there facing them until they either move or make their move!"

A low murmur went up as word of what lay ahead traveled to the back edges of the marchers.

Leeta leaned forward as Hank approached. "I don't see any Texas Ranger lawmen down there, do you?" she asked.

"No, and there's sure to be trouble if they don't show up. Most that bunch ain't from Vander County. One of our Rose Hill folks coming home from his night job at the depot this morning said there are horse trailers parked all over the side streets in town, most of them from out of the county. Unfamiliar cars parked everywhere, too."

"Oh, my," Justine said, pointing at the Klan. "That one in the gold robes and on that big white horse is the Exalted Cyclops of the Knights of the White Camellia himself! It's said he's from San Antone. It seems word about our march has traveled far."

"That truly is him, all right ... the Klan's exalted cyclops," Clara said. "I know this because when Justine and I were children, Poppa took us to the Battle of Flowers parade in San Antonio and when it was over, here comes the Klan down the same street and Poppa said 'there is their leader, the Exalted Cyclops.' Poppa certainly had no affection for the Klan. Momma said his refusal to join them was why his cotton gin business went broke. Of course, that was back in the day when Texas had as many Klan members as it had coyotes and rattlesnakes."

Justine added, "According to Vernell Watson, whose brother was once a Klan member until his family threatened to disinherit him, Vander County has less than a hundred members. If that's true, there must be over two hundred out-of-towners down there."

Hank nodded. "Yes, ma'am, and they aren't here to escort us *peaceably* to the courthouse. That's why I want you ladies to stay back here. When the way is clear, you can come on."

Clara smile sweetly at him. "Thank you for your concern, Hank, but Rudolph is getting impatient. He may just decide to go straight through their middle. We shall see if they want to try and stop *him!*"

Hank's eyes suddenly locked on Leeta and the wooden croquet mallet in her hand. "Now what do you think you're gonna do with that?"

"Whatever I need to do with it, that's what."

"You're gonna stay back here, Leeta."

"I don't recall putting it up to you whether I could go or not, Hank Posey," she said, narrowing her eyes at him.

Justine reached down to the floorboards and came up with a crochet mallet of her own. "We are *all* going, Hank Posey! Today's event is going to be enormously significant to Vander County's future, and Clara and I intend to be a part of it, just as our grandfather became a part of Vander County history when he founded the town. Besides, Clara and I need to pay our poll tax for this year, and there is no better time than the present." She waved the mallet over her head. "We have come prepared!"

Mary held up a mallet, as did Aunt Lucy. "Don't worry about us, Hank. We will not get out of the Buick, and we will not let anyone get in it."

"Jack wouldn't want you going down there, Miss Mary."

"Well ... he can tell me *that* when he gets home. Maybe we will have our first ever fight over it," she added, here blue eyes suddenly shining with moisture.

"Okay. I ain't gonna say nothing more about it 'cause I know it won't do any good." He eyed Leeta. "Don't be using that stick on nobody, honey. We're going peaceably to the courthouse, like Jack planned." With that, he waved the procession slowly forward.

Rudolph Valentino, apparently feeling that he'd spent enough time on the road to Hesterwine this morning, forged to the front.

"You'd better slow him down, Clara!" Justine yelled.

"I'm trying, but he seems to have a mind of his own today," Clara replied, but she was grinning ... and *jiggling* the reins rather than pulling back on them. Fifty or sixty marchers rushed to catch up to the old Buick and then lined up to trot alongside it, while cautiously giving the massive, wicked-looking bull all the room he needed out front.

When less than a hundred feet separated the Klan from the oncoming throng, all went deathly silent on both sides. The only sound came from the hooves and whinnying of the Exalted Cyclops's horse as the animal danced nervously about on the pavement.

"The poor horse is afraid of Rudolph," Justine said. "He doesn't know Rudolph adores horses."

Clara corrected her. "Rudolph adores *donkeys*, not horses."

"Well, maybe he thinks that horse favors Lionel a little," Justine snapped.

The Exalted Cyclops unsheathed a sword from a jeweled sheath that girded his robe and waved it over his head, and then yelled at the top of his twangy voice, "You niggers and Meskins better turn back or there is gonna be hell to pay!"

"Giddy up, Mr. Valentino!" Clara cried as she snapped the reins harder. The bull, seeming to grasp Clara's aggressive intent, bellowed, lowered his head, and charged at the white line blocking the road. When he was almost upon them they scattered, and then were further prompted to vacate the road by the startling blast of a siren coming from behind them, the shrill warning instantly followed by a Cavalry-style bugle call. The latter sound, though a bit crackly, suddenly put an even wider smile on Clara's face. She pulled hard on the reins and yelled for Mr. Valentino to halt.

Moments later, the entire hoard of Klansmen were pushed aside to fill the ditches as the Hesterwine Medallions, in full costume and carrying their traditional blackthorn shillelaghs over their shoulders, came marching spryly down the center of the road, Vernell pumping her bugle high in the air as if it were a baton. Laughing, Justine hugged Rube.

Behind the Medallions, with sirens occasionally bleating, rolled four 1941 black Plymouths with white sidewalls. Four solemn-faced Texas Rangers—Stetson hats sitting squarely on their heads, and big .357 Magnum Revolvers strapped to their hips—strode beside each vehicle, their knee-high boots scarcely making a sound on the pavement. A cheer went up from the marchers. The twenty-four-strong team of legendary lawmen, plus the pair riding in each Plymouth, was more than enough *Ranger power* to handle the three hundred Klansmen that now packed even tighter into the ditches. The white-sheeted mob shrunk yet farther back as the unlikely entourage of Hesterwine Medallions and Texas Rangers continued their advance.

"Jesus Pete, I feel like I just woke up in the Wild West," Leeta whispered to Mary as she stared at the Rangers. Fresh cheers rose up from the marchers as the Rangers' cars made U-turns in the road and the Hesterwine Medallions executed a military-style about-face and lined up behind them. With a siren blast from the lead Plymouth and a drum roll from the Medallions, they led the marchers into town, the statue-still Klan silently looking on.

"Why don't the Rangers arrest those Klu Kluxers?" Leeta wanted to know.

"I suppose because all they are doing now is staring daggers at us through those cowardly little peepholes in their hoods," Justine said.

Leeta laid aside her mallet. "I almost wish we could have put knots on a few heads before them Medallions and the law showed up."

"I'm thinking like you, girl," Aunt Lucy said. "It'd be worth a few nights in jail just to give that Exalted Cyclops the biggest headache he done ever had." She looked longingly over her shoulder at him. He had dismounted his horse and was sitting on the ground, leaning against a telephone pole. As they passed, he waved his arms at them in a tirade of curse words.

"Forget it," Leeta said. "What we set out to do is gonna be done, and everybody that's on this march today will vote in the next election and Jack Dunston will be sheriff."

"He gonna be sheriff iffen he make it bac—" Aunt Lucy looked regretfully at Mary. "I could bite my tongue, Miss Mary."

"You shoulda bit the damn thing off," Leeta said.

Mary patted Aunt Lucy's knee. "You only said what all of us are thinking, Aunt Lucy ... even me."

After an awkward moment when nobody spoke, Leeta poked her fingers into her ears. "I wish two-ton Bessie would quit beating that damn Medallion drum!"

"I'm thinking like you on that one, too, girl," Aunt Lucy said.

They were approaching the intersection to Hesterwine's main thoroughfare, and when they turned the corner, they were stunned to see the sidewalks lined with townsfolk; men, women, and children waving and yelling out words of encouragement. Both sides of the street leading the four blocks to the courthouse brimmed to the curbs with people, familiar faces and unfamiliar faces. Scattered among them, a few silent onlookers stared broodingly at the marchers, obviously not so supportive. No doubt one or more of their male family members had been among the white-robed greeting committee at the edge of town.

"My! Look at that crowd!" Justine said as she waved gaily. "I wouldn't be a bit surprised if the Hesterwine Medallions encouraged the townsfolk to greet us today."

Clara turned on the seat as she swept her arm toward the crowded streets. "See, girls? Not everyone in Vander County is a racist, and the ones who are can just lump it."

Leeta leaned close and whispered, "I can think of something else they can do, but Miss Clara wouldn't like me saying it."

"I bet you can," Mary said, and smiled at her. "But you know what? Despite those few glum faces in the crowd, there is something very appealing about Hesterwine, Texas, today. Either it is like Miss Justine said and the Medallions did another good deed ... or the folks waving and cheering us on saw all those Klansmen in their town today and decided to form a greeting committee of their own—a committee more reflective of the heart and soul of the little town of Hesterwine, Texas. Either way, I think this 'colorful little garden of a town, with its mixed bed of flowers,' is on the verge of finally getting rid of its stinkweeds."

The county tax office added extra clerks to handle the massive number of registrants, and the tax assessor collector, himself—obviously not a member of *the powers that be*—agreed to keep the doors open past closing time until the last person had paid his or her poll tax and registered to vote. Crowds of people on the streets joined the lines, obviously to pay their poll tax as well. There were four service windows in the tax office and so four lines formed on the courthouse lawn, all four extending three blocks down the street. The mood was jubilant. Change was in the air.

A group of Hesterwine's enterprising townsfolk, seeing the overflow crowds of onlookers, seized the opportunity to make a few dollars by quickly setting up portable food booths selling sandwiches, sodas, popcorn, and hotdogs. A three-day Cutting Horse event at the County Fairgrounds on the edge of town had just ended, and now the crowds from there, as well as festive-looking chuck wagons and miniature food courts, rolled onto Main Street with their wide selection of fare. Balloons on sticks, cotton candy on funnels of paper, costume jewelry, toys, trinkets, photo booths, and sketch artists created a carnival atmosphere that filled the streets with cheerful noises. Few of the marchers could afford to patronize the booths, but they didn't care. The Klan had failed this time, and they were doing what they'd set out to do.

On the courthouse lawn facing Main Street, the conjunto band members and the Blue Creek Trotliners took turns playing their special brands of music, greatly pleasing the crowds that gathered to dance in the street. A Mariachi band that had entertained at the fairgrounds during the horse show strolled the streets, their lively Mexican folk music adding to the gaiety that filled every avenue.

Leeta and Hank stood at the bottom of the courthouse steps, reminding registrants to keep their poll tax receipts in a safe place because they would be required to show them on Election Day if they expected to vote, and if they had lost their receipts, they would be turned away.

"I can't believe this, can you, Hank?" Leeta said. "We were expecting the worst, but the people of Hesterwine did everything but give us a key to the city."

"We got lots of fair-minded folks in Hesterwine and over the county, Leeta. They want Bloot and his crowd out of office, and with Rose Hill's and La Villita's help, they're gonna get what they want." He paused. "I hate to say it, but we'll have to find another candidate to run for sheriff, if—"

Leeta pressed her fingers to his lips. "Don't say it, Hank."

"Leeta, honey, we gotta face it. Jack might be dead."

"I said don't say it!" Her eyes were brimming. "That can't happen ... 'cause that would mean ain't nothing fair in this world, and Mary would be...!" she trailed off.

"Okay, honey. Let's don't think about it. Let's just enjoy what's happening right now." He waved his arm at the cheerful scenes around them.

She nodded, obviously eager to put Jack's fate from her mind. A group of little boys lit a string of firecrackers nearby and they both turned to watch as the firecrackers exploded on the ground with a rapid *Pop! Pop! Pop!* and the stench of burned black powder drifted to them. Leeta fanned her hand in front of her nose.

"I hope they don't blow their fingers off with them things," she said, turning back to Hank. "We couldn't afford firecrackers when I was a kid, could you?" she said, and then frowned. Hank was staring strangely at her.

"*Hank!*" she screamed, clutching at him as he fell forward, blood staining the front of his shirt.

South Texas sizzled in August, and close to sundown Mary, Clara, Justine, Aunt Lucy, and the entire body of Hesterwine Medallions sat on the long benches beneath a huge grape arbor on the west lawn of Hesterwine Regional Hospital, fanning themselves with straw fans handed out to them courtesy of Brown & Sons Funeral Home of Rose Hill. After three hours of sweltering in the colored waiting room alongside Leeta and Reverend Posey, the entire body of women had opted for the cooler ninety-eight-degree temperature outdoors the instant Leeta and the Reverend were allowed in to see Hank.

No one outside knew yet what was going on inside until the Texas Ranger who had loaded Hank into his car and sped him to the hospital came out to the arbor and said, "Anything larger than that twenty-two bullet would have killed him for sure. It was right next to his heart, but he's gonna be fine."

Another Ranger captured the shooter—a sixteen-year-old boy riding a bicycle and with a twenty-two rifle dangling from a strap over his shoulder. He was Joe Setler, the teenager that had beaten Flaco Rosales so brutally and knocked Leeta unconscious the day he and his crowd destroyed the watermelons. Joe was also the youngest son of Klan member Mr. Setler, whose big toe Jack threatened to shoot off the night of the dance. "The apple never falls far from the tree," Vernell Watson commented with a sniff when she heard the boy's name; after which, a hushed argument ensued among the Medallions when several of them stated that the apple tree analogy wasn't always reliable.

Thank God, Hank would be okay. Mary felt relief, but even as worried as she had been at the possibility of Leeta losing Hank to a hater's bullet, her thoughts of Jack were always present, her despair shining in her eyes like muted sobs. Knowing that Miss Clara and Miss Justine were devastated by the upcoming loss of their cherished ancestral home and the treasures within, she felt she should be comforting them instead of being so preoccupied with her own misery. The pair said nothing of their despair today, but Mary knew that their minds never strayed far from tomorrow morning when they would close Hesterwine Place's doors behind them for the last time. They would summon a taxi to take them to Mrs. Harvey's boarding house in town, leaving behind all they loved, including their animals, except for Rube and Etta Ruth's cat, Beelzebub. Rudolph Valentino and the Buick were listed on the mortgage, as were the cow, Lillian Gish, and the donkey, Lionel Barrymore, as well as the peacocks, chickens, pigs ... *everything*. Before Jack disappeared, Mary had listened sympathetically as Clara and Justine spoke of Rudolph, Lionel, and Lillian as if they were cherished family members. Without their beloved Hesterwine Place, tomorrow would be the end of a happy life for Miss Clara and Miss Justine. And if Jack did not come back to *her*—!

She was not aware that she had sobbed aloud until Miss Clara and Miss Justine suddenly scooted closer and put their arms around her shoulders. Mary dropped her head to her chest. "He should have been back by now. If he was all right, he would have called me." She wept on Miss Clara's white lace collar as Justine pressed her cheek to Mary's shoulder. Moments later, the Hesterwine Medallions gathered around the trio, most of them wiping tears.

Vernell Watson, dry-eyed as a devil's advocate as usual, spoke up. "Now let's stop thinking the worst, ladies. Jack Dunston is as tough as nails. He's got all sorts of rescue equipment on that plane of his. If he landed on water, I'd bet my flap he'll be rescued while floating leisurely around on one of those nice, comfy little rafts."

"You'd win that bet, Miz Watson," said a familiar voice from behind the crowd of Medallions. "Now, if you sweet ladies will step aside and give me a path to my girl..."

Mary screamed and jumped to her feet as the women parted and Jack, missing his artificial leg and on two crutches, swung toward her, a wide grin on his heavily sunburned and blistered face.

# 33

THAT NIGHT THE HOUSE WAS EMPTY, except for Clara and Justine. Leeta was at the hospital with Hank. Aunt Lucy had gotten a ride from the hospital to Rose Hill with her brother, Reverend Posey. Mary and little James had gone to town with Jack to have supper with his sister, Linda. Tomorrow was moving day, and everyone was packed.

In the kitchen, Justine poured tea. "I think it is so romantic of Jack wanting to wait until his new leg arrives before getting married so that he can dance with Mary on their wedding day."

He's a sweet boy," Clara replied.

"Heavens, Clara, I shiver every time I think of him having to crash-land his plane on the ocean, and him and his copilot being tossed around in that raft for four whole days before being rescued. What was that Jack said? In the storm, they lost their water supply and if it hadn't rained, they would have been in trouble?" She rolled her eyes as she set the teapot down. "*Then*, just as Jack was climbing into the Coast Guard rescue boat, that huge shark popped up and bit off his artificial leg. Heavens! It could have just as easily been his good one!"

"It could have just as easily been *him*, Justine," Clara said.

"Oh, Lordy, Clara, can't you just imagine that big shark swallowing Jack whole?"

"No! I can't and I won't," Clara said crossly. "Why don't you just stifle that imagination of yours? I am quite sick of it."

Justine tightened her lips. "Why are you biting my head off? Oh, you don't have to answer that because I know why, and I am just as upset as you are that this is our last night in our beloved home! It is all I can do to keep from crying."

"Then why don't you shut up and start crying?"

"Oh, Clara, sometimes you are so mean! I swear, lately I don't see any difference between you and Etta Ruth except that she's *notably* cracked."

"Well, guess what! With all that has happened to turn our lives upside down lately, I indeed *feel* cracked! I'm just not cracked enough yet to take a swan dive off the windmill, but I *am* as sick and tired as Etta Ruth was, I'm sure."

"So am I, but I try my best not to take it out on you."

"Ha! You need to try harder."

"Oh, Clara, you really are—"

Just then, a loud knock sounded on the front door.

"Who could that be? Lately, I don't like it when someone knocks on our door. It never has a good outcome," Justine said as she raised her cup for a sip, making no effort to get up.

Clara slammed down her napkin. "I'll get it. By all means, Justine, sit there and drink your tea, and get in a better mood while you're at it," she said, and then added dryly, "Maybe it's the grim reaper knocking at our door this time."

"I'm not the one who needs to get in a better mood, Clara," Justine said and then called after her, "If it's the grim reaper, see if he's got six hundred dollars!"

The porch light was on and, making her way down the long foyer, Clara made out the silhouette of a rather slightly built man standing on the porch just outside the screen door. The figure looked like no one she could recognize.

Always cordial to visitors, she peered through the screen at him. "Yes?" she said, all traces of her former mood dissipating for appearance's sake. The little man slowly removed his Panama straw hat and ducked his head almost shyly.

"Don't you recognize me, Clara? It's me, *Boyd Pendleton.*"

Clara found the great need to catch hold of the doorframe to keep from keeling over. It took a few seconds to recover, in which time her owl eyes grew larger and larger as they crawled over him. *Everyone changes with the metamorphosing tricks age plays on God's creatures*, she thought, *but this is perverse!*

Boyd Pendleton was indeed only a shadow of his former self. *The Pendleton heir with the savoir faire* was a stoop-shouldered little man with an exceedingly rutted gray face and a nose and ears that must have continued to grow while the rest of him shrank. His nose, in particular, stood out in more ways than was ordinary, covered as it was with a neon map of red and purple spider veins, and nostrils that needed a haircut. As to hair, where was that glorious blond mane he once sported, a sweet, curly lock of which he could never keep off his forehead? Clara adjusted her glasses and, tilting her head back, peered through her bifocals at the few strands that remained. *My God! He's dyed those pathetic little strings jet-black and...good grief!...his scalp is stained with dye!*

"Clara, I said 'don't you recognize me'?" He was staring forlornly at her.

She smiled. "Of course I recognize you, Boyd." She started to push the screen open but quickly pulled it shut again. "Uh, would you mind waiting there a moment? I'll be right back." She hurried to the kitchen.

"Hurry, Justine! Come with me!"

"Heavens, Clara, you look ... *strange*. What is it?"

"It's hard to explain, but you'll see."

At the door, Justine's reaction was a short scream, and then Clara locked her elbow through Justine's to hold her up.

Excusing themselves "for a moment," and leaving Boyd standing under the porch light, the two women ducked around the corner into the parlor where, obviously thinking the same thoughts, they clutched at each other like adolescent schoolgirls sharing a startling revelation, and then burst into smothered bouts of hysterical laughter.

"I don't remember him being so *short*, do you?" Justine asked, giggling behind her hand and trying to calm herself.

"Or so *repentant*! He was gaping at me through the screen like a puppy that's soiled the rug and is sorry for it," Clara said, trying to control her sniggering but was as unsuccessful as her sister was.

"Do you suppose he doesn't know he has all that hair growing out of his ears?"

"And his nose?"

"Are those *eyebrows* or wooly black tomato worms on his forehead?"

"He's dyed his hair, too, what's left of it—*and* his scalp," Clara whispered, barely understandable. "I don't mean to be unkind, but ..." She slapped a hand over her mouth and the other hand on top of it, once again victim to another fit of sniggering ... the sounds escaping through her nose in loud snorts that made them both laugh even harder.

They were having glorious fun at Boyd Pendleton's expense, their half-century quarrel over him suddenly drolly irrelevant.

Finally, Clara composed herself and shushed Justine. "I suppose we should invite Boyd in for a cup of tea."

"Yes, let's do!" Justine said, but then frowned. "But just one cup, Clara—we certainly don't want to *reward* the man."

When all three were in the parlor, Boyd got right to the reasons for his visit, the first being he was moving back to Hesterwine and wanted lodging.

"This is no rooming house, Boyd," Clara said.

"I understand. But I thought, for old times' sake, you might consider it."

"No."

"Then allow me to get to the other reason I'm here. I want to apologize to you both for ... well, I don't have to remind you, do I? I suppose some things are better left unsaid. Even so, I think in this case, we ought to talk about it."

Boyd Pendleton's insistence on dragging them into the mortifying past was annoying, to say the least—especially since they were still absorbing the jarring revelation they'd shared in the parlor only moments before about a very much *mythical* Boyd Pendleton and themselves. Justine seemed particularly angered.

"*Some things* certainly are better left unsaid, Boyd Pendleton, so *don't* say them!" She glared a warning at him.

"I loved you both, Justine," Boyd replied. "I am sorry, but that's the way it was."

Justine's mouth gathered into a pout. "That's ridiculous! It's impossible to *truly* love two women at the same time."

Clara nodded. "Justine is right. It's impossible."

"No, it isn't. Clara, I loved *you* for your intelligence ... your, er, *purity*, and your determination to stay that way no matter how much in love we were." He turned to Justine. "And I loved *you*, Justine, for..." He paused, his pasty face actually flushing with color. "Well, for ... *you* know."

"I knew it!" Clara hissed, her owl eyes bulging at Justine and then at him.

Justine sighed as if finally caught sneaking in the back door after being out all night, then she glowered at her old rendezvous partner. "You are not a gentleman, Boyd Pendleton! Telling on me like that! Get out of this house!"

"Indeed, Boyd, get out," Clara said, then stuck out her open palm and quipped in a jokingly cynical tone, "Unless you can pay three months in advance for the room, which for *you* is three hundred dollars cash, plus three hundred more for meals and laundry service. All told, exactly six hundred dollars. You can't afford it? Fine. There's the door." She pointed the way, her raised chin chronicling her anger at him and her sister.

"I can afford it," he mumbled as he reached into his breast pocket and drew out his wallet. "But it seems awfully steep, Clara. Three times what I normally pay for room and board."

Both women dropped their jaws at the same time as they converged on him to peer down at his wallet, and then eagerly watched as he removed six one-hundred-dollar bills from the fat stack of green folding money. Almost subconsciously, Clara and Justine slowly locked elbows, the look in their eyes as they stared at each other saying it all—*Saved! And just in time to pay Banker Prickett's widow at nine o'clock in the morning!*

Mollified to the point of being weak-kneed, Clara clutched the bills to her bosom and sank onto a chair to reconsider her hostile attitude. An instant later, she smiled forgivingly at Justine. *Life is too short to mull over the past,* she decided, her fingers caressing the slender stack of paper currency pressed to her chest as if it were a favorite kitten.

Boyd stepped to Justine's side and grasped her hands.

"I was the happiest man in the world when I found out you never divorced me, Justine, sweetums."

"Whaaat?" Clara was unable to say anything else because she was choking.

Boyd, almost starry-eyed, continued, "I checked the county records today and knew there must be a reason you didn't seek a divorce. It's because you still love me, don't you? I told myself on the way here, 'Boyd, Justine and Clara have always had lots of class, and they're not about to make a scene over a couple of things that happened twenty or thirty years ago—they've probably forgotten all about it."

As he babbled on, Justine stared horror-struck at Clara as if Clara was metamorphosing into Lon Chaney's werewolf character and was about to rip out her throat. "Damn you, Boyd Pendleton, now you've done it!" She jerked her hands from his.

"You mean you never told anybody we got married in Mexico, Justine?" Boyd's crestfallen countenance seemed to enrage both women even more.

Now it was Justine's turn to look like Lon Chaney. "You old fool! I was too ashamed to tell anybody, and Clara would have *killed* me!"

"I want your forgiveness, sweetums. Yours, too, Clara ... and I don't mind paying for it." He extended his wallet. "There is more where that came from."

"How dare you suggest we could be influenced by—" Justine began, but was cut short by Clara's: "We'll take it," as she snatched the wallet from his fingers, removed five more hundred-dollar bills, then handed the considerably thinner wallet back to him.

"Clara!" Justine stared in disbelief at her.

Clara jutted out her chin. "We haven't paid Aunt Lucy and Flaco in months, and we'll want to give our Mary a proper wedding. The outside shutters need fixing, plus the second-floor balcony needs work. And then there's the painters we'll have to hire. First off, those screeching windmill blades are being replaced. There's work to be done if we are to turn Hesterwine Place into a first-rate *hotel/boarding house.*"

"What? We are going to rent rooms?" Justine cried, waving her hands to keep Boyd from grasping them again.

"Now that we know our home is secure, we shall make certain our future is as well." Clara glanced at Boyd as she poked the crisp green bills down the front of her dress. "We shall need more money, Boyd. However, it can wait a day or two."

"Clara!" Justine again stared at her in disbelief.

Boyd patted Justine's arm. "It's all right, sweetums. Though unlucky in love, I've been outstandingly fortunate otherwise—oil and gas, stocks, and a coal mine in Virginia."

Justine slapped her hands to her cheeks. "You're a *Republican* now? Oh my! Poppa would not be happy."

"I am *practical*, Justine dearest, as is Clara ... another of the things I always admired about her."

Clara grinned wickedly at her sister. "Yes, indeed, I am the practical one and *you*, Justine, are the lucky one—you now have *Boyd.*"

Justine's face quivered, her big eyes squinting oddly as she looked Boyd Pendleton over, as if trying to determine if she could tolerate him.

Clara's grin spread wider. "Show your husband upstairs to your room, Justine. And since he is now the man of the house, you can get that old cigar box of bills from the kitchen and hand them over to him."

"*My* room? But-but it really isn't all that large. I don't think it can accommodate *two* people."

"We don't need a lot of rooms, sweetums, remember?" Boyd had managed to grab her hand again and was rubbing it slowly and methodically.

Clara was close to beaming. "See, sister, *dear*? Everything is working out just fine, and Boyd doesn't intend to take up much space at all in that lovely bedroom of yours."

Justine, looking as if she were hanging off a cliff by her fingernails, took a giant backward step away from both of them. "But, Clara, we can't have a rooming house... because... because..." She was clearly grappling for anything she could think of. "Have you forgotten? Sheriff Bloot and his county commissioner friends would never allow it! They'd give us another one of those *Writ of Mandamus* things!"

"They will be voted out of office in a month," replied Clara.

"If not," Boyd said, waving his wallet, "I've learned in my business operations that money talks to politicians like nectar talks to honey bees."

"Influence like that is what the upcoming election is going to do away with in Vander County, Boyd Pendleton," Clara said. "Go ahead, Justine. Show your husband to bed. He looks like he hasn't had a night's sleep in fifty years." She gave him a quick once-over, then rolled her eyes toward Justine as if to say, *he's all yours.*

Justine's shoulders slumped. If she intended to say anything it was curtailed as Mary, Jack, Leeta, and *Hank*—with a sling holding his arm to his chest—came into the room, and then stopped short to gaze curiously at the strange man in the house.

"Hank! What are you doing out of the hospital?" Clara cried.

"The doctor said all I needed now was bed rest. I can get all the bed rest I need at home, and it's free. The hospital ain't."

"We couldn't let you be alone on your last night in the house," Mary said.

Then, to Clara and Justine's astonishment, Etta Ruth stepped out from behind the little crowd of visitors and hooted, "My God! It's *Boyd Pendleton*! Somebody tie Justine down!"

Mary and Leeta stared briefly at him and then at each other, as Etta Ruth continued.

"You look like hell, Boyd. Don't let my cat see you or he'll think you're supper." She winked at Justine. "Are you going to throw away that old Hamilton Beach electric *backache massager* now that lover-boy is back?"

"Go to hell!" Justine cried.

Clara, puzzled to see Etta Ruth out of jail, looked to Jack for an explanation.

"She's a free woman. The chief of police found the car jack that killed Prickett hanging in the bushes and figured out that he died accidently the way Miz Morley said he died. We spotted her on the highway trying to hitchhike out here. We told her there wouldn't be anyone living on the place after tomorrow and offered to call Clarence Jr. to come get her, but she wouldn't have it."

"Nope," Etta Ruth said. "I'll damn well hop a freight train out of town before I let that greedy pup drag me off to you-know-where."

"Yes, well, Etta Ruth, good news," Clara said. "You don't have to go anywhere you don't want to go." With a wide sweep of her open hand, she pointed at Boyd. "Everyone, this gentleman is Justine's long-lost *husband*, Boyd Pendleton." She looked at Mary and Leeta. "I'm sure you've heard of him," she added in a comical tone that made them grin.

Etta Ruth cackled. "Good grief! You mean the *Pendleton heir with the savoir faire* and the floozy have been married all these years? Now we know why you left town, Boyd. Why are you back? Senile dementia?"

Clara put up a hand to stop whatever Justine was about to reply. "Boyd is paying off Hesterwine Place's debts and then some, Cousin Etta—as he very well *should* do, for many reasons, the least of them being, as Justine's husband, he is now the responsible *man* of the house. And since we won't be moving to Mrs. Harvey's in town after all, your old room awaits you."

"Why, thank you, Clara," Etta Ruth said. "I shall try not to make y'all any more miserable than I ever did—except you, floozy," she added, glancing at Justine.

Justine glowered at her. "I'll tell you right now, Etta Ruth Morley, if you want to remain in this house, you will stop calling me names."

"I calls 'em as I sees 'em."

"No, you will not!"

"Yes, I will."

Mary jumped to her feet and hugged Clara and then Justine. "I am so happy I don't know what to say!"

"Me, too," said Leeta. "Jesus Pete! This has been a great day all 'round ... even if Hank did get shot."

Little James, in Jack's arms, woke and began to cry. Everyone tried to mollify him at once, jabbering baby talk and making faces, even Boyd Pendleton. All the chattering and up-close faces descending on him seemed to make him cry that much harder.

Clara stood back watching them, suddenly reminded how lonely she and Justine had felt at having no family, other than Etta Ruth, of course ... until Mary and Leeta came into their lives and eventually brought Jack, Hank, and little James into the circle. Now—especially tonight—the once ominously silent old mansion was alive with the noise of family. The months of worry over losing Hesterwine Place had been dreadful, today's activities exhausting, and now the racket her *family* was making over little James was deafening, but she watched with approving eyes, adoring them all ... except maybe Boyd.

Just then, a knock sounded on the front door.

"I'll get it," Clara said, wearily happy.

Justine, still glaring at Etta Ruth, waved a hand. "Go ahead, Clara. Maybe *that is* actually the grim reaper this time ... come to get *you-know-who*."

*Hesterwine Place is a popular place tonight*, Clara thought on her way to the door. She half-hoped this new visitor would be Sheriff Bloot come to remind her that tomorrow morning was the deadline to vacate her home. However, she knew he would not be out of the hospital for a while. Just the same, she would have liked to thank him for saving Etta Ruth's life, and then she would have liked to see his face when she told him that she and Justine would not be losing Hesterwine Place to Betty Prickett and the bank after all. *What a day*, she thought, longing for bedtime and silence, even though she knew she would lie awake all night gratefully running everything over in her mind ... and glad that there was nothing else with which to be shocked.

*Hesterwine, Texas 1943*

She realized how wrong she was as she peered through the screen door at Fritz Von Heuvel, alias Gustave Herrmann, standing under the porch light dressed in a gray suit, vest, and tie, neatly shaven, eye patch in place, and trimmed hair combed straight back as he'd worn it when much younger. Despite the scarred side of his face, he was recognizable as the fiancé she had deserted nearly twenty-nine years before in Germany.

She pushed open the screen door and he handed her a small jewelry box—the one she had left behind with her engagement ring and the fine baubles he had gifted her. She locked eyes with his one good eye and they stood thusly for the longest time. Finally, she spoke.

"Tea, Fritz?"

"Coffee, Clara. I have brought za Cognac." He touched his coat pocket.

"I remember. Black coffee and a splash of fine Cognac after supper," she said, as she pushed the screen door wider.

Fritz pulled his shoulders back and scarcely limped as Clara looped her elbow through his and guided him into the parlor. She had almost forgotten how tall he was.

Little James stopped crying to stare curiously at the man with the black patch covering one side of his face.

Clara put out a hand. "Justine ... Boyd ... Etta Ruth ... Mary ... Leeta ... Jack, and Hank, I want you to meet my fiancé, Doctor Fritz Von Heuvel, formerly of Aachen, a town in North Rhine-Westphalia, Germany."

The stunned silence was almost like an explosion in the room. Even Etta Ruth's mouth, like Justine's mouth, hung open with nothing coming out.

Clara smiled. "Since you have nothing to say, Justine ... Etta Ruth ... why don't you two trot on out to the kitchen and make a very large pot of coffee, and then we shall all sit down and get acquainted."